THE TRUTH ABOUT MURDER

THE TRUTH ABOUT MURDER

A captivating crime mystery full of twists and turns

CHRIS COLLETT

First published 2019
Joffe Books, London

ISBN 978-1-78931-293-5

Join our mailing list to receive free Kindle crime thrillers, detective novels, mysteries and romances, with new releases every week.

www.joffebooks.com

PROLOGUE

July burns with a suffocating heat, which only becomes more oppressive as the month progresses. These are turbulent times, with unemployment, inflation and poverty high. A sharp rise in the birth rate has created anxiety about how limited resources and public services can meet the population's needs, so prejudice grows.

Inside the Bishop's Palace it is cool but airless, and for days now a headache has gripped my temples, making it impossible for me to marshal my thoughts coherently. Rumours have been circulating for some time now, but unsubstantiated as they are, it has been easy enough to ignore them in order to protect the reputation of an increasingly fragile institution trying to stay afloat in a chaotic world. At our last meeting, the Fulda bishops agreed to resist challenging the status quo when the Church itself is so vulnerable. Nevertheless, the chatter becomes more insistent. Visits from Heinrich Lackmann and Sister Baudelerta have uncovered some disturbing developments, and now I face a challenge from within. One of my most popular young priests threatens to leave his calling because of a crisis of faith and I have so far let him down. If ever a man was born to his vocation it was this man. His intellect and charisma have strengthened the Church's position in the parishes he has led. In him I have seen echoes of myself as a younger man — the same integrity, the same conviction — at least until now.

1

CHAPTER ONE

Walking from one side of the ward to the other, Rita Todd was alert to the percussive music of the various machines beeping as they registered the vital signs of her tiny patients. She wondered, as she had on many occasions, whether it would be possible to do this job if she was tone deaf. They were full to capacity, as always, even though they'd managed to ship one patient out to a more specialised hospital in the next county, and only this morning — too early in Rita's view — Baby Rushton, barely twenty-three weeks when he came in, had progressed on to the recovery ward, now relocated to a different wing of the hospital. It was a practice Rita had yet to get used to. Each time a child went from her care, Rita's unease grew a little more. Her discomfort was compounded by what lately seemed to her to be the almost inevitable outcome — that the transfer to the 'recovery' ward marked exactly the opposite, and instead was the beginning of a fatal deterioration. The rationale was, of course, that the prognosis for severely premature infants was poor anyway, and that moving them on would at least free up space to admit a child with more chance of survival, like Verity, the little scrap before her now. The tiny human being that looked nothing more than a new-born rodent with her raw red skin and tiny row of ribs that stood out like the breakwater on a beach every time she gasped for breath.

The only other adult in the room, Verity's mum, Fay, sat on the opposite side of the cot, gazing unblinkingly down at her precious daughter, the bond so strong between them it was almost tangible. The other parents were not far away, trying to grab a few hours' rest in the family room along the corridor, or collecting siblings from school for the weekend, a reminder that beyond the confines of these walls, life had to go on.

Fay glanced up. 'They work you hard, don't they?' she said, a comment on Rita's continual presence on the ward this week.

'It keeps me out of mischief,' was Rita's much-rehearsed rejoinder. What she really wanted to do was wholeheartedly agree. Almost in response, and mesmerised by the rhythmic bleeping, she felt a wave of fatigue crash over her. She'd agreed to stay on for the graveyard shift for the third consecutive night only because, once again, they were short-staffed. Since the latest reorganisations they were spread so thinly she seemed to do more extra cover than regular hours, though no one in management seemed to notice — or, more to the point, *wanted* to notice.

She was shaken from her thoughts by the urgent squealing of a monitor across the ward: Baby Carew's oxygen levels had dipped suddenly and dangerously low. As Rita hurried across the room, the door swung open and junior nurse Ellen Campbell, alerted by the sound, appeared from where she'd been snatching a few minutes' break in the staff room.

Words were superfluous, and the two women worked in silence, their eyes fixed on the array of screens and digital markers. Rita was all too aware of the anxious looks cast across from Fay. Every crisis in here was a painful reminder of the tenuous grasp on life all these children had. When she'd first qualified, Rita's pulse used to accelerate to keep pace with the urgency of the machines, but after seventeen years she'd learned to check the anxiety and remain as calm as possible. She and Ellen worked quickly and quietly through the procedure, tension seething beneath the surface as it always did, but after only minutes the baby began to stabilise, the machines resumed their regular beat, and the danger had passed. As she turned back to the ward, Rita saw that the door was open, framing the stocky figure of paediatric consultant Mr Leonard. He had a medication records file tucked under his arm, she noticed, and his expression was grim.

'Can I have a word, Rita?'

'Yes, of course.'

'You go ahead, I'll be fine here,' said Ellen, oblivious to the sudden thickening of the atmosphere. And it was now, as Rita crossed the room to follow Mr Leonard, that her heartbeat began to pick up speed.

CHAPTER TWO

It was a Friday unlike any other, which is no doubt why I ended the working day feeling like my head had been used to score the winning goal for the opposition. It traced back to those moments in the courtroom before the verdict was pronounced, when the only discernible sound was the creak of ancient timber doing battle with an overzealous heating system. Along the row I could see Mr Asif's fingers tangled in his lap, his knuckles white.

'Not guilty.'

At the delivery of the verdict, there followed a collective exhalation of breath from across the chamber, and I looked across to see Councillor Ashley Curzon exchange a look with his solicitor. He wasn't crass enough to gloat — if anything he looked relieved — but there was a hint of a smile behind the eyes, too. He'd got away with it, and he knew he had. On our side of the courtroom, Mr Asif's shoulders slumped. Jake was leaning in to him, doubtlessly with words of apology and sympathy, knowing that Asif would now have to go home to his wife and tell her that the death of their baby boy was down to nothing but a collection of unfortunate circumstances. Never mind that they were circumstances constructed through negligence and greed. Instead, the jury concluded, it had been a tragic accident. Taken in by the defence barrister's tale, they decided that the outcomers had brought it on themselves. Even though it had been established that the central heating boiler was a cheap, knocked off import from Eastern Europe, health and safety officers could find no fault with it, nor in the way it had been fitted. They did however find the house to be poorly ventilated, with no open windows, leading over time to higher levels of carbon dioxide, which were enough to overwhelm a delicate child. The tiny boy was premature and in poor health anyway. And never mind that Asif was a qualified engineer, the family — being new to the country — could not be expected to understand the workings of the modern central heating system, suggesting a strong possibility that on this occasion the pilot light had gone out (or been extinguished). Certainly, it had been decided that there was no criminal case to answer. The only representative remaining here from the police was a scruffy looking individual, who hadn't even been required to give evidence.

As papers were tucked back into briefcases and tablets were shut down, Curzon and his team got to their feet and were first out of the courtroom, Curzon pausing only to throw a penetrating stare in our direction.

'And so he goes on, his reputation unsullied,' muttered Jake, watching them go. Generally irrepressible, in another life, Jake would have made an excellent spiv. Today he wore his customary uniform: dark suit, tie at half-mast and desert boots. All that was missing was a trilby perched on the back of his head. As it was, he'd grown up in what he called a posh suburb of Liverpool. Until meeting him I hadn't known there was any such thing.

'How can a guy that hot be so cool?' my friend Laura had wanted to know, after the one and only time she met him. It was a mystery, but something Jake could never resist turning to his advantage, which is why one of the early divorces I'd done the grunt work for was his. I'd kind of hoped that some of Jake's success with women might rub off on me, but so far that had yet to be realised

'So that's it?' I said, still stunned that it was all over so easily.

Jake nodded slowly. 'It was going to take rather more than we managed to find to bring down the reputation of Ashley Curzon,' he said. And he was right. For all that he was rough around the edges, Curzon was a local boy made good, his success founded on the housing squeeze back at the beginning of the century. He'd been responsible for the construction of almost all the town's new developments, based on his supposed belief in high-quality social and affordable housing, most of which he still owned. The jewel in his crown was the small complex set aside for newly arrived refugees from war-torn Syria and his very public undertaking to allow them to get on their feet before any rent was required. The philanthropic gesture made the national news and had secured Curzon a strong influence within the local council. Long-term it had probably nailed him a knighthood, too. But behind the facade of publicity, Curzon, it transpired, had been far from mindful of the welfare of his tenants. He hadn't factored in Mr Abdul Asif, who two months ago had walked into the offices of Perry, Goodman and Wright (PGW, as we're known locally), to sue him for negligent manslaughter. There had been too little evidence for the police to take much interest — we had done what we could, but it wasn't enough.

'Well,' Jake said, now on his feet and stowing files into a messenger bag. 'I think we can treat ourselves and take the rest of the day off.'

'It's ten to five,' I pointed out.

'There you are then. I won't even dock your wages.' But as is so often the case, it didn't quite work out like that.

The offices for PGW are located in a former Victorian townhouse we share with a small IT company, along a back alley off the high street. We're one of a handful of law firms in the town that have evolved broadly designated roles. Ours had started out small, specialising in divorce, with the occasional employment litigation case. But the lines were blurring. Fewer people were getting married, so the divorce rate had dropped correspondingly, and with local jobs scarce, those who had them liked to hang on to them and dared not risk taking action against employers, present or past. But we like to think that, unlike some of our competitors, we're ethically sound. We don't chase ambulances, even metaphorically, nor do we promise guaranteed pay-outs, which means that slowly and incrementally our work opportunities are shrinking. My task as the firm's one remaining paralegal is to research cases, put together the paperwork, and on rare occasions talk to clients.

After such a tense afternoon, I looked forward to getting back to the comforting, familiar smell of furniture polish and old paper and the air of peaceful calm. It wasn't to be. We could hear the raised voices before we'd even opened the door. Barbara, our main administrator, was standing in the cramped outer space that we laughably call reception, coat on and bag over her arm, ready to leave, but was apparently being prevented from doing so by the more pressing commitment of refereeing two other women who were engaged in a heated discussion. For once in her life, Barbara looked harassed.

'No, I've made up my mind. It's a fuss over nothing,' the other, older woman was saying.

'Oh, come on, Mum!' The younger woman was clearly exasperated. 'Now that we're here . . . It's just a few minutes of your time!' She was dressed for business, in a suit, with subtle make-up and groomed, shoulder-length hair. Her towering heels went some way towards compensating for her slight frame, and she was taking charge.

'I'm sorry,' Barbara intervened. 'In any event, you will need to . . .' Hearing us, she swung round, sagging with relief.

'What's going on?' asked Jake.

'I was just explaining to these ladies that because of the time, they will need to make an appointment to come back on another day.'

Jake made a show of looking at his watch, though I knew what was coming next and I understood. It would be nice to end the day by doing something positive for someone.

'Actually, Barbara,' he said. 'Our last meeting finished a bit earlier than expected, so I've got a few minutes to spare. It's OK, you get off home. We can handle it.' As Barbara hurried out with a grateful smile, Jake turned the full beam on the two women. 'Now, what can we do for you?'

After a pause of two or three seconds, it was the younger woman who spoke up, shooting her mother a meaningful look as she did so. 'I'm Andrea Todd and this is my mum, Rita. She needs you to help her keep her job.'

The older woman rolled her eyes. 'Don't be so melodramatic, Andrea.'

Her daughter sighed a weary sigh. 'Just talk to the man, Mum. Please?'

Jake, meanwhile, was looking from one to the other, trying to assess what exactly was going on. In the end he settled on the mother.

'Why don't you come through to my office and we can . . .'

But Rita Todd stood her ground. 'No offence,' she said. 'But if we must go through with this charade, I don't want you.' She switched her gaze to me. 'I want him.'

Well. That was a first.

Jake raised his eyebrows at me. My head throbbed, the pain blossoming out from the base of my skull, but this was a potential client. Tired though I was, I nodded. A quick chat and a date in the diary. I could do that, even after five on a Friday afternoon. I walked past Jake towards my office.

'I'll hang around for a bit,' he murmured.

'I'll wait for you outside in the car,' Andrea called after her mum. 'Then I can drop you back home.'

'No thanks, love, I'll walk,' came the response, with more than a touch of belligerence. 'I don't mind a bit of rain and it'll clear my head.'

CHAPTER THREE

For practical reasons, my face-to-face contact with clients is rare, and consequently I inhabit an office that's poorly designed for it. My desk takes up one corner beside a window that overlooks the narrow yard and next door's fire escape, with most of the other space taken up with filing cabinets and archive boxes. It meant that Rita Todd and I ended up sitting with our knees almost touching.

Up close and personal, I got a better sense of her. Late fifties, or perhaps even early sixties, she was attractive in an impish kind of way, with a slim, boyish figure and improbably dark, close-cropped hair. I could imagine her being at home behind a bar. She wore jeans and a V-necked pullover, and I knew at least one of my colleagues who would have approved of the Doc Martens. Sitting down, she seemed to have as much difficulty keeping still as I did. While we talked, her eyes ranged around the room and every couple of minutes or so, she picked up the tiny crucifix that hung around her neck, pulling it up over her chin and running the cross back and forth along its fine silver chain. She caught me watching her at one point and, as if it was some guilty secret, hastily dropped it. Perhaps she could feel the atheist vibes coming at her from my direction and was afraid it might prejudice her chances.

'Right, tell me how I can help. Is it Miss or Mrs Todd?'
I turned to clear a space in the papers on my desk. I found it
usually helped to give people a few seconds to adjust to my
laboured speech patterns, but when I glanced up, she was
entirely composed.

'It's Mrs,' she said. 'But Rita will do.' She was foraging
in her backpack and finally brought out a pack of cigarettes
and a lighter. 'Don't suppose I can . . . ?'

'Sorry, one careless move and this lot'll go up like a tin-
der box.' She smiled and replaced them. No problem with
her understanding me either, then.

'I'm going to be straight with you,' she said, fixing me
with her blue-grey eyes. She didn't wait for a reply. 'This
is a waste of your time. But if we could just sit here for a
few minutes, make an appointment like your boss said —
perhaps you can put it on one of those little cards? — then
I'll have done what I promised to do and Andrea will get
off my back. I don't know. My first time off in God knows
how long and this is where she brings me. Other daughters
would take their mum out for lunch or to a spa or something, wouldn't they?'

I sensed her custom — and fee — slipping away, and
Jake wouldn't thank me for that. 'Why *did* your daughter
bring you here?' I asked.

'You heard — she thinks I'm about to lose my job. And
my pension.'

I opened my mouth again to ask but she was one step
ahead. 'I'm a paediatric nurse up at the John Skidmore.'

'And is your daughter right to be worried?'

With a light shrug, Rita picked up the crucifix and
dropped it again. 'I suppose it's possible,' she conceded. 'You
know what things are like these days. Is there anyone who can
say that they're truly safe?'

'But that's exactly what we're here for,' I said. 'We might
be able to do something.'

She smiled. 'That's kind of you, but honestly, I can fight
my own battles. I really don't need you or Andie to do it for

11

me.' She glanced out of the window and the glance lengthened into a stare at nothing in particular.

I stifled a yawn, suddenly feeling exhausted myself. I wanted to go home and it felt as if she did too.

'OK,' I said. 'Let's make that appointment, and in the meantime, you can think things through and decide if you'd like our help.' It seemed to satisfy her so I went and fetched the office diary (Barbara still likes things 'written on a real page'). We settled on the following Wednesday to give Rita the chance to mull things over — and, I suspected, to cancel on us. It would also allow me to work out what the bloody hell, if anything, I could do to keep her on board. For form's sake, along with the appointment details I gave her a business card, more out of habit than out of any hope that it would be used. 'And is there a number I can reach you on, should I need to?' I asked in return.

She gave me a landline number. 'I won't bother you with the mobile,' she said. 'I hardly ever have it on.'

Obligations fulfilled, she reached down and picked up the backpack. 'Now perhaps Andrea'll leave me in peace,' she said with a wry smile. 'Funny thing is, some proverbial faecal matter *is* about to hit the fan, but not at all in the way she thinks.'

On another day, or at a different time, I might have probed to find out exactly what she meant. Instead, as she stood up to leave, I asked, 'Why us? There are plenty of other law firms in town. Or was it Andrea who chose?'

She shook her head. 'Mr Asif told me about you.'

'You know him?'

'I cared for the baby when he was first born.'

* * *

'That was a strange one,' observed Jake, after I'd seen Rita out. He leaned back in the chair in his rather better-appointed office, squeezing a stress ball in the palm of his hand. 'What's your gut feeling?'

'Hungry,' I said, though that wasn't what he meant. 'Beyond that, I really couldn't say. She wasn't exactly forthcoming.'

'Did you get anything?'

'A commitment to come back in a few days. But apart from that, not much more than you heard. Her daughter thinks her job might be under threat.' I relayed the rest of my short exchange with Rita.

'What did you think about her?'

'I don't know . . .'

Jake raised his eyebrows.

'I liked her. She was upfront and I don't doubt that she can fight her own corner. But she did agree, in theory, to come back again.'

'OK.' Jake seemed satisfied with that.

'I don't get why she wanted me, though,' I said, still baffled.

'You're the handsome one,' said Jake. He threw the stress ball in my direction. 'Now piss off home, before I start getting a complex.'

CHAPTER FOUR

When we were young, my best friend Laura had a string puppet. You rarely see them now, but this was back in the days
when kids used to play with proper toys instead of relying
on the virtual world for their entertainment. The puppet was
made from wood, with a bright green felt hat atop a perfectly
spherical head, and a dopey expression painted on his face.
She said he reminded her of me. Not because of the hat, or
even the dopey expression, but because of the way he walked.
Sometimes when she was bored with plodding him up and
down, she would yank the strings hard, up through the wooden
X that controlled him, bunching him into a knot of arms and
legs, the strings contracting so much that they almost broke.

Laura was right, I thought, wiping the rain out of my
eyes. I was a lot like that puppet, and never more so than on
this Friday night, when there was so much tension in my
sinews, I thought they might snap. I needed a fix. Walking
home, my line on the pavement ranged unevenly from one
side to the other, and I had to work hard to avoid knocking
into anyone. If there's one thing total strangers don't like,
it's unsolicited physical contact. The effort made my head
throb even more, though after a day confined to the harsh
strip lighting and stuffy atmosphere of various offices, it was

a relief to at least be outside, even in the middle of the sort of sharp shower that had dogged the last few days. Crossing the stone bridge, I glanced down at the river, which flowed high and fast, brown waters surging by. Debris was accumulating round the supports and I watched a branch as big as a sapling being carried down from upstream.

Arriving at my apartment block, I managed to stab pretty accurately at the security pad, but it took me three exhausted attempts to get my key in the lock of my front door. Once inside my flat I poured myself a drink before switching on my laptop — two meaningful emails amongst all the spam. One from Laura, asking me to confirm that I'd be round for supper tomorrow night, the other from 'Crusader' comprising four words: *knight to king four*. Some of us are old school, and the chessboard was set next to my laptop. Scanning it first to refresh my memory, I slowly moved the corresponding piece. Interesting — it was not what I'd expected and right now it was hard to work out what it meant. The important things taken care of, I collapsed into my favourite recliner to give my next move some thought. (Laura would also say that I'm getting middle-aged.) What I needed now was a good woman and some chemical relaxation. A couple of hours later they both appeared, as arranged.

'Hi.' Letting herself in with the key I'd given her, Keeley walked into the lounge, from where I'd barely moved in two hours, and slipped off her jacket. The sight of her snug-fitting, low-cut dress began to shunt the blood around my body just a little bit quicker. She'd pinned up her dark hair tonight and looked more than ever like an exotic long-necked bird parading its plumage to attract a male. It was doing it for me.

'You look nice,' I managed to say.

'Thanks,' she smiled in appreciation. 'I'm sure I must be putting on weight though.' Frowning, she reached down to pinch an imaginary fold of skin between finger and thumb. 'Could hardly get into this.' The beige dress, cinched in at the waist with a wide, shiny black belt, seemed to me to cling in all the right places.

'Don't worry . . .' I began.

She flashed me a humourless smile. 'I know. *I won't be staying in it for long.*'

She dumped her bag beside me on the sofa. 'So, what first?' she asked, but a glance at my crotch told her all she needed to know, and in one smooth movement she was on her knees in front of me, sending shock waves the length of my thighs.

In phase two of this therapy session, Keeley took out of her bag a small polythene pouch of neatly rolled cylinders, thirty in all. 'Thought you might need to stock up,' she said.

I'd tried a DIY roll-up a couple of times, but too much of the good stuff had ended up on the floor. This way was far more satisfactory. She put a joint between her lips and held a lighter to it before handing it to me. I took a long drag and the remaining tension began to slowly ebb away, my muscles easing. Over time, Keeley and I had perfected a routine that worked well, and when the spliff was spent we retreated to the bedroom.

Much later, while I showered, Keeley disappeared into the kitchen and not long after, her disembodied head appeared through the steam.

'No milk,' she said. Bugger. Although it didn't matter now, it would in the morning. Plus, I was low on cash and was going to owe Keeley more than usual for the 'extras'. When I was dressed, I left her to freshen up and pulled my leather jacket on.

'Back in five,' I told her — as it turned out, somewhat optimistically.

Outside, the nip in the night air was enough to cloud my breath, but in my newfound relaxed state, I hardly noticed the cold. This was the one time of the week when life was good and from the inside at least, I felt like the me I was always meant to have been.

I noticed the gang of youths loitering outside Davey's supermarket from some distance away. They fell quiet as I approached, triggering an unwelcome murmuring in my gut and unwanted memories of the school playground. One of them said something to make the others laugh, and as I drew parallel with them a gobbet of spit arced out of the huddle, landing on the pavement just in front of me, just close enough for it not to have been random fire. Fighting the urge to shoot back an insult or even a punch, I forced myself to nod a civil greeting towards them and pushed my way into the shop.

I went to the cashpoint first. It meant paying a transaction fee, but at least the retinal scanner here was reliable. In the couple of years since they'd introduced them, they hadn't yet got the technology right and it seemed like half of them either malfunctioned or had been vandalised. I withdrew three hundred. Davey, or so I'd always assumed him to be, smiled from behind his counter as usual, and waited patiently while I fished out the loose change I needed for the milk.

Despite my determination not to be intimidated, it was a relief when I emerged from the shop to find that the youths had gone. I wasn't about to let the incident ruin my evening, but I'd already decided that tonight Keeley and I would go for dinner somewhere we were known. By the time I reached my building, I had relaxed again. Perhaps if I hadn't been in a haze of dope I might have seen it coming, but I was putting my key in the door when something slammed into me from behind, smacking my face into the reinforced glass and sending a judder through my jaw. I was spun around, my shouting cut short by a blow to the stomach that knocked the air out of me and bent me double, pushing bile up into my throat. As I lurched forward, a foot hooked under my shin and brought the pavement rushing up to meet me. My skull reverberated as my head hit the concrete. Dazed, I had a vague impression of two, maybe three dark shadows dancing around me and I knew instinctively that they were young males. The icy concrete stinging my face, I thought vaguely of the items of worth in my pockets: my wallet stuffed with twenty pound notes, my mobile phone and house keys. I hugged my arms around myself to protect them. But the pummelling blows continued until my only conscious sensations were a searing pain in my chest, a fire between my legs and a metallic stickiness in my mouth. Then, when I could bear it no more, the pain began to dissolve and somewhere in my field of vision, a brilliant light appeared. Beginning as a pinprick, it grew ever more intense, giving off a warmth and glowing comfort that drew me compulsively towards it. I floated towards the light, with that same euphoric lightness that comes on the cusp of sleep. Then a sharp, hot force smacked me in the ear and a foul smell invaded my nostrils, dragging me back to cold, painful reality. In desperation, I flailed my arms to grab at the light, but as I did it began to recede, getting dimmer and dimmer, until the blackness overcame me and I slipped into the void.

CHAPTER FIVE

When the light snapped on again, it was dizzying and painful. A weight on my chest held me down and my arms were pinned by my sides. A faint smell of citrus wafted in the air as a young woman leaned over me, and my head rolled uncomfortably on the pillows beneath. Everything in front of me seemed a long way off and slightly out of focus, as if I was looking the wrong way down a telescope.

'Hello there,' she said brightly, her voice ricocheting around inside my head. 'You're still with us, then.' She stepped back and her form became clearer, a smile spreading across her pale, freckled face. Policemen weren't the only ones getting younger. Nurses were, too. Despite the jagged pain inside my skull, I struggled to arrange my facial muscles to reciprocate — unsuccessfully, apparently, because it seemed to frighten her off, and she backed away. But then, after a murmured conversation somewhere outside my vision, she came back, followed by an older man whose hair was too long. I had a sense of black clothing and a white collar. A priest? Was I about to be given the last rites? Or had I already bypassed that bit? He smelled of the outside world and didn't look as if he'd shaved recently. If I had died and gone to heaven, St Peter was looking distinctly rough.

'Hi Stephen, how are you feeling?' His voice was too loud and his smile seemed overloaded with sympathy because I'd been hurt, or maybe just because it was me.

'Stefan,' I tried to correct him, but it was even harder than usual to get my mouth around the word. He leaned in towards me, his face creased in a frown of concentration as I breathed in stale air, but after my third unintelligible attempt he gave up and put a comforting hand on my shoulder.

'Never mind, son. You're finding it hard to talk. I'll come back another time.'

If he was anticipating any improvement in the interim, he was going to be in for a big disappointment. But I was glad he went, as it meant I could slide back into my cocoon again. When I next awoke, the room was dimly lit and quieter, and I felt a little more present in it. For a moment I thought I was alone, but then I felt the movement beside me and looked up into another woman's face, as a cloying perfume wafted my way. I'd caught her scrutinising me. She was smartly dressed but with no white coat, so I was guessing not medical staff.

'Everything all right, doctor?' a female voice inquired. OK, so I'd guessed wrong about that, put in my place by Freckle-face, who was suddenly in the doorway. 'Doctor' muttered something in reply that I couldn't hear, and when he retreated, so did I. The next time I saw the world, it was in the form of a fleeting glimpse of a ginger scalp, more dark clothes and a different aftershave, but this time I couldn't even summon enough energy to break the surface.

* * *

I was concentrating on my book when I sensed rather than heard it — a subtle change in breathing pattern, nothing more. Was he awake? Keeping my eyes fixed on the page I was reading, I listened carefully. The disturbance passed and regular rhythm resumed. I risked a sideways glance. No, his eyes were still closed, his breathing steady again. The momentary surge of adrenalin subsided and I felt ludicrously grateful for the reprieve. Coward. The sooner he regained consciousness, the sooner I could get this over with. It was long overdue.

I had Denny Sutton to thank for this. He'd come here to interview the victim last night but found him still out of it and pretty much unable to speak. He'd assumed it was because of the beating and the medication until the nurse had put him straight. At that point, Denny decided that this case was better suited to a junior officer.

'Good luck,' he'd said, with a smug grin. Not his fault, really. Denny Sutton was a product of his time. He couldn't get his head round 'all the political correctness bollocks.' There didn't seem much point in him trying now either. Two weeks and he'd be gone, retired with the lovely Mrs Sutton to sunny Portugal, where he could be as un-politically correct as he liked.

In every other respect, Denny was a good copper, at least that's what everyone kept telling me. He'd stayed on the front line, garnering bucketloads of respect along the way. It wasn't that I didn't believe it, more that I hadn't seen much evidence. Sure, he'd been accepting enough of me turning up from the other end of the country to fill the gap left by his old partner, Kevin Booth, and there were plenty who wouldn't have. But that was as far as it went. It wasn't made any better by everyone telling me what a dynamic team Denny and Booth had been. At first, I'd naively hoped that some of that expertise would rub off on me — I was keen to learn — but so far Denny was keeping me too much at arm's length to make that happen, and we were fast running out of time. I'd even found myself envying the easy banter between Denny and the paramedic who'd attended the scene on Friday night.

'Another one for you, Den,' the ambulance man had said. 'If we keep meeting like this, people will talk.'

Mostly Denny seemed to prefer to work alone, his philosophy being that we should each play to our strengths, which, according to him, was why I was sitting here instead of him, nervous tension clamping my insides. I suppose it was marginally better than being out on the streets on this wet late winter night.

It was important to keep a sense of perspective. After Denny had given me the background, I don't know what I'd expected when I got to the hospital, but it was a relief to see a relatively ordinary guy lying there. I mean, he hadn't got two heads or anything like that. He was just another crime victim, and I would just address him in the same way as I would any other member of the public.

When I was absolutely certain that the breathing had settled again, I looked up. Pale, with blond hair cropped short and looking like a cornfield after a storm, where the nurses had not completely succeeded in washing out the blood. After three days the stubble on his chin was poking through, and my Sonia would probably say he was not bad looking underneath all the bruises. He took up the length of the hospital bed, which must make him a slim six feet, and apart from the tics and twitches, you couldn't tell really that there was anything wrong with him. Poor bastard. I went back to my book.

'Anything?' The nurse who'd shown me down here appeared in the doorway.

I shook my head. 'When he does come around . . . is there anything I should know . . . I mean, how to . . . ?' I tailed off, not really knowing what I was asking, but somehow she worked it out.

She came over to the bed and started tucking in an imaginary loose corner. 'I've been told he's a bright guy and not to underestimate or patronise him. Apparently, he hates it.'

No pressure, then.

* * *

I seemed to drift in and out of the world for a couple of days, making fleeting contact, until finally I re-entered civilisation for good on Tuesday afternoon. Scoping the room, my eyes fell again on the shaven ginger nut. He must've heard me this time because he looked up, hazel eyes in a chubby pink face, a half-smile full of uncertainty. Welcome to my world.

'Hello,' he said, putting to one side the paperback he'd been reading. I didn't catch the title, but it was substantial. The dark clothes made sense now: a bulky stab vest with all the hardware, over a white shirt. St Peter was a cop. He cleared his throat, casting about for a distraction. Nerves. Someone must have told him about me. He said something, but so fast and with such an impenetrable Scots accent that I didn't catch it. I'd have laughed at the irony if I hadn't hurt so much.

Seeing the blank look, he tried it again, this time more slowly, clearly, loudly. 'I'm Police Constable Mick Fraser,' he said, like the outfit didn't speak for itself. He leaned back on the chair next to the bed, relieved to put some distance between us, and rifled through his pockets for something, finally holding out a warrant card for my perusal, his eye contact fleeting and evasive. 'Can I get you anything? Some water perhaps?' He mimed drinking, evidently now thinking I was deaf, too.

But I was glad he could read minds, because while I was asleep, in addition to everything else, someone seemed to have plugged my mouth with superglue. When I nodded, PC Mick Fraser stood up, picking up the jug from the bedside table, but regarding its murky contents said, 'Yeah, this has been standing here a while, I'll go and get you some fresh.'

While he was gone, I tried to drag myself up on the pillows to a kind of sitting position. *Aagh!* The slightest movement set off a chain reaction, starting in my neck, spreading across my shoulders, down my spine and round to my ribs, and ending up in my balls. He came back in and clocked the grimace.

'Painful, eh?' He glanced towards the door, as if hoping that one of the nurses would appear, but no one did, so gingerly (as it were) he reached out and tugged at the pillows, in a vague attempt to help. 'Here, let me . . .' Without having to actually touch me, he managed to wedge a pillow behind my back and then, recognising it as the only possible course of action, held the glass of water awkwardly to my lips. It was going pretty well until my tongue and throat got out of sync, then I coughed, spraying it everywhere. His colour rose. 'Sorry, I'm crap at this. Not cut out for nursing. Is that enough for now?'

I nodded, and lay back again, exhausted by the manoeuvre.

'Are you comfortable? Anything else before we start?' Fraser asked.

I had, in the last couple of minutes, become aware of a nagging urgency in my bladder. I hadn't been catheterised, but I was pretty sure that getting up to go to the bathroom wasn't a realistic option right now either. Scanning the room, my eyes alighted on a side-lying wide-necked plastic bottle, clearly left there for the purpose. Fraser, following my gaze, saw the same thing. *Oh crap* passed across his eyes like a banner across the sky. Not part of his job description, nor my idea of fun either. Fortunately, we were both saved the embarrassment of that particular intimacy by the timely reappearance of Freckle-face.

The operation over, Fraser settled back into his seat, which he'd left to go and lurk discreetly in a corner of the room. 'Right, Stefan,' he said. 'I need to ask you some questions about your attack. That OK?'

I nodded again. This was going to be fun. 'Thanks,' I said. It came out as 'hang'.

Surprise crossed his features. 'What for?'

'For getting — my — name — right.' It took forever to say it, shaping my mouth around the words as clearly as I could, with no guarantee that he'd get it, but miraculously, he did.

'No problem,' he replied, with enviable ease. 'It's a pretty fundamental starting point.'

Not for your colleague, I wanted to say, but it wasn't worth the effort.

'Now, are you OK talking about it?' he asked, producing from his pockets a notebook and pen, something else to focus on.

How are your listening skills? I wanted to ask, but it would have wasted too much time. 'I — don't — remember much,' I told him instead.

'Sorry?'

Oh, here we go. 'I — don't — re*mem*ber much.' I strained to enunciate the words.

'Ach, don't worry, that's not uncommon in these situations. We'll start with what you can recall and build on it as things come back to you. And as soon as you start to get tired, we'll stop.'

But I already was.

CHAPTER SIX

'So, in your own time,' he said. 'What do you remember about the attack, maybe starting from when you left your flat?'

I recounted what I could of my walk to the corner shop, which took an eternity, even though my memory of it was sparse. To his credit, Fraser seemed to keep up, though I noticed that after the first couple of utterances he'd abandoned the notebook, concentrating instead on my contorting mouth, which he had to study for additional clues. I wish I'd had the chance to clean my teeth. I described my walk to Davey's and the reception committee waiting outside.

'They saw you go into the supermarket?'

'Yes.'

'How many were there?'

'Two, maybe three.'

'Could you describe any of them? Height, skin colour, hair colour, clothing?'

'I didn't look at them. Didn't want to draw attention to myself.'

'Not sure that it worked,' he said, drily. 'There's nothing you can tell me about them?'

But I hadn't singled any of them out for special attention, so could give only the vaguest of descriptions: jeans, hoodies, shaven heads. Talk about stereotyping.

'What about age?'

'I don't know. Late teens, early twenties?'

'Did you feel threatened by them?'

'One of them spat at me but . . . ' I tailed off.

He seemed taken aback, sceptical even. 'Spat at you?' He wanted to make sure he'd heard me correctly. 'Why?'

'You haven't seen the way I walk.'

'You make it sound like this has happened before.'

I said nothing.

'Jesus.'

His naivety would have made me laugh, but the pain in my ribs put a stop to that. 'I'm fair game,' I slurred. 'What'm I gonna do, fight back? Give them a verbal lashing?' The words came out painfully slowly, proving my point.

Maybe Fraser didn't catch all of that, but he got the gist. 'That's bad.' I liked the way he said it, not in that pitying 'oh, poor you' kind of way, but as statement of fact.

'It's the way it is.'

He gave a wry smile, rubbing a hand over his scalp. 'Yeah.' That he understood. 'But it doesn't make it right.'

I shrugged. Who said it did?

'Could it be the same group of youths who followed you?'

'S'possible. They were outside, but they might have seen me use the cashpoint.'

'Were you aware of being followed?'

'Not at all.' In reality, I had little memory of anything prior to the attack.

'Davey might be able to help,' Fraser said. 'If they were hanging around his shop, he might know them. Do you remember seeing any of them before?'

I shook my head again. I was getting tired now.

'From what you say it sounds like an opportunistic attack. I think it's likely these guys outside the shop saw you withdrawing the money and pounced.'

'They got my wallet?' His nod confirmed it. They must have waited till I passed out, as I had a sudden memory of hugging my jacket around me.

'Were you carrying anything else of value?' Fraser asked.

'Phone,' I said. 'And my watch.' Suddenly I noticed its absence on my wrist. It was a gift from a friend, and an expensive one at that.

'We didn't find those on you, so I think we can assume that this was a particularly brutal mugging. Don't worry, we'll take it very seriously. Spitting is one thing, aggravated assault is something else.'

I couldn't argue with that. No, really, I couldn't argue.

'This appears to give us a pretty clear motive, but for the record, can you think of anyone who'd want to hurt you?'

'Me? I'm not important enough . . .' I started to say, but as I did, an image of Ashley Curzon floated into my head. Would he? No, he'd have more important things to occupy himself with. And he'd certainly have no interest in my pathetic belongings. 'Who found me?' I asked, the thought suddenly occurring.

'Sorry?'

'Who—?'

'Oh, found you? A woman called it in.' He flicked back through the notebook. 'Keeley Moynihan. You know her?'

I nodded. Of course, she'd have wondered where I'd got to. Fraser didn't ask about our relationship and for some reason, I felt reluctant to offer him that information. In any case, who should appear in the doorway at that moment but the woman herself. Today she was casual, skinny jeans tucked into high boots, with a man's shirt belted over the top. She still looked as if she'd just stepped off the catwalk, and suddenly I realised I'd ceased to be the object of Fraser's attention. He jumped up from his seat, almost tipping it over in his eagerness, but Keeley was homing in on me like a surface-to-air missile.

'Hi, you. How are you doing?' She came over to the other side of the bed and kissed me long and slow, and with enough heat to make it clear to Fraser that we were already acquainted. It had exactly the effect she was aiming for.

When I came up for air, Fraser was struggling to wipe the look of near astonishment off his face. He closed his notebook. 'I guess that's enough for today,' he said, obviously completely distracted. 'I'll leave you to it.'

'I've been helping him with his enquiries,' I told Keeley. It was predictable as lines go, but they were both polite and patient enough to wait for me to say it.

'I'll be in touch,' said Fraser. 'And will let you know when there are any developments.'

Later that evening, after Keeley had gone, Freckle-face returned to dig me in for the night. She tucked the sheets in so tight, I could feel my lungs expand every time I breathed.

'You're a popular guy,' she said. 'Someone called Laura came to see you too — oh, and a guy called Jake, with his daughter. She's a piece of work, isn't she?'

His daughter? Jake would be thrilled to hear Plum called that. But I sensed that Freckle-face was testing me out. She wanted me to tell her that Plum wasn't Jake's daughter, and that Jake was single. I decided not to disabuse her. It was for her own protection.

CHAPTER SEVEN

On the drive back to the station I was relieved, almost to the point of euphoria. OK, I hadn't caught everything he'd said, but enough to not make it awkward and I'd got some decent notes to be going on with. And as we'd talked, I'd relaxed. He was just a guy. I tried to imagine coping with his situation all the time.

It was no surprise to find when I got back that Denny was in a meeting with Chief Superintendent Bowers — Bowers clearly doing what I wanted to do and picking Denny's brains. They seemed to have developed quite a friendship, now that Denny was cruising towards his exit. Well, no matter. I went straight to my desk and, logging on to the system, scrolled the Intranet to pull up the file on Stefan Greaves' mugging and add in the first interview notes. I did a search of Greaves' name to begin with, but no results came up. I went to last Friday night's incident log page and found a couple of burglaries, and sure enough the assault was listed, along with the crime number. The 999 call was logged at 10.24 p.m., but when I searched using that, again no file appeared. I worked through the list of newly created incident files, scrolling up and down several times, before accepting that there was nothing there. There was no getting away from it — details of the attack hadn't yet been recorded. There was bound to be an explanation for it, so I just had to bide my time and wait for Denny to reappear. Meanwhile, I put a call through to one of my favourite people. She wouldn't like me nagging her, but Natalie from the private forensic service would know if they'd had anything.

She picked up immediately.

'The gorgeous Natalie,' I said. 'Hi, how are you? It's Fraser from OCU2.' I can't remember who started it, but although we'd hardly spoken and never met, somehow our established habit was to indulge in a bit of gentle flirting on the phone.

'I'm good.' She was smiling. I could hear it. 'How are you, handsome Fraser from OCU2?'

'Yeah, I'm OK. I wanted to check on the processing time for clothes belonging to an assault victim, Stefan Greaves.' I gave her the crime number. 'They will have been submitted sometime since Friday evening.'

There was a pause while Natalie looked it up on the system, taking enough time for me to have drawn a little stick man hanging from a noose. Whatever had brought that on?

'Can you give me that number again?' Natalie asked. I repeated it for her. Another pause, producing the executioner in a hood, carrying, for some reason, a scythe. 'I'm sorry,' she came back. 'I haven't got any record of that name or number. Are you sure they came here?'

'You're our favourite people. We send everything to you,' I said, reminding her of the station details.

She sighed. 'Well we don't seem to have anything relating to that incident. We are pretty swamped at the moment though, and what with the weekend, there's a backlog and it might be that they just haven't been checked in yet.'

'OK, thanks.' She was right. Everyone's resources were overstretched, including ours. It could easily mean a simple delay in admin. Denny might even have held on to the clothing for now. But a check with the property store log turned up big fat nothing, nor did there seem to be anything on or around Denny's desk, which was puzzling.

When Denny finally appeared, late in the afternoon, he was preoccupied and I had to wait while he made a couple of phone calls before he even acknowledged me. Five foot nine and heavily built, from the belt on his trousers holding up his middle-aged paunch to his weatherworn face, he looked every one of his fifty-seven years.

'All right?' I asked, when he eventually got off the phone.

'Eh, oh, yeah.' Now that he'd noticed me, his grey eyes were shrewd and watchful beneath untamed brows. He could see that I was waiting for more. 'The chief wanted a bit of local knowledge, something he's got coming up.' Chief Superintendent Bowers, like me, was a relative new boy in the area. Typical of current police management, he was a fast track ex-public school copper with a double first in criminology and psychology who, if station gossip was to be believed, preferred his police work to be conducted from behind a desk.

'Oh yes, what's that then?'

'Oh, just a thing.' He couldn't have been more vague if he'd tried, but I let it go. I couldn't be arsed playing games.

'I've not long got back from interviewing Stefan Greaves,' I said instead.

'I know that name.' Denny frowned.

Seriously? 'The guy who was assaulted on Friday night,' I reminded him, trying to keep a lid on my impatience.

'Oh yeah, right, how did it go then?' He was trying to sound interested. I could hear the effort going in.

'Very well, actually.' I tried not to sound smug. 'The woman who found him came to visit.' I thought back to that kiss. Jesus, what a kiss. 'I think she must be his girlfriend.'

'Get away.' Denny looked up. Now I'd got his attention.

'Why shouldn't she be?' I didn't like to admit that I'd been surprised too.

'I don't know,' said Denny defensively. 'Still, he's a lawyer, isn't he? Must be worth a bit.'

I decided to ignore the crass assumption. 'Anyway, he doesn't remember too much yet, so I'll need to go back. Meanwhile we may have another witness. Davey, proprietor of the supermarket on Dog Lane. There was a gang of youths hanging around outside when Greaves went in to use the cashpoint. It's possible they might have followed him from there, or been lying in wait. I'll go and talk to him.'

'All right. If you think it'll do any good.' Talk about passive-aggressive. Maybe he was miffed that I hadn't completely cocked up. He'd hardly sat down and now, before five, he was reaching for his coat. 'I'm off,' he said, as if I hadn't noticed. 'I'll see you in the morning.'

There had been a change even in the short time I'd known him, I thought, watching him go. When I first got transferred here, Denny seemed to be a permanent fixture, the first one at his desk in the morning and usually the last to leave at night. Not anymore. These last few weeks, there was every indication that retirement couldn't come soon enough for him. I'd known from the start that I'd never to step into Booth's shoes. He and Denny had worked together for years. But I hadn't expected to be quite so comprehensively left out in the cold. Still, only a couple more weeks and hopefully I'd be able to make a fresh start with a new partner.

It wasn't until after Denny had gone that I realised I'd forgotten to ask him about Stefan Greaves' clothes. I briefly considered getting him on his mobile, but that would probably irritate him even more, so it would have to wait another day. The last thing I did before leaving was to phone the neighbourhood security division of the council — the team who now had responsibility for the remaining CCTV cameras in the town, though I held out little hope. Since the demise of the New Labour obsession with surveillance, most of the cameras had fallen into disrepair or been decommissioned. Sure enough, on Meridian Crescent, the war with vandalism had been waged and lost. I would have to depend on Davey and hope that his security cameras were operational.

I took a tablet from the store and drove home past Davey's, but he had a shop full. Tax on the poor in action, people were queuing up to buy their midweek lottery tickets, doubtlessly attracted by the poster in the window declaring that no fewer than three customers who'd bought tickets there had enjoyed substantial wins. There was no point stopping there now.

CHAPTER EIGHT

'I still wish you'd come and stay with us for a few days,' Laura said. Hers was one of the faces that had floated before me in my days of semi-consciousness, but now here she was, in the flesh, packing up the few belongings I'd accumulated during my hospital stay.

'I'll be fine,' I said, perched on the edge of the bed, wrestling my way into a shirt, trying to ignore the fact that my hands were shaking more than usual. I'd been X-rayed, scanned, poked and prodded, and so far as anyone could tell, there was no reason to keep me in hospital any longer. With resources stretched as they were, they couldn't wait to get rid of me so that someone else could have the bed.

The idea of being looked after by Laura for a few days was, in truth, an attractive one. But at the risk of sounding chippy, I didn't know if I could stay in such close proximity to the kind of cosy domesticity that was becoming ever more elusive with every passing year. 'Anyway, you're supposed to be taking it easy,' I reminded her, adjusting the cuff.

An abrupt laugh exploded from her. 'Adding you to the family won't make much difference. Besides, I'm only about fourteen weeks. There's a long way to go.'

'Exactly.' I looked up at her. 'Really, I'll be fine.' I picked up the coat she'd brought. 'What happened to my clothes, the ones I was wearing on Friday?' I asked, thinking of my leather jacket. I'd had it for years and was very attached to it. 'I suppose the police took them?'

Laura looked surprised. 'No, one of the nurses gave them to me the first time I visited. She didn't know what else to do with them, so most of your stuff is somewhere in our wash. I sent your jacket to the cleaners,' Laura went on. 'They couldn't be sure of restoring it to mint condition, but they said they'd give it a go.' Having finished what she was doing, Laura stood, arms folded, patiently watching me but knowing better than to offer any help. 'If you change your mind about staying with us, we're only a phone call away.'

'I know.' I decided not to mention the conversation I'd had with the doctor who'd brought the discharge medication earlier that afternoon.

'Some painkillers until the bruising subsides, and what do you take for the seizures?' he'd asked.

'I don't have seizures,' I told him, confidently. In that regard, I was one of the lucky ones.

'You had one on Saturday night. Didn't anyone tell you?' He glanced up from my notes.

Fuck. 'No.'

Picking up the chart at the foot of the bed, he flicked through the pages to show me. 'Recorded as a *grand mal*.' He glanced up. 'You're sure you haven't had them before?'

I nodded emphatically.

'Well, it was just the one,' he confirmed. 'You don't seem to have had any more, which means it might have been a one-off, resulting from the head trauma. They gave you a drubbing, didn't they?'

I assumed the question was rhetorical.

'You're going to need to be careful for a few days,' he went on. 'Is there someone you can stay with who can keep an eye on you?'

'Yes,' I'd told him. Technically it was true. I was simply choosing not to take advantage of that fact. He wasn't to know that.

'Good.'

Something else had been bugging me, but I wasn't sure whether to raise it. The doctor looked up and caught my eye. 'Yes?'

'When I was being attacked,' I began, unsure of how to proceed. 'Just before I passed out, I saw this kind of bright light in front of my eyes, a sort of way off, along a tunnel. I felt drawn towards it, as if it was inevitable, as if . . .' I stopped, feeling foolish.

'As if you were crossing to the other side?' He gave a wry smile.

Hearing it out loud it did sound ridiculous, but that's what I'd meant. 'Yes.'

'I'm not surprised,' the doctor said, as if it was the most natural thing in the world. 'It was a brutal attack. They nearly killed you, and I'm pretty sure that was their intention.'

I snorted. 'All for a few hundred quid.'

'Maybe they just got carried away. There isn't any evidence from the test results to indicate that your heart stopped beating, but it may have come close. Your body might have started to shut down. What you describe isn't new. Other patients have reported similar sensations, sometimes after tricky operations.' He smiled. 'Count yourself lucky, Mr Greaves, you've had a narrow escape. I'll see you back in a few days to make sure that everything's healing as it should. Do you need anything to help you sleep?'

'No. Thanks.'

And with that, he shook my hand and left.

* * *

Laura had thought of everything, including some much-needed cash — 'Oh yes, and something to put it in.' She dug into her handbag and retrieved a tiny, pink, bejewelled purse. 'Grace insisted that I offer you this. Or on the other hand, there's this, an old one of Simon's.' She matched the purse with a battered black wallet.

'Tell Grace I'm very touched by her offer.' I smiled, taking the wallet. 'Will she cope with the rejection?'

'She'll have forgotten all about it by now,' Laura said. 'Oh, and I've cancelled your credit cards too, so you'll need to arrange replacements.'

'What would I do without you?' I said, with feeling. On our way out, we stopped by the nurses' station to say goodbye and to thank Freckle-face.

'It's a pleasure.'

'Be seeing you,' I said, noticing now that her name was Claire.

'You'll have to be quick,' she said, with a grin. 'I'm leaving next month for Australia.'

'Their gain is our loss.' In a strange way, I felt genuinely saddened by the news.

'In the meantime, anything you need, you know where we are.'

* * *

The rain was lashing down as Laura stopped off at the supermarket on the way home, and I was glad of the trolley to lean on, disappointed at how unsteady and unnerved I felt. The outside world seemed louder and brasher than it had been four days ago. And was it my imagination, or was the stare-count particularly high today? Automatically I checked my flies, but of course they were safely zipped. Other people's curiosity was one of those things I had learned to live with but had never quite got used to. As youngsters, Laura and I had measured reactions on what we called the 'Gobsmack scale'. My mother always regarded it as something to be proud of, reminding me that celebrities attract the same kind of interest. 'Just imagine you're a famous film or sports star,' she would say, while we both ignored the obvious ironies therein. 'Now you know how they feel.' When my resilience is intact it's easy to deflect the unwanted attention, often with what I consider to be my most disarming smile, which tends to scare the shit out of people.

But today was different. I felt unusually self-conscious and awkward. In the checkout queue, as I wrangled Simon's wallet out of my inside jacket pocket and painstakingly plucked out a couple of banknotes, one middle-aged woman kept up an unblinking vigil throughout the whole manoeuvre, until eventually Laura asked, 'Something we can help you with?'. The woman was forced to look away but did so without a shred of shame.

Entering the front of my building, we had to walk past the spot where just a few nights previously, I'd lain helpless on the ground while a group of thugs kicked the living crap out of me. Even though the memories were hazy, I was surprised at how powerfully it unsettled me, and hurried past as quickly as possible. I opened my mouth to tell Laura about what I thought I had experienced, but stopped before any sound came out. Even with that endorsement from the doctor, I knew with absolute certainty that Laura would find the idea of my 'crossing over' to the other side hilarious, attributing it to some kind of mental breakdown. And the whole episode was humiliating enough as it was.

Laura helped me unpack the shopping and put it away, then she made a cup of tea. 'Do you want me to make you something to eat?'

'No, I'll be fine, thanks.'

'Sure?'

'Yes, I'm sure.' It came out more irritably than I'd intended, because the truth was, I didn't want her to go.

She gave me a measured look. 'Well, I'd best go and get Grace from the outlaws.'

I gave her a hug. 'Thanks. I'm grateful, really I am.'

'Well, what are mates for?'

And that was the point, really. Having her take on the role of caring for me in this big sister kind of way just brought to the surface my deep disappointment — and let's face it, resentment — that it was Simon she'd married and not me. Although in many ways Laura was like my twin sister, I'd long harboured the hope that it wouldn't always be that way. We had been close for as long as I could remember, growing up next door to each other only a couple of miles from where I now lived, going to the same toddler groups and primary school. She knew me as well as I knew myself, accepting me for what I am. But then the compensation came through, and I was sent to a private school that would 'better meet my needs'. We grew apart during those crucial teenage years and by the time we reconnected, Laura had already met Simon.

Throughout our childhood she'd been a brilliant advocate and supporter, and for a long time it must have seemed like one-way traffic until finally I was able to be there in her hour, or rather weeks, of need. The tearful phone call came late one Friday night, her second term into university in London. 'I'm pregnant,' she'd sobbed. Initially, Simon, who was beginning to develop his reputation as a journalist, freaked out and it looked as if Laura would be abandoned. But then he came to his senses and fifteen years later here they both still were, back in Charnford, with as decent a marriage as I've seen anywhere, along with two ravishing daughters and another baby on the way.

It felt weird being at home in the middle of a Wednesday afternoon. I paced around the flat a couple of times, reacquainting myself with everything. What the hell was I going to do? I never usually smoked during the week, but my nerves were jangling and the stash of roll-ups was conveniently still lying there on the sofa where Keeley had left it. I hadn't paid her for them yet, I realised. Taking one into the kitchen, I lit it by holding it shakily to the flame on the gas cooker. I needed it. It was the only thing that dissolved the tension in my muscles. Swimming helped too, but I realised that with the current state of my body, going to the public baths would be off the agenda for a while.

Feeling more chilled, I switched on my laptop to check my messages. Naturally, Crusader was already waiting for my next move. I had a look at the board, made my move and messaged him back. The response was instant, as if he'd been waiting for me: *What kept you? Afraid of what I might do?*

He always managed to sound vaguely menacing — if Crusader was a 'he', of course. I had no way of knowing. Occasionally, online opponents were inclined to chat, and we'd exchange a few personal details, but that wasn't Crusader's style. He preferred mystery. His next move was already planned, and he made it straight away, a move that was predictably unpredictable. Ordinarily I'd have tried to figure out what his overall strategy might be, but today I couldn't concentrate. Standing over the chessboard, a sudden, vivid sensation had come back to me: the unpleasant smell that had, if I was right about it, brought me back from the brink of death. I should have been grateful, but even the memory of that rank odour almost made me gag. The smell, real or imagined, had re-entered my nostrils and I couldn't clear it. It was further compounded by the overlay of *eau d'hôpital*, which meant that every time I inhaled, I was reminded of the attack. I was overcome with a sudden impulse to wash off every trace of it. Having only recently got dressed, the prospect of going through the whole rigmarole again was an exhausting one, but I knew that until I did, I wouldn't settle. Getting the water as hot as I could bear, I ducked into the shower and scrubbed at the left side of my face until it was sore and my ear throbbing.

CHAPTER NINE

On my way to work the next day, I called in at Davey's supermarket, in the hope that things there would be a bit less fraught. Back where I came from, a business like this would have been owned and run by an Asian family. I understood that this one had been once but the Guptas had departed not long after a botched firebomb attack had highlighted their vulnerability, and Davey had taken it on. My calculation was sound — the shop was much quieter than last night, with just the odd customer calling in for fags or a newspaper on their way to work. Even so, I had to wait a few minutes until Davey was free. I showed him my identification.

'Do you know about the assault that took place not far from here, on Meridian Crescent, last Friday night? It was a guy called Stefan Greaves, he'd just been in to use your cash machine.'

'I heard about that. It was a terrible thing.' Davey was all sympathy. 'He often comes in here. He's all right.'

'Do you remember him coming in on Friday?'

'Yes, he bought some milk.'

'He said there were some kids hanging around outside your shop when he came in. Any idea who they might be?'

He shook his head dubiously. 'When it's dark and I'm back here, you can't really see much out there. There are often people around.'

'They might have been into the shop too, though. Do you remember serving any customers immediately before Mr Greaves?'

He was dismissive. 'Friday's always busy — people come in to pick up last-minute groceries for the weekend, or for their lottery tickets. It's hard to remember from one day to the next exactly who's been in.' He seemed to be finding eye contact a challenge. But what he said wasn't unreasonable. I couldn't decide if he was telling the truth or he was simply worried about possible reprisals.

'Was anyone else serving in the shop with you that night, at about ten?'

'The missus was here earlier in the evening, but by that time it would have just been me.'

'What about the cameras?' I nodded towards the CCTV.

He shook his head. 'Stored on the hard drive. I wipe them every twenty-four hours. I didn't hear about the attack until Sunday so by then it was too late.'

I held up the tablet. 'Would you look at some pictures for me, see if you recognise anyone?'

Davey was hesitant. 'I'm not sure I can help you. I told you I don't really remember who else came in the shop on Friday. The days all merge into one.'

'I know, but just humour me, will you?' I said. 'You'd be surprised at how often a picture can just spark something. You may be the closest thing to a witness we've got.' And even if he didn't admit recognition, his reactions might be telling.

'OK.' He didn't like it, but really, how could he refuse? He called a young woman through to the shop while we went behind the counter and into a room that smelled strongly of detergent. We sat on a sagging sofa, surrounded by stacks of toilet rolls and cardboard cartons of stock for the shop. I booted up the tablet and we began scrolling through pages of mug shots. I'd rounded up images of the local lowlifes aged between fifteen and thirty-five who weren't currently serving time. It was a gruesome gallery. On page three we scored a hit of sorts. Although he said nothing, Davey's body stiffened almost imperceptibly. Resisting the urge to pick up on it, I continued on. A couple of pages later, the same thing happened.

This time I pounced. 'Someone you know, Davey?'

He shrugged. 'I'm not sure. Maybe. He could just be a customer. Since the lottery wins, we're very popular.'

'Which one?'

He indicated the young man in the bottom right hand corner, with cropped mousy hair, sharp features, and a tattoo to one side of his throat.

'You think he was in the shop on Friday evening?'

'He might have been. Like I said, it's hard to remember.'

I backtracked to page three. 'You recognised someone here, too. Which one?'

The man he indicated looked barely out of his teens, olive-skinned, his head shaved. 'Have you ever seen these men together?'

'I don't know. Maybe.'

'Any others with them?'

This time just a shrug.

I was getting desperate. 'Is there anything you can tell me about them, what they were wearing, what they bought, anything?'

'I don't remember what they bought, it could have been crisps or something. I think they were quite boisterous, a lot of banter and that. I think they're off the estate.'

When I was growing up, 'estate' was simply the descriptive word for a housing development, but in recent years it had become so much more loaded.

'Thanks, Davey, it's a start,' I said. 'Would you be prepared to come into the station and see if you can pick them out from a line-up?'

'I don't know about that.'

'Davey, Stefan Greaves was badly beaten up. He could have died. I want to get these guys off the street. They wouldn't see you, or be able to identify you.'

'I'll think about it.'

I had to settle for that. 'Great,' I said, with more enthusiasm than I felt. 'I'll give you a call when we can set something up.'

* * *

Back at the station, I looked up the two men that Davey had identified: Sam Bostwick and Evan Phelps. The names didn't ring any bells, but then I still had a lot to learn about the local colour.

'What have you got there?' Suddenly, Denny was at my shoulder, looking at the picture of Evan Phelps. When I explained, he was far from excited about my two newly identified suspects.

'It won't be either of them,' he said, instantly crushing any hopes I might have had. 'I know Bostwick, and I vaguely remember Phelps getting caught up in something or other, but I don't think they even know each other.'

'It doesn't mean they don't,' I returned. 'Davey was pretty certain with his identification.' I was laying it on thick, but Denny wasn't taken in.

'What, that they were outside his shop? So what?' He moved round to sit at his own desk. 'I've known Bostwick for years,' he went on. 'He's a troublemaker all right, but apart from anything else he wouldn't be in Greaves' part of town. He doesn't stray that far from his patch — too parochial. Plus, he wouldn't have it in him to initiate something like that.'

'Could easily have been an impulsive thing,' I challenged.

Denny shook his head regretfully. 'Your witness has made a mistake. You have to be mindful of that. Witnesses often want to please you. The human brain likes to make connections where it can — often they're not exactly lying but their eagerness causes them to jump to false conclusions.'

I felt a stab of annoyance. I might not know either of these men, but I didn't need a patronising lecture. I was well aware of how witnesses could behave, and I was convinced it didn't apply in this case. I was half inclined to mention Greaves' clothes, and see how Denny wriggled out of that one, but this was the longest conversation we'd had in days, and though he seemed in a pretty good mood, he remained volatile. I didn't want to upset things by pointing out what was at best an oversight, and at worst a mistake. Especially as it was probably too late now to do anything about it. It occurred to me in that moment that maybe Denny was one of these coppers I'd heard about who is actually frightened of retirement, worrying about how he'd fill the hours after the job came to an end. It might account for the reticence and negativity. If that was the case, then criticism of his handling of the job was the last thing he needed.

Besides, at that moment, Bowers strolled in.

'Denny,' he said, casually. 'When you've got a moment.' He dipped his head towards his office.

'Blimey, what does he want now,' I muttered, more out of frustration than anything else.

'To discuss arrangements for Operation—' Denny's head snapped round, guilt all over his face. He'd let that slip unintentionally.

'Operation what?'

'Doesn't matter, it's nothing. A visitor, that's all,' he said, managing to look as awkward as a six-year-old caught with his hand in the biscuit tin. Suddenly he was preoccupied with rearranging random sheets of paper in his tray stack.

'Well that's hardly unique,' I pushed. 'What visitor?'

He went on rearranging. 'Someone who doesn't want a lot of fuss made.'

And yet he or she commanded their own ops title. 'When's this, then?'

'Not sure exactly, a couple of weeks or so. It's been in the planning for some time. I suppose it's never certain if these things will come off. Anyway, on the off-chance it goes ahead, the chief wants some local knowledge, and a bit of security support. He's keen to get it right.'

I'll bet he was. From what I could tell, schmoozing dignitaries seemed to be Bowers' favourite occupation by some distance and I could imagine a visit by any VIP would be a dream come true for him. No prizes for guessing where all his energies would be centred for the immediate future.

'Why all the secrecy?' I asked.

'No secret,' Denny said. 'They just want to keep below the radar, that's all. Forget it, will you? It's no big deal.'

So why was I left thinking exactly the opposite?

* * *

Despite what Denny had said, after he'd gone, I logged onto the Police National Computer (or PNC, as we call it) to see what we had on Bostwick and Phelps. No harm in educating myself, I thought, though at first glance I had to concede that Denny might have had a point. For one thing, they didn't look a very likely pairing. Bostwick was white and the older of the two — early thirties — and lived in one of the remaining down at heel areas of the notorious Flatwood estate. He wasn't listed as having a regular job. But then, from what I'd heard, there wasn't much in the way of prospects for kids growing up on the Flatwood. Detail was sparse and Bostwick didn't at first glance have much of a record. A habitual offender when he was in his teens, between then and now, either he'd stopped altogether or, what was more likely, he'd got good enough at it to fly under the radar. I wondered what might have prompted the move to aggravated assault at this point in his life. There was a queried annotation 'WA?', which must have been local code and meant nothing to me. I'd have to ask Denny at some point. It was a bugger we didn't have Greaves' clothes. Who knew what they might have yielded?

Evan Phelps, on the other hand, had an address on the smarter side of town and had only just turned twenty. His sole misdemeanour was a burglary three years ago, which had been called in by a Mr Hywel Phelps of the same address, which suggested to me that Phelps might have been turned in by his own father. That in turn suggested a possible drug dependency problem that could have resulted in him stealing from his family. Phelps had been arrested along with another unnamed — so presumably innocent — youth of the same age, and got a caution for his trouble. So why was Phelps hanging out with Bostwick last Friday night? Was Davey mistaken, or had he been stringing me along to get rid of me?

What might settle it, I decided, would be to run the same catalogue of faces past Stefan Greaves. If he picked out Phelps and Bostwick too, then I might be onto something. But when I turned up at the hospital, I learned that Greaves had already been discharged.

CHAPTER TEN

Emerging from the shower, a towel around my waist, this was the first time since the mugging I'd looked in a mirror. The one clear bruise on my face, from when I'd been slammed into the wall, had mutated to an impressive dark purple, with a speckled graze that ran down the length of my cheek. Maybe that's what the woman in the supermarket had been drawn to — I couldn't say I blamed her. I was admiring the rest of the handiwork, including the multicoloured ribs and abdomen, when the door buzzer sounded. Shit, who could that be? Standing frozen by the sink, I realised that I was slightly afraid. It occurred to me for the first time that my attackers had struck, almost literally, on my front doorstep. They knew the block where I lived. Did they also know which flat was mine? Fraser had intimated that he thought the attack was random, but they would know by now that I was easy prey, virtually incapable of defending myself. They might also think I'd seen enough to shop them. What would stop them from coming back for another try? This feeling of vulnerability was new and unwelcome, and I considered ignoring the buzzer. I could at least establish who it was, though. Limping through to the hall, I pushed the intercom button.

'Hi Stefan, it's PC Fraser.' The Scots accent was immediately reassuring. 'Those pictures. Would it be convenient to come in for a few minutes?'

Relieved, I debated whether to make Fraser wait the ten minutes it would take me to get dressed again, or even a couple of minutes while I battled my way into my boxers. But I was decent, just about if I kept hold of the towel (no mean feat), and as a police officer he'd hardly be green around the gills, so I simply said 'yes' and let him in, though not before throwing the bag of roll-ups into a drawer and wafting the air around a bit with a cushion. Understandably, he was a little disconcerted when I opened the door.

'Don't panic,' I said, letting him in and taking him through to the living room. 'I'm not coming on to you. Just inspecting the damage.'

But by now he was distracted by the sight of my multi-shaded body.

'Christ, they really made a mess of you, didn't they?' He averted his gaze.

'You think I could flog it to the Tate?' It was an offbeat comment and I didn't expect him to understand what I was saying, but he laughed.

'You could enter for the Turner Prize.'

'I'll go and get dressed.'

'No hurry,' he said, lifting his right arm and a tablet. 'This is running a bit low, I'll plug it in to charge.'

'Make yourself at home.' Directing Fraser to the nearest electric socket, I retreated to the bedroom, all too aware of the lingering smell of weed. By the time I had laboriously pulled my clothes back on and returned, exhausted, to the living room, he had set up the computer on the dining table.

'Interesting room freshener you use,' he said, without looking up from the screen.

'Cuts down on the spasms. Helps me relax,' I said, keeping my tone casual. He responded with the slightest nod of the head. He wasn't going to make anything of it. It was time to fess up. 'I'd been smoking on the night I was attacked,' I told him.

Now he looked at me. 'You were stoned?'

'As a raisin. You going to arrest me?'

He shook his head. 'I don't think so. Not this time.'

'It might explain why my memory's a bit hazy.'

He shrugged. 'Yeah, that or the fact that the bastards beat you senseless.'

I decided I liked this guy. 'You want a beer?'

'Nice thought, but no thanks. I'm on duty. A coffee would go down all right though.'

It took me a while, but he didn't seem to mind the wait. Coming back into the lounge, there was something else I had to get off my chest. 'I remembered something else when I came back here,' I said, putting his coffee down within reach.

'Yeah?'

I had considered the possibilities and decided to go with the one that was most palatable. 'I think one of them threw something bleachy on me,' I said.

Now he was sceptical. 'Jeez. No one said anything about that. Are you sure?'

'I remember a kind of burning sensation, and the smell. It came back to me when I walked past the spot earlier. Now it's like I can't get it off me.' The shower hadn't made much difference, I realised.

He pulled a face. 'Well that's good . . . I mean, not good that they did it, obviously, but it might give us a lead, especially if it's been a factor in any other assaults.' His turn to look awkward now. 'What happened to the clothes you were wearing that night?'

'One of the nurses gave them to my friend Laura, so she took them home to wash. All except my leather jacket, and that's gone to the cleaners.'

'Shit.'

'So you *did* want them for forensics.'

He sighed heavily. 'Yeah, slight communication break-down there. I suppose I thought Denny, my partner, had collected them, and I guess he left it to me.' He looked puzzled. 'Laura's not the girl who found you.'

'No, that's Keeley. Laura's another friend.'

'You have a lot of women running around after you,' he observed. 'Do you know if she's actually washed them yet?'

'I would think so. She's pretty efficient and she did mention it when she picked me up this morning.' So — we both knew — any useful samples would have been eliminated. 'I can double-check with her, if you like?'

'Yeah, might be worth a try.' Fraser handed me the tablet. 'Meanwhile have a look at these — some possible candidates. It's a long shot, but sometimes seeing the face again can just jog the memory.'

He brought up a grid with nine mug shots, without exception as unflattering as the average passport photo. I didn't recognise any of them. For the next while, I swiped across page after page of similarly anonymous faces in near silence, the only rhythm provided at the end of each page by a shake of my head. The parade seemed to go on forever, and after a while they all began to blur into one another, with their mostly shaven heads and grim expressions. A couple of times a spark of familiarity flared, until I realised it was just my short-term memory playing tricks. Finally, Fraser sat back.

'That's it,' he said. 'The full extent of our rogues' gallery.'

My sigh was pure frustration. 'It could have been anyone,' I grumbled. I felt sure that there were one or two faces I could have seen before, but I couldn't definitively place any of them in the context of Friday night.

'Don't worry about it,' Fraser said, philosophically. 'It might just be too soon. We'll try it again in a week or so. For what it's worth, Davey at the supermarket has picked out a couple of possibilities.'

'Really?'

'Don't get your hopes up. I haven't had the chance to check them out yet. Might be nothing. Do the names "Bostwick" or "Phelps" mean anything to you?'

They didn't, and my disappointment must have been crystal clear.

'Like I say — may turn out to be nothing anyway,' said Fraser. He powered down the tablet and unplugged the cable. Sipping his coffee, he cast a look around the room. 'Nice place you've got here,' he said.

'You're wondering how I can afford it?' It was a touch defensive, though I hadn't meant it that way.

'Of course not. You're a lawyer, aren't you?' But he'd coloured a little. It had crossed his mind.

'I'm a glorified clerk. Let's be accurate about it. I don't blame you. There was a compensation settlement,' I said. 'My mum invested it in a trust fund, and enjoyed her own pretty lucrative career.'

'She was a lawyer too?'

'Not exactly. She was a model.'

'Wow.'

'Yeah, how about that?'

'Well, thanks for the coffee.' He took his mug through to the kitchen, passing the chessboard on the way. 'You're in the middle of a game,' he observed.

'An online game,' I said. 'Quite often, I can hold the moves in my head, but this one's more of a challenge. He's a strong opponent, so I need to play it out.'

'Who is he?'

'I don't know anything other than his pseudonym, Crusader. He could be anyone, anywhere in the world.'

'You don't know anything about him?'

'Only his nickname and his chess ranking, which is about the same as mine.'

'Does he know anything about you?'

'Hardly, he's not much of one for chat. Do you play?'

'Not really. I'm more of a five-a-side man, me.'

'Oh, I was a footballing legend too, but tough choices and all that . . .' At that moment a motorbike outside backfired and I leapt. Fortunately, I'd drunk my coffee so nothing got spilled.

'You OK?' Fraser asked.

'Yeah, it's just spasms. They happen to me. It's nothing to get alarmed about.'

'Looked like more than that to me,' he said, astutely.

'I felt safe here.'

'Not now?'

'It happened just outside, a bit close for comfort.' I was disappointed to realise that going out by myself after dark was not something I would relish in the immediate future, and I was dismayed by my apparent lack of resilience.

Fraser was reassuring. 'Feeling vulnerable isn't uncommon,' he said. 'Victims of these kinds of crimes often get a dip in confidence immediately after the incident. It'll come back. Your girlfriend doesn't live here with you, then?'

'My . . . ?' I had to think for a minute. 'Oh, Keeley? No, no she doesn't.' I'd assumed that he might have worked out who she was by now, but as he hadn't, I wouldn't disillusion him just yet.

I walked with him to the front door. 'I know it's what everyone asks, but are you likely to catch them?' Posing the question, I was fully aware of my own shortcomings as a witness.

'Honestly? I don't know. We've got Davey's leads to follow up, which might help us with the lads who were hanging around outside his shop, but there's no CCTV outside your building, and we've got no other witnesses who would have got a clear sighting.'

His mobile rang. 'Sorry,' he said, glancing at it. 'Denny. My partner. I need to take this.'

'Sure. I appreciate you stopping by,' I said, and meant it.

'No problem. Look, my experience tells me this was a "wrong place, wrong time" opportunistic attack. I can't see them coming back. Really.'

'I'm sure you're right,' I said, though I wasn't convinced.

CHAPTER ELEVEN

Denny. First time for everything. Calling to tick me off for wasting my time, probably. He kept it brief and to the point: 'Where are you?'

'Meridian Crescent. Just about to leave.'

'Well step on it. We've got a shout.'

'Ten minutes,' I said, and ended the call.

Something felt odd, driving back to the station, the rain drumming on the roof of the car. I couldn't work it out to begin with, then I realised that the weird thing about it was Denny calling on me for assistance. The rain had slowed the traffic to a crawl and my ten minutes became twenty. As soon as I drew up in the car park, Denny came running from the building and threw himself into the passenger seat, cursing.

'What took you so long?'

'Flooding,' I said. 'You might have noticed it's raining, again. What's the panic?'

'A body's been found on the riverbank by a couple of water company surveyors, a mile or so downstream of the town.' He broke off briefly to give me directions. 'Our involvement will be a formality, so I want to get it over with.' This last was said with authority, as we idled in a traffic queue where temporary lights had been set up around a flooded stretch of road.

'Why a formality?' I didn't doubt him for a second. Even with his years of experience, he'd never struck me as one to race to judgements.

'It'll be a jumper.'

'How can you be so sure?'

'We haven't had one for a while and we generally get one every few months. Short of the likes of Beachy Head or Clifton Suspension Bridge, the Charn is the next best thing, especially at this time of year when it's in full spate. There are some fierce currents.' He stared out at the rain running down the gutters. 'Bet you a tenner.' I wasn't going to take him on, but once again felt a twinge of regret that I'd been somehow cheated of the benefits of his knowledge. It explained why Bowers was so keen to keep Denny close. The lights changed to green and I drove cautiously through a puddle that must have come halfway up the wheel arches.

'What were you doing at Meridian Crescent, anyway?' Denny asked. I sensed he was passing the time rather than genuinely interested.

'I was at Stefan Greaves' place.'

There followed a pause, after which he asked, 'What for?'

'I thought I'd see if he could pick anyone out.'

'And did he?'

'No,' I admitted with some irritation. 'And it's unfortunate,' I went on. 'Even if we had DNA on file for the perpetrators, we didn't get Greaves' clothing, so there's nothing to compare it with.' I let it hang for a moment.

'You didn't take his clothes?' Denny asked, innocently.

'I wasn't the first at the hospital,' I reminded him, doing my best not to make it an accusation. 'I guess I thought they'd already been processed.'

'Ah well, it's unlikely we'd have got anything anyway,' said Denny, finding a renewed interest in what lay beyond the window. 'You want my advice, you'll spend your time on other cases. That one isn't worth pursuing.'

'Why not?' There were so many things wrong with that statement that I didn't know where to start. Mostly, I was angered by the implications of the word 'worth'. Did Denny really believe that for whatever reason, Stefan Greaves wasn't a 'worthwhile' cause?

'You're never going to get a conviction without material evidence, are you?' Denny said. 'Not in a million years, and no one's going to thank you for wasting your time on it. You'd be better off focusing your energy on something that will get you a result.'

'But surely . . .' I tailed off. I wanted to say that we ought to try anyway, that no victim was of any less value than another, but he was *right about the politics. There was always pressure to solve the more serious crimes and — though nobody said it out loud — the ones we were sure to get a conviction on. With budgets tied tightly to results, as they had been the last ten years, it was all anyone upstairs was really interested in. I could have pointed out that had Stefan Greaves' clothes been sent straight to forensics as they should have, getting DNA might have given us our material evidence. But my feeling was that Denny had simply forgotten and that this casual dismissal was to cover his embarrassment. Although his attitude was infuriating, perhaps it was inevitable. He was starting to wind down, his mind elsewhere, and I didn't want to get into an argument with him, so that was the matter effectively closed.*

'I bet you won't be sorry to leave this behind,' I said to change the subject.

'What, the traffic or the weather? You can say that again.' Then he answered my real question. 'I can't imagine I'll be sitting on my sun lounger thinking longingly of cadavers either.'

'Has the paperwork all gone through?' The purchase of his villa on the Algarve, I knew, had not been a straightforward one.

'At long last. And we've got a date to hand over the keys to the house here, so there's no stopping Sheila now. She's throwing stuff out like the world's about to end. If I sit in the same place too long, she'll probably have me carted off to the charity shop too,' he chuckled. It was good to see his spirits lift and glimpse the Denny everyone had told me about when I first arrived.

'When do you leave England?' I had a good idea but wanted to prolong the bonhomie.

'End of next month. About six weeks. We're going to have to lodge with Sheila's mum for a couple of weeks, but even that will be worth it. I can't wait.' It was the most heartfelt statement I'd ever heard him make.

* * *

Our time in attendance at the deposition site was, by some margin, in inverse proportion to the time we took to get there. The strobing lights of the response vehicles, parked higgledy-piggledy along the grass verge, cast an icy flicker over the gloomy scene. The SOCOs (scenes of crime officers) seemed to have beaten us to it. Denny wouldn't be happy about that. I pulled in at the back of the row and, donning waterproof jackets, we set off on foot — or at least tried to. There was no real path through the undergrowth, just a narrow corridor of flattened and broken greenery sitting atop a quagmire. Slipping and sliding with each step, it was as much as we could do to stay on two feet, while wet foliage slapped at us from all directions. Before we even got within sight of the body, we were met at the makeshift cordon by the police surgeon, Dr Shea, who advised against going any further. At this point, he more or less had to shout at us over the combined sound of the rain and the rushing river, and I didn't catch everything, but we got the gist. Deposition site unstable . . . chunks of riverbank breaking away . . . too close to the fast-flowing river . . . impossible to construct a tent . . . any physical evidence almost certainly compromised. 'We're going to have to move him as soon as the SOCOs have finished filming and photographing!' he yelled in conclusion.

Denny nodded. 'Suicide?'

This time it was Shea's turn to nod. 'Most likely. He's been in the water a while.'

'Any ID?' asked Denny.

A shake of the head from Shea.

So Denny's assessment of the situation had been accurate. All we could do now was dry off and wait for the post-mortem for clues as to whom the deceased might be. It was a depressing end to the day.

CHAPTER TWELVE

Opening the front door of our house, a three-floor modern build, I was greeted by the smell of frying onions and garlic. 'Hi, sweetheart,' I called.

Sonia popped her head out of the kitchen, where, from the sound of it, she was cooking some kind of stir-fry for supper, the radio chattering in the background. She was flushed from the cooking, her wayward hair pushed back, and she looked gorgeous. We'd been together seven years now and I still couldn't really believe my luck.

'You're late,' she said, though it was nothing more than an observation. 'And wet,' she added, taking in the slicked-down hair. 'What kept you?'

'A suspected suicide.'

'How horrible. How did they—?'

I gave her the bare facts such as I knew them and she was silent for a moment. 'Are you OK?'

'Aye.' She wasn't convinced. 'Really.' I added.

'OK, well, go and get dried off. Dinner will be on the table in ten minutes.'

* * *

'Mum called earlier,' Sonia told me as we sat down to eat.

'Are they all right?'

'They're both fine. But it'll be her birthday the week after next. I wondered if we could go up and see them sometime.'

'Sure.' It would mean a drive up the motorway to near Blackburn. 'I'll just need to see how my shifts are.'

'OK, but soon, eh?'

'Yeah.' I tried to sound keen. I had no objection to visiting Sonia's parents in itself, but I knew that the minute we got there, her mum would start turning the screws (in her own subtle way, of course) about grandkids. Now that we'd actually made the decision to go ahead with that, I could do without the extra pressure.

'How's the rest of your day been?' she asked. 'With the lovely Denny?'

'Och, he's OK.'

'Still not cutting you much slack?' Perceptive as ever, my missus.

'I really hoped when I started the job that we could work well together, y'know? But it's becoming more and more obvious that he's just biding his time till retirement and doesn't really give a toss about me. We seem to be having less and less to do with each other, and now the super's got him working on preparations for an upcoming visit by some mysterious VIP.'

'Who?'

'That's the point. Denny won't say. I don't think he even meant to tell me that much, though I definitely get the impression it's someone important. God knows why he, or she, might be coming here.'

'Why not?' said Sonia. 'Charnford's as good as anywhere else, better than a lot of places, you might say. We moved here,' she pointed out.

'Yeah, but that was for other reasons, wasn't it? And as I've learned over the last few days, it's not exactly a crime-free zone.'

'Have you made any progress on that mugging you attended?'

'Maybe,' I said, trying to muster some enthusiasm. 'I ran some potential suspects past the guy in the supermarket and he definitely reacted to a couple, but I'll need more before I can bring them in.'

'No DNA?'

'There might be something on the National Database, but nothing to compare it with, thanks to a screw-up with collecting Greaves' clothes.'

'What kind of screw-up?'

'I'm not exactly sure. I assumed Denny had taken them for forensics, so I didn't bother asking at the hospital, but he hadn't. I think he forgot.'

'Have you tackled him about it?'

'Sort of. But it's too late to rectify, and all it would achieve is making Denny even more antagonistic towards me in his last couple of weeks in the job. What good would that do? I went back to talk to the victim, though, Stefan Greaves.'

'Is it going all right with him?'

'What do you mean?'

'You forget how well I know you, Michael Fraser,' she said, with a smile. 'You weren't looking forward to that first interview, were you?'

'I don't know what I was worried about. It was stupid. He's an all right bloke — of course he is.'

'Does he know how you felt?'

'I don't think so.'

'Well, no harm done, was there? He's got to you though, hasn't he?'

'I'd like to find out who did him over, if that's what you mean. But I'd feel that way about any victim. Although Denny's made it clear that he doesn't have much confidence in my ability to solve the case.'

'All the more reason to prove him wrong, then. And isn't it better that he trusts you and leaves you to get on with your job rather than breathing down your neck all the time?'

'Aye, I suppose.'

'And once he's retired you might get a decent partner you can build a real relationship with.'

'I know, but it still feels like a missed opportunity. I could have learned such a lot from him, if he'd let me.'

'He hasn't got much longer now, has he?'

'Week after next. Tomorrow night's the first of his leaving bashes. I'll be late home. Naturally, I've got the job of babysitting him for the day so that they can organise it while he's out of the way.'

'Very subtle,' she chuckled.

'Yeah, well that's the police for you.'

CHAPTER THIRTEEN

Early that evening, the phone rang. It was Laura.

'Are you checking up on me?'

'As a matter of fact, I am,' she said, candidly. 'How are you doing?'

'I'm OK. Police came to see me again.'

'Good. Anything?'

'Not really. Unreliable witness.'

'Just unreliable, you mean,' she joked. 'Listen, I meant to ask you earlier about supper on Saturday night. You were otherwise engaged last weekend. Want to come this week instead? Do you feel up to it?'

'I might, just about.'

'Great, we'll see you at about seven then. And you're sure you're OK on your own tonight? It's not too late to change your mind. Simon hasn't left work yet, so he can quite easily—'

'Really, I'll be fine,' I lied and she rang off.

In the ordinary course of things, I would have been fine. I'd kind of got used to being on my own. Kind of.

Did I fancy some company tonight? Nah, Keeley would probably be busy, and while some parts of my anatomy might be (quite literally) up to it, I wasn't sure if the rest of my battered body could take it. Instead, I spent a restless night. I spent more than an hour or so gazing at the chessboard trying to work out Crusader's strategy, but my mind kept wandering back to that Friday night. Nothing on TV held my attention for very long either, so in the end I settled on an early night. Once in bed, though, I started to think back to the doctor's words and lay there for a long time wondering if I was about to have another seizure. I wished I hadn't declined those sleeping pills.

I was determined to make it into work on Thursday morning. I'd go stir-crazy if I had to spend any more time cooped up in the flat on my own. A gang of teenagers got on the bus at the stop after mine, loud and jostling for space. They were school kids, that was all, but I made sure I steered clear of them. A couple of them eyed me up as they walked up the aisle to the back seats, and again it was hard to deflect the unwanted attention. Suddenly I was fearful of provocation.

As I walked into reception, Jake looked up from the wad of letters he was flicking through.

'What are you doing here?' he asked, with a hint of accusation.

'I still have a job, don't I?'

'But shouldn't you be resting or something?'

'Staring at four walls, you mean? Not really for me.'

'How are you?' Beneath her stiffly coiffed hair, Barbara was all sympathy, which was the last thing I needed. She'd got used to having me around now, Barbara, but she was of the generation who still thought I was 'terribly brave' to venture into the outside world and try to earn a living.

'Walk this way,' said Jake, leading into his office. Still preoccupied with the mail, he waited until I was inside, kicking the door shut behind us in a deft manoeuvre that I envied. 'Have the police been in touch? Are they looking at anyone?' he asked. He flopped down behind his desk, casting aside the pile of post. It landed in the miniscule space between the blocks of files that covered the rest of its surface. Even though it wasn't yet nine o'clock, his tie had slipped a couple of inches below his unfastened top button and I wondered what time he'd left the office last night.

'They've been to see me a couple of times,' I said, lowering myself carefully into the chair opposite, my ribs protesting all the way. 'A Scot called Fraser.' His slight incline of the head indicated that Jake didn't know him, although he was acquainted with many of the local police. 'But I can't give them much. It all happened pretty fast, and it was dark, so I still can't remember enough to give a clear description.'

'Well, it might come back to you.'

'That's what Fraser said. You came to see me in the hospital too?'

He looked slightly embarrassed. 'Yeah, you were a bit out of it.'

'Sorry about that. I'd have made more of an effort if I'd known. You made an impression, though.'

'Eh?'

'One of the nurses. I think she took a shine to you.'

'My natural charisma,' he said. The remark might have been tongue-in-cheek coming from anyone else, but not from Jake. He frowned. 'And you're sure you're OK to be here?'

'I need to be.'

'One condition then: that you start with short days today and tomorrow and go home if you need to.'

'All right.'

A brief nod. Jake trusted me to make my own decision and accepted it. In a nutshell, he treated me like a grown-up and always had. In the months after I graduated with first class honours, I'd sat in front of numerous interview panels that had ranged from the mildly condescending to the downright offensive, and discovered in a few short weeks what a pile of crap all the 1990s' equal rights legislation had been. Out of desperation, I'd ended up taking a low-level administrative job working for a voluntary organisation. My qualifications seemed to count for nothing. I'd set out with high ideals about being honest right from the start, but that didn't last long. Even though I hadn't explicitly disclosed anything on my application form for PGW, Jake had displayed absolutely no reaction when I'd shown up for the interview. Throughout the meeting, he'd allowed me plenty of time to speak, and from his responses I could tell he'd had surprisingly few problems with understanding me. When he did miss something, he'd simply asked me to repeat what I'd said. At the end, when he'd asked me the standard 'anything else you'd like to tell us' question, I'd felt compelled to mention the elephant in the room.

'OK,' he'd said, so deadpan that I had been convinced he was taking the piss. 'How does that affect your work?'

To indulge him, I'd stated the obvious: speed and communication.

'Well, thank you for pointing that out,' he'd said. Then had come the blow. 'I should warn you that we're interviewing another strong, highly qualified candidate this afternoon.' So he'd put me through all that just to give me the brush off right at the end, probably just so that he could feel good about doing his bit for equal opportunities, I'd thought. I'd left the offices seething. That evening, Jake rang to offer me the job.

'What about the other strong candidate?' I'd asked. 'Qualifications not stand up?'

There had been a short pause while Jake deciphered what I'd said, always harder on the phone.

'Oh yes,' he'd replied eventually. 'But he was a twat.'

Just a few minutes after I was installed behind my desk, Plum sauntered in and was equally surprised to see me, a reaction she did nothing to hide. Despite having been with us a couple of years now, we all still referred to Plum as the 'work experience girl', because that was how she'd started, Jake doing a favour to his ex-wife, who counselled at a local rehabilitation centre. At the time, it was a gamble. All we had known about Victoria, as she was known then, was that she'd run away from home aged thirteen and spent a couple of years on the streets with her new best friends — industrial strength cider and skunk — before the project had taken her in.

You'd think that I of all people would have given the kid a break, but when she walked in on her first day, all dreadlocks and piercings, I'd inwardly recoiled, same as everyone else. Maybe it was the boots she wore, which would have looked more at home on a deep-sea diver, and reminded me uncomfortably of my Piedros, the orthopaedic shoes I'd been forced to wear as a kid.

A pale wisp of a thing, Plum's eternally surly expression came with an attitude to match. I'd come across the term 'emo', of course, but this was my first real-life encounter with one. Plum had clearly never come across anyone like me before either. After all, freak shows went out of fashion years ago. Consequently, for the first few days, as we carefully stepped around each other, I was subjected to intense and uninhibited scrutiny, while she chomped down on an ever-present blob of chewing gum. Whenever we were in the same room, Plum seemed to be watching me. After a while it got tiresome, even for me, so I began glaring back, but she remained totally unfazed. Then it dawned on me that life was going more smoothly. After the first couple of days, I rarely had to repeat myself to her and, without being told, Plum delivered my coffee in a large mug, to the right side of my desk and never more than two-thirds full. When I went through the post, I began to find the envelopes discreetly slit open, the contents intact.

'Did you get her to do that?' I asked Barbara. But she hadn't.

Over time, I found that I only ever had to say something to Plum once and it was done. To begin with, Jake put her on basic office junior stuff — filing, the post run and making tea, but despite a somewhat unhurried approach, Plum tackled everything she was required to do with the same level of quiet commitment. I remarked on this once to Barbara.

'Of course she does,' she chuckled. 'She's got a crush.'

I followed her gaze through to Jake's office, where he was talking Plum through some kind of admin task. The two of them stood so close that her arm brushed against his, and plainly she was hanging on his every word. It was obvious, now that it was pointed out.

When it became apparent that Plum's two-fingered typing was also accurate, she progressed to taking on the occasional correspondence when Barbara was overloaded. Then, one lunch time, I came out to ask Barbara to make a phone call for me, a sensitive call to someone I'd never met. I didn't want to risk any misunderstandings. But Barbara had gone out to do some shopping.

'I could do it for you,' Plum offered, the indifferent shrug clearly anticipating polite rejection. But then I thought about it. What was the worst that could happen? Carefully primed and prompted by me as she went along, she did it pretty much to perfection. And gradually, Plum had slipped into the role of my personal assistant.

Although there had been a brief fad at the start of the century for celebrities naming their offspring after random pieces of fruit, Plum was just a nickname, for which I had to take full responsibility. Victoria somehow seemed altogether too decorous for this pragmatic girl. Plus, even after years of speech therapy, I've never held much affection for the labiodental fricative. The first time I called her Plum I was tired, it was shorthand and it was a pathetic joke, but she hadn't seemed to mind, so it stuck. Lately, she'd even started to match her lipstick, thickly applied, with the name.

Today she was back to close scrutiny again, her masticating jaw reduced to slow motion, the gum languishing in the corner of her mouth.

'Christ, look at the state of your face.'

'Memorise the details,' I said, turning my attention to what had dropped into my in-tray over the last few days. 'I'm going to test you on it later.'

I looked up to see her tilting her head and squinting at me. 'Isle of Skye,' she said.

'What?'

'The Isle of Skye.' She raised her thumbs and index fingers in front of her face, framing my left cheek like a film director might. 'If you discount that straggly bit at the bottom.'

'Yes. Thanks. How about we get down to some work now?' A name sprang out at me from my diary. 'Do you know what happened with Rita Todd? She was meant to come in and see me on Wednesday. Did Jake talk to her?'

'Nah. He told me to cancel, so I left a message on her answer machine. She didn't show, so I guess she must have picked it up. You want to reschedule?'

'Yeah. I feel bad — I don't think I exactly gave her my full attention last time she was here. Let's find out if she wants our help or not.'

Plum punched in the number. 'Not answering,' she said, after a couple of minutes. 'Shall I leave another message?'

'Yes. She must be expecting to hear from us at some point.'

CHAPTER FOURTEEN

When I arrived at Fulford Road on Thursday morning, Denny was closeted with the Chief Superintendent again. Well, stuff him. I didn't have to agree with him about Bostwick. The guy looked like a thug, exactly the kind of thug who would get a buzz out of beating up some-one who couldn't defend himself, especially for material gain. If he was prone to the short fuse, having a bit of an off day was probably all it would take. Also, despite what Denny had said, Davey's supermarket wasn't that far away from the Flatwood estate, and like everyone else, Bostwick would have seen the posters advertising the recent lottery win-ners. If the reputation of the shop had spread, people like him would travel much greater distances to increase the odds of buying a winning ticket. Whatever Denny's opinion might be, there was nothing to stop me pursuing that particular line of enquiry until it ran out of steam.

To get to the Flatwood I had to drive across town and, in doing so, it occurred to me (as it had done on many occasions) that Sonia was right: we could have ended up in worse places. In the national economic dip that had characterised the end of the twentieth century there were towns like this all over Britain that had lost their core manufacturing base — carpets, shoes or whatever the commodity might be. Rapid decline had followed as the population deserted, followed by the businesses, leaving run-down husks where the rich stayed rich — usually by commuting to lucrative jobs elsewhere — and the poor remained poor, materially and in aspiration, barred from all but the most meagre opportunities from the start. Charnford somehow seemed to have avoided that for the most part and was a tidy town, with a growing population of about 15,000. It had originally developed from the merger of a number of smaller communities and had somehow retained that rural backwater feel. It wasn't exactly small enough that everyone knew everyone else, but it was underpinned by connecting relationships, large enough for anyone to remain anonymous if they wanted to, but small enough to navigate easily after only a few days. The geography of the place helped with that, bisected as the town was by the River Charn that cut through the centre, delineating the social mix as well as the landscape. The most desirable dwellings in the town were the riverside properties, from the converted mill in the centre with its luxury apartment balconies, to the larger detached houses towards the outskirts of the town that spread out to the north.

South of the river, the Flatwood estate, comprising about two hundred social housing dwellings, lacked such genteel charm and retained a slightly menacing feel, despite the recent efforts at regeneration whereby some of the social housing had been replaced with buildings owned by a private association. In one corner next to Millpool Primary School, there was a small, spanking new development that included housing for newly arrived refugees. Elsewhere, however, the rebuild was a cut-and-paste job. Squat maisonette blocks had been pulled down and replaced with three-storey townhouses in red brick and stucco with tiny wrought-iron balconies, which continued to rub shoulders with the seedy-looking older generation terraced and semi-detached brick and clapboard houses, which you just knew would be plagued inside with damp.

It was in one of these that the Bostwick family lived, situated opposite an abandoned kids' playground in the smaller of the town's two parks, made even more dismal today by the nondescript weather. The curtains of number thirty-five Talbot Way were closed upstairs and yellowing nets obscured the ground-floor room. As there was no doorbell on the mud-stained UPVC door, I knocked as hard as I could on the glass, bruising my knuckles in the process. From somewhere at the back of the house came the gruff bark of a large dog, but otherwise there was no response. Repeating the exercise was no more productive, nor were there any friendly neighbours on hand to discuss the matter with, so with a backward glance at the first-floor windows, I headed back to my car.

The estate where Evan Phelps lived was about as far from the Flatwood as it was possible to get, both geographically and aesthetically. North of the river, sprawled over a rise, these private houses languished at the end of fifty-metre front drives, concealed in the main by mature trees and hedges.

Fourteen High Close was a half-hearted attempt at a mock Tudor with a double garage, its condition as immaculate as the properties on either side, but with a 'For Sale' sign planted in the front garden. Phelps didn't, on the face of it, look quite as desperate for a lottery win as Bostwick might be.

The Mini and the souped-up Corsa parked on the drive were encouraging, and this time when I rang the bell, a figure appeared almost immediately behind the frosted glass door. The girl who opened it could have been anything from late teens to mid-twenties and the familial resemblance in her skin and hair colour told me this was Evan Phelps' sister. The family would have stood out in this town, as the children were clearly mixed heritage and therefore a rarity.

Seeing the uniform, the girl was immediately cagey, the door inching back just a little, which made me wonder if she was used to visits from the police or maybe just Jehovah's Witnesses. I switched on my broadest smile.

'Hi, I'm PC Mick Fraser.' I held up my warrant card for her to see. 'I wondered if Evan Phelps was at home. I'd like to have a word.'

'What's it about?'

'I just want to ask him a couple of questions. Is he here?' I glanced behind her into the empty hall.

'Questions about what?'

'It's all right, Billie.' Over her shoulder, I saw a lanky figure descending the staircase. 'You can leave this to me. Go back to your revision.'

Billie did as she was told, but not without an anxious glance towards her brother, who took her place in the doorway. A slim and healthy-looking six feet tall, his hair cut close to his scalp, Phelps wore a loose T-shirt and sweatpants and leaned on the door frame, his arms folded, the picture of relaxation. It didn't look as if I was going to be invited in, but I could live with that. I guessed the parents were out at work.

'So, how can I help you?' Phelps asked, with just the right tone of polite deference. The carefully modulated voice spoke to me of a private education.

'Where were you last Friday night, between ten and eleven p.m.?' I asked.

Pursing his lips, his eyebrows drew together in a frown while he considered the question. Smart move to think about it before answering. The mistake most guilty people make is to answer straight away — usually untruthfully. It was further demonstration that he wasn't perhaps entirely new to this situation.

'Ten and eleven on a Friday night? I'd have been at the Drum and Monkey.' I recognised the name, a pub-turned-bar a little way out on this side of town.

'And you're sure about that particular Friday?'

'Yeah, been going there most weeks for ever.'

'And you were there all evening?'

'Absolutely.'

'There are people who can vouch for you?'

'Loads.' He brightened suddenly. 'I'll tell you what, a couple of your brothers were there. A bit of a scuffle kicked off and two officers came in to sort it. I spoke to one of them, so he might remember me.'

Shit. So that would appear to be that. I'd ask some questions to check it out back at the station, but that would be a pretty stupid thing to lie about. I took my final weapon out of my pocket and held it out to him.

'Do you know this man at all?'

He studied the photo of Sam Bostwick coolly, before slowly shaking his head. 'No, don't think so.' Again, he was nice and casual, not too eager. 'Just so that you know, I'm clean. Haven't touched the stuff for years. Learned my lesson you might say.' The assured smile almost had me convinced.

I had nothing left. 'OK, thanks for your time, Mr Phelps. You've been very helpful.'

'No probs.' He allowed himself a smile. I turned and walked back down the drive. There was one interesting thing, though. He hadn't apparently been curious enough about my visit to ask why I was so interested in his whereabouts on Friday night.

CHAPTER FIFTEEN

It wasn't until the next morning that I managed to track him down, but when I caught up with Sam Bostwick, I had to seriously reconsider whether Denny might have been right about him and Phelps. What had been hinted at by their places of residence was thrown into stark relief face to face. Chalk and cheese didn't even begin to describe the differences between the two men Davey had identified. Bostwick was a whippet to Evan Phelps' elegant Weimaraner, and not a very well kept one at that. It was hard to believe that Phelps was the younger of the two by several years. Small and under-nourished, Bostwick was a bundle of nervous tension, his pale, washed-out eyes never lingering on anything for long. His bitten-down nails were grimy, and faded homemade tattoos across the knuckles of both hands (I eventually figured out) spelled 'immortal'. Looking at the state of him, I wouldn't be placing any bets on that being true. The aroma surrounding him was organic and slightly unwashed. Another equally faded tattoo to the left of his prominent Adam's apple indicated an allegiance, some decades too late, to the Waffen SS. That kind of affiliation would surely put Bostwick and Phelps on opposite sides of the fence.

We were sitting in a lounge, ten by ten at most, and crammed with a cheap leather sofa, fifty-inch flat screen TV and assorted junk, including, incongruously, a crate stuffed full of what appeared to be children's toys. The air was stale, and the windows looked as if they hadn't been opened in a long time. The dog that had sounded so fierce the first time I'd rung the bell turned out to be a soft old Staffie bitch with sagging teats and kept coming to nuzzle my leg. Bostwick eventually managed to tear himself away from the video game he was playing, but he also had an alibi of sorts for the Friday night.

'I was babysitting,' he said, when he finally dragged his attention from the screen, where the image of a warrior being blown to pieces was frozen mid-air. 'I fetched a takeaway for me and the wife to have before she went on her night shift, then I stopped in with the kids and sank a few cans.'

When I showed him the picture of Phelps, though, he blinked hard at it, before denying all knowledge of him.

'Are you sure about that?' I persisted.

He gave it another cursory glance. 'Yes,' he said, but he squirmed as he said it.

Something on the sofa crackled and a baby monitor came to life with the grizzling of an infant. Bostwick threw down the controller and got to his feet. I heard him climb the stairs and his voice in the distance. When he re-entered the room, it was with a small baby in his arms.

'Sorry, I've got to get the oldest one from nursery in twenty minutes,' he said, glancing at the clock. 'And this one wants changing, as you'll soon find out.' He gave the baby a tender smile and rubbed noses, to make it giggle.

I saw myself out, though the dog waddled hopefully with me to the front door, and on the way back down the footpath a scrap of coloured paper caught my eye — a spent lottery ticket. I picked it up.

By now I had also checked out Phelps' story with the beat officers who'd attended the incident at the Drum and Monkey on the Friday night. When I'd showed them the picture, one of them categorically remembered having a conversation with Phelps.

'Seemed a pleasant sort of lad,' he'd said. 'He certainly did everything he could to co-operate. What's he done?'

'Probably nothing,' I'd said, miserably.

I considered what I'd learned about Bostwick and Phelps. The only thing that might possibly bring them together could be drugs. Illegal substances have a way of crossing boundaries in a way that any amount of multicultural awareness doesn't. The officer who'd dealt with Phelps' little drug misadventure was Sergeant Sharon Petrowlski, back when she was still a PC. Friendly in a practical kind of way, Petrowlski had a reputation for being a safe pair of hands. An experienced officer in her forties, she gave off an aura of dependability, and whenever we'd spoken she'd demonstrated an encyclopaedic knowledge of current cases. I'd hoped that this extended to past ones too and she didn't let me down. Sharon had investigated the burglary at the Phelps address.

'I didn't have to look far,' she'd said. 'Within five minutes, Mr Phelps senior had told me that his son was responsible and offered up items from the boy's room for fingerprinting purposes. Phelps himself never denied it.'

'But his father pressed charges?'

'Insisted on it. Was hoping to teach the boy a lesson, I think, and it seemed to work. It scared the crap out of him. He was given a caution and as far as I know, he hasn't been in trouble since.'

'And the drugs?'

'Possession only. Weed and a bit of skunk. Phelps didn't look as if he was on the hard stuff but, even if he was sticking to the nursery slopes, someone must have supplied him.'

'Any thoughts who that might have been?'

'He gave me a flat number in Ebury House, one of the blocks on the edge of the Flatwood, but that could have been misdirection. There's a pair of sneakers slung over the telegraph wires outside, so everyone knows it goes on there.'

'Any association that you know of with a man called Bostwick?'

'Bostwick? I'm sure I've heard that name in connection with the White Angel lot.'

WA — so that's what the note on his record had meant. It had the ring of a supremacist organisation, which Petrowlski had confirmed. I made a note to check if there was any other sign of their involvement, and if there was it would surely put Phelps in the clear.

'They've gone very quiet of late, if they ever even existed,' Petrowlski had told me.

'How do you mean?'

'There's been talk of such an organisation for years but I've never come across an actual card-carrying member. And I didn't get a sense of anyone else there that Phelps was connected with.'

Shame, but she hadn't made it sound incontrovertible. Out of interest, I then ran the two number plates from the Phelps drive through the ANPR. The Mini, as I'd deduced, belonged to Phelps, and the Corsa to a Tyler Curzon. He was the same age as Phelps, so presumably a mate. I wondered if he was any relation to the local councillor.

* * *

Plum tried all Thursday and Friday morning, and still there was no response from Rita Todd. 'Could be her phone's not working,' she suggested. It was unlikely but a possibility.

By the middle of the afternoon, my ribs were complaining painfully and I decided to take some paperwork home and make up the time in relative comfort.

'I'll stop off at Rita's place on the way,' I told Plum.

'Want me to come too? I can drive you.' The offer was grudging, but it was there nonetheless.

'OK, thanks.'

Plum's car was a scruffy old banger of a vehicle and she treated it accordingly, that is, with minimal respect. In order to sit down I had to clear the front passenger seat of an old computer hard drive, bits of dried flowers, a couple of children's crayons and a tin of beans (unopened), along with assorted sweet wrappers and crisp packets. When she turned the key in the ignition, music blasted out of the speakers at ear-bleeding volume. Seeing me wince, she doused it straight away, but not before I'd caught the climactic bars of the 1812 Overture. She was full of surprises.

Encouragingly, as we drew up outside, Rita's house was one of the few in the little terrace of two-up two-downs that had light shining from behind the flimsy curtains of the ground-floor windows. But several pushes on the doorbell summoned no one and it began to look as if the light was a security precaution. While I continued to wait, Plum tried next door, but the young woman who appeared, carrying a toddler on her hip, didn't know where Rita might be.

73

'We don't see much of her at all these days. Usually it's just a wave through the window as she's off out. Don't get me wrong — everyone deserves a social life, but we used to rely on Rita for babysitting, so we're a bit stuck now.'

It occurred to me then that we knew nothing about Rita's family circumstances. 'Is there a husband or partner?' I asked, over the trimmed privet.

'No one I know of, although I have wondered just lately if she might be seeing someone. She's got a grown-up daughter who lives somewhere not too far away. We see her now and again.'

'What makes you think Rita could have someone she's seeing?'

'She never used to go out much of an evening, but these days she does. And she's dressed up like she's going somewhere special. She did tell me where she was headed one time.' She frowned. 'Barney's I think it was — some bar in town, I suppose. I've never heard of it, but then I'm way out of touch with Charnford's nightlife, thanks to this one.'

The toddler, who had been staring unblinkingly at me, was getting bored and starting to wriggle.

I gestured to Plum, who handed over a business card.

'When you next see Rita, could you tell her we stopped by and ask her to give us a call?'

The toddler looked all set to demonstrate his lung capacity, so his mum took the card and with a brief, apologetic smile, went back in and closed the door.

'Should we call the police?' Plum asked me, keen to crank up the drama.

'Only if we want to get an earful for wasting their time,' I said.

'We could ring round the hospitals.'

'I'm not sure that that's necessary yet either. We'll put a note through the door. Have you got any paper we can use?'

'In the car.'

But while Plum was rummaging around, another vehicle pulled into a space a little way down the street and Andrea Todd got out. She called over as she headed towards us.

'Can I help you?' As she crossed the road, the wind swept her hair over her face. Pushing it back, she saw and recognised me. 'Oh, hello,' she said, holding me under scrutiny for just a little too long. 'You've been in the wars.'

'I can be clumsy sometimes,' I said, hoping that would cover it. 'But it means I've been off work, so I had to cancel your mother's appointment. I've been trying to contact her to make another, but without success, so we came to see her in person.'

'Me too,' said Andrea. 'Have you tried the bell?'

Plum joined us in the small garden. 'Loads of times. But no one's answering.'

Andrea gave her a long look, before turning her attention to sorting through the keys on her laden key ring.

'When did you last see her?' I asked.

'Last Friday, when I left your office,' she said, finally isolating the key she wanted. 'I called her, but her answer machine doesn't seem to be working.'

'We had the same problem.'

Andrea unlocked the door and, stooping to pick up a handful of letters from the mat, she called out to her mum, even though her absence seemed to be confirmed.

'Looks as if she's gone away,' said Andrea. 'She did text me over the weekend to say that she might. That was a miracle. She hardly ever uses her mobile. She bought herself a smartphone not long ago — a complete waste of money.'

'Is it unusual for her to be out of touch for this long?' I asked.

Like her mother, Andrea didn't appear to have any difficulty understanding me. 'Not at all.' She seemed very relaxed with it. 'What *is* rare is for her to get any time off work, so I imagine she's making good use of it. She's got friends in Hoyland so I'm guessing that's where she's gone. I was at a conference near here today, so it was convenient to stop off on my way home. I knew there was a chance she wouldn't be here.'

We followed her inside and found things neat and orderly, with nothing overtly out of place. Looking through to the kitchen, I could see that the washing up had been done and left in the drainer.

A picture on the wall caught my eye: a framed photograph of two children, a girl of about four with a chubby infant lain across her lap. The older child looked very like Andrea, even down to the hairstyle.

'Yes, me and my little brother, Martin,' she obliged. 'The picture was taken shortly before he died. He had a life-limiting condition.'

'I'm sorry.'

'It was a long time ago.'

Half a dozen thank you cards were displayed on the mantelshelf and on a side table stood a bouquet of flowers, still in their delivery box and beginning to wilt.

'From grateful families,' said Andrea. 'She gets that all the time.'

'May I?'

Her nod said, 'Go ahead', so I picked out the card that sat wedged between the blooms.

My thoughts and prayers will be with you always FRA xx

'FRA?'

She shrugged, unable to elucidate.

'Your mum is Catholic,' I said, noticing that one of the cards had a religious theme.

Andrea seemed amused by the statement. 'Not really,' she said. 'Not anymore. I mean, we used to go to Mass every week when I was a kid, all done up in our Sunday best. But when my grandparents died, we stopped all that. Between what happened with Martin and what Mum had to put up with from Dad, it was enough to make anyone lose their faith. As for me, I'm a complete lost cause and will no doubt burn in the fires of hell.'

'What happened with your dad?'

'We left him when I was still quite small, shortly before he drank himself to death,' she told us, with a note of defiance. 'It's been just Mum and me for a long time now.' Something in her voice made me hold back from probing further.

'Your mum hasn't had other relationships?' I queried. 'Her neighbour seems to think she might be seeing someone.'

'It's not impossible,' Andrea conceded. 'After Dad, it took her a long time to trust again, but she's looked after herself and she can be quite the flirt when she feels like it. So yes, there have been men from time to time, although she hasn't necessarily lost the knack of choosing unsuitable ones. Sometimes it feels like I'm the responsible one.'

'So you wouldn't know who she might be seeing?'

'Sorry.' She shook her head. 'If past form is anything to go by, I'll be the last person to know.'

'Why did you bring Rita to us?'

Andrea sighed. 'I think she's being forced out of her job. She needs someone to have her back. Someone she'll listen to, before she gets herself in too deep.'

'Into what too deep?'

'She didn't explain? I mean, I don't know the full story, but what with all the cuts, Mum's been working ridiculous hours. This is the first time off she's had in I don't know how long. I know some of the practices have changed too and, according to her, not for the better. Mum can be quite forthright if she doesn't agree with something. And obstinate. She digs her heels in. She let slip a couple of weeks back that she's had a run-in with management, and as an experienced and therefore expensive member of staff, it would suit them to get rid of her. I'm worried that she could go the same way as her friend Delores and, to be frank, Mum can't afford that.'

'Delores worked with her?'

'For years. She was the other senior nurse on the ward. She'd been having quite a lot of time off to look after her elderly mother, and I understand it was suggested to her in the strongest terms that it was time she retired, which she did. From what Mum told me, she wasn't given much choice.'

'But if your mum is being badly treated, if her workload is excessive . . .' I began.

'That's a matter of perspective, isn't it?' said Andrea. 'Do something for me, would you? Stick with her, just for a little longer. Persuade her to keep your appointment and try and get her to open up and talk to you about what's been going on.' She nodded towards the cards. 'Mum's good at her job, you can see that.'

'Of course.' I didn't like to tell Andrea that I'd planned to persevere with Rita anyway — because we needed the business. But whatever our next move was, there was nothing to be done until she was home again.

By the time Plum had dropped me off at my flat in the early evening, I was shattered and my back and limbs ached. What I'd planned as a short nap went on a bit and I woke as it was getting dark. I didn't want work spilling too far into the weekend, so once I'd eaten and pinged my next move back to Crusader, I reluctantly got out my bag to do the work I'd brought home with me. The mugging had made me jittery, but somehow I was going to have to learn how to relax again.

CHAPTER SIXTEEN

It was Friday morning and our last ten till six shift of the week. I was under strict instructions to keep Denny away from the station while preparations were going on for the first of several surprise retirement parties that he pretty certainly knew all about. I was then required to deliver him back to the nick promptly at the appointed time. But it was late morning before he surfaced from Bowers' office, looking more crumpled and careworn than ever. He'd have to smarten himself up if he was to host this VIP, I thought, uncharitably.

'Productive meeting?' I asked him.

'Hm,' he said, and that was that.

The afternoon was a quiet one and we only needed to put in a couple more hours before we could go back. To avoid returning to the station too early and blowing the 'surprise', I talked Denny into some R & R at the Rose café, a greasy spoon just off the high street. It was nearly six o'clock and starting to get dark when a call came through from the dispatch centre about a Liam Archer making a nuisance of himself outside the hostel for the homeless.

'He must have a sixth sense,' Denny said, with a sour look on his face. 'I can't believe he's doing this again. He was only in the cells a couple of nights ago and this time he'll really be in trouble.'

'Do I know him?' I asked. Like so many others around here, the name wasn't familiar to me.

'You'd probably recognise him on sight,' Denny said. 'He's one of that little crowd that used to hang around in the park all day. He's been a lost soul since . . .'

'What?'

'Since forever. Archer's pretty harmless until the drink takes over.'

'What's his problem?'

'I'm not sure that anybody knows, really. Basically, his head's not right and he likes a drink. It's a combination that gets him into trouble from time to time. He's easily led. I've known him for must be going on twenty years now. He was one of the first round here to be let out under "care in the community".'

'That's obviously working, then.'

'Yeah, turns out that we're the ones who have to do the caring,' Denny said with a sneer. 'It'll probably mean another night in the cells while he sobers up.' He gave me a searching look. 'Wouldn't be surprised if someone's put him up to this, to get me a harmless last collar.' His gaze lingered on my face for a moment, but if this was a set-up, I knew nothing about it.

Turning into the end of the road, even though a couple of the street lights were out, we immediately saw a giant of a man, going on six and a half feet, and bundled up in a parka and woolly hat. Clearly inebriated, he was lurching all over the pavement, scavenging the verge for missiles to throw at the hostel windows, in between shaking his fist and swearing, apparently at the building. We cruised slowly to a stand-still and gradually, as he took in the vehicle and who was in it, Archer started to back away down the street until he finally turned to run. As we came to a standstill Denny and I both started to get out of the car, but Denny put out an arm to stop me.

'I'll go after him. You go and see what damage he's done to the hostel.'

'You sure?' It was tempting to point out that I was younger and fitter, but I thought it politic not to do so.

'He's pissed out of his brains,' Denny said. 'He won't get far. I know these streets better than you do, and I know how to handle Archer.'

I couldn't argue with that, so I let Denny go after our offender and walked up the path to the hostel, a converted Victorian house, where, aside from a broken window, there seemed to be little damage.

The manager, Doug, saw me approaching and came to the door. He seemed pretty cool about the incident.

'It's not like it hasn't happened before,' he said. He was standing in front of a row of photographs pinned to the wall, showing more staff than I'd have expected in a place like this. Some of them looked as if they'd been taken by our photographer.

'What provoked it?' I asked, knowing that it might not have been anything.

'He did,' said Doug pointing down the garden, where, for the first time I saw the dark coloured mongrel standing patiently beneath a laurel tree. Deciding that neither of us was of sufficient interest, it lay down and put its head on its paws. 'He sleeps under there when Liam uses the hostel,' Doug said. 'That's what kicked off the row. Liam doesn't get that Jacko can't sleep inside, even in bad weather. I've called the RSPCA. They'll have him overnight.'

It seemed that Archer had arrived at the hostel drunk just as it was getting dark and, finding Jacko barred again, he began shouting abuse and throwing anything he could get his hands on at the windows.

'That's when I called you,' said Doug. 'This is a residential street, so we have to be mindful of the neighbours.'

I reported in, then waited for Denny to come back with Archer. After ten minutes, I began to think that Archer must have outrun him. Somewhere in the distance, a powerful car engine revved and a dog barked. Jacko lifted his head for a moment. At this rate, I could be here all night. Locking the car, I headed in the direction they had gone, to what looked like an industrial area. Rounding the corner, I came to an expanse of lumpy wasteland in front of a couple of big, prefabricated hangars. A security light blazed out from the side of one of them, the distant glare half blinding me. I strained my eyes in the semi-darkness, weighing up the most likely direction they'd have taken, but this was new territory for me. I could just about pick out a street sign to the side of the security light, so, regretting that I hadn't brought a torch, I aimed for that, stepping out across the rough ground. I had no idea what I was treading on and a vision flashed through my head of broken glass and needles, ready and waiting to pierce my heavy-duty boots at any moment. Instead, my foot caught on something inert and sent me sprawling. My landing was, fortunately, soft soil and clumps of grass, but as I cursed my clumsiness, I heard a horrible low moan coming at me from close quarters. Turning, I realised I'd tripped over my partner.

'Denny? Oh, fuck! Denny!'

He was lying curled in a foetal position, groaning and muttering something I couldn't hear. I knelt down beside him, putting my knee in something sticky and disgusting in the process. Ugh, dog crap. Ignoring it, my voice shaking with emotion, I spoke into my radio.

'Urgent assistance needed — industrial estate at the back of Vesey Street. Officer down.'

Denny moaned again.

'Where are you hurt?' I put a hand to his face and it came away slick with a dark, syrupy substance. Archer had found the one place not covered by Denny's stab vest. He was leaking from his jugular, his blood oozing all over the ground and now me. Suddenly the moaning faded to an awful gurgling and he fell silent.

'Denny!' I yelled in his face, my own voice echoing back at me from the surrounding buildings. 'Denny! Hang in there, don't leave me!'

It seemed an age waiting for the ambulance to come. I knelt on the icy ground, feeling the life seeping out of my friend, praying that help would come soon. I looked around me at the deserted streets. Archer had vanished, but he couldn't go far. Whatever happened, we'd find him.

CHAPTER SEVENTEEN

The side room at the hospital seemed to be getting smaller with every circuit I made, and the waiting was driving me mad. I'd been shunted in here over an hour ago, shortly after we'd hit A&E, and no one had been near me since. I couldn't get my head round the idea that just a few short hours ago, Denny had been whole, and on his way to retirement. A couple of times I'd stuck my head out into the corridor, but everyone I saw was going about their business as usual. I was about to walk along to the reception desk again when I saw a doctor approaching from the opposite direction. I recognised him as one of those who'd come out to attend to Denny when we'd first crashed into the hospital, and he was coming straight for me. No doubt he would try to persuade me to go home and get some rest, because Denny would be in surgery for hours. But I had no intention of leaving yet. I wanted to wait until Sheila got here and until I knew Denny would be all right. Then the doctor was standing next to me, his hand gripping my arm.

'I'm sorry,' he was saying. 'There was nothing more we could do.'
'What?' I heard myself say.
'PC Sutton passed away fifteen minutes ago,' the doctor repeated patiently, accustomed to this ritual. 'We couldn't save him.' His sympathetic hand was still on my arm. 'I'm very sorry, constable.'
I felt numb. How could this have happened so quickly, and with his family still on their way to the hospital? Suddenly I became aware

that Denny's wife and sons had appeared at the other end of the corridor. My eyes met Sheila's for an instant. I didn't want to have to face them but fortunately, Superintendent Bowers arrived at the same time and I was saved that particular confrontation. Like the coward that I was, I ducked back into the waiting room and flopped down onto a chair. I don't know how long I sat there, immobile, but eventually the door opened and Bowers appeared, all concern and sympathetic smiles.

'Come on, son, let's get you back to the station,' he said.

'We should let Kevin know,' I said, vaguely.

'Kevin?'

'Booth, Denny's partner. Ex-partner.'

'Of course,' he soothed, as if I was the casualty. 'Plenty of time for that.'

* * *

Back at Fulford Road, everyone was in shock, the office still obscenely decorated for Denny's party, though a couple of the lads were hurriedly trying to snatch down the balloons and bunting. People kept their distance, apart from CID who subjected me to an hour and a half in the interview suite. It had to be done, of course, as quickly as possible, and they were gentle on me.

'We just need to know what happened from your point of view. It's a witness statement, that's all. No one's accusing you of anything.'

They might as well have. I felt responsible. My only task had been to keep Denny safe for just a couple more hours. How could I have failed so appallingly?

'You mustn't blame yourself,' I was told, more than once, but to no effect. 'It's just one of those things.'

Liam Archer was nowhere to be found. A bloodied knife had been found not far from where Denny fell and it would doubtless have Archer's prints all over it, but the chances were that even when he did turn up, he probably wouldn't be charged. If, as Denny had told me, he had a history of mental health issues he would probably spend some time in a secure hospital, where he'd be looked after. Meanwhile, who would look after Denny's family? Mercifully, after the interview, I was told to go home.

Sonia had a miserable weekend in my company. When I went to bed, exhausted, sleep wouldn't come, and I lay awake much of Friday night rehearsing the events of that evening. The next day, any conversation we had just kept returning to the same old ground and finally, in an attempt to distract me, Sonia suggested we make a start on redecorating the spare bedroom. We'd already agreed on colours so all it took was a trip to the DIY store to buy the paint. But while I trailed after Sonia up and down the aisles looking for the exact shade of yellow (how many could there be?), I couldn't stop thinking about what kind of Saturday Sheila and her sons would be having. I couldn't let go of the idea that I shouldn't even be at home, but should be out there doing something. Bowers had ordered me to take a few days' leave, but what was the point? It wasn't going to bring Denny back, was it? It was one of the longest weekends of my life. On Saturday evening, we went out for a meal.

'I feel bad for grumbling about him now,' I told Sonia.

'It was justified,' she said immediately, coming to my defence, as I knew she would. 'It's not your fault that he kept his distance. From what you've told me, you've barely seen him in the last couple of weeks.' We were coming to the end of our main course and Sonia put her hand over mine, a mischievous smile playing on her lips. 'Go and pay the bill,' she said, nodding towards my almost empty glass. 'I know just the thing to help you relax.'

She was right, of course, as she so often is, and as I lay with my arm around her much later, the world seemed, if only temporarily, a better place.

'This could be it,' Sonia said, taking my hand and placing it on her stomach. 'Even now there could be a little Fraser beginning to take shape in there.' She put her hand over mine.

'Wouldn't that be a bit quick?' She'd only stopped taking the pill a few weeks ago.

'You never know. In fact, I think he is. I can feel him.' She was doing her best to keep my mind off Denny, and I loved her for it.

'Oh yes? It's "him" this time, is it?' I played along, as I had before in the weeks since we'd decided the time was right to start our family.

'Yes, definitely.'

'And what's he called tonight?'

85

Duncan.' She giggled.

'Duncan? Ach no, that's a terrible old-fashioned name. It's puny, too, and my boy's not going to be puny.'

'No, he's going to be six foot three, handsome and muscular, with blue eyes and strawberry blond hair.'

'And he'll play for Glasgow Rangers and Scotland.'

'He might prefer ballet.'

'He can do anything. I don't care.' I remembered Stefan Greaves' crack about the five-a-side. 'What if he turned out to be disabled?' I said.

'That's a funny thing to say. We'd love him just the same,' she said, straight away. 'But it doesn't happen that often and there are tests they do—'

'I mean, what if we did all the tests and they showed that there was something wrong?'

She was thoughtful for a minute. 'Honestly? I don't know. I'd like to think that it wouldn't make any difference, but you just know that his life would be tougher. Perhaps it's one of those decisions that you can't make until it actually happens.'

'Perhaps it is.'

CHAPTER EIGHTEEN

I was dog tired by the weekend and the last thing I felt like was socialising, but I'd promised Laura, so I went to her house as planned on Saturday night. My spirits sank further when I saw a second, unfamiliar car parked on the drive of the Victorian semi, yet another of Laura's female friends who, she would no doubt claim, had 'just happened to drop by'. I'd tackled her more than once about this impulse to keep trying to fix me up.

'I'm not!' she would insist. 'I'm just introducing you to like-minded people and broadening your social circle. It's good for you.'

'So is cod liver oil, but I opted out of taking that a long time ago.'

The air of exaggerated bonhomie when she let me in confirmed my fears. I followed her through to the lounge, where immediately the woman curled on the sofa got to her feet, hooking dark wavy hair behind her ear. She had an open, slightly tanned face, with green eyes and a wide smile. Barefoot, she came to just below my chin.

'Hi.' She came towards me, hand outstretched. 'You must be Stefan. I'm Cate, with a "C".'

'Hello.' I reserved judgement for now. I mean, she was pretty enough, the heart-shaped face subtly made up, but the smile was just a little too wide, the greeting slightly over-enthusiastic. Maybe I'm a little hypersensitive, too. I was fairly certain she'd had work done to her nose and fillers in the chin. With most people you can tell. My back stiffened a little. Cosmetic surgery always feels like a personal insult.

'Cate's quite new to the area,' chirped Laura.

'Hardly,' said Cate. 'It's been more than eighteen months.'

'Really?' Laura seemed genuinely surprised. 'How time flies.'

'Anyway, it's good to meet you,' said Cate. She grasped my arm and making me wince.

'Sorry, Laura may have told you, I got duffed up last week.' Her smile slipped a little as she watched my face contort around the words, though that could have just been concentration. Smiles to sympathy in a split-second, but because of the beating or the way I struggled to talk? Oh, who the hell cared?

'She did,' Cate replied. So, at least she understood me. 'That must have been terrible.'

'Anything new on that?' Laura asked. But before I could answer, a volley of footsteps drummed on the wooden floor behind me and the force that struck me almost knocked me off balance.

'Uncle Stefan! I've been waiting for you. Come here!' Reaching down, I unwrapped my three-year-old goddaughter from my legs and she crawled up me until I was holding her, none too securely, in my arms.

I kissed her nose. 'You women, you're *so* bossy,' I said.

Grace giggled. 'I'm not a *wimmin,* I'm a little *girl!*' she protested. 'Come on, now!' Squirming free, she gripped my hand and dragged me through the kitchen into the playroom, talking all the time as if she was afraid her voice might run out. In those few minutes she leapt from one topic of conversation to another at breakneck speed — what had happened at nursery, the latest steps she was learning at dance class (complete with demonstration) and had I *seen* what

Tinkerbell (the cat) had done to Mummy's favourite blue cardigan?

Tonight I was truly honoured, and after her bath and while Laura cooked dinner, Grace presented me with her bedtime story book and hauled herself onto my lap, stepping heavily on my groin as she did so, to make herself comfortable. Oof. I began the story.

'Uncle Stefan, you're not *saying* it properly!'

There followed a small hiatus, during which Laura broke from her conversation with Cate. 'Grace,' she warned, gently.

'But he's not!' my goddaughter insisted. 'He didn't do the "munch munch" at the end.'

'So not just bossy, but pedantic too,' I said, pouncing on her tummy, tickling her and making her shriek. 'Munch, munch, MUNCH! There, how's that?'

After the story, Grace also insisted that I should put her to bed. As I came down the stairs, I couldn't help overhearing Laura in the kitchen.

'He has a lot going for him, if you know what I mean — a *lot*,' she was saying. I hesitated for a moment outside the door.

'You don't have to sell him to me,' Cate replied. 'I like him. He's lovely with Grace.'

'Thank God. She's wearing me out at the moment.'

'Yeah, well that's how it is,' Cate said. 'You're past the twelve-week mark?'

'Yes, if we've got the dates right.'

'Have you had the results of the prenatals yet?'

'A few days ago. Everything came back fine,' Laura said, clearly wanting to move on.

'That must be such a relief,' said Cate. 'The risk gets higher incrementally as you get older and you wouldn't want to . . .' She broke off as I made my lopsided entrance into the kitchen.

'Have one like me?' I finished for her. It was a bit harsh and to her credit, Cate did look pretty mortified. Reaching out to touch my arm, she looked me straight in the eye.

'Stefan, I'm so sorry, that was completely tactless. That's not what I . . .'

Of course not.

'Forget it,' I said. I took another beer out the fridge. 'Nothing wrong with my genes anyway. Mine was a baggage handling cock-up.'

'Anyway,' Cate said to Laura. 'It's no wonder you're tired. Are you still working?'

'Just the odd couple of days here and there. Supply teaching's good money. We can't afford to turn it down, and it's usually either at Millpool or St Barnabas, so they're both quite handy. It would be nice to get some work up at Cavendish, but it's pretty much a closed shop.'

'St Barnabas? You must know the wonderful Father Adriano then. I hear about him a lot. To hear some of my patients talk, you'd think he was the Second Coming personified.'

'He's a charmer, all right,' said Laura. 'He takes assembly once a week and has the kids eating out of his hand. I've never seen them so rapt.'

'And what about the staff?'

'Well let's just say he's livened things up for us, too. I have one or two colleagues who would quite happily encourage him to break his vows. Although he's not nearly as much fun as he used to be . . .' Laura lifted her eyebrows suggestively. 'Perhaps he's had his wrist slapped.'

'What is it with priests?' mused Cate.

'Yeah, what is it?' I asked, genuinely mystified.

'The uniform,' said Cate and Laura in unison and laughing. They must have seen my blank face.

'It's the black clerical garb,' said Cate. 'Dead sexy on the right man.'

'I think it's that thing of being a priest too, the frisson of being off-limits,' Laura added. 'If Father Adriano really is . . .'

'What do you mean?' Cate looked scandalised.

'Oh, you know,' said Laura. She shrugged. 'There are rumours.'

'Well, I'm sure none of my patients are aware of that. He would go down in their estimation.'

'You're a doctor?' I surmised.

Cate nodded. 'A GP.'

'Which is why she's constantly clucking over me,' said Laura.

'Someone has to,' said Cate. 'You must take it easy — get Simon to do more around the house.'

Laura laughed. 'Simon? You're kidding, aren't you? He never did it for Zoe or for Grace, so he's hardly going to start now.'

'He's such a dinosaur!' Cate exclaimed. 'I can't believe you let him get away with it!'

'I knew what I married,' Laura said. 'Too late to change him now.'

'It doesn't have to stop you trying. I think I'll have a word with him. You need to be looked after.'

'Yes, doc!' Laura mimed a mock salute.

'Have you heard from Zoe?' I asked. My other goddaughter was eighteen now and in her second term at university.

'Not lately,' Laura said. 'Which usually means that she doesn't need anything. I expect she's too busy with the social life.'

It was late when we sat down to eat, and even then Simon almost didn't make it, his job as sub-editor on the local weekly paper keeping him out until all hours as usual. He hurried in as Laura was serving up, joining us at the table after a quick wash and goodnight kiss for Grace.

'Life still pretty hectic then,' I said, as he sat down.

'Yes, and not likely to change much. Competition from the internet is fierce.'

'Thanks for the mention, by the way,' I said, in reference to the short report on my mugging that had made the week's edition.

'No problem, and sorry I couldn't get you on the front page. Have the police had any response on the contact number we printed?'

'Not as far as I know.'

'Hm, why am I not surprised? You need to keep on at them.'

'I will. My liaison officer seems to know what he's doing, and he's been good at keeping me up to speed.'

'I still can't believe it happened,' Laura said. 'Not round here.'

'I don't see why not,' Cate said. 'It happens everywhere, doesn't it?'

'Not according to Ashley Curzon,' said Simon. 'The way he has it, the streets of Charnford are paved with gold.'

'And we all know who he credits with the improvement,' I added. 'To hear him speak, you'd think he was the sole saviour of our little town.'

'You can't argue with what he's done, though,' Laura said. 'When we first came back here, the place was pretty rough around the edges, but that's changed, now. People are moving in.'

Simon rolled his eyes. 'They can't stay away from the hanging flower baskets and painted railings.'

'Oh, come on, it's more than just cosmetic, isn't it? Even the Flatwood looks a bit tidier.'

'And why is that? Nothing to do with the fact that the social housing is being bought up bit by bit by private landlords. They up the rent, forcing out the poorer families in some attempt at gentrification. Up the rent, ship them out and rid us of the scourge of the poor.'

'Isn't that where Curzon grew up, though?' said Cate. 'He must still have roots there.'

'Not that you'd know it.'

'But the town's a friendlier place,' insisted Laura.

'Apart from the odd mugging,' I felt compelled to add. I didn't go as far as mentioning the death of a refugee baby in the poorly maintained housing. That would have crushed the evening flat.

'Well, yes, of course . . . yes, there's that,' Laura admitted.

I relaxed as the evening went on and the booze went down — mostly mine and Simon's work, given that Laura was pregnant and Cate driving. It made it easier to cope with the embarrassment when Laura started singing my praises, as she always did, especially to her female friends.

'Though I wish you'd get a job with a proper law firm,' Laura said, as she did on a regular basis. She didn't mean it.

'I like working for Jake,' I reminded her. 'And your memory is short. Think back to what things were like when I was looking for a job. There wasn't a great deal of choice.' With an unsteady hand, I refilled Cate's glass.

'What is this?' She held it up for inspection. 'It's good.'

'It's wine,' Laura said. 'Beyond that, I have no idea. Stefan brought it.'

'Excellent choice,' said Cate.

I didn't like to tell her it was a purely random selection.

'He's a connoisseur of the well-rolled spliff too,' Laura added with a wink.

'For therapeutic purposes,' I added quickly.

'It's a good relaxant,' Cate agreed, without missing a beat. 'I'm not sure that outlawing it has ever been a good idea.'

'Would you prescribe it then?' asked Simon.

'I'm not allowed to. But if it's what works . . .' She shrugged.

'Nothing better,' I told her. 'That and swimming. Though I won't be doing much of that for a while. I'd scare everyone out of the pool.'

'I'll dig out Grace's paddling pool for you,' Laura offered.

'You could come and use mine,' said Cate.

'You've got your own swimming pool?' Even Simon was impressed.

Cate laughed. 'Not exactly. But there's a residents' pool in the basement of my building.' She turned to me. 'You could come as my guest. It's generally pretty quiet in the evenings.'

I could see that she meant it. 'Thanks.'

It was just after one in the morning when Cate offered to drive me home and while I mostly prefer to assert my independence, at that time of night it would have been foolhardy not to accept.

'Thanks for the lift,' I said, as we drew to a halt outside my building.

'No problem.' She turned off the engine. 'I've really enjoyed meeting you and I'm glad for the chance to apologise.'

'For what?'

'Being so over the top to begin with. I didn't know what to expect.'

'I get that a lot.'

'No, that's not what I mean. It's just that Laura has done this to me before — "Why don't you come for lunch or dinner?" Followed by the phone call a week later . . . "Oh, by the way Tom/Dick/Harry will be there. I don't think you've met him. You two will really hit it off." And somehow I always feel I have to "perform".'

I couldn't help laughing. 'She does that to you too?'

'God, yes. Let me think . . . this must be at least the fourth time.'

'She's getting desperate, then, if she's down to me.'

'Oh no, quite the reverse. I got the feeling I had to get through the preliminary rounds before I was deemed to be good enough for you.' She seemed sincere. 'But I'm glad we got there in the end.'

'Me too.' Buoyed by the alcohol, I leaned over, intending to give her a chaste kiss on the cheek, but at the last instant she turned towards me so that our lips made contact. Nothing heavy. Just a couple of seconds. Just a kiss, but it was definitely deliberate. 'Goodnight, Cate,' I managed to stammer.

'Goodnight, Stefan.' She placed a hand on my arm. 'And don't forget that swim. I meant it.'

'I'd like that.' I clambered out of the car.

'How about Friday?' she called after me. 'We could have dinner afterwards?'

'That would be great.'

'Come over at about eight.' She recited her address.

If I could have managed a hop, skip and jump into my apartment, I would have, but instead I had to content myself with enjoying a warm inner glow. Maybe Laura's efforts were finally going to pay off.

CHAPTER NINETEEN

Despite Superintendent Bowers' encouragement to take a few days off, I couldn't stay away. I needed to be doing something useful. I'd braced myself for the snide remarks I expected to come my way when I returned to the station, but as it turned out it was almost worse. People all but ignored me. I couldn't really blame them — had I been in their position, I wouldn't have known what to say to me either. A pall hung over Fulford Road. In my limited experience it was always the same when a fellow copper died. Most people were busy out looking for Liam Archer or gathering statements pertaining to Denny's murder. I wasn't allowed to be in on the action, of course. Instead I was put on 'light duties', as if I was ill or something.

My intention was to do more work on the Stefan Greaves case, but in reality, I spent most of the morning gazing out of the window, watching the frequent comings and goings in the car park below and tuning in and out of the conversation going on around me.

It was only when I looked up and caught Bowers on the far side of the room watching me that I was able to galvanise myself into actually doing something, to avoid being sent home again. Denny had been an experienced copper, but despite the fact that the last few days had elevated him to sainthood, it was important to remember that he wasn't infallible. And while he didn't think a mugging was worth the effort, some of us did. The only other possible witness to Greaves' attack was via Keeley

Moynihan. Although she'd been the one to find him, she hadn't yet been asked to make a statement, further indication of Denny's apparent complete lack of interest. But I hadn't talked to her properly yet either. I didn't have her address to hand but had made a note of her mobile number. When I called it, her voice came at me from a hubbub of background noise.

'Would it be convenient for me to call round for a chat?' I asked.

'I'm out shopping,' she explained. 'But I'm not far from the police station. You're at Fulford Road, right? I could stop by there when I've finished, in about an hour, if you like?'

'That would be great.' My stomach had started to growl and this arrangement would allow me time to make inroads into the sandwiches Sonia had made for me. I was sitting at my desk trying to not spill crumbs all over the computer keyboard when I had the call up from reception, pretty much at the time Keeley had promised.

'Someone to see you, Mick,' Ed Farlow said. 'Though looking at her, I think she must have got the wrong bloke.'

I went down to meet her.

'PC Mick Fraser,' I reminded her, as we shook hands.

'Yes, we met at the hospital, didn't we?' She was dressed in fake fur today, a short jacket that finished just above the hips, topping off long legs that were encased in skintight leather stiletto boots. Not many women could carry off that look with class, but she was one of them.

'That's right. Thanks for coming in, I appreciate it.'

'Anything I can do to help catch the bastards who hurt Stefan.'

All along the corridor and across the office to my desk, I felt eyes swivel in our direction, and I was fairly sure they weren't looking at me.

Once we were settled in one of the informal interview rooms, which was light and tastefully decorated with low furniture, I took her back to the night of the attack. 'So you didn't see or hear anything after Mr Greaves went out?' I checked again.

'No. We had been . . . occupied for a couple of hours and were getting ready to go out to dinner. I was in the shower when Stefan left the flat. I dried off, put on my make-up and did my hair. I mean, I heard voices at one point — a group of lads going past, laughing and talking. But it was the start of the weekend, it's what people do.'

'So what time was this?'

'By the time I was ready, it was about ten. I remember looking at the clock and thinking Stefan had been gone quite a while. But then the queues at the cashpoint on a Friday night can be horrendous, and of course everything takes him a little longer, so I waited another ten minutes, then I went out to the main entrance hall to see if I could see him. I had to be discreet. He'd have hated the idea that I was checking up on him, and even then, I nearly didn't notice him. It was dark and I was looking out to the street, but then a movement caught my eye and I realised there was something on the ground. I didn't think it would be Stefan. I rushed out and he was just lying there, sort of curled up and by then he was completely still.' She paused to catch her breath. 'That scared me — he's never completely still, even when he's asleep — but when I leaned over, I could hear him breathing. I had to run back inside to get my mobile and call for an ambulance, then I came back and sat with him, talking to him, until the medics and then you came.'

'And you didn't notice anything else, anyone hanging about?'

'No. I suppose I was too preoccupied with looking out for the paramedics to notice much else.' She closed her eyes briefly. 'There was actually a moment when I thought he might be . . .' She shivered.

I produced the mug shots of Bostwick and Phelps, placing them on the table in front of her. 'Do you know either of these two men? Have you seen them hanging around that area at all?'

She studied both, her gaze lingering a little longer on Phelps. 'I'm not sure. He does look a little familiar, but I couldn't tell you where I've seen him. Do you think it was them?'

'They've been picked out by the owner of the supermarket Mr Greaves went to, but I don't know for sure yet.'

She took a surreptitious glance at her watch. 'Is there anything else? I'm really sorry but I'm going out tonight, so I should be getting on.'

'No, that's fine. Thank you. You've been really helpful.'

* * *

Plum had continued to spend the morning, almost non-stop, trying to get through to Rita Todd.

'Look, I'm due at the hospital for a check-up later today,' I told her. 'Why don't you come with me?'

She looked at me as if I'd gone mad. 'You want me to hold your hand?'

'Not exactly. It's been over a week, so Rita must be back at work by now. We could stop by her ward, see if she's there. See? Two birds, one stone.'

'Great,' she said, with all the enthusiasm I'd come to expect. 'I'll sharpen my pencil.'

It's hard to say which of us attracted the most attention as we sat in the outpatients' waiting area, and the inevitable lengthy wait meant that we were subjected to the public gaze for quite a while. Plum was fidgety and uncomfortable.

'You don't like hospitals?' I surmised.

She visibly shuddered. 'Hate them.'

'I've never understood that,' I said, knowing at the same time that she was far from alone. 'They're places of healing.'

'Not always. Sometimes they're just dumping places for the damaged,' she said.

I looked at her.

'I spent a bit of time in hospital when I was a kid,' she said, as if that was in the far distant past.

'I didn't know that.'

Without taking her eyes off mine, Plum began, wordlessly, to roll up the sleeve of her jumper. It hadn't occurred to me until that moment that I had only ever seen Plum in long-sleeved garments, usually hanging way down over her hands. The reason soon became clear. Just above her pale wrist were a dozen or so delicate, thread-like scars that disappeared up under her cuff.

'Bad karma,' she said. 'Jake saved my life,' she added. 'I mean, literally, man.' Had we been cartoon characters, hearts and chirruping bluebirds would have been circling her head.

Not for the first time, I didn't know what to say to her. Instead, for some reason, I slipped an arm awkwardly round her shoulders and squeezed. 'We're only visiting this time,' I said. And Plum did something I've never seen her do before. She blushed, as dark as her name.

This effectively, if somewhat awkwardly, ended the conversation, so it was something of a relief when just a couple of minutes later my name was called. I was subjected to all the usual checks: blood pressure, reflexes, eyes and ears. It was a different doctor, of course, but for once, he'd read my notes.

'Have you had any further seizures?' he asked.

'No.' To tell the truth, I'd forgotten all about them.

'And how do you feel in yourself?' he asked finally.

'I'm OK,' I said. It was true. Apart from those wobbly couple of days immediately afterwards, I felt pretty normal again.

'And you're taking it easy?'

'Oh, yes.'

Afterwards, I went back out to Plum in the waiting room.

'Wonderful news, darling,' I said. 'I'm going to live.'

She forced a weak and mirthless smile. 'Can we go now?'

'Of course, after we've stopped off at Rita Todd's department.'

'Which is what?' she asked, walking over to the ubiquitous multicoloured wall plan.

'The neonatal unit.'

Plum wrinkled her nose. 'What's that when it's at home?'

'Sick babies.'

CHAPTER TWENTY

The phrase 'stopping off' turned out to be something of an understatement. It felt as though we pounded mile upon mile of sterile corridor, hiking virtually the length of the hospital site to get to the right department, but eventually we came to the Neonatal Intensive Care Unit where Rita Todd worked. In the interests of simplicity, Plum approached the nurses' station, where a harassed young auxiliary, whose name badge identified her as Shelley, was fielding phone calls with impressive efficiency. We waited our turn. At last, when there was a break in the traffic, she looked up at Plum, the disdain barely masked. It was a minimalist conversation.

'Can I help you?' Shelley asked.

'Is Rita Todd at work today?' Plum asked in response.

'No.'

'When will she be back?'

'I don't know.'

'Who would?'

'I'll go and find out.' She disappeared for more than five minutes. 'Sorry, nobody seems to know.'

I was beginning to feel fobbed off, which made me all the more determined not to leave empty handed.

'Do you work with Rita?' I asked her.

'Yes,' she said, a touch defensively.

'We think she may be in trouble.' It was over-egging it a bit, but I was looking for a result and she didn't contradict me. Maybe Andrea was closer to the mark than we'd thought. 'Do you want to help her?' I asked.

It took a while but eventually she nodded, which in itself was interesting.

'Well, we'd like that too. But she's away and if we're going to stand any chance, it would be really useful to talk to someone who knows something about what's going on. Is there anyone who can do that? We can wait as long as you like.' I ignored a glare from Plum.

Shelley sighed. 'I'll see what I can do.' She pointed back the way we'd come. 'There's a staff room down that corridor and on the right. You can wait in there.'

'Thank you, it's much appreciated,' I said, though I'm not sure she got that.

* * *

Clearly the hospital personnel were not expected to enjoy much in the way of breaks. All they had was a functional box room, with steel lockers lining one wall, half a dozen stained and threadbare easy chairs surrounding a square, utilitarian coffee table, its surface covered with an untidy pile of dog-eared gossip magazines. A notice board on one wall displayed flyers for social events that had been and gone, along with a collection of faded postcards and a number of aphorisms that might, on the first reading, have been vaguely amusing: *You don't have to be mad to work here...* etc. Oscar Wilde wasn't under any threat.

Ten minutes stretched out to almost half an hour, during which time my stomach and Plum's competed to produce the loudest hunger growl. I was about to give up and go — they were taking the piss. But then the door swung open on a young woman, short and sturdily built, her mousy hair elaborately plaited around her head. She looked red-faced and flustered and barely seemed to register our presence, heading straight for one of the lockers. She opened it up to retrieve a handbag, which she rifled through fruitlessly, sniffing while she did so. I fished in my pocket and came out with a clean handkerchief.

'Here.' I held it out to her, and she turned and took it.

'Thanks.' With a wan smile, she blew her nose.

I gave Plum a meaningful look, hoping she'd pick up the cue. She did.

'Is everything all right?' she asked.

If this girl was being put under excess pressure too, we might be home and dry.

'We just lost a patient,' she said. 'We seem to be going through a bad patch at the moment, but the frequency doesn't really make it any easier. You have to hold it in when you're with the parents, but—' She dropped into one of the chairs across from Plum and me. 'Poor little mite, she didn't have much going for her, but it still breaks your heart.' She blew her nose again, then, making a visible effort to shake herself out of it. 'Sorry, what are you doing in here?'

'It's Ellen, right?' I said, reading her name tag. 'We're waiting to talk to someone who knows Rita Todd. We wanted to see Rita herself, but I understand that she's not back from holiday yet. Do you know her?'

'Yes, of course. We work on the same ward together. Um, who are you again?'

'Rita came to us for help. I'm her lawyer.'

Seemingly for the first time, she looked at me properly, taking in the suit and tie. The double take only lasted a split-second.

'Oh, right . . .' Too late, she recognised her reaction as insensitive and gave a helpless shrug. 'Rita said her daughter was trying to get her to go to a lawyer. Poor Rita,' she said, recovering. 'I was just thinking about her this morning. How's she getting on?'

'She seems to be doing OK, considering.' I recalled Rita's straightforward manner and her dignified air of resignation as she left our offices. 'She's given us her side of things, of course. But it would help to get another perspective.'

'I can't tell you much,' she said. 'Mr Leonard's the one you want to talk to,' said Ellen. 'But he's the consultant in charge, so he's a very busy man.'

'We plan on talking to him, too,' I said. I nodded towards Plum to make a note of that name.

Ellen looked from one of us to the other. 'So, what is it you want to know?'

'For a start, why did you call her "poor Rita"?' I asked.

'Well, nobody wants to get suspended, do they?'

Suspended? I had to stop myself from repeating the word out loud. I wondered if Andrea knew, or was this the matter about to hit the fan that Rita had mentioned? But she hadn't seemed worried by that, instead she'd been almost defiant.

'Why?' I asked.

'I don't exactly know. Babies were dying who shouldn't have died — something to do with their medication. But I'm sure it can't have been Rita.'

Shit. This was far worse than I could have imagined. 'Has someone said that it was?'

'Well, not as such, but the day after the last . . . incident, Rita didn't turn up for work and we were told she wouldn't be in for a while.' She looked doubtful. 'You start to put two and two together, don't you?'

'Do you think Rita's capable of that, causing the death of a patient?'

'No! That's what I'm saying. Not intentionally.'

'You mean it could have been an accident? That Rita might have made a mistake?'

'Maybe. This job, it can be relentless. And there's fewer of us to do it. Since we got restructured, quite a few people didn't like it, so they left. They haven't been replaced with permanent staff. The trust buys in agency staff to try and fill the gaps but the temporary pay and conditions are pretty crap, so they don't stay. By the time they get used to how we do things, they've gone and there's someone else in their place. And they don't take on the same level of responsibility, so that gets left to the rest of us. I mean, Mr Leonard helps out when he can but, as I said, he's a very busy man.'

'And what about Rita?' If we could demonstrate that she was under undue pressure, we might have a chance.

'Well now that Delores has gone, she's the only senior nurse on the unit, so she has to do a lot of cover. She used to say she didn't mind, on account of her daughter being grown up and all that, but you've got to have a life, haven't you? It was starting to get her down.'

'Was it? What makes you think that?'

'She's been a bit distant, like she's got a lot on her mind. I wondered if she'd started seeing someone. Except . . .'

'What?'

'She seemed kind of sad about it. I heard about what her ex was like and I was hoping it's not the same thing again.'

'Do Rita and Mr Leonard get on?'

Ellen's eyes flicked anxiously towards the CCTV camera that was monitoring our every move. 'They used to. When I first started here, it was a really good atmosphere. We were a much bigger team, and we looked out for each other. There was a lot of banter and leg-pulling that went on. It can be a tough job sometimes, especially like today when you lose a patient. Because it's happening more than usual, it makes everyone tense. Sometimes you need to be able to let go a bit and have a laugh. Rita and Mr Leonard, they used to be the worst. Same sense of humour.'

'But not anymore.'

'I suppose because she's the senior nurse, Mr Leonard is on Rita's back more than the rest of us. It's stupid things, really. If he can't find the notes on a patient he's looking for, or hasn't got the right equipment to hand, he can be a bit sharp. I mean, technically Rita's the next in line, of course, so she's the one who cops for it. But she just gets on with the job and never complains.'

'Mr Leonard sounds quite a difficult man to work with,' I said. In my limited experience, medical consultants could have egos the size of Canada and behave accordingly. Should it come to that, this could all be evidence for Rita's defence.

But, disappointingly, Campbell responded with an emphatic shake of the head. 'Oh no. Most of the time he's great — a really nice down to earth guy. And he's brilliant with the families. He's just . . . he has a lot of responsibilities.'

'When do you think things between him and Rita started to go wrong?'

'When the department got reorganised. I think Rita thought that Mr Leonard could have stood up to the hospital management to resist it. I overheard her telling him once that he was betraying his profession and betraying the families.'

'It wasn't Mr Leonard's idea, then? The directive for that came from higher up management?'

She wrinkled her brow. 'Yes, I mean, nobody seemed to want it, but it just sort of happened.'

At that moment, the door burst open and another young woman put her head in.

'Ellen, can you come?' She was breathless, either with haste or anxiety. 'Things are kicking off out here.'

She was instantly on her feet and moving towards the door. 'Sorry, got to go.'

'Is there anything else you think we should know?' Plum called after her, but she'd gone.

'Thanks for your time,' I murmured as the door swung closed behind her.

'What do you reckon, then?' Plum asked as we started out on the trek back to the main entrance, negotiating our way out through the warren of corridors.

'I'm still reeling from finding out that children have died. Rita kept that quiet.'

'So why didn't she tell you any of that? Why hold back?'

'Well the obvious conclusion is that she's guilty. If she knows she hasn't got a leg to stand on it would explain why Andrea had to drag her kicking and screaming to us. But I don't get it. She was so . . . calm. She said she'd deal with it and didn't need anyone else to fight her battles. We certainly need to speak to her again, and urgently.'

Instead of heading towards the exit, I started back to the department's reception desk.

'What are you doing?' said Plum.

'Striking while the iron's hot,' I said. 'We might as well see this Mr Leonard while we're here. It sounds as if he's in the thick of it. Though none of this will be at all relevant if Rita insists on going it alone. We could just be pissing in the wind.'

We went back to the desk where Shelley was stationed again.

'We were hoping to speak to Mr Leonard, too,' said Plum, making it sound like an entitlement. 'Is he on duty today?'

'Well, he is,' Shelley said uncertainly, as if we'd just asked for an audience with God. 'But I'll have to see if he's available. He's—'

'—a very busy man,' Plum finished for her, adding a sardonic smile. 'I know.'

Shelley disappeared for some time. When she came back, she was apologetic. 'He's in a meeting,' she said. 'I'm afraid he hasn't got time to see anyone today.'

Of course he hadn't.

CHAPTER TWENTY-ONE

I was at my desk when I became aware of someone standing over me. It was one of the constables from the incident room, assigned to Denny's case.

'I was asked to work through PC Sutton's in-tray and I came across this,' he said. 'I've tried phoning back, but no luck so far. Does it mean anything to you?'

What he handed me was a phone message slip asking Denny to call the mortuary regarding the fatality last Thursday. I had to think for a minute what that was. Then I remembered. It was the John Doe suicide we'd attended the afternoon of the day before Denny was killed. God, it seemed a lifetime ago.

'It's OK,' I told the constable. 'You can leave it with me.'

He looked uncertain.

'Really,' I said. 'I'll get back to you with whatever I find. Promise.'

I tried phoning the mortuary first, but like my colleague had said, they must have been rushed off their feet, because there wasn't even space to leave a recorded message.

The mortuary was way down the list of places I wanted to go right then. Apart from anything else, I couldn't shake the thought that it was where Denny would be. But a trip to the hospital would give me something to do and get me away from the oppressive atmosphere of the station.

Visitor parking at the hospital was always at a premium and I'd turned up at what was probably the busiest time of day. I cruised slowly up and down the rows a couple of times until finally conceding that there were no free spaces, even for anyone there in an official capacity. I drove off-site, into a residential side street, finally finding a gap about a quarter of a mile away. When I got to the basement mortuary, there was no one around. The pathologist and his staff were obviously otherwise engaged, so I picked up a cup of typically unappealing vending machine coffee and took it to the waiting room, where I absently flicked through a couple of tattered magazines put there for the purpose. I'd only ever been here a couple of times and could never quite shake the feeling of slight apprehension, even though outwardly it was just another set of offices and waiting space. I'd been there about twenty minutes, and was thinking of giving up, when I heard the banging of a door and a mortuary assistant — Sammy, if I'd remembered correctly — walked past the open door, saw me and retraced his steps.

'Constable Fraser?' he queried, as unsure as me, though he'd remembered my relationship with Denny and followed up with what had become the routine commiserations.

'How can we help you?' he asked.

I explained the mystery message, omitting the main reason why I'd come along in person.

He grimaced. 'I'm sorry, you've had a wasted journey,' he said. 'I only called to let PC Sutton know that there would be a delay on the post-mortem. We had a couple of unexpected deaths ourselves the night before, on Ward Nine.' He saw my blank face. 'Geriatrics. It set us back a bit. And now . . . your partner . . .'

Of course. Denny would have been fast-tracked. I wondered what he'd have thought of that.

'Tell you what, though—' Sammy brightened at the prospect of offering up something. 'We've got the clothes and stuff bagged up for your suicide. You could take those?'

'Any ID?' I asked hopefully, when he returned. There wasn't, but the personal effects would help for verification when an anxious friend or relative fetched up at Fulford Road to report a missing person. Sammy also tracked down a facial photograph, which he'd slipped into an envelope.

109

'Not a pretty sight.'

'Thanks,' I said.

'No probs,' said Sammy. 'And don't worry. We'll look after him.' I wasn't sure if he meant Denny or our suicide, but, having seen the mortuary team in action before, I had no doubts that both would be afforded the same level of respect.

Even so, I didn't like to think of Denny subjected to the indignity of a post-mortem, and it occurred to me that if I'd been a bit more insistent about going after Archer, he wouldn't have to be. I climbed the stairs to the ground floor, working hard to dispel the unwelcome images that had come into my head, so didn't hear my name called across the atrium until it was bellowed at close range. Looking up, I was puzzled to see the owner of the voice — a striking young woman whom Sonia would have described as 'alternative'. Then I noticed the distinctive gait of her companion, Stefan Greaves.

'Everything all right?' I asked, as we came face to face.

He replied with a thumbs up. 'Clean bill of health, near enough,' he said.

'That's great.' I was pleased for him. 'Look, I'm sorry I haven't got back to you yet, but there's a lot going on.'

'No problem. It was hardly the crime of the century.' He was more reasonable than I had a right to expect. He gave me a curious look. 'You look like shit,' he observed. 'Has something happened?'

I forced a smile. 'Yeah, you could say that.' I rubbed a hand over my shaven head. 'You heard about the officer stabbed to death off Vesey Street?'

He nodded. 'It's been all over the news.'

'It was my partner, Denny. You remember the other guy who came to talk to you in the hospital?'

I missed what he said in reply. I mean, it sounded like 'Saint Peter', but that seemed unlikely. The next bit I did get.

'I didn't know that,' he said. 'Were you there when it happened?'

'Right beside him.' Something nudged me in the stomach. 'It's on a loop in my head. I mean, it was dark, so I couldn't see clearly, but I could hear him. First this moaning noise, but then it was just this awful rattling sound in time with his breathing. Every time I close my eyes it comes back to me.' I realised suddenly what I was saying. 'Sorry, that must be like a flashback to what you went through.'

A shake of the head. 'It's fine. They said on the news that the guy who attacked him had mental health problems.'

'Mainly a not so friendly relationship with alcohol,' I told him. 'But yeah, he's a few spanners short of a full toolkit.'

'Has he been picked up yet?'

'Not as far as I know. They've taken me off it, of course.'

The girl standing beside Greaves appeared to be scowling at me, though it could have been simply her natural expression. Her jaw worked hard on a piece of gum.

'This is Plum, my assistant,' Greaves said. 'Plum, PC Fraser, my police liaison officer.'

'Hi,' she said, but it took some effort, so I didn't like to ask about the name.

'Are you here about . . . ?' asked Greaves. He didn't have to say Denny's name.

I shook my head. 'Another one I couldn't do much about, unfortunately,' I said, nodding towards the stairwell I'd just ascended.

'That's tough.'

'Aye, it's the incident I got called to from your flat, and the last one Denny and I attended, so it would be good to find out what happened. No ID yet, but I'm working on it.'

'Good luck with that,' said Greaves.

I lifted a hand to bid them goodbye. 'I'll be seeing you, then.' But as I made to move off, Greaves seemed to freeze.

'What's that?' he asked, looking at one of the evidence bags in my hand.

'Effects of the deceased.' For the first time, I looked properly at the two bags. One contained what looked like nondescript high street store clothing, the other a couple of personal items. 'Not much to show for a life.'

He swallowed. 'It's just, I've seen one of those very recently.' He was pointing at a fine silver chain, which had a tiny cross attached. 'Shortly before I got my head kicked in.'

'Your attackers?' My heart did a little leap, but he shook his head.

'No, before that. A client we've been trying — unsuccessfully so far — to get hold of over the weekend.'

'Who is he?'

'It's a "she",' said Plum. 'Rita Todd. Works here, funnily enough.'

'Ah, well this one's a . . .' I was about to say 'man' but then realised that we hadn't had confirmation on that. Could it possibly be? Then I remembered I was also carrying the manila envelope. 'I've got a picture here,' I said. 'It won't be a pretty sight.'

I was right about that. It was a gruesome image, the face grey and distended from prolonged time spent in the water. But it wasn't disgust he recoiled in. It was recognition.

'I'm sorry. Suicide's looking pretty definite,' I said.

'Suicide? Shit.' They exchanged a look.

'Is there any reason to think she might have come to harm that way?' I asked.

'No. I don't know.' Greaves looked bewildered. 'I just had one brief conversation with her.'

I was still trying to get my head round the possibility. 'Take another look, if you can,' I said. 'You really think it could be her?'

'How did she . . . ? I mean, what were the circumstances?' asked Greaves. 'Can you say?'

'There's not much more to tell. She was found by a couple of river authority guys, down near Mill Lane on Thursday afternoon. It's what I got called to when I left your flat. Nothing yet suggests anything other than suicide. I understand it's not uncommon around here — a couple or so every six months. Was Rita Todd in that kind of state?'

Another look passed between them, but it was Greaves who spoke again. 'I don't know. Her daughter had persuaded her to come to us because of trouble at work, but Rita implied that it was an overreaction. She seemed . . . fine. Together.'

'We did just find out that she might have been suspended, though,' Plum reminded him.

'Yeah, that's something she forgot to share with me.' I could see him replaying the conversation with Rita Todd in his head, struggling to recall any clues.

112

There was an easy way of determining this one way or the other.

'Look, I have no right to ask this, but how would you feel about doing a preliminary identification?' I asked him. 'It would save putting the family through any unnecessary pain and . . .' But he'd already agreed. 'She has got family then?' I confirmed.

'Just the daughter — Andrea — as far as we know.'

'Well,' I said. 'No time like the present.' They came with me back to the mortuary, where Plum waited outside.

'Have you ever done this before?' I asked Greaves before we went in.

'Once,' he said. 'My mother.'

That wouldn't have been a happy memory, but this wasn't the time to ask about that. I was still trying to get to grips with the potential coincidence of all this.

'She'd spent some considerable time in the river,' I warned him. 'So, like in the photo, she's really not looking her best.'

The attendant lifted the sheet and Greaves' reaction was instantaneous, leaving no room for doubt.

'It's her,' he confirmed, flinching a little. 'Rita Todd. And it's definitely suicide?'

'We're pretty certain,' I said. 'Although there's always the possibility of an accident, of course. Have you got contact details for her daughter?'

He nodded, dazed. 'You said she was found on Thursday?'

'Well, it's difficult to tell where water is involved, but speaking from my limited experience, I'm guessing she could have been in there for up to a week. When did you talk to her?'

'Oh Christ, I could have been among the last people to see her alive.'

'It's possible,' I had to concede. 'But not inevitable. Try not to have nightmares, eh?'

He gave me the kind of look that that deserved.

As we left the mortuary, I called the number Greaves had given me. Naturally, Andrea Todd was a in a shocked and delicate state when I picked her up from her workplace, and I was glad I had arranged for a family liaison officer, PC Emily Kendrick, to meet us at the mortuary.

113

Miss Todd was keen to do the identification right away. She was hoping, of course, as relatives so often did, that we had made a mistake, even though I knew that we hadn't. Afterwards however, she was unexpectedly calm — just utterly certain that her mother would not have taken her own life. I went along with it for now. There was no point in causing her further distress.

CHAPTER TWENTY-TWO

Plum and I returned to the office, utterly stunned by this development. We had spent much of the drive back in silence, both wrapped up in our own thoughts, even Plum short on cynical observations about the world in general. In my case, it meant turning over in my mind the meeting with Rita Todd and wondering how I could have failed to realise how vulnerable she was. It explained why she was dismissive of any offers of help — she must have known that she wouldn't need it. All I could think of was what I could and should have said to her that afternoon that might have stopped her from taking her own life.

Jake, too, was silent as he absorbed the news.

'Did you get even the slightest hint that she was suicidal?' he said after a while.

'Not at all,' I said, doubts beginning to creep in. 'There was an impatience about her — a kind of nervous energy, like she was wired. But then, she wasn't exactly straight with me about her situation. What we've been told this morning puts a different spin on things, too.'

'Meaning what?'

'Rita wasn't on leave, as she implied. She'd been suspended from work.' I recounted our conversation with Ellen Campbell.

'Shit. Why?'

'That we don't know exactly, but one of her colleagues has linked it to the deaths of babies on the ward.'

'Christ.'

'There's obviously tension in that department. There's been some radical restructuring, which doesn't sound like it's been to the benefit of the existing staff. Rita and her boss, a Mr Leonard, had fallen out about it. While she was here, she told me that "the faecal matter is about to hit the fan, but not in the way Andrea thinks". Now I don't know if that was about the suspension from the hospital, or what she was intending to do. Either way, I badly missed an opportunity.'

'You weren't to know that,' Jake said immediately.

'I tried to talk to Leonard, but when they checked, he was too busy.'

'Avoidance?'

'Possibly, but in fairness, as a consultant he would be in high demand.'

'Well, it's all immaterial now anyway, isn't it?' said Jake. 'There will be an inquest, which will determine Rita's state of mind. We might find out more then. There's more bad news too,' said Jake, after a moment. He passed me a letter. 'Mr Asif and his family are leaving town. Too many bad memories here.'

And who could blame them?

CHAPTER TWENTY-THREE

Having identified Rita Todd, all I could do was wait now for the pathologist to do his stuff. But I was still having trouble focusing on anything useful. Most of all I wanted to do something for Denny, but I was barred from both the investigation and the funeral arrangements and I could see that his desk had been cleared. There was, however, one place left. I half expected, when I got there, to find his locker clean and bare, but was ludicrously pleased to find it in its usual chaotic state. This was something I could do. The family would want to take his belongings from here, too, so it wouldn't hurt to be prepared.

Tacked to the inside of the locker door alongside the usual family line-ups were a couple of photos of Denny with Kevin Booth. I'd never studied them before, but saw now that they were taken in happier times at social events. Both featured a number of empty or half-empty glasses in front of them, which had undoubtedly been instrumental in Kevin Booth's drink problem. It made me wonder again what it was that had prompted his sudden departure. Dependence on alcohol was hardly something novel in this job. But those I'd spoken to had hinted that there was more to it than that. The few direct enquiries I'd made had met with a brick wall, meaning that people had liked Booth and were reluctant to bad-mouth him, which was interesting. And now that Denny had gone, I was unlikely to learn anything more.

Like any copper's locker, Denny's was a repository for useless odds and ends: curled up copies of Police Review, *a couple of crumpled and dusty T-shirts, a sports flask with the stopper missing, a ball of crushed plastic carrier bags. At the bottom, under it all, was a nylon drawstring bag with a sports logo on the side. That raised a smile. I couldn't imagine Denny had ever done anything remotely athletic in his life. His boast was always that the closest he got to any physical activity was when he pressed the button to change channels on his television.*

I should have simply dumped the bag in the archive box along with everything else. What Denny chose to keep in his locker was nothing to do with me. But something — idle curiosity, I suppose — made me pull open the neck of the bag. What harm could it do to look? I tugged at the cord and peered inside. It took me several moments to make sense of what I saw, and although bewildering and initially meaningless, the contents made my heart thud with apprehension. Inside was a miscellaneous collection of purses, wallets and mobile phones, and a clear plastic bag stuffed with jewellery. I realised I was holding my breath.

There had to be a rational explanation for this — lost property, perhaps, that Denny had forgotten to check in. Except that didn't make sense. No one simply handed lost property to a copper, not in this quantity. This had to be more than oversight. And it was clear from its location that it had been deliberately stashed away from prying eyes. I stared uncomprehending for a couple of minutes, then, with clumsy fingers, reluctantly picked up one of the wallets and opened it up. It appeared intact, with credit cards but no cash and, according to the Visa debit card (which had recently passed its expiry date), belonged to Mr L. Jones. I tried another. It was old and battered, but again contained bank cards, library cards, a couple of minutely folded press cuttings, and a strip of pictures from a photo booth. All of which apparently belonged to an I. Whiteacre. I tried the phones. A couple of them were smartphones but the rest were old-fashioned mobiles. Most were dead, but one, the newest looking, had some life left in it.

The contacts list was just names and numbers, but they were somehow less random than I had expected and halfway down I felt a horrible pang of recognition that made my stomach lurch. Fumbling through the remainder of the wallets, I came to the one that was thickest. Unlike the others, this one still contained a wad of cash, as well as the mandatory

118

credit cards. By the time I took one out and read it, I'd already worked out whom it belonged to, courtesy of that address list. Stefan Greaves. I felt sick. What the hell did this mean? Greaves had been mugged and beaten for his wallet, watch and phone. Denny had told me that himself. So how had they all ended up at the bottom of his locker? He must have taken them from Greaves when he got to the scene, before I arrived. I thought back to how it had played out that evening.

I seemed to remember that Denny had been typically uncommunicative that night, and more than a little on edge, another of those things I'd put down to retirement nerves. We'd done the usual circuit of the Flatwood when Denny fancied a coffee. As he was driving at the time, he pulled up outside the high street fast-food place so that I could go and get us a couple of takeouts. Afterwards, he'd decided we should go and take a look up at the south end of the town. Anomaly one. I'd joked that the most we were likely to see up there was a bit of wife-swapping, but Denny had insisted we go on the grounds of some vague spate of burglaries, and convinced me that it was a reasonable use of our time. It was how we came to be so close to Meridian Close when the call came through from dispatch.

Anomaly two: after establishing what was going on, Denny had sent me back to the car for the spare torch because his wasn't working properly. By the time I returned, there was also a blanket covering Greaves, meaning that Denny must have sent Keeley away to fetch that, too. Left on his own with an unconscious victim, he would have had ample time and opportunity to relieve Greaves of his possessions and hide them about his person. Oh Denny, what had you been doing?

The obvious conclusion was that this was about money, but it smacked of desperation and Denny surely wasn't that desperate. He was retiring on a good pension and he'd told me himself that he and Sheila were minted when they'd sold the house to buy the property in Portugal. Besides, the cash was still here in Greaves' wallet. It made me wonder if Denny had been having some kind of mental breakdown, but there would surely have been other visible symptoms. It might, however, explain why he had failed to take Greaves' clothes for forensic examination. Was he completely losing the plot and I hadn't noticed? Even if that were true, there was nothing to be gained by discrediting the man now. Turning these in would shatter his reputation, and for what?

Denny had been a lot of things, but I felt certain that bent wasn't one of them. There had to be some explanation. In addition, the discovery raised questions about Stefan Greaves' attack. If he hadn't been set on for his possessions, then what was that all about?

I glanced at my watch. The locker room was quiet right now but there was a shift change due in about ten minutes. I needed time to think through all the possible implications before doing anything rash. There was no one around to see, so I stashed the bag inside my hold-all back in my own locker. Then I gathered all the other things from Denny's locker and put them into the archive box to await collection.

* * *

On Friday evening, after what had seemed like an eternal week, I arrived at Cate's flat at the appointed time. Her building was more upmarket than my place, with plush carpeted hallways and a proper concierge. When she opened the door to me, she had already changed, her towelling robe hanging open over a dark one-piece swimsuit that, from what I could see, accentuated all the right places.

'The poolside facilities aren't that great,' she explained. 'We're better off getting changed up here.' She handed me a robe almost identical to hers. 'My sister and her family often come to stay. It's a treat for the kids. So I keep spares,' she added, in case I got the wrong idea. She directed me towards the guest bedroom, which, like the rest of her flat, was modern, functional and minimalist except for the framed photographs on almost every surface, one or two featuring Cate herself but most showing friends and family.

'It'll take me a few minutes,' I warned her.

'We've got all night.'

Jesus. I hoped she wasn't expecting too much. When I was ready, we went down to the basement in the lift. It being the middle of a Friday evening, there were only a handful of other people swimming, and unlike the local public baths, this was a very adult affair. Everyone was sedately swimming lengths and keeping their own distance, and all were too polite to take much notice of me, which was nice. There were no children. We joined in and gradually the pool emptied, leaving us and a lone middle-aged man in a hat and goggles ploughing up and down. Cate joined me in the shallow end.

'How was that?'

'Fantastic.' It was no exaggeration. The water had a way of both supporting and relaxing me and I felt better than I had all week.

She reached out and touched the bruising on my stomach.

'Couple more weeks and it will all be gone.' Despite the cool of the water, her touch burned into my flesh. I caught her hand, locking my fingers awkwardly around hers. The air sizzled a little between us. Seeing the other swimmer heading away from us towards the far end of the pool, I leaned forward and kissed Cate. At first she moved in, pressing her damp body against mine, but then she broke it off. Unimpressed by my technique, perhaps? But, as if reading my mind, she nodded at the CCTV camera high on the wall. 'Strictly no petting in the pool,' she said. 'You'll get me evicted.'

We went up in the lift, each clutching the plastic bags that contained our costumes to avoid dripping all over the hallways, the air dense with anticipation in the knowledge that underneath the robes was nothing but bare flesh. But thanks to another camera, there would be no funny business in here either. Inside her flat, Cate headed for the kitchen.

'Make yourself comfortable,' she said.

I did as I was told and sank down into the soft leather sofa. She reappeared minutes later with two glasses of red wine.

'I know how partial you are to a nice burgundy,' she said, handing one to me. 'Cheers.'

'Cheers.'

We clinked glasses. Cate placed down her glass on the coffee table, then unfastened her robe, shook it loose from her shoulders, and let it drop.

I gaped at her, and suddenly she was self-conscious.

'What is it?'

'You're so . . . perfect,' I whispered. See, there's the rub. Despite all my own shortcomings, I'm a sucker for perfection, just like anyone else.

Sitting down beside me, she tugged the belt on my robe and pulled it open.

'Well,' she murmured, moving her mouth towards mine, and running her hand up the inside of my thigh. 'Laura wasn't kidding. You *have* got a lot going for you.'

Maybe she'd elaborately engineered it that way, but not having to wrestle with clothing made it the simplest and most relaxed foreplay I'd ever experienced and Cate seemed to read me faultlessly, allowing me the initiative, yet conscious of my limitations. We never made it as far as the bedroom, and afterwards lay on the sofa, limbs intertwined and wrapped in a blanket.

'I should cook dinner,' she said, eventually, sliding out of the blanket and into her robe again. 'Don't worry, it won't take long.'

'Want any help?'

'Give me ten minutes and then you can set the table.'

I was nervous about the meal, hoping that my body wouldn't let me down by making me spit dim sum all over her. But if I did, Cate seemed to take it all in her stride. We sat at the table for a while after we'd eaten, until I started to get uncomfortable.

'My ribs,' I said, which was partly the truth.

'Do the police have any ideas about who attacked you yet?' Cate asked when we'd settled back on the sofa.

'Not really. They took my wallet, watch and phone so chances are it was theft, probably drug-related.'

'Hmm, so the voluntary sterilisation programme hasn't started to take effect yet.'

'The *what*?'

'Yes, I was rather shocked too,' she said, swirling her wine in the glass. 'A memo got circulated a couple of months ago from the health trust, giving GPs the opportunity to sign up to a pilot scheme that would offer voluntary sterilisation to people with drug and alcohol abuse issues — smackhead begets smackhead is the theory — and pay them accordingly. See, if I had signed up, maybe you wouldn't have been attacked.' Her sardonic expression said she didn't really believe it.

'That sounds pretty radical.'

'It's come over here from the States, of course. It's quite popular there, I understand.'

'Are you going to sign up?'

'Absolutely not. There are all kinds of ethical issues I would struggle with. I've dealt with my fair share of substance abusers and I don't know how anyone could be sure that they were in a condition to make a rational decision about something like that, especially when there are financial rewards on offer. It plays to their addiction because naturally, in the short-term, they'll take the money and run. On the other hand, the argument is that it would reduce the numbers of children being born with drug dependency and foetal alcohol syndrome. That's where it gets tricky, when you have a chance to alleviate the suffering of children. Ultimately, you're balancing the rights of the unborn child against those of the adult. It's a very controversial scheme, which is probably why it's only been suggested as a pilot so far.'

'Do you know if anyone is taking it on?'

'Not yet, although even if they were, I'm not sure it's something that colleagues would openly admit to. I think some of them might privately be in favour of it and there are some tempting funding incentives attached. On the other hand, it can be very costly, supporting addicts. I've heard rumours about having some kind of central facility in the area to manage it, presumably because on an individual level people are reluctant. Anyway,' she added, with a smile, putting a hand on my thigh. 'This is all getting a bit too much like work, and I thought you'd come round to play.'

* * *

123

I'd been slow to catch on with the concept of brunch, and I hadn't remembered ever having had it before, but when Cate suggested at about ten thirty on Saturday morning that we get up and go out to eat, it seemed like not a bad idea. She took me to somewhere new — always a challenge, but good for me.

We found a booth towards the back of the restaurant, Cate facing the door. Brunch turned out to be less of a deal than I expected. Coffee and pastries was about all we could manage. We were on our second round of cappuccinos when the door pinged and a couple entered the restaurant.

Cate exclaimed in recognition. 'Guy! Joss! How lovely to see you!'

They came over to our table, all smiles. We both, in my case rather awkwardly, got to our feet and there were hugs all round. Then Cate turned to me.

'This is Stefan — Stefan, meet some old friends of mine.'

'Hey, less of the "old" if you don't mind,' Joss said. She rolled her eyes at me. 'What is she like? Good to meet you, Stefan.'

'You too,' I said. What with Cate and me standing next to them, this was a good place to play compare and contrast. Joss was larger than life, tall in stature and with a big personality, while Guy was diminutive in height and seemed the more serious of the two. To their credit, they seemed completely unfazed by me.

'Why don't you join us?' Cate said. She shot me a questioning look, as if to check.

'Oh, we're not staying,' Guy said, apologetically. 'We're on football duty this morning. Just came in for a sideline takeaway.'

'And a blast of warm air,' smiled Joss, hugging her coat round her. 'Our twins both play football so this is the Saturday morning endurance test,' she told me, by way of an explanation. 'I'm glad to have run into you, though, Cate. I've been meaning to call. We're having a bash for Guy's fiftieth next weekend, Saturday from eight. Come, both of you.'

'Of course.'

'Nice people,' I said, after they'd gone.

'They are,' Cate said. 'Joss and I were at uni together. Both medics, of course. Sorry, you'll get sick of us after a while.'

After a while? It had a ring of permanence that I liked. My mind turned over the coals of the previous night, and warm embers glowed in the depths of my belly.

I took hold of her hand. 'Oh, I don't think so.'

CHAPTER TWENTY-FOUR

Each time I went back to my locker that day, it felt like that draw-string bag sitting in my hold-all was so incendiary, it must be giving off a radioactive glow. I needed to do something with it, so that evening, short of any better ideas, I took it home. Sonia was going out with a couple of workmates, so I waited until she'd gone and then got it out and emptied the contents onto the coffee table in front of me — phones, wallets and jewellery. The only timepiece here was an old-fashioned pocket watch, which surely wasn't what Stefan Greaves would have been wearing. Rufus the cat came and sniffed at the pile for a moment but, unimpressed, wandered away again.

First off, I made a note of all the ownership details. Between them, the wallets, purses and phones gave me a list of four people: Stefan Greaves, Lloyd Jones, Ian Whiteacre and J. Marshall. The expiry dates on the credit cards also suggested a time frame going back as much as three years, though of course it could be less. That was the easy part. The provenance of the jewellery was less clear. It wasn't expensive stuff from what I could tell, though Sonia might have a better idea. The assumption was, of course, that J. Marshall must be female but there was nothing to verify that. I was picking it over when I heard the front door slam and Sonia came in, much sooner than I'd expected.

'You're back early.' I must have looked guilty, though I don't know why I felt that way.

'Just tired,' she said, her attention instantly drawn to the treasure trove on the table.

'Don't worry,' I reassured her. 'I haven't swapped sides.'

Sonia stared. 'I'm glad to hear it. There had better be a good explanation, though,' she said, in a good imitation of role reversal.

'It's not what you think,' I said, not really knowing what she might be thinking. 'I found it.'

'Found it?'

'In Denny's locker.'

'My God. Where's it come from?'

'That's what I'm hoping to work out. Crime victims are looking the most likely right now.'

'You think Denny stole it?'

'No, I can't believe that. But it has made me wonder about how well I really knew him.'

Sonia took off her coat and came to sit beside me. 'Can I touch it?'

'I don't see why not. It's too old to be of any use to forensics.'

She picked up one of the half a dozen or so gold and silver necklaces.

'Are they genuine?' I asked her.

'They look and feel like decent quality,' she said, 'and see here . . .' She indicated the tiny emblems on one of the clasps. 'They're hallmarked. These are beautiful.' She picked up one of the rings that had a row of three sparkling stones and put it in her palm alongside a plain gold band. 'This is rose gold, and see how thin they've worn? I bet these belonged to someone's parents or grandparents. In fact, most of it looks a bit dated.'

'So it's probably inherited rather than recently bought.'

'I would say so, unless it belongs to someone who collects vintage stuff. It's very popular right now.' She picked up the pocket watch. 'Though I don't know anyone who wears one of these any more, do you?' She looked up at me and asked the million dollar question. 'What will you do with it?'

'The wallets have named credit cards in them. I'll try and track down the owners through the PNC.'

'You think they're definitely related to robberies?'

127

'I know at least one of them is.' Sorting through the pile, I came to Stefan Greaves' wallet and removed one of the credit cards, which I held up for her to see.

'Greaves?' she said. 'Wasn't that the guy who was mugged the other weekend? That's bizarre. What was Denny up to?'

What indeed.

* * *

I was still preoccupied with the hoard when I stood in the church at Denny's funeral on Monday morning. Expedited because of his role as a serving officer, it was always going to be a big affair. Despite these austere times, the police service liked to be seen to be looking after its own, though it felt slightly obscene that so soon after we were organising his retirement parties, such a different send-off should be taking place. I didn't know if Denny had ever gone regularly to church but today the big Anglican nave was packed with uniforms, mine among them, with Sheila sitting at the front, flanked by her two grown-up sons and other members of the family.

'What an ordeal for her,' I heard someone behind me murmur. 'She must have thought they were on the home straight, to have got through all those years safely, only for him to be taken from her in his last week. Life is so cruel sometimes . . .' The voice broke off suddenly. 'What's he doing here?'

At first I thought they were referring to me, and an unwelcome heat flared inside my collar, but when I turned and looked back down the aisle I saw that Ashley Curzon was making an entrance. I didn't realise that Denny had known him, unless it was something to do with that mysterious VIP visitor, but the service would of course be reported in the media, perhaps even nationally, so it would be in Curzon's interests to show his face.

It wasn't an easy service. This was a man cut down too soon, before he'd had the opportunity to reap the rewards of a long working life. As the superlatives flowed, I couldn't help thinking about what the various speakers would make of what I'd found in Denny's locker.

After the service, Denny's son Tony approached me. We'd met once before.

128

'I'm really sorry,' I said. It was inadequate.

'I know. And bloody awful timing. He so very nearly made it to the end.' He glanced over to his mother. 'I think that's the hardest thing for Mum to bear. He should have quit before. They could have managed.'

'I should have looked out for him,' I said, voicing what I had wanted to for days.

Tony grasped my arm. 'No, mate,' he insisted. 'That wasn't what I meant at all. It's not your fault and nobody blames you. You must believe that. This kind of crap, it's part of the job and Dad knew that.' I could find little comfort in his words. 'To be honest, he was never the same after Kevin left. I mean, no disrespect to you or anything. Dad tried to stick it out, but he should have jacked it in at the same time Kev did.'

'Booth left under a bit of a cloud, didn't he?' I said. I was just making conversation, really.

'You could say that,' said Tony. 'It goes with the territory, of course, but Kevin's drink problem had got the two of them into trouble a couple of times. I think Dad thought it might be easier after he'd gone, but the job was different, too. He said that it had changed beyond all recognition. He was getting increasingly disillusioned and according to Mum it was starting to keep him awake at night for the first time ever. It had never got to him like that before.'

While we were talking, Bowers walked past. 'And as for him . . .' Tony muttered under his breath.

'But I thought they got on well,' I said. 'Your dad had been spending a lot of time with him just recently.'

Tony flashed a cynical smile. 'Dad was old school,' he reminded me. 'He'd been around long enough to know that he had to play the game and get along with those he had to, but he didn't have much time for what he called the "over-educated" lot. Yeah, he should have got out when he had the opportunity.'

'Would it help if the man who did it was caught?' I asked him.

'It might bring closure of a sort, I suppose,' Tony admitted. 'But from what they've told us about Archer, he was a lost soul anyway. It's doubtful that he was even aware of what he was doing. And I don't know if that makes it better or worse.'

'No.' I couldn't come up with a better response. 'Look, if there's anything I can do,' I offered, lamely. 'I took the liberty of clearing your

129

dad's locker for you — thought it would be easier if I did it. His personal things are all boxed up and ready to collect whenever you feel ready.'

'Thanks, I appreciate that. I'll come and fetch them myself. It's not something I'd want to leave for Mum to do. How would tomorrow morning suit?'

'Perfect,' I said, even though we both knew it was about as far from perfect as it could be. 'And I really am sorry.'

'I know.' He nodded, we shook hands and he re-joined his family.

What Tony had said was interesting. I knew Denny was losing momentum somehow, and had assumed it to be a natural consequence of coming to the end of his working life. But where did the treasure haul I'd found in his locker fit in? It got me wondering again if Denny had been headed for some kind of mental implosion. Scanning the room, my eyes came to rest on the superintendent, who was in a tight huddle with Ashley Curzon. They seemed to have a lot to talk about.

It was early the next morning when I was summoned to reception, where Tony Sutton was waiting to collect his father's belongings. Leaving him in an interview room, I went and fetched them.

I put the box on the table in front of him. 'Here you go, then.' Tony took off the lid and peered inside, staring at the contents for a long moment.

'So this is it.' It was a statement, not a question — but he looked up and held my gaze and for one crazy moment, I wondered if he knew about the drawstring bag. But then he blinked hard and the emotion was clear and obviously unrelated.

'A bit pathetic, isn't it?' he went on. 'Not much to show for a thirty-year career. I'm glad Mum didn't have to do this.'

I nodded in agreement.

'Thanks for sorting it out. I know you didn't work with Dad for long, but he thought a lot of you.'

That was a surprise. It had so often felt as if Denny barely noticed me. An impulse came over me.

'You wouldn't happen to have contact details for Kevin Booth, would you? No one here knew where he was to get hold of him for the funeral, but it seems only fair to let him know what's happened.'

'Yes, Dad would have had his address, or at least a contact number somewhere. I'm sure they kept in touch for a while. I'll have a look for you and give you a call.'

'Thanks.'

Walking back up to the office, I passed Superintendent Bowers on the stairs. Our eyes locked for a second.

'It was a good service yesterday, I thought, sir,' I said, short of anything more original to say.

'Yes, son. They did him proud.'

Of course they did. It was what people said. We each made to continue on our way, but before I moved on, I turned to him again. 'Did anyone let Denny's partner know, sir?'

'His partner?'

'Well, ex-partner, Kevin Booth. He and Denny worked together for years. I wasn't sure if he would be there yesterday.'

'Excellent point, Fraser. I'll make some enquiries, see if anyone's been in touch. Though he's an old soak, from what I understand, went pretty downhill when he left the job and cut himself off. Very sad.' He paused. 'I suppose PC Sutton's locker will need to be cleared at some point.'

'I've done it, sir,' I told him, feeling efficient for once.

'Already?' Bowers looked a little startled. Perhaps he felt it was too soon to be respectful.

'Yes, sir. His son Tony has just been in to collect his dad's things. I got the idea he wanted to get it over with.'

Recovering, Bowers put a hand on my shoulder.

'Ah, yes, well, understandable in the circumstances.' He seemed to think for a moment. 'Sutton's phone found its way back to IT, did it?'

I could understand the concern. There were always worries about compromising security and confidentiality. Normal procedure was that at some point the SIM would be replaced and the phone recycled.

'As far as I know, sir, but I'll check.'

'Good, well, er, well done, Fraser. Never a nice thing to have to do.'

'No, sir.'

Before returning to duties, I made a detour via the IT department, where I spoke to Rob Docherty, the technician responsible for phones and personal radios.

'Has Denny's mobile been processed yet?'

'I haven't done it,' he confessed. 'Been putting it off, if I'm honest, you know?'

Yes, I did know. Nobody wanted to be reminded that a colleague was dead. But now I was there, he went and got the phone for me and opened it up.

'That's weird,' he said. 'The SIM has gone. Do you know if anyone took it out?'

I didn't, and told him so. He checked the work log, but there was no record of anyone else having tended to Denny's phone. 'Very strange,' he reiterated.

'A mystery,' I agreed, noting at the same time how clean and unused the phone looked.

CHAPTER TWENTY-FIVE

'You're disgustingly chipper today,' said Jake, when I got to the office on Monday morning. 'Good weekend?'

'Outstanding weekend,' I said. I was grinning like an idiot.

He regarded me with suspicion.

'What's going on?' Light dawned. 'Hah! You got laid. Who is she? Got a white stick and a dog?'

I flashed him the most sarcastic smile I could muster, but really my heart wasn't in it.

'A friend of Laura's.' I gave him what I was prepared to share about Cate's background.

'Well it's about time, that's all I can say.'

'What is?' Plum slouched in, all ears.

'Stefan got his end away at the weekend.'

Plum blushed and frowned, and I wished Jake hadn't been so blunt.

'Well, whoopee doo,' she said, deadpan, and hurried into the office we shared. By the time I followed her, she had her head down, deep in paperwork.

* * *

I heard the hubbub in the outer office first of all — Barbara was trying to calm someone, a woman who sounded very angry. Then my office door was flung open and Andrea Todd marched in, Barbara trailing helplessly behind.

'My mother did not kill herself!' Andrea exclaimed, without preamble. Her eyes were red-rimmed and bloodshot.

'I'm sorry . . .'

'It's fine, Barbara,' I said. 'Could you bring us a couple of coffees, please?'

Plum made to follow her out, but a signal from me kept her where she was and, taking out her pad and pencil, did what she was good at — pretending not to be there.

'Please sit down, Miss Todd.' I gestured to the chair opposite mine.

'She absolutely wouldn't have done that.' She paused momentarily as Barbara came back in with two mugs of coffee.

'I'm so sorry about your mother, Andrea,' I said, when Barbara had retreated. 'But this isn't my job,' I reminded her. 'The police will be conducting an investigation on behalf of the coroner.'

'They're not,' she retorted. 'They've already made up their minds.' She sipped at her coffee. 'They told me it was you who first realised it must be Mum.'

'It was just an extraordinary coincidence, a chance conversation with an officer I've got to know. I really wish it hadn't turned out like this.'

'But they're wrong,' she said, her eyes shining. 'You must know that. You talked to her.'

'For about five minutes,' I reminded her, not wanting to commit myself. 'We had a single, brief conversation.'

'And how suicidal did she seem then?' she demanded.

'You told us yourself — she was having difficulties at work, but she told me very little. As it happens, we've since spoken to one of her colleagues, who agreed that your mother was under a lot of pressure. Maybe she . . .'

Suddenly she saw where this was headed. 'No! Mum had coped with all kinds of crap her whole life. She wouldn't have given in to a bit of stress. She was more resilient than that.'

'Did you know she'd been suspended?'

Her face said it all. 'What? She can't have been.'

'It's what we've been told, though we don't know the precise reason. Having said she'd be straight with me, your mum was anything but. There's a suggestion that her suspension followed on from the deaths of two babies.'

That really floored her. 'No, Mum would never . . . That can't be right.'

'Maybe it isn't, but whatever the reason for the suspension, it wouldn't have been good. Perhaps for your mother, that was the final straw.'

Andrea was shaking her head, but with less commitment now. 'No, if she thought she was being treated unfairly she would fight it, she wouldn't fold. And Mum was Catholic, remember?'

'But you said it yourself, she had lapsed.'

'You don't get it. She might not have been practising, but she still believed in the fundamentals. She refused to divorce Dad in spite of all that happened, and I know she believed in the sanctity of life. As far as she was concerned, only God has the power to end it.'

'Suicide isn't the only possibility,' I reminded her.

'I know,' she said. 'The police say it could have been an accident. But that doesn't add up either. They found Mum in the river. I don't know what she'd have been doing anywhere near it. She wasn't a strong swimmer, so I'm sure she wouldn't have taken any risks.'

'I don't suppose she was expecting to fall in. Andrea, this is all speculation. You need to talk to the police. They'll explain their thinking to you.'

'I've tried, but they just keep saying the same thing. There's something about this that isn't right. I know it, and

I think you do too.' She frowned, deep in thought, before looking up at me. 'This friend of yours, in the police . . .'

'He's not so much a friend. We met through . . . through something else.'

'But you could talk to him?'

'I don't know how that would help. Believe me, the police know what they're doing. And I heard it from the pathologist. There's no reason to suspect that there are any other complications to your mother's death. It was either suicide or a terrible accident. And as I've said, it's not my place to investigate.'

'You're a lawyer, aren't you, and you were going to represent Mum? You're meant to find out things. Can't you do it for me, and for her?'

That was the killer, as it were. There was still a part of me, whatever had happened, that felt I had somehow let Rita Todd down. If she really had been suicidal on that afternoon, then I should have recognised that and been able to do something to dissuade her. At the very least, I should have made more effort to find out more about her situation.

Andrea got up to leave. 'My mum was a good and dedicated nurse,' she said, 'who died in strange circumstances. Talk to your police friend. Please.'

* * *

Plum showed Andrea out, so I was left alone for a while with my thoughts. After some time, I picked up the phone to talk to Mick Fraser. I had some difficulty getting past a receptionist who clearly thought my garbled speech was that of a pervert, but eventually I managed to convince her it was a legitimate call and Fraser's voice came on the line.

'Stefan, what can I do for you?'

'I wanted to ask you a favour,' I said. 'Rita Todd's daughter came here. She's upset about the suggestion of suicide.'

'Och, I know, she said the same to me. It's a tough one to hear, especially for loved ones. They can blame themselves.'

136

'But you're sure about it?'

'Well, as I said, the other possibility was an accident, but that's looking less solid. The toxicology results have come back and there are high levels of venlafaxine in Rita Todd's blood. Did Andrea tell you that her mum was on antidepressants?'

'No.' Did she even know? But it could explain why Rita hadn't seemed particularly low when I met her.

'Rita was found in the river adjacent to one of the fields off Mill Lane,' Fraser continued. 'So forensics worked out that she must have gone in somewhere between there and the town centre bridge. Some of our lads walked the bank and found Rita's backpack a little way upstream at the spot where she must have gone into the water,' he said. 'It had been carefully positioned, partially concealed, as if whoever left it there didn't want it found immediately, which suggests that she had time to take it off and place it first. The riverside path is pretty sound at that point so it's doubtful that she could have fallen in by accident, and the SOCOs have done a light touch search of the area and found nothing to indicate any kind of struggle or anything else that would point to foul play. Her bag was intact too — purse, money and credit cards all untouched. We haven't recovered her phone, but Andrea received a text from her mum at around ten on Friday evening. That seems to be the last anyone heard or saw of her, so although we can't exactly pinpoint the timing, the probability is that it happened sometime after that.'

'What did the text say?' I hoped that somehow it might exonerate me from blame.

'Just that as Rita was off work, she might go and stay with her friends in Hoyland. We checked with these friends and they knew nothing about her plans, so that would point to Rita buying herself some time. Perhaps at that stage, she hadn't made up her mind. There'll be an inquest, of course,' Fraser reminded me. 'All the evidence will be looked at.'

'Do you know when?'

'Not yet, but I'll let you know as soon as there's news.'

137

'Thanks, I appreciate that.' I ended the call as Jake appeared, and relayed both conversations to him. 'So it looks as if the most likely explanation is suicide,' I finished. 'Sometime just after she came here.'

'Rita didn't kill herself because of you,' Jake said.

'I didn't exactly make much effort to uncover what was happening to her, though, did I?'

'That's not the business we're in,' said Jake. 'You gave her the chance to talk and she chose not to take advantage of that. What else could you have done?'

'I might have been the last person she spoke to.'

'Not necessarily.'

'Ellen Campbell even presented us with the mitigating factors. Tension running high on the ward, excessive work-loads — especially for Rita, victimisation by the head consultant. I mean, she didn't put it that strongly but . . .'

'And what about if Rita was guilty, if she had caused the deaths of those infants?' said Jake. 'I know you don't want to believe it, but you have to at least consider it. Even if she only thought she did, it would all have contributed to her state of mind. She's walking by the river, perhaps a little numbed by the medication, and suddenly sees a way out of it all. No, it's not an easy thought, but it does make some kind of logical sense.'

'Except for one fly in the ointment,' I said. 'Rita was Catholic. Andrea maintains that although Rita had ceased practising, she still held to the main tenets.'

'Andrea is clutching at straws,' said Jake, only voicing what was obvious. 'Having her mother return to Catholicism would conveniently help to rule out an inclination to suicide. And the police are as certain as they can be that it wasn't an accident?'

'It would seem so,' I said. 'They've found Rita's back-pack carefully arranged on the riverbank.'

'So the alternative is what? That someone helped her on her way?' He was right, that would be ludicrous. 'If there is any change to what the police think, I'm sure Fraser will keep you informed,' Jake said. 'He's a good contact to have.'

CHAPTER TWENTY-SIX

When I went to my locker on Friday morning, I got the strangest feeling that it had been gone through. My habit was to leave my spare shirt lying on the top where it was least likely to get creased, but today I found it buried under other things, halfway down. I dismissed the idea almost immediately as paranoia. The last few days, my head had been all over the place and keeping my locker tidy had definitely not been at the top of the list of priorities.

A message had been left on my voicemail from Tony Sutton, giving me an address for Kevin Booth, but no phone number. Whatever had happened here with Booth, he had certainly wanted to get away from it all. I'd never heard of the place Tony named and when I entered it online I could see why — the location was what looked like a farm in a remote, unpopulated area adjacent to the Forest of Bowland, just south of the Lakes. Policing to farming signalled a radical career change, too, and made me all the more curious about what had prompted the move. Sonia might get to visit her parents sooner than she'd expected, though I'd need to be subtle about it.

And that wasn't the only research I had planned for today. Superintendent Bowers was out at the weekly council meeting, sucking up to Ashley Curzon, so I could take advantage of not having him breathing down my neck for at least a couple of hours. Taking out of my pocket the list of names I'd made at the weekend, I logged onto the

PNC. I had no case numbers yet, but I was hoping that the names alone would be enough.

I got a hit on the first query. According to the incident report, Lloyd Jones was an eighteen-year-old who had been set upon as he returned home from an early evening computer club, eight months previously. He'd been to the chip shop and then got on the bus coming out of town. In her statement, his mother had been particularly distressed because it was unusual for her son to get the bus. On most occasions she drove him to the club and picked him up afterwards. Jones had been attacked just a street away from his home, but no one had heard the commotion and no witnesses had come forward, despite a number of appeals. He'd been kicked and beaten, and had banged his head so hard on the pavement, he'd sustained a massive blunt force trauma and subsequent brain haemorrhage, which had put him into a coma, or 'pervasive vegetative state' as it was so poetically called.

Although a couple of leads had been followed up, they'd run out of steam early on and no arrests had been made. According to the report, Jones' wallet and mobile phone had been stolen, so the incident was recorded as aggravated theft. Except that as I now knew, they hadn't been stolen at all. Instead, they had found their way into Denny Sutton's locker.

Ian Whiteacre had been stabbed and killed while walking home from the pub. Details of this were even more sketchy — even some personal details such as place of employment had been overlooked. As with the Jones case, no persons of interest had been identified. As his wallet, phone and a gold chain from around Whiteacre's neck had been 'taken', homicide with aggravated theft was the recorded crime.

J. Marshall turned out to be a female, Jodie. This crime was recorded as homicide and her attack had a completely different MO. She lived alone and her house had been broken into. During the course of the burglary she had been assaulted and fatally injured. Marshall had also been subjected to a sexual assault and had then been strangled with a pair of tights. Bruising on her body indicated that she had struggled and made attempts to fend off her attacker, but at 'five foot three and of a slight build' she probably wouldn't have stood a chance. It must have been terrifying, poor woman. According to the report, no conclusive DNA material had been recovered. Since her ground-floor flat had been ransacked and her sister had reported a number of personal items, *including jewellery, to be missing, despite the seriousness of the physical assault, once again the incident was recorded as homicide with aggravated burglary. I felt sick thinking about the hoard from Denny's locker.*

There seemed to be nothing to connect the victims, although there were a number of depressing commonalities in the way that the cases had been handled. All were unsolved, yet, despite this, there was a marked absence of any follow-up activity beyond the first week or two. I was reminded of what Denny had said about prioritising investigations that would get a result. Did that explain it? All the incidents had been described as theft, even though I now knew this to be a false classification. They had all occurred within the last four years, but happened in different parts of the town, and with different MOs, though interestingly I noticed from the log that the response times were all very short, an indication that Denny and his partner had been close by when the emergency calls were made. That could, of course, be simply coincidence — there were not enough incidents to prove that one way or the other, and it was hard to know how Denny and Booth would have known where to be when the calls came through, unless they were getting some kind of tip-off. But if they were, what was special about these particular crimes?

Denny seemed to have taken responsibility for writing up the final crime reports, though he had not necessarily been the sole attendant. Mostly he'd been with Booth, the man who had abandoned his career in the police force to go to a remote dwelling in the far north, six months ago. I wondered if Booth had believed at the time, like I did, that the victims had simply been robbed.

The question that just kept screaming out at me was why Denny had taken things from these particular victims, and why now? He would have been at dozens of similar call-outs over the years, so why these? One possibility was opportunity. Perhaps these were the occasions when, at some point, he'd found himself alone with the victim and had taken the chance. While I was on the system, I did a search of Denny's incident attendance. There had been a number of assaults in the past, but that was nothing unusual, in fact it would be par for the course. There was that spate of them two or three years ago, but again, it didn't necessarily mean anything.

It's well known that trends in petty crime are changing all the time. House burglary and car theft have declined in favour of easier thefts of mobile electronic devices that can be easily sold on. The pattern of incidents here could simply reflect that shifting pattern. When had the pattern changed for Denny? Out of curiosity, I looked up the assault case recorded that immediately preceded Lloyd Jones. The victim's name was Richard Donnelly. It was another street attack, but it appeared that no trophy had been taken on that occasion. Of course, it could have been that Denny was doing it over time, but that he'd offloaded or cashed in his haul prior to this.

Despite the contents of Greaves' wallet, there was a slim possibility that money was behind this and there was a simple way of ruling it out. The property cage was quiet when I went down there, the civilian clerk updating records in her efficient way. I gave her the crime numbers and she turned to her computer screen and the database that recorded logged property. Nothing had been checked in for those crimes.

'What were you after?' she asked.

'Just checking if Denny Sutton logged anything for those incidents,' I said.

'I can do a search using his name,' she offered. 'Yes, here we are.' A couple of small amounts of cash had been submitted, attributed to other random incidents. I'd have to look them up and do the sums, but I was pretty sure that Denny had at least checked in some of what he'd taken. It was a relief of sorts and I felt it was enough to allow me to rule out the possibility of Denny lining his own pockets. But if Denny hadn't taken the wallets for the money, then what the hell had he taken them for, and why keep them? These incidents had been dressed up to look like theft, but why?

I must have missed some detail that would point to the common factor. With neither Booth nor Denny available, the only other option open to me was to approach the victims' relatives. I was hesitant. It was pretty likely that the emotions would still be raw, but I couldn't see any other alternative.

The contact details for Lloyd Jones were for his parents. His mother answered the phone. Naturally, her first anxious question after I'd introduced myself was, 'Have you caught them?'

'I'm sorry, Mrs Jones, we haven't yet,' I said. 'But I wondered if I could just ask you a couple more questions? How is your son doing?'

'What?' After a pause, there was scuffling at the other end of the line and for a moment I thought we'd been cut off, but then a male voice came on the phon.

'Who is this?' he demanded.

'I'm PC Fraser from Fulford Road,' I said. 'I was just following up . . .'

'Have you found our Lloyd's killer?'

For a second too long, I was speechless. 'I'm sorry, I thought . . .'

'Oh, I'm sure you did. Yet another example of the wonderful communication within your department, no doubt. His mother and I were persuaded to turn off his life support two months ago. Until you catch the bastard who murdered our boy, we have nothing else to say to you.'

He put the phone down on me. Shit! Why hadn't I thought to check that out first? So much for sensitivity. Until that point, I hadn't thought too much about the fact that these crimes had not been referred to CID — there were no leads to investigate. But this one had become a homicide. The case should have been reopened or, at the very least, re-examined.

Jodie Marshall's sister's response was also lukewarm, if more politely framed.

'Unless you have anything positive to tell me, I'd really rather not talk about it,' she told me, and put down the phone.

I tried ringing Ian Whiteacre's home next, and got through on the third attempt, but the lady I spoke to had only moved into Whiteacre's flat a couple of months ago, and was certain that the previous occupant had been another single woman on her own. Whiteacre had apparently moved on some time ago and failed to leave a forwarding address.

The responses didn't come as any great surprise. These were people who were justifiably aggrieved, and though they couldn't know the reason for it, the lack of any kind of closure would have made matters worse. There was a phone number listed for the neighbour who'd found Jodie Marshall. Chances were, she would be a little more emotionally distanced and therefore more cooperative. And so it proved: she agreed to see me the following morning.

I was just considering whether to enter the appointment into my electronic diary when I looked up to see Superintendent Bowers looming over me from the other side of the desk.

'How are you bearing up, Fraser?' he asked, as he had done almost every day since Denny's murder. On the previous occasions, I could do no more than give the automatic response 'Fine', while barely

143

thinking about it. But this time, in a fit of pique, I made my views about my lack of involvement in Denny's investigation known. There was an inevitability to Bowers' reaction, though at least he had the courtesy to listen first.

'Sorry, you know better than that, Fraser,' Bowers said, after my rant had come to an end. 'You're way too close to it, as well as being a key witness. What are you working on right now?' he asked, not because he really wanted to know, but to engage with one of his officers, deemed to be 'vulnerable'. I gave him a brief outline of the Greaves case and he indicated some vague recognition from keeping up with the daily bulletins. 'Ah yes,' he said. 'I remember PC Sutton mentioning that. How's it going?'

'Bit of a non-starter, to be honest, sir.' I thought it better not to mention the drawstring bag. 'We have a witness who identified a couple of possible suspects, but Denny didn't see them as likely for it, and he seems to have been right. Both are alibied for the night in question. Since then, nothing, really.'

Bowers gave a knowing nod. 'Come up to my office, would you?'

I'd never really studied Bowers before, beyond the sharp suits, haircut and clipped accent that set him out as ex-public school. He was way above small fry like me and in addition, Denny had placed himself as a barrier between us, as if for protection, though I'm not sure for whom. The furnishing in Bowers' office was spare and disciplined, much like the man himself. The only indulgence he allowed himself was the handful of framed photographs on his desk: attractive spouse, photo-genic offspring and a faithful hound. On the walls were the certificates reminding us lesser mortals that he had been educated, via University College London, to postgraduate level. With distinction. He sat down in an ergonomic chair that would've looked at home in the control room of a spaceship, and invited me to take the bog-standard one opposite.

He leaned back in his seat, hands over the armrests and frowning at me, as if he was working out a complex problem.

'I think you need a diversion,' he said, finally. 'Something to take your mind off things.' So now him, too. Everyone thought I needed distracting.

'I know Denny thought a lot of you, Fraser. He told me that you have great potential.'

144

'Did he?' Like Tony's remarks, this came as a genuine surprise. I didn't like to tell Bowers that, thanks to him, I felt Denny hardly knew I was there.

In a creepy bit of telepathy, Bowers then said, 'I'm sorry, I realise that in the last few weeks I rather monopolised PC Sutton's time. He was working on something for me, which perhaps got in the way of you two getting to know each other. But trust me, it was for a good cause. Denny may have mentioned to you that we have someone rather special visiting Charnford very soon.' He had my full attention now, along with a hefty dose of curiosity, and the sense that a poisoned chalice was heading my way. I assumed what I hoped was a blank expression.

'Denny was working on the security arrangements,' Bowers went on. 'And was going to take care of our guest while they're here. Our visitor is coming alone, and likes to travel independently. How would you feel about taking over the reins?' I realised I was meant to be flattered.

'Um . . . yes, sir. I mean, I'd be honoured, sir,' I said. It was a bit left field, but it would do my career no harm to be working so clearly under the watchful eye of the superintendent. It might give me an opportunity to prove to him what I could do.

'In terms of the actual organisation there isn't a lot left to do, just a few remaining specifics to confirm. Denny had arranged most of it. But I think it would be appropriate for you to see it through for him. You're smart and clean-cut. I understand you're pretty handy. The plan was that Denny would act as a kind of body man for our visitor and I think you'd make a perfect replacement. Have you got a decent suit?'

'Yes, sir.'

'Perfect. As I said, most of the graft has been done in terms of planning, but it's important that it all goes smoothly, as Denny would have wanted. That means attention to detail. You'll need to focus all your energy on it, so it would be best if you handed over the Greaves case and any other outstanding work to another officer, for the duration.'

'Oh, I don't think there's any need for that, sir. I'm sure I can handle both at the same time.'

'Just temporarily,' Bowers insisted. 'Until this visit is over. We shan't know until the last minute when exactly it's going ahead, so I need you on standby. And I don't want you to be sidetracked.'

I hesitated. 'Am I allowed to know who this visitor is?'

'Naturally. All in good time.'

It seemed a good opportunity to ask. 'And why exactly is he — or she — coming here, sir?'

'You may not realise this, Fraser, but our humble town has a lot going for it,' said Bowers. 'Essentially, we want to show off what we have — a strong local economy, with low crime and high conviction rates, few social problems, lower rates of benefit claims. Our local authority and health trust are amongst the most cost-effective in the country, and improving. The government is keen to support areas that are helping themselves and this will be our chance to secure future government investment.'

So that was what it was all about. The claims were pretty impressive. I couldn't help but wonder how the superintendent knew all of that, but I supposed he would have been brushing up in readiness for the visit. But if that was all it boiled down to, it did make all the cloak and dagger seem completely unnecessary.

There didn't seem much option but to do as he suggested and bow out of the Greaves case, but it just might take me a little time to decide who was best to hand it over to, especially now that it was getting interesting. The main thing was the obligation I felt towards Greaves himself, but I felt sure he'd understand. This kind of thing happened all the time. If I was careful about whom I chose to hand the case on to, I'd be able to stay involved on some level. And as Bowers himself had said, it was only temporary.

CHAPTER TWENTY-SEVEN

'Do you want me to file this or shred it?' asked Plum. It was customary for us to spend the last hour of the day doing routine filing, leaving the deck clear for a fresh start in the morning, and she had in her hand the flimsy folder that contained the brief notes I had taken on Rita Todd.

'Doesn't seem much point in holding onto it.' But something made me hesitate. I sensed the same in Plum too.

'It's not fair,' she said. 'If all everyone knows is that Rita got suspended after two babies died then they're going to think it was down to her, even if it's not true.' Plum's sense of fair play rivalled my own. 'And if it happened because someone was giving her a hard time, they shouldn't get away with it. Isn't there anything we can do?'

'Not unless we can prove that someone else's behaviour is what drove Rita to suicide, and I don't know what we could possibly achieve, even if we did have all the facts.'

Taking the folder from Plum, I read through what I had noted down following that short exchange with Rita. I tried to remember her demeanour as she spoke, but still there was nothing I could recall that even hinted at what she was about to do. I would have felt a whole lot better, though, if I had known that I wasn't the last person she talked to. If I was honest, at the time, I was flattered that Rita chose me. This reluctance to let go was vanity as much as anything.

'That Delores might be worth talking to,' said Plum.

'She's in the Caribbean,' I said. 'I don't think Jake is likely to cough up for a research trip there, do you?'

'What about this bloke Rita was seeing, then? He must know something. She'd have talked to him.'

'I'm sure you're right,' I said. 'Except no one apart from her neighbour has so much as mentioned him. No, Jake's right. We have to let this one go.' Handing back the folder, I could see that she was disappointed.

'Got any plans after work?' I asked.

'Not especially.'

'Fancy coming for a walk?'

She hesitated. 'All right,' she said.

* * *

Rita had set off on foot from PGW and had somehow finished up by the river close to the bridge, so when we left the office that afternoon, that was where we headed to.

'What is it we're looking for?' asked Plum.

'I've no idea,' I admitted. I could only hope that we'd know it when we saw it. 'The woman next door to Rita said she went to Barney's bar, didn't she? I thought we could look for that to begin with.'

The route took us along the main high street past shops, restaurants and the occasional pub. But after only twenty minutes, we'd walked the length of the street twice and there was no sign of a Barney's anywhere. We even stopped and asked a couple of people, but no one seemed to know it. Plum got her phone out. She was more dextrous than me.

'Anything?' I asked.

'Loads,' she said, still frowning at the phone. 'There's a few Barney's Barber Shops and a Barney's Bar in Amsterdam or Lanzarote.'

'But nothing in Charnford,' I surmised.

She looked up. 'Sweet FA.'

We'd reached the bridge by now and were none the wiser about where Rita might have gone. My back to the wall, I turned 180 degrees, studying the surroundings for inspiration, and there it was — a square, white brick building, constructed in the 1960s and set into a small graveyard.

'Rita didn't go to Barney's bar,' I said, mostly to myself. 'Come on,' I said to Plum. 'We're going to church.'

She turned and shot me exactly the kind of look I'd have expected if I'd told her I was taking up Christianity again, but agreed to come in with me for translation purposes.

With some effort, I pushed open the heavy wooden door to St Barnabas church. Inside was dark and hushed, and at first glance seemingly deserted, but we could hear sounds coming from the direction of the altar. We walked to the front of the church, where the sound seemed to be emanating from a side door, and a short passageway led to what must be the vestry. Through the open door we saw a man sorting through piles of books and packing them into boxes. I tapped lightly on the wood panelling and he looked up.

'Hello. You're the priest here?' I inquired, though the dog collar was something of a giveaway.

'Father Adrian,' he said, with the hint of an accent. 'Adriano, really, but most people here call me by my English name.' Perhaps fifty or so, he scrutinised us with brown eyes in a dark and handsome face, reminding me of what Laura and Cate had said about him. 'How can I help you?'

'We want to ask you about one of your flock,' said Plum, casting a look in my direction that said *See? I've got the lingo*. 'Rita Todd.'

'Ah, Rita.' Closing his eyes momentarily, he crossed himself and murmured a few words, ending with 'Amen'.

'You knew her, then?' said Plum.

'Not well,' he said, quickly. 'I met her perhaps once or twice, but I haven't seen her for a little while now. I read about her death, though. It was a shock. It's a terrible thing for anyone to be so in despair . . .'

'When did you last see her?' I asked. 'Did she come to Mass?' It might signal a return to her faith, if that was the case.

Bringing his palms together under his chin, he took a breath.

'Not exactly.' He seemed to hesitate, choosing his words carefully. 'Rita had struggled with her faith in the past, so had stayed away from St Barnabas for a long time. But like so many others, she was looking for a way through what can be a troubling world. She thought that I could help her. She came to the church just a few times in the evenings, when she had finished working. I think we might have prayed once, but mostly she wanted to talk, about the things that preoccupied her. She told me about her job and the challenges it presented. I listened. I offered what support I could, but I feared it wasn't enough.' His eyes glazed over and he became lost in his own thoughts, seemingly oblivious to our presence. 'I couldn't live up to what she wanted from me,' he said, mostly to himself. 'I hoped that we had reached an . . . understanding, but now it seems I failed her.' Suddenly he remembered we were there and his eyes met mine. 'I don't have the Lion's courage, you see.'

He walked back up the church with us, and as we approached the door a thought struck me — Father Adrian. Not 'FRA' but 'Fr A'.

'Did you send Rita some flowers?' I asked.

He seemed taken aback by the question.

'No.' I wasn't sure that I believed him. He narrowed his eyes at me. 'I'm sorry, you are Rita's family?'

'I'm a lawyer, Stefan Greaves. Rita came to me for help, but of a more practical kind. I'm afraid I let her down, too.'

He nodded. 'She will be in our prayers.'

There seemed nothing more to say. As he bid us goodbye, a mobile phone rang, which, it soon became apparent, was the priest's. With a brief apology, he took the call and Plum and I watched as he turned and strode down the nave towards his office, his vestments billowing out behind him.

'She got to him, didn't she?' said Plum. 'Even though he'd only known Rita a little while.'

'I feel bad enough having only had one short conversation with her,' I pointed out. 'And he's a priest. He must feel even worse that he didn't see it coming.'

But Plum had a point. I thought about Father Adrian and Rita spending evenings in the church, discussing their faith, and I considered the priest's reaction to our questions. And the thought that had threatened to germinate began to put down roots, until it was almost impossible to ignore. Unnatural death, it is said, is usually about one of three things: money, revenge or sex. Nothing Rita had said, nor anyone had told me about her, remotely suggested that the first or second of those was a factor, which left me with the third. Was Father Adrian's reputation deserved, or was I just letting my overactive imagination run amok?

'One question, though,' Plum was pensive as we walked back through the streets. 'Where does *The Wizard of Oz* come in?'

CHAPTER TWENTY-EIGHT

Coming out of Bowers' office, I stopped by at Denny's old desk and searched through his in-tray for the folder detailing the mystery person's visit. Operation Beagle, it was called — named after Bowers' dog, I supposed. Sweet, Sonia would have said. Now I saw the schedule for the first time. Whoever this VIP was, he or she was to be in Charnford for three full days and was timetabled for the usual grip-and-grin type visits. Just a few lines in, I was thinking 'politician', though hard to say of which persuasion. The venues were pretty eclectic, from an old people's home and a school, to the police headquarters itself. Essentially, it appeared that Denny's role was to be the driver — hardly the high profile job that the superintendent had indicated. Seeing it set out in black and white, it was hard to understand why he'd insisted I give up my other work. Most of the visits were self-explanatory and our guest would be staying at a five-star hotel a little way out of town. If I was going to drive him or her there, I'd need to find out where it was.

Bowers had been right in that Denny had done all the hard, preparatory work negotiating the timings, leaving the schedule complete but for a short 'to do' list. Using this, I made a couple of calls to the contacts he'd established to ensure that things were in place and to confirm times for the visit. If my first call to the Fletcher Lane seniors' residence was anything to go by, this VIP was in for a thrilling time. The various establishments had, however, come up with the kind of data that Denny had requested. For instance, I could see that when he or she came to Fulford Road, local councillors and community leaders had been invited along to discuss the crime prevention plan and how that was going. In the file was a report marked, unnecessarily, it seemed to me, Strictly Confidential, *which seemed to contain nothing more than a compilation of crime figures for the year along with costings relating to the annual budget. I skimmed the first few pages, suppressed a yawn and tucked it back into the file. Bowers was no longer around — I'd seen him go out shortly after our chat — so it meant that I could get back to doing what I wanted.*

* * *

Jodie Marshall had lived at 12 Church Road and her neighbour, Tracy Carrick, still lived next door. I drove to the small complex of apartments and rang the doorbell of number 14.

'Who is it?'

I held my ID up to the peephole. 'Miss Carrick? It's PC Mick Fraser. I called you about Jodie.'

Tracy Carrick was about forty, slim and willowy, with long, dark hair. She came to the door in jeans and a T-shirt and was barefoot. On a day that hadn't yet seen the sun, and was unlikely to any time soon, she was wearing sunglasses. Feeling fragile after a heavy night, perhaps. She invited me in. Her deliberate progress along the short hallway, occasionally relying on the walls for support, seemed to confirm it. We arrived in a small, neat lounge with a galley kitchen off to the side.

'Would you like a coffee?' she asked.

'No, I'm fine, thank you,' I said. 'I won't keep you very long.'

'Do you mind if I do? I'm gasping.' So, definitely a rough night.

'I understand that you were the one to find Jodie.' I ran through the notes as she headed for the kitchen to make the coffee. 'That must have been upsetting.'

'It was. We had keys to each other's flats, so when I couldn't reach her that morning, I just went in. To begin with, I thought she had collapsed. But then I found Rory . . .'

'She had a child?'

Tracy came back into the lounge with the same cautious gait and lowered herself into the seat opposite me.

153

'No, Rory was her dog. There was quite a smell. I think the poor animal must have lost control of his bladder. Fear, I suppose. He must have been terrified and distraught that he couldn't protect Jodie. That was when I realised something dreadful had happened.'

'Did you have any thoughts about who might have wanted to do that to Jodie?'

'No. Your colleagues at the time were pretty certain that it was just a random opportunistic burglary gone wrong, someone after drug money most likely. Jodie used to suffer terribly with migraines, so she sometimes went to bed quite early. It's possible that whoever broke in thought there was no one at home.'

'But what about Rory? Wouldn't he have reacted?'

'Rory was getting old, and he was going a bit deaf. Jodie should have let him go, but they'd been together a long time and she didn't want to part with him.'

'And you don't have any idea who it could have been?'

'None at all. A bit before that, we'd had some problems with a nasty little group of thugs who used to hang around the flats hurling verbal abuse at people on a fairly regular basis, but the police didn't seem to think there was a connection, and shouting names at someone is a long way from strangling them.' Not so different from what I'd said to Stefan Greaves. 'Jodie used to chat to people online sometimes, so I did wonder if it could have been someone she'd met that way, but I know she was really careful not to give away too many details about herself. I mean, we all do it, don't we? Anyway, your guys took her computer and said they didn't find any clues on it.'

'Did you report the harassment?' I asked.

'Oh yes, on several occasions.'

I couldn't think of any more questions.

'Well, thank you for your time, Tracy, and if you should think of anything else, please get in touch.' I gave her my card and she lifted it to look at, squinting against the light. I wondered if I should offer her some paracetamol.

When I got back to the station, I tried to find the records of the reported harassment, but drew a blank with both the women's names and addresses. There was something at the heart of this that was frustrating me at every turn. And as Denny wasn't around to explain it, I'd *have to try his partner — his other partner. I'd maybe take some mug shots around to Tracy Carrick, too, and see if the faces rang any bells.*

* * *

That evening when I got home, as luck had it, Sonia was chatting to her mum on her laptop.

'Hello, Michael!' she called out, her enlarged face bobbing around on the screen.

'Hello, Meg,' I said. I decided to go for it. 'How would you like some guests this weekend?'

Sonia swivelled round, a questioning look on her face.

'That would be super!' Meg exclaimed, as I'd known she would. 'You're always welcome. What time shall we expect you?'

'How about Saturday lunchtime?'

'Lovely!'

Leaving Sonia to plan the weekend with her mum, I went to get showered and changed.

'That came a bit out of the blue,' Sonia observed later, with a wry smile. 'What do you want?'

I put my arms round her. 'Nothing I can't have anyway.'

'Well, it's a nice surprise,' she said. 'I can get her a decent birthday present to take up with us now.'

CHAPTER TWENTY-NINE

It was years since I'd been to a proper party and even driving over to Joss and Guy's place on Saturday evening with Cate at my side, I couldn't help feeling a little apprehensive.

'It'll be fine,' she said, reading my thoughts. 'I can guarantee it will be a very middle class affair and everyone will be terribly polite and politically correct.'

'So any personal remarks will be discreet and behind my back,' I added. 'I don't know which is worse.'

We drew up a little way down the street from a well-lit, Edwardian villa.

'There's no pleasing some people,' she said. She slid her hand along my thigh and up between my legs, cupping a hand over my crotch and gently squeezing. 'Although I'll do my best later.'

I leant in for a kiss. 'Can't we just skip the party?'

'No! We are going to be sociable.'

And sociable I was. It wasn't even too bad and, despite the noise, I managed to hold reasonably intelligible conversations with at least three people. After a while, though, the strain began to take its toll and I retreated to the kitchen, where I wrestled for several minutes to get the top off a beer bottle. When it finally flew off, some of it spattered over a pile of junk mail and flyers that had been cast aside on the windowsill. I got a bit of kitchen towel and dabbed at them, and in doing so managed to knock the whole lot onto the floor. As I was picking them up, I couldn't help but notice the recipient's name on one of the envelopes: Mrs J. Leonard. I looked up for Cate to confirm it, but she was nowhere to be seen. The man himself, however, was heading — if a little unsteadily — my way.

'Cheers!' He held his beer bottle up to mine.

'Happy birthday,' I said. 'It's quite a party.' He frowned slightly, working out what I had said.

'Glad you're enjoying it,' he responded eventually. 'Stefan, isn't it?'

'Yes. I didn't know your surname was Leonard,' I said, casually. 'Are you the same Mr Leonard who runs the neonatal department at the hospital?' I asked him, barely able to believe my luck.

He flashed me a bleary-eyed smile. 'For my sins. And let's be honest, there are plenty of those.'

'So, you must have known Rita Todd,' I tried to keep it light.

The smile faltered, and for a split-second I think he hoped he might have misheard me, before it became obvious that he hadn't.

'Yes, of course, Rita worked in our department for a number of years. It was a tragic loss . . . a shock to us all.' He hesitated, deciding whether to pursue it or to let it drop. 'Did you know her?'

'Not really. I didn't get the chance. Her daughter thought she was being treated unfairly at work, possibly even forced out, so she approached my law firm for representation. I didn't know at the time that Rita had already been suspended.' I paused, in the hope that he might deny it, or protest Rita's innocence, but he just nodded a brief acknowledgement. 'Could I ask you a few questions?' I tried to make it sound casual. 'I'd be interested in getting another perspective.'

He blinked a couple of times. 'Surely now that Rita's . . .' He raised the bottle again. 'Your services won't be needed.'

'That's true. This would be purely in an unofficial capacity. Call it curiosity. I promised Andrea I would try and find out as much as I can, and this seems just a great opportunity. I'd like to understand more about what was going on.'

Perhaps if he'd been sober, he would have put up more of a fight, but instead he just sighed.

'All right, but not here, eh? Come with me.'

He was going to make me work for it. Pushing through the noisy throng in the hallway he started up the stairs, and I clomped up three flights behind him until we emerged into an office created in an elegant loft conversion, with dormer windows overlooking rooftops towards the town centre. The many bookshelves were crammed, and what little wall space remained was crowded with family photographs and what might be considered tasteful modern artwork. An ornate soap-stone chess set was set up beside the desk, a game in progress.

'An online game, "Chesschallenger dot com",' said Leonard, even though I hadn't asked. 'Do you play?'

I gave the slightest nod. 'The same site. What's your username?'

'The Doctor. Hardly original. So, Rita.'

'I understand you and she were good friends at one time,' I said, lightly.

'We were work colleagues, but yes, we got on all right.' He smiled at the memory. 'Rita could be fun.'

'But you had a falling out?'

'Who told you that?' He waved his beer bottle. 'Oh, what does it matter? Rita had worked at the hospital for years and she was set in her ways. She didn't like the changes we'd introduced to the department, because basically it meant a dilution of responsibilities. And there were some . . . professional differences of opinion about the line we took with supporting parents. Happens all the time. And if one's mind isn't one hundred per cent on the job, mistakes are made.

Rita allowed her personal experience to cloud her judgement when she should have left her private beliefs at home. We're treating very ill and vulnerable babies, so it's inevitable that some of them don't make it. Often you realise that for some of them, it's the best thing.' He held my gaze for just a beat too long.

'Did Rita think you were selling your patients short?'

'Rita was naive. She got too emotionally involved with the patients and their families.' He broke off, a rant brewing. 'And she could be stubborn. She didn't have a sense of the broader picture, nor did she have to satisfy the demands of people higher up the rankings. Money is tight and the impact is felt everywhere. Whole wards have been closed, for God's sake.'

'Is that why you picked on her?'

'Is that what she told you?'

I recalled what Ellen Campbell had told us.

'You didn't like what was happening any more than she did, did you?'

'Sometimes? No. But we're all accountable to someone.'

'And you answer to hospital management.'

'Along with the ethics committee. I don't know how familiar you are with the health services, but the committee wields a great deal of power. A devil on each shoulder, you might say.'

'What kind of power?'

'The power that agrees or cuts budgets, renews contracts, approves salaries and research. And our chair has very firm ideas about the way we run things. Likes a tight ship. So, we do as we're told.' He gave a little mock salute.

'Even when it means your staff are so exhausted, they start to make mistakes?'

'Hm, is that what Rita told you happened?' His eyes narrowed, almost as if he suddenly realised what we were talking about. 'Listen matey, take it from me, you don't have a clue, you really don't . . .' He swayed slightly and for a moment I thought he was going to pass out, but he roused himself again.

159

'Is he here?' I asked.

'Who?'

'The chair of the ethics committee?' I became aware of footsteps on the stairs.

This time he laughed. 'Are you serious? *She* wouldn't mix socially with the likes of me. And frankly, I wouldn't want her to. Oh, no. Margot Warren-Byrne plays in a much higher league than with mere mortals like me.'

The footsteps got louder and Joss appeared.

'What are you two doing hiding away up here?' she said, feigning disapproval. 'Someone said they'd seen you climbing the stairs.' She studied me, weighing me up. 'I just can't keep him away.'

'Stefan wanted to see the conversion, darling,' Leonard said smoothly, 'And our splendid view. He's thinking of getting one, aren't you?'

'Oh. In a ground-floor flat? That *would* be unusual.' Joss had been talking to Cate. She glanced coolly between us, gauging the atmosphere. 'Well, whatever you've found to talk about, it all looks far too serious for a birthday party. Come on darling, we're waiting for you to cut the cake.'

After we'd all sung and gorged on too-sweet sponge cake, I went to find Cate.

'Right, I've done my bit,' I said. 'Can we go?'

I don't know if she read or understood the tension in my face, but she didn't demur.

When we got back to her flat, Cate and I couldn't wait to get our hands on each other. Tonight, of course, we were restricted by clothing. It's one of the times when I really curse my useless muscles, but Cate was very patient and finally it was done. It was going pretty well until the rocking of the bed jolted the lamp off the bedside table with a crash, and I went into total spasm. By the time I could relax again, I'd completely lost my rhythm, and my erection. I swore and rolled off her, my limbs still twitching.

'Sorry.'

'It's OK,' she said, stroking my face. 'We've got all night.'

I looked across at her. 'What have I done to deserve you?'

She smiled, then tucked herself in beside me. 'You could get something done, you know.'

'What do you mean?'

'They're developing a procedure to repair the damaged neurons. I mean, it's still in the experimental stage, but in cases like yours they've seen amazing results already.'

Cases like yours? It was like a slap to the face. *I like you a lot, but would you mind having invasive surgery so that you conform to my standards?* Up till now there had been no hint that she had any issues with who I was. How wrong could I have been?

I somehow managed to swallow back my anger. 'I don't know,' I said. 'I've kind of got used to being the way I am.'

'Of course.' She leaned up and kissed me. I kissed her back, but felt oddly detached.

CHAPTER THIRTY

*The journey up to Blackburn went pretty smoothly, the motorways rel-
atively clear for a Saturday morning.*

'There's something I need to do this afternoon,' I said to Sonia.

*'Ah, so now we get to it,' Sonia smiled. 'I should have known
there'd be an ulterior motive for spending the weekend with my parents.'*

I grinned. 'It won't take long, I promise, and it is important.'

'I'll take your word for it. Is it work?'

'Sort of. It's a bit unofficial, though.'

*She gave me a sideways look. 'It's not going to get you into any
trouble, is it?'*

'No, I'm just doing a favour for someone.'

*I've never really understood the adversarial position some men
adopt with their in-laws. Although I probably wasn't their ideal choice
of son-in-law, Sonia's mum and dad had always made me feel welcome
and today was no exception. We got there in time for lunch and, as
usual, Meg had provided enough food to feed us along with the brood of
kids we didn't yet have.*

*'Got to build you up,' she smiled at me. 'Sonia says you're trying
for a baby.'*

I caught Sonia's eye. Oh great, so no pressure there then.

*'How's work?' Keith asked, smoothly changing the subject. 'It
must have been a shock, what happened to your colleague.'*

'It was. I'm still taking it in, really, but we're getting on with things. Life has to go on and all that.'

'It's an ill wind indeed if nothing positive comes out of it,' Sonia said. 'Mick's been given responsibility for overseeing a VIP visit.'

'Who's that then?' asked Meg.

'He's such a VIP I haven't been told yet. It's all a big secret.'

'Security, I suppose.'

'Something like that.'

'You must have had some thoughts,' Keith said.

'I think it's probably a politician,' I hedged. 'But honestly, beyond that . . .' I shrugged. It was all speculation. Secretly, I'd wondered if it could go up as far as the PM, but it seemed improbable, and I'd look pretty stupid if I was wrong.

* * *

After lunch, Sonia and her mum embarked on the usual trip to the local retail park (which just happened to include a mother and baby store). I tried to ignore this when I gave them a lift before going on, Sonia told her parents, to look up an old friend who I'd recently found out had moved to the area. The 'old friend' part was pushing it a bit, but deflected any awkward questions.

Kevin Booth's farm was in a remote corner of the Forest of Bowland, which occupied the blank space between Blackpool on the one side and the Yorkshire Dales on the other. Even from Sonia's parents', it took me about an hour to drive out there and I was apprehensive about what sort of reception I'd get. Knowing what I did about Kevin Booth, it seemed a good idea to pick up a bottle, which I did at the supermarket on the way out of Blackburn. After that I headed away from the tourist trail, where sweeping fields were broken up by dry stone walls and the occasional clump of trees. As the satnav took me nearer to my destination, the roads got progressively smaller, until I was clattering along a single-lane cinder track across exposed moorland. I rattled over cattle grids as the wind strengthened. I could feel the car juddering with each gust. The track delivered me to a greystone farm with assorted outbuildings, but not to Kevin Booth. Instead, the young woman who emerged from the house directed me back to a neighbouring field. Kevin

163

Booth hadn't actually taken up farming — or if he had, it was as a casual labourer — and his home was a caravan in the corner of a sheep pasture that was open to the elements, protected only by a wooden fence that ran around three of its edges, creating a small enclosure. I left the car by the fence, which was leaning in the strong winds. One corner panel was hanging loose and flapping noisily.

I stopped beside a five-bar gate and, climbing the adjacent stile, walked the last few yards across uneven, rutted terrain, through grass that brushed my calves. He'd seen me coming and the caravan door swung open before I'd even knocked. I couldn't help wondering what Booth's sanitary arrangements were, but judging from his appearance they must have been adequate. Of average height, slim and pale, he was neatly groomed, his hair clipped short to disguise male pattern baldness, and he had a neat goatee. He wore jeans and a sweatshirt that were clean and pressed. He still looked every inch a copper, albeit one that was in need of a good meal and a good woman. I almost wished I'd brought him a food parcel.

'Kevin Booth?'

'That's me.'

'I'm Mick Fraser, a police constable down in Charnford.'

'Oh yes?' Suddenly, Booth was wary.

I pressed on. 'Up until he died a couple of weeks ago, I partnered Denny Sutton.'

Booth squinted at me, making sense of what I'd said, suspicion routed by disbelief.

'Denny's dead? You're kidding me. How?'

'Killed in the line.'

At that moment, a raw gust of wind made me lurch and rattled the door on its hinges. Booth held it back to let me through.

'You'd better come in.'

The inside of the caravan was ordered and clean, to an obsessive degree, and reminded me of my first experience of a traveller van. Booth gestured me to the living area, a couple of built-in couches at one end. It was well insulated, too. Despite the buffeting of the wind outside it was warm and snug inside, the heat coming mainly from a three-bar electric heater.

'So what happened?' Booth asked, when we'd sat down on the benches at right angles to each other. I described the incident with

164

Archer, the emotions returning unbidden as I talked. Booth shook his head in disbelief. 'Liam Archer. I knew that would come back to bite us. He was an accident waiting to happen — should have been taken off the streets years ago. Liam was never the same after he lost his drinking pals.'

'Lost them?'

'To a wicked spell of cold weather we had, a couple of winters ago. It was tragic. The homeless hostel was out of commission because the council had finally stumped up enough funds for them to do a well-over-due refurbishment. Some of the regulars had the sense to move on to somewhere they could get shelter, but two were found in the park, one dead and the other barely alive. He didn't make it . . . Liam blamed everyone for it, including the police. He can be a regular conspiracy theorist sometimes.' He shook his head sadly. 'Poor Denny. I suppose the funeral . . . ?'

'It was last week. I'm sorry. No one at the station seemed to know where you were. It took me until now to get hold of you. You're a hard man to track down.'

'Yeah, well, that was the general idea. I probably couldn't have come anyway. I don't own a suit anymore, and I don't socialise much these days. I'll write a note to Sheila, though. Maybe you could take it for me?'

'Sure.'

It was much too early in the day for me, and I was conscious of my car parked down the field, but I had a few questions for Booth and knew that joining him might oil the wheels a little, so I took the bottle out of my pocket.

'I brought this for you — thought we could drink a toast to our ex-partner.'

Booth looked momentarily embarrassed.

'That's nice of you,' he said. 'But I don't do that anymore. Can I make you a cup of tea instead?'

'That'd be great,' I said with some relief. 'Milk, no sugar, thanks. You and Denny worked together for quite a while,' I said, minutes later, taking the mug from him.

'Twelve years,' he said.

'Wow. You must have built up a good partnership.'

'I guess so. We had a few laughs along the way, too.'

'So why the sudden departure?'

There was the beat of a pause, during which Booth glanced across at the bottle.

'I decided that the job, and the habits I'd developed to cope with it, weren't doing either of us any good anymore.'

'It's true, then.'

'Regrettably, yes. Denny had to cover for me more than once. In fact, it was getting to be a regular occurrence. I had become a liability. It was time to go, for Denny's sake and for mine.'

'And you don't drink at all now?'

'Haven't done since I moved here.'

'That's impressive.'

The shrug was self-effacing. 'I've met a nice woman up in the village and, well, the relationship looks like it might have a future. I count myself lucky that the booze didn't entirely wreck my life. So,' he held my gaze for a moment. 'Why are you really here? It isn't just to tell me about Denny, is it? You could have written to tell me that.'

'I'm interested in a couple of particular cases you and Denny worked on.'

Booth snorted. 'Well, you can ask, but I find the memory sometimes lets me down these days, for obvious reasons.' I didn't believe that for a moment, but sensed that he might be preparing the way for selective recall.

'They were aggravated assault cases. The victims were Lloyd Jones and Ian Whiteacre.' I gave him the dates. Jodie Marshall's attack I knew had happened shortly after Booth's departure.

There was a flicker of recognition, I thought, but after a moment's studied thought Booth shook his head.

'Nah, don't ring any bells. What's special about those two?'

I took care choosing my words. 'Something about them is puzzling,' I said. 'They were logged as robberies, but when I cleared Denny's locker, I found their stolen possessions stowed there.'

Booth looked away and out of the window, suddenly fascinated by a thicket of trees in the far distance that were billowing and swaying in the wind.

'You know something about it, don't you?' I pressed.

Without a word, Booth stood and walked up the van, disappearing into one of the rooms at the other end. He was gone a while, and I began to wonder if I had outstayed my welcome and was required to leave. When he reappeared, I was relieved that all he carried in his hands was a shoebox. I'd half expected a shotgun. He passed it to me and I lifted the lid. Inside were two wallets and a mobile phone.

'You might like to add these to your collection.'

'But I don't understand,' I said. 'Why have you got them?' I held his gaze. 'Why did you really leave? Tony Sutton hinted that you lost your nerve.'

He let out a derisive laugh. 'Is that right? It wasn't anything to do with losing my nerve. It was more about a loss of faith.'

'Come on, you have to tell me more than that.'

Booth considered for a long moment before finally yielding.

'Like I said, my drinking was increasingly getting the better of me, if you know what I mean, and I'd got into trouble a couple of times. To be honest, the next step was likely to be dismissal. There had been a couple of complaints from members of the public that they could smell alcohol on my breath, that kind of thing. Then one night, I was off duty, round at a mate's and I'd had a skinful but decided to drive home anyway, thought I could handle it. I couldn't. I rolled the car over into a ditch and was lucky not to kill myself or anyone else. If I'd been breathalysed, that would have been the end of me, but I called Denny. He came and fetched me and sorted out a mate of his with a tow truck to pull me out. We seemed to have got away with it at the time, but then somehow, months later, Bowers got wind of it. Instead of hauling me in front of a disciplinary, he called Denny into his office and told him there was a way out for us. One of our local councillors was making a lot of noise about what seemed to be a fast-growing crime rate in Charnford. You're familiar with the Flatwood, of course?'

I nodded.

'Well, grim as it is now, it used to be far worse. Practically all of the town's social problems were centred there. Drugs had long been an issue, and circulation of a contaminated batch had put a few people in hospital. Violence amongst the rival factions vying for control of the supply chain had escalated, culminating in a couple of homicides, but we couldn't get any witnesses to come forward. Bowers was a relative new *boy, so eager to make his mark. His strategy, or at least someone else's idea that he latched onto, was what he euphemistically called a "light touch" approach based on an unspoken theory that eventually the estate would implode, problem solved. Certain crimes — particularly those centred on the Flatwood that involved physical violence but were not domestics — were to be classified as "Code B", whatever that meant. We would respond and go through the formalities, but there would be very little in the way of follow-up afterwards. Most of the victims were pretty sad losers themselves anyway, and perceived as troublemakers. So generally, no one made a fuss.'*

'Do you think the same people were responsible for all the Code B attacks?'

'That's what makes most sense to me. Rumour was that there was some kind of gang going around targeting selected undesirables.'

'The White Angels?'

'So you've heard of them. I don't really know where the name came from. Talk was that Bowers had harnessed a little squad of self-appointed vigilantes, but no one could ever pin down exactly who they were, and we were told to stay out of it. I'm pretty sure it was them who torched an Indian-run supermarket, but the only witness statements we could get were either totally useless or were mysteriously withdrawn. We could barely accumulate enough evidence to bring anyone in for questioning, let alone conviction. Meanwhile we focused our attention on any crimes we could press charges on and our conviction rate started to look pretty impressive.'

'But you had no idea who the White Angels might be?'

'We were discouraged from finding out. But gradually, the victim profile seemed to change. That was when it started to get uncomfortable.'

'So how did it work?'

'Where the incident looked like outright assault or homicide, the procedure was always to be the same. First thing was to remove any valuables, so that the crimes could be recorded as straightforward robbery or aggravated robbery. Cash was signed over to Bowers, who kept count of it. He told us to get rid of the other stuff.'

'Why didn't you?'

'We did, to start off with, but then the last few . . . I guess it just didn't seem right.'

168

'And for going along with this approach, you were let off the hook?'

The view outside became suddenly compelling again.

'We got an additional "incentive payment" in our pay packets too, for processing these crimes as instructed and assuming this "additional responsibility" as part of a new initiative. It was sold to us as something upfront and legitimate, a pilot scheme. It even had an operational name, some kind of animal, as I remember it. But the name was irrelevant. It was implicitly agreed that these cases were low priority, so we were less than rigorous with our enquiries.'

'But how could you go along with it?'

'Bowers had me. If I didn't play ball, I'd be off the force altogether and lose my pay and pension. I'd have survived, but Denny had incriminated himself by now, too. He only had a short while to go, and neither of us wanted to jeopardise his future either. I felt terrible about it. I'd got us into this mess, after all. At the time we tried to rationalise it, behaved as if it was no big deal — it was just a question of reclassifying some crimes and massaging the figures a bit. Bowers' reasoning was that it allowed us to use our resources more effectively elsewhere, and I suppose on one level, he was right.'

'Sharon Petrowlski implied that the White Angels don't exist anymore.'

'If they ever did,' said Booth. 'Certainly, things on the Flatwood calmed down. Key players were rubbed out, or moved on, and we stopped hearing anything about them.'

'So what made you quit?'

He indicated the wallets and phone he'd just given me. 'Because the Code Bs didn't stop. Milo Ferguson and Jeffrey Kingston-Blake, another couple of names to add to your list.'

'But the victims I've looked up just seem like ordinary people—' I began, interrupted by a sharp 'crack' like a gunshot from outside the van.

'Bugger!' Booth, who was facing the window, jumped up and I looked out to see what he had, a large fence panel snapped by the wind, cartwheeling across the field towards us. Booth flung back the door and we both rushed out. The panel dropped to the ground and we pounced on it before it could take off again, wrestling against the

169

gale which seemed to have gathered still more force in the short time we'd been inside. Somehow between us, we managed to wedge it in a safe place between the rest of the fence and the stone wall, but it would need to be secured.

'I need to fix this before the sheep get in here,' said Booth.

'Anything I can do?' I asked, knowing that my skills would only extend as far as holding the nails. But he shook his head.

'Won't take me long.'

But it signalled the end of our conversation.

'Thanks for all your help,' I said, raising my voice above the howling winds. 'It's been good to meet you.' I meant it. It put into perspective the man I thought I'd been competing against these past months.

'You're not going to try and solve these cases, are you, Fraser?' he said. 'Think about Denny's reputation and your own future.'

'What's happened isn't right,' I pointed out. In truth, I didn't know what I was going to do. Booth turned to head back to his van. But something must have jogged his memory and he spun round again.

'Ian Whiteacre was knifed, wasn't he?'

'Yes, that's right.'

'Poor bugger had been pissed on too.'

'Pissed on?' I remembered what Greaves had said about the smell, and what Tracy Carrick said about Jodie Marshall. 'The report doesn't say anything about that.'

'I wouldn't know. I don't remember writing it up so it must have been one that Denny did. But it's not something that you forget.'

* * *

When we got home on Sunday night, I was doing a reasonable impression of watching TV, but the reality was that those cases were going round and round in my head. Sonia was sorting out the washing.

'These are a write-off,' she said, coming into the living room with a pair of trousers. 'I don't know what you've got all over them, but I've washed them three times now, and these stains won't come out.' She indicated a dark patch on the knee.

I tried to remember the last time I'd worn those trousers. Then it came back to me.

170

'Oh Christ,' I said. 'It's blood, Denny's blood. Ditch them.' After that, my concentration was completely shot and I was back there on that night, kneeling on that scabby piece of wasteland in the dark. I had a feeling that Sonia had said something of the utmost importance, but I couldn't pin down what it was.

CHAPTER THIRTY-ONE

Rita Todd was getting her day in court, it just wasn't the one any of us would have imagined. The inquest into her death was held in a large room in the basement of the law courts in the centre of town, an old wood-panelled building with leaded windows, which felt overheated and oppressive on this sunny spring morning. The courtroom was about half-full with a few faces I recognised — including, towards the back, one I couldn't quite place, but which triggered a distant but elusive memory.

The coroner opened the proceedings by describing the circumstances in which the inquest was being held and briefly explaining how things would play out. The medical evidence and testimony from the pathologist I'd met briefly at the identification reflected what Fraser and I had been told at the time.

'Death was by drowning sometime between four p.m. and four a.m. on the night of Friday the fourth of March,' he said. 'There were no indications on the victim of foul play, though there were signs of some historic injuries, a broken arm and cheek bone some time ago, but nothing recent. Traces of a prescription medication, taken for depression, were found in her bloodstream, along with evidence of

172

sleeping pills. I understand from the police that these were consistent with medication that was found at the deceased's house.' I glanced over at Andrea Todd. She wasn't surprised to hear any of this. Someone had enlightened her beforehand.

'And what effect, in your opinion, would the quantity found have had on the deceased?' the coroner asked.

'It would have been sufficient to take the edge off her concentration.'

'So a walk down by the river wouldn't have been the best idea.'

'It probably wasn't wise, no. Another explanation might be that Rita Todd had resolved to take her own life and took the sedatives in order to make that process easier.'

'Thank you, Dr Shea.'

A police officer I didn't recognise then gave evidence.

'It has not been possible to ascertain precisely where Mrs Todd entered the river, but according to the current and flow, we made an estimate and found Ms Todd's backpack close to this area.' He pointed on a map to the stretch just below the bridge. 'The riverbank deteriorated rapidly in the adverse weather, but there's no evidence in that vicinity that any kind of struggle took place. Statements from those who knew Mrs Todd have concurred that she was, at the time of her death, under some stress as she had been suspended from her job pending an investigation into allegations of professional misconduct.'

So that was it, a formal rationale for Rita's suspension. Why on earth had she chosen to keep that from me? Guy Leonard came next, looking rather more in command of his faculties than the last time I had seen him.

'Mr Leonard, you were Mrs Todd's employer,' verified the coroner.

'I was her line manager, Your Honour. Rita was employed by the health service.'

'Of course. I understand that she had been suspended pending disciplinary action. In your opinion, how much of a threat to her livelihood was this likely to be?'

'I have no doubt that Rita could have fully accounted for her actions,' Leonard said with confidence.

'So it is likely that she would have been exonerated and reinstated?'

'I think so, yes.'

Hm, easy to say now.

'And do you think Mrs Todd was aware of this?' the coroner asked.

'I'd had no contact with her since her suspension, so I had no way of knowing that. But Rita was an excellent nurse and I had no reason to doubt her general competence.'

'Then why the allegations?' I murmured to myself.

Andrea Todd at last had an opportunity to speak.

'Miss Todd, you are the victim's daughter, and I understand that you would also like to make a statement?'

'Yes, Your Honour.' She gave her evidence, her voice clear and steady. 'My mother was Catholic by faith. Although she had not practised actively for a number of years, I am certain that the idea of taking her own life would have been abhorrent to her.'

'You spoke to her about this?' the coroner asked.

'Not explicitly, no.'

Were I a police officer, this is where I could have interjected to request an adjournment while lines of enquiry were pursued. But the coroner was quick to reach his conclusions.

'I record a verdict of death by misadventure,' he said. 'I think we have enough evidence to indicate that Rita Todd was in a depressed state due to her job situation. Combined with the post-mortem report that tells us that she had quantities of sedative drugs in her bloodstream and a lack of evidence of any kind of foul play, it is likely that she fell into the river and drowned.'

As the coroner spoke, I saw Guy Leonard turn and exchange a glance with a woman standing towards the back of the room. Wearing a troubled expression, she acknowledged him with the slightest incline of the head, then slipped through the crowd and walked out. As I watched her go, another stricken face briefly passed my line of vision, Father Adrian also hurrying out without speaking to anyone.

Outside, I caught up with Andrea Todd.

'How are you?'

She shrugged. 'Hardly the outcome I wanted, though I suppose it could have been worse. You were right about her suspension from work.' Delving into her bag, she brought out an envelope, torn open along one side. 'This came through to Mum from the Royal College of Nursing. It details the allegations against her.'

'Do you believe they were serious enough to tip her over the edge?'

'I think all they prove is that someone had it in for Mum at the hospital and was trying to force her out. See for yourself. Take it,' she added, as I fumbled to try and take it out of the envelope. 'You can let me have it back whenever. What I really can't understand is how Mum had got herself into such a mess. She wouldn't deliberately harm those children. But it's made me think. We never talked much about Martin, but when we did, I always got the impression that Mum felt, awful as it was, that it was for the best. It's made me wonder if she was trying to save other parents the trauma of having to make the same appalling decision that she and Dad were forced to make.'

'For what it's worth, it looks as if your mum had gone back to the church for help, too,' I said.

'Really?'

'I don't think she'd got as far as recovering her faith, but she had been going to see the local priest in the evenings. Clearly there were things bothering her.'

'Something else I didn't know,' she said, shaking her head. 'God, I wish she'd been straight with me . . . and you. Anyway, none of it really matters now, does it? Did you get to speak to Delores?' she asked, almost as an afterthought.

'She's in Jamaica,' I reminded her.

175

She handed me a slip of paper with a phone number on it.

'She came back two days ago.'

* * *

When I returned to the office at lunchtime, I had to let myself in. Everyone else appeared to be using their midday break to catch up on errands. I slumped down at my desk and picked up the envelope Andrea had given me. Grappling with it, I managed to slide out the concertina of paperwork.

The covering letter was addressed to Rita and dated three weeks ago, though the postmark indicated that it had been franked only a few days previously. From the Royal College of Nursing, it confirmed that Rita was suspended from her job as a senior paediatric nurse, with full pay, pending a disciplinary hearing to investigate several alleged counts of misconduct. These were detailed in bullet points on a separate sheet and appeared to have varying degrees of seriousness: two counts of administering the incorrect dosage of medication to a patient, two counts (presumably relating to the first) of doctoring records to indicate that the correct dosage of medication had been given, and one count each of behaving in an unprofessional manner and compromising patient confidentiality.

At first glance this was pretty straightforward. Either Rita had or hadn't done what was alleged. The only charge that could be subject to interpretation was 'behaving in an unprofessional manner', and it was likely that there would be guidelines to clarify that one.

I was studying it when Plum returned from lunch.

'How did it go this morning?' she asked.

'Death by misadventure. And listening to the evidence, the coroner didn't have much choice.'

'Is that good?'

'Not really, but it's better than a definite verdict of suicide.'

Plum spotted the address on the envelope. 'What's that, then?'

'The reasons Rita was suspended from her job.' I didn't see what harm it could do, so I passed it to her to read herself.

'Not good, is it?' said Plum, after a few minutes' silence.

'It's not,' I agreed. 'My first thought was that Andrea might be right. None of that adds up with what we know about Rita's professional commitment.'

'She's biased, though,' Plum pointed out.

'True. But all those thank you cards we saw at her house can't be exceptions.'

'Ellen Campbell said that Rita was "brilliant at her job", too.'

'These allegations don't make sense, unless, for some reason, Rita's mind wasn't really on her job. I mean, this first thing — giving the wrong dose of medication — could have just been a mistake, a lapse of concentration, the sort of thing you might do if your mind is elsewhere. But to do it twice, and to each time cover her tracks?'

'What do you think was the distraction?'

I sighed. 'We're not likely to find out now, are we?'

'So that's it then,' said Plum. 'Case closed.'

CHAPTER THIRTY-TWO

It wasn't until I was driving into work on Tuesday morning that it came to me. I'd knelt next to Denny in much the same way as Keeley Moynihan must have knelt beside Stefan Greaves. I remembered the sticky mess I'd assumed to be dog crap that had turned out to be Denny's blood. If Greaves had, as I thought, been peed on, then Keeley might have knelt or stood in something too, something that could give us a DNA profile. Denny would probably have noticed it, but of course he'd have said nothing as part of the big cover-up. I still had Keeley's card in my pocket, so pulled over where I was and gave her a call. It took a while for her to answer and when she did, she sounded groggy. But she agreed to see me.

She lived in a modern flat in a good part of town. I hadn't expected that she'd be able to see me during the day. The company on her business card sounded like a lawyer's and I'd surmised that work was what had brought her and Stefan Greaves together. But maybe it was her day off or, given how rough she sounded, maybe she was off sick. The ring on the doorbell didn't produce an encouraging response and I was getting my phone out when the door opened. She looked different from the last time we'd met, less polished. The vague expression and messy hair suggested I'd got her out of bed. She squinted at me, trying to work out who I was.

'Oh, hi.' The recognition wasn't entirely convincing, but it was enough for her to allow me in. 'I need coffee,' she said. She led the way

down a stripped pine hallway and into a glossy kitchen that was all stainless steel and black granite. 'Want some?'

The coffee brewed, she handed me a mug and we went through to the lounge, which was dominated by cream leather recliners and a fifty-inch plasma screen that was tuned to a twenty-four-hour news channel, where we could sit in comfort and talk. She flicked off the TV.

'Actually, I'd been thinking about getting in touch with you. The police, that is. I've had some not very polite letters,' she said, sipping from the mug clasped in her hands.

'Do you want to show me?'

She went over to a white cabinet and rummaged around in a drawer for a couple of minutes, before passing me an envelope containing a folded sheet of paper onto which had been typed in a large font: TAKES A SICK BITCH TO FUCK A SPAZ.

'How many of these have you had?'

'Three. The first one came just after Stefan was mugged, the last one on Tuesday. I've never had anything like this before.'

'All saying the same thing?' I studied her, but she seemed relaxed about it.

'More or less.' She flashed a weak smile. 'Not much imagination.'

'You mind if I keep this?'

'Be my guest.'

I pocketed the letter. 'It's Stefan I came to talk to you about,' I said. 'I wanted to ask you something about the night he was attacked. When you went out and found him on the ground, did you notice anything else?'

'Like what?'

'I know this sounds like a weird question, but was he wet at all?'

There was a pause. 'Actually, yes, he was. I'd forgotten that. It must have rained. I got my knees wet when I first knelt down to him. And when I stroked his hair, it was damp from it. There was an unpleasant smell too, kind of ammonia-like.'

'I suppose you've washed the clothes you were wearing that night.'

She flashed an apologetic smile. 'I have. Is it important?'

I grimaced in anticipation of Keeley's reaction.

'It hadn't rained for hours by that time,' I told her.

'What, then?'

'I think one of his assailants may have peed on him.'

'Ugh! Oh God. That's disgusting.'

'Maybe, but if we could get hold of some DNA, we might make some progress. What about your shoes?'

'I don't know, but I suppose it's possible. I crouched down right beside him.'

'It's worth a try. Could I borrow them for a couple of days?'

'Sure.' She disappeared into the bedroom and there followed the distant sound of light swearing and the clomp of footwear being discarded onto the wooden floor. Eventually she returned bearing a pair of heeled ankle boots. They just about fit in the brown paper evidence bag.

'How's Stefan doing?' she asked, manipulating the boots into the bag.

'How do you mean?' It seemed an odd question coming from her, and I wondered for a moment if she was asking me about the progress we'd made on the case.

'Well it's a while since I've seen him.' She looked up. 'The hospital, in fact. I thought you might have . . .'

'Is everything all right?' I asked.

'How do you mean?'

I was treading personal territory here.

'Between the two of you. Have you split up or something?'

'Split up?' Suddenly she laughed. 'My relationship with Stefan isn't like that.'

'How do you mean?'

'Stefan is a client. Ours is a professional arrangement.'

Shit. Why the hell hadn't I seen that?

'It's true, we've got quite close over time,' she went on. 'I'd say that I'm more of a "friend with benefits" these days. But I'm hoping it's good news that he hasn't been in touch,' said Keeley. 'Makes me think he might have someone else. I hope he has. He's a good guy and he deserves it.' She clicked her fingers, remembering something. 'Oh, by the way, I remembered where I'd seen that boy.'

It took me a moment to figure out who she meant.

'Evan Phelps?'

'I'm sure he used to be a waiter at the restaurant Stef and I often go to — the Thai place just off the high street.'

As soon as I got back to the station, I sent Keeley's boots off to the lab, with a note for Natalie that emphasised the urgency. Sharon wasn't about so I dropped her a text too, telling her what I'd done. After that, all I could do was wait.

CHAPTER THIRTY-THREE

It was the evening of Laura and Simon's antenatal class and I'd agreed to collect Grace from nursery and take her home. I couldn't help but feel self-conscious waiting with all the other parents (largely mums) outside the school gates, at the same time wishing, not for the first time, that the child I was meeting was mine.

The air was fresh and breezy, so it didn't take much persuasion from Grace to stop off at the park on the way home. As we walked, Grace grabbed my good hand and swung it, skipping along beside me, while I limped along beside her. We must have made a cockeyed sight, but Grace is the one girl in my life who remains oblivious to my differences and who makes no judgements at all. That would change, of course. It was just a question of when. Zoe, her older sister, had gone through that tough stage of being embarrassed to introduce me to her friends. I'd mentioned it to Laura once.

'Don't flatter yourself,' she'd retorted. 'She's thirteen. We're all an embarrassment.'

The phase hadn't lasted long and Zoe had emerged on the other side an independent and broad-minded young woman, but it had happened, nonetheless. She'd simply succumbed to that primal biological need, common to so many teenagers, to conform and be part of the tribe. I wondered which Grace would outgrow first, the park or me.

At the adventure playground, she dashed from one piece of equipment to another without stopping.

She yelled to me from the monkey bars. 'Look at me, Uncle Stefan, look at what I can do!'

'Clever girl,' I said. 'Wish I could do that.' I pushed her on the swing a bit and she shrieked as it wobbled from side to side. 'Now you do it,' I said. 'Got to build up those muscles.'

* * *

We got home shortly before Laura and Simon.

'How did it go?'

'Good,' Laura said. 'Everything's in order. How's it going with you and Cate?' she asked, a glint in her eye.

'Fine.'

'Fine? I spoke to her yesterday. She thinks you're wonderful. And all you can say is "fine"?'

'But that's what it is. What do you want me to say?'

She gave me a look. 'I might have hoped for a little more enthusiasm, that's all.'

'Well, sorry I can't manage to live up to your expectations either.' The bitterness erupted with more bile than I had intended.

'OK, spit it out. What's going on?'

I told her what had happened.

'The truth is that now I don't know what to think. It's always been my rule that I will only go out with someone who accepts me for what I am.'

Laura laughed. 'What a prima donna! Didn't you know it's every woman's duty to change her man? Think yourself lucky it's the cerebral palsy, otherwise it'd be something else, believe me.'

Was it so different, then, with Cate and me? Were Laura and Fraser right, and I was making too much of this? It was time to change the subject.

'When I was last round at yours, you and Cate were discussing the priest up at St Barnabas, Father Adrian.'

'Hmm, we were, weren't we?'

'Do you really think the rumours about him are unfounded?'

'Why?'

'Oh, just something that came up at work.' Laura waited me out. 'A client,' I said. 'A nurse who died shortly after I saw her — committed suicide. It seems she'd spent a lot of time at St Barnabas recently.'

'Perhaps she needed to if she was suicidal,' said Laura. 'Really, I'm sure there's no credence to the gossip at all. Idle staff room chit-chat, that's all. I mean, there was one of the mums. But that was just people drawing their own conclusions simply because the whole family is blonde and Scandinavian-looking, while the new baby has jet black hair and olive skin. It's a joke.'

* * *

'I've been thinking,' Plum announced the following morning. 'What if this distraction of Rita Todd's wasn't a *what,* but a *who*? What if Rita and Father Adrian were doing more in the church in the late evenings than just talking . . .' She tailed off. 'What?'

'I've been wondering the same thing,' I admitted.

'I mean I know it's not *allowed*—'

'It's not against the law,' I pointed out. 'It's just not compatible with his calling. Doesn't mean it never happens, though.'

'It does happen,' said Plum, with some satisfaction. 'I looked it up. There are support groups and everything, for women who, like, fall in love with their priest. It happens all the time. Perhaps Rita did. I wouldn't blame her. He's lush, for a vicar.' Her brow creased. 'What I don't get is, if they were, you know . . . why would she kill herself?'

If nothing else, that at least was obvious.

'Because unless Father Adrian was willing to give up his vocation, there was never going to be in any future in it, was there? That could explain why he felt he'd let her down. It's more likely that Rita had just developed an infatuation, one that was, and would always be, unrequited.'

'What's that?'

'He didn't feel the same way. Andrea said her mum had a knack of choosing unsuitable partners. Maybe this time it was one who was unattainable. Perhaps, with everything else going on in her life, it was enough to tip Rita over the edge. Maybe when she came to see us here, she'd already decided, but she couldn't come out and tell me why because she didn't want to drop Father Adrian in it. Ellen Campbell told us how loyal she was.'

'So you don't think it's a nuts idea?' said Plum.

'Not entirely,' I said. 'We should go and talk to Father Adrian again.'

'What, and ask him if he's been shagging one of his . . .'

'Flock? We might need a bit more evidence first.'

But the more I thought about it, the more I realised that so far all we were doing was speculating. Father Adrian was the only person who could confirm or deny it, even if that was simply through his behaviour. Sounding him out was the only sensible thing to do.

* * *

This time, when I attempted to push open the heavy, wood-panelled door, it flew back to reveal a tall, gangling man, with dull, reddish hair, a long, thin face, and the kind of complexion that usually comes twinned with an inhaler.

'Oh, I do apologise,' he exclaimed.

'We were looking for Father Adrian,' I said.

'Ah, I'm afraid you've missed him. I'm Dean Robert. Can I help at all?'

'What time will he be back?' I wasn't really up for a lengthy wait.

'No, you misunderstand.' The curate wrung his hands together in a very priestlike gesture. 'Father Adrian has left the parish. He was recalled to Rome.' His smile was fleeting and didn't reach his eyes, which blinked rapidly. 'It all happened quite quickly, in the event, but . . . um . . .'

'The Lord works in mysterious ways,' said Plum.

'Quite,' said the curate, clearly, like me, trying to judge whether Plum was taking the piss.

'Why?' I asked.

'Sorry?'

'Why did he go?'

'Oh. I'm not sure that . . .'

'Was it anything to do with Rita Todd?' I persevered. 'It's just that I understand she had been spending a lot of time with Father Adrian. When we told him that she had passed away — killed herself — he seemed to take it very . . . personally.'

'I'm sorry, I don't understand . . . Oh.' And then, even though it seemed impossible, his skin paled even further. 'No. I'm certain you're mistaken about that. Father Adrian would never . . . He is absolutely devoted to the Church. Naturally, he would be upset to lose a parishioner, especially like that. But he would never exploit such vulnerability. It would be immoral.'

'So why has he been recalled?'

'It could be for a number of reasons,' blustered the curate. 'Father Adrian is a respected member of this community, and of the Catholic faith. He has responsibilities.'

'Did you know Rita?'

'I wouldn't say that I knew her, but I occasionally came across her in the church, of course. I was here on the last evening she was seen, I believe. Father Adrian was out and I could tell that she was disappointed. She was hoping to make one last attempt to "change his mind".'

'Is that what she said? Change his mind about what?'

'I really don't know,' said the curate. 'She stayed here for a while anyway, sitting on her own in the church as she sometimes did. She only left when it was time for me to lock up.'

'Did you see which direction she took when she left?'

'No, but she met someone outside. They were standing talking by the gates.'

'Someone she knew?'

'I would think so. Though I heard Rita greet whomever it was quite loudly, as if she was surprised.'

'Was it a man or woman?'

'It was impossible to tell. It was dark and they were both bundled up in winter clothing. But Rita seemed happy to see whomever it was, there was something in the tone of her voice. When I left the church myself, a few minutes later, I saw the two of them walking together quite companionably towards the town centre.'

In the opposite direction to Rita's house. 'What time was this?'

'It would have been around eight o'clock.' He waited for my next question. 'Was there anything else?'

'No. Thank you.'

* * *

This was something I felt sure Mick Fraser didn't know. As far as he was concerned, the last person Rita had seen on the night she died was me. I rang Fraser, but he was out of the office, so it would have to keep for now.

Plum and I made our way back to the town centre.

'What do you think?' I asked her. 'He was cagey about why Father Adrian has suddenly scarpered.'

'In fairness, it is none of our business.'

Recalled — like a faulty car. Or at least, one that's not behaving in the way that it should.

CHAPTER THIRTY-FOUR

*When I arrived at Fulford Road the following morning, I saw that
Stefan Greaves had phoned and called him back as soon as I'd had
my coffee.*

*'Did you know that Rita Todd went to the church on the Friday
night after she left my office?' he said.*

It was news to me.

*'She met someone when she left, too. The curate saw her. They
went off together.'*

'Did he see who it was?'

'No, it was too dark.'

I had to ask. 'Where are you going with this?'

*'I don't know. I just thought it might be worth getting the full story
and trying to ascertain who it was that she met. They might know more
about what was going through Rita's head at that time. They could have
even witnessed what happened.'*

*He was right, of course. If Denny hadn't been killed when he
had, I would have made more of an effort to trace Rita's last known
movements. But from the start it had seemed a straightforward case,
and it was hard to believe that having either the priest or this unknown
person at the inquest would have changed anything. I had to recognise
this for what it was — Greaves was desperate to know that he hadn't
played a role in Rita Todd's demise. Clearly it was important to him,*

188

and it wasn't as if we'd come up with much regarding his own attack, so I offered a suggestion.

'We still have some CCTV in the town centre. I could have a quick look if you think that would help? I've been meaning to anyway. Only thing is, I've got a lot going on just now, so it might have to wait a couple of days.'

'Of course, no problem.' He seemed disproportionately pleased. I glanced up as I heard a shout from the incident room and saw several of my colleagues reaching for hats and Kevlars before racing out of the room.

'Sorry,' I said. 'I've got to go . . .'

Ringing off, I wandered over to the doorway, where a couple of the civilian admin staff sat at their workstations.

'What's going on?' I asked.

The nearest looked up from her screen. 'The animal rescue centre called in,' she said. 'Liam Archer's turned up there.'

It was impossible to get on with my work again. I'd be on tenter-hooks till I knew an arrest had been made. But they were back all too soon. As the first one came into the office, he saw my face.

'He'd scarpered before we got there,' he said, aggrieved. 'Must have realised that the manager was calling us.'

'He'd gone to collect his dog?'

He shook his head. 'Just visiting. They wouldn't let him take the dog, the state he was in. Sounds like he's barely managing to take care of himself. The manager said he was rambling, and reeked of booze even at this time of day. He thinks Archer is sleeping rough. Our bad luck that the manager also let slip that people were looking for him. He suggested that he turn himself in, which is probably what frightened him off.'

'Rambling about what?' I asked.

'Denny Sutton. He didn't know that Denny had died and it scared the life out of him. Kept saying "they made him" do it.'

'Who did?'

'The voices in his head, I guess. The same voices that kept telling him he was going to win the lottery. That didn't get him very far, did it?'

* * *

It was more from hope than expectation, but on my way home that evening, I called in at the hostel, just on the off-chance. Archer wasn't there, of course. While I waited in the hall for Doug, those head shots stared down at me.

No one at the hostel had seen Archer since the night of Denny's attack, something that Doug was clearly worried about.

'I know you're the wrong person to say this to, but Liam's not dangerous,' he said. 'He's vulnerable, and easy prey to others.'

'I understand he hears voices?' I said.

'I've never seen any evidence of that, but I suppose, given his history, it wouldn't come as a total shock either.'

'Would any of the other staff know?' I asked, nodding towards the row of mug shots.

Doug forced a laugh.

'They're not staff,' he said, pausing to study the pictures. 'They're some of our regulars who've passed away over the last few years. Too many, just lately. We realised that no one apart from us even noticed their passing, so decided to create a memorial wall. If we didn't make an effort to remember them, no one would.'

It was a moving tribute, simple but effective.

'If you're interested, we're holding a vigil for them in the market square this Friday evening,' he added. 'We do it every year.'

'I'll think about that,' I said. 'What happened to them?'

He pointed out two men who had succumbed to a bad lot of drugs, and three more, a woman and two men who had perished in bad weather.

'Someone told me about that.'

'Yeah, it was terrible. A local builder, Ashley Curzon, offered to do up the hostel at cost price, but he had a limited time frame, so we had to grab the opportunity. It was appalling luck that it coincided with such a cold spell.'

* * *

Back at Fulford Road, I bumped into Chief Superintendent Bowers on the stairs and got my second invitation into his office inside of a week. Once I was seated, he closed the door.

'Time to let the cat out of the bag,' he said, with barely concealed excitement. 'Have you heard of a man called Matthew Westfield?'

It was like asking me if I'd heard of Jack the Ripper. 'The politician, you mean?'

'The very one,' he said. 'We've had word that he's available, so it's all systems go for tomorrow.'

'Right, sir.'

'Can you spare a few minutes to go over the schedule?'

'Yes, of course.'

It wasn't a big task, now that all the planned visits were confirmed.

'We might need to fit in a couple of extra meetings — there are some local dignitaries who might get upset if they don't get to meet him. You know how it is,' said Bowers. 'But we've added in a formal reception on the last night — a black tie event at Mawton Manor — so that we can mop up anyone who feels they may have missed out. Our last opportunity, you might say. And we're hoping to end with something quite special.'

Bowers then stressed again the need for discretion, though I couldn't understand what all the fuss was about.

He shepherded me to the door. 'The media can be tiresome,' he added. 'There's a particular local hack who does a good job of making a nuisance of himself.'

'In what way?'

'Oh, you know, putting two and two together to make five. If you ever come across Simon Montgomery, give him a wide berth.'

* * *

I decided that if I was going to be spending time in his company, it would be good to find out more about Matthew Westfield, beyond what I'd seen in the tabloids and on TV. I typed his name into a search engine and an overwhelming number of news stories flooded onto the screen, the most recent ones predominantly concerned with current government health policy.

The more reliable content picked up the trail some six or seven years ago, when Westfield met and formed an alliance with the now prime minister. There was plenty about how he'd masterminded and

191

orchestrated the premier's rise to power and helped to shape the man into a world leader. The most commonly used epithet seemed to be 'Machiavelli', which was hardly ever meant as a compliment. But then it was well known that Westfield didn't court the media. His bullying tactics and abrasive manner at that time were well-documented, and appeared not to concern him in the slightest. And he was vindicated shortly afterwards by an admirable demonstration of the capriciousness of the British public and press corporations, who dramatically changed their tune when his long-term partner, Amelie Ghestin, became ill with motor neurone disease. Her deterioration was rapid and for several years, Westfield all but withdrew from political life. His reappearance was marked by a couple of controversial speeches on assisted dying and after her death, it was reported that she had spent her last days in Switzerland. Westfield had a reputation as a straight talker and that had never been more evident than when he'd described in graphic detail the last, miserable stages of his wife's illness. It was widely reported that the prime minister missed his friend and advisor, and it was no great surprise that shortly after Westfield's wife's death, the pair were rumoured to be spending time together again.

However, Westfield's only public appearances since his wife's death seemed to be his regular participation in marathons to raise money for various MND charities. And now he was coming to Charnford. The big question was: why here and why now? Was there about to be a major policy announcement, or was this Westfield signalling the low key resumption of his political career?

I scrolled down the pages of hits, trying to glean more about the man, but there wasn't much. According to his somewhat sketchy bio, he was a scholarship grammar school boy, who'd progressed to the London School of Economics in the late 1980s and worked his way to a first class degree, alongside a number of extracurricular activities. The piece included a list of societies he'd belonged to, the debating society among them of course, along with others whose names gave away little about their purpose.

I nearly wouldn't have recognised Westfield in photographs from that time. His hair was blonder and hung almost to his shoulders. Someone else in the picture caught my eye. I couldn't be certain, but the similarity was there, and it was surely too much of a coincidence. I clicked on the photo and was taken back to its original source, where a caption listed the people pictured. I'd been right. Unfortunately, it only specified those in the centre of the picture, but I had a plausible explanation now for why Westfield had shown such interest in Charnford. It was why Bowers had been looking forward to Westfield's visit so much: they were old chums. Suddenly a whole lot of stuff that had been bothering me became clear. Closing the web page, I turned my attention back to Westfield's timetable, double-checking that everything was in place. At least we wouldn't have to clean up the streets in preparation for the visit. Nature, or, at least, the climate had effectively done that for us.

I'd become so absorbed in the information search that I hadn't realised how quiet the office had become. Checking the clock, I realised the afternoon had gone. It was time to go.

CHAPTER THIRTY-FIVE

When I arrived at work the following morning, the first thing Barbara said was, 'You have a visitor.'

A woman who had been sitting in one of the visitor chairs got to her feet.

'I'm Delores Mbegu. Andrea Todd asked me to come and talk to you.'

Unlike Rita, Delores was solid and matronly and looked her age, though she evidently took great pride and care with her appearance, wearing a smart wool coat and patent, heeled shoes.

I invited her through to my office, where she declined any refreshment, but took the seat beside my desk. She seemed contained, clutching her handbag in her lap and a tissue wadded in her hand, which she used from time to time, still coming to terms with the death of her friend, I supposed.

Plum was hovering by the door and on my signal, took up her note-taking post, though I wasn't at all sure why I thought that might be necessary.

'I appreciate your taking the time to come in to see me,' I began, unsure of how this was going to help anyone. 'We're all very sorry about what has happened to Rita. It came as rather a shock to us too, as you can imagine, though I only met her on one occasion.'

Delores sniffed and pinched her nose with the tissue.

'I feel so bad for her. I might have been partly responsible.'

'In what way?'

'Because I wasn't here for her. I knew she was getting into some kind of trouble.'

Another member of the growing band who thought they had let Rita down. I was familiar with that feeling, so the least I could do was hear her out.

Plum gave me a questioning look. Where to start?

'One of your former colleagues, Ellen Campbell, told us that Rita was suspended after a couple of babies died on her ward,' I began. 'I've seen the formal allegations.' I gestured to where the envelope still sat on my desk. 'There's nothing in them to contradict that.'

Delores glared at me. 'Rita wasn't killing babies — she was desperately trying to keep them alive.'

'Could she have made mistakes, though? We got the impression she was under some duress.'

'Of course she was!' said Delores. 'The team had been decimated. And even before I retired, I was having a lot of time off, which put added pressure on everyone else. After I left, I know things didn't improve. They didn't bring in a proper replacement.'

'Ellen Campbell told us a bit about that, and about the restructuring. Did that have anything to do with your retirement?'

'Well, my mother was ill. But yes, the changes made my decision much easier, and I wasn't exactly discouraged from leaving. We had always been a strong unit, a tight unit, you know? The reorganisation undermined that.'

'How?'

She shrugged. 'Divide and rule — that was what they wanted. Up until the changes, we were all part of one big team that worked across two wards exactly the same. It was a "key worker" system, so we were allocated children at the acute phase, as soon as they were admitted, so we would be there from the very start of the treatment and stay with them right through to recovery until they had been discharged. It meant that we got to know the child and the family really well and could ensure that the care plan was meeting their needs, and that everything was in place for when they went home. It gave us and the families continuity and allowed us to build strong relationships. When the reorganisation came, the team was split and the wards renamed "Holly" and "Ivy".' She shook her head in contempt at that. 'Euphemisms for "acute" and "recovering". The idea was that at the appropriate time, the child passed from one ward — and one team — to the other.'

'Why did that matter?' I asked.

'It meant that we only dealt with one stage of the process, depending on which ward we were assigned to. With Rita and me it was the acute ward. When the patient transferred, we passed them on to someone else. It's frustrating because you only get a snapshot view of what's happening to the child, and often the families have just got used to one clinician and suddenly they have to start all over again. There's meant to be a handover meeting when information is passed from one nurse to the next, but in practice there's never time to do it properly. The closure of some wards and the relocation of others doesn't help, it just makes it easier for things to get missed or forgotten.'

'What was the rationale for it?'

'*Efficiency,* of course,' said Delores, with a sniff. 'It was felt that if we were overseeing a smaller number of children it would lighten the workload. Ha! As if that would make any difference.'

'It sounds as if it made the job harder,' I said. 'Could it account for the mistakes that Rita was alleged to have made?'

'Hm, if they *were* mistakes,' said Delores. I'd expected her to back up her friend.

'I don't understand.'

'After I left, Rita began to notice a rise in the number of children who were passing away. Children she had been

196

responsible for, who'd had a good prognosis, were dying unexpectedly during recovery.'

I felt a murmur of foreboding. 'Isn't that inevitable with such vulnerable babies, though?' I recalled what Guy Leonard had said.

'Yes, of course. The children are, by their nature, very fragile. But Rita had concerns about the way in which decisions were being made.'

'What kinds of decisions?'

'About what kind of care a child should have. We've known for a long time now that the advances in medicine mean that our capacity to keep a patient alive often exceeds our ability to cure the underlying condition. Sometimes you get to a point where it becomes obvious that the child is unlikely to ever improve and that their quality of life is severely limited, and difficult decisions have to be made. Any life support can be ended in favour of palliative care. Rita believed strongly, like I do, that decisions like those should be made together, with the parents, not just the professionals. She'd had experience of it on the other side — her little boy, Martin, was very poorly. Rita knew first-hand how important it is for the family's wishes to be given full consideration.'

'And she didn't think they were?'

'All referrals go to the VPB.' Delores saw my blank face. 'The Vulnerable Persons Board. But now, in the name of efficiency and "to spare the parents distress", these decisions are increasingly made without their input. There's discussion of how the family is coping, and the short and long-term impact of the child's condition on the family unit. The idea is that it provides an opportunity to discuss treatment in an objective way, in terms of benefits versus burdens. By burdens they mean cost, of course. But the main thing is that it's become a discussion *about* the family, not *with* them. Once the decision is made, it's much easier for the consultants to frame their conclusions in a way that informs parents it's for their own good, and their child's. The rationale is that in taking that decision-making responsibility from the parents, it absolves them of any guilt they might feel.'

'But aren't there guidelines for these things?' I asked.

'Of course. There are guidelines about neonatal care for premature babies and criteria for when care should be withdrawn. But these are human beings we're talking about, so sometimes it's not so straightforward. In rare instances the decision is black and white. More often than not, it's a confusing shade of grey. A lot of sick babies come into that unit, Mr Greaves, those born prematurely and older children with complex medical needs. The machines keep them alive, but sometimes it's clear either that life is being prolonged artificially,' she hesitated, 'or that if the child does survive, he or she will be so disabled that their quality of life will be poor.' For a second or two she found it hard to meet my gaze, and we both did our best to ignore the elephant that had just strolled in and plonked itself down in awkward proximity. 'There's a fine line, isn't there?'

'Yes,' I said. Our eyes met. 'I sat on it once.'

Delores was firm. 'Rita didn't make any mistakes,' she said.

'I don't understand.'

'Rita tried to alert Mr Leonard to the increased mortality rates, but he wouldn't listen. Instead, he began to make Rita's life a misery. She tried to get hold of some hard, statistical evidence, but met a brick wall. I even think she'd started taking copies of individual patient records.'

'How?'

'I think she was photographing them on her phone.'

Rita's phone, the smartphone she didn't need. Probably somewhere at the bottom of the Charn now.

'And she took alternative action.'

'How?'

'A child can't be deliberately killed, of course, but pain-relieving treatments can be administered to hasten death. It remains lawful if the doctor doesn't intend death and is guided by the best interests of the patient. Life-shortening pain relief is seen as being morally acceptable. It was one of those rules that increasingly we were required to breach. The truth is, some parents welcome it. Rita realised that where a child might need long-term interventions, higher dosages of diamorphine were being prescribed. In large enough quantities, especially where a child has breathing difficulties, it's enough to kill.'

'So that's why Rita reduced the dosage, of her own volition?'

'Yes.'

'But why did she draw attention to what she was doing by altering the records? If she'd noted the prescribed dose, instead of what she'd actually given them, no one would have been the wiser.'

Delores fixed me with a gaze that said I was being particularly slow. 'This was her protest. Rita didn't want to get away with it,' she explained, patiently. 'She wanted to be called in front of the disciplinary board because she saw it as an opportunity to highlight what was going on. She couldn't amass the evidence she needed, so she wanted to speak out in a public forum.'

'There was another allegation,' I said. 'Rita was charged with compromising patient confidentiality. Do you know what that was about?'

'Yes, that was Baby Dawson. She broke the rules, but again she felt justified.'

'What happened?' I asked.

'There was a dispute about Baby Dawson's treatment that bothered Rita. I don't know exactly what.'

'But that was the breach of confidence?'

'I think it must have been. You should talk to the parents, Mr Greaves.'

'I'm really not sure that—'

'It wasn't an isolated case,' Delores cut in. 'There were others. We had already been lectured by Mr Leonard on the perils of raising parents' expectations. It was an insult. He said we should be realistic, that it was impossible to grasp what it could be like caring for a child with a lifelong disability

199

and how much suffering it could cause, both for the patients and their families. He even used the word "viability".' She shuddered. 'Now there's a word I hate.'

'I doubt I would be able to get hold of the Dawsons' details without arousing suspicion,' I said.

'Perhaps I can get them for you,' said Delores. 'I know this might sound like an overreaction, Mr Greaves, but after what has happened . . . I was afraid for Rita's safety. She had exposed herself professionally, and I know that she felt she was being watched.'

'Did she say by whom?'

'No. But she was convinced that there was more going on than even we knew. She sent me rather an odd text just before I went away. I saved it.' Delores scrolled down the messages. 'Look.'

I took the phone from her. The message was short and to the point: *I'm right — it's pure strategy.*

'What do you think she meant — that the strategy is being put before patient welfare?' I couldn't imagine that it was anything new.

'That's what it says to me. Rita felt they were being sold an idea on the grounds of efficiency and sustainability. But vulnerable human beings shouldn't be viewed in those terms and someone should answer for it. If nothing else, they shouldn't be allowed to get away with the way they treated Rita.' She looked down at her lap. 'I should have done more — she needed my support.'

'Did you know Rita had gone back to church?'

'I thought she might have,' said Delores. 'The priest came to the hospital once, and she went to speak to him. They did seem to have a lot to talk about.'

'This was Father Adrian?'

She frowned. 'I thought Rita mentioned Father Frank, but perhaps I was mistaken.'

She got up to leave. 'One last thing: shortly before I made the decision to retire, I was offered an alternative way out, a newly created post in a proposed new facility.'

'What kind of facility?'

'One specialising in the care of patients with complex medical needs, of all ages. Rita warned me against it.'

'But why? It sounds like a positive thing.'

'Perhaps. But it was odd. I was told that if I wanted the job, I would have to sign a non-disclosure agreement.'

'Why do you think that was?'

'I really don't know. In the end it didn't matter, did it? I chose to retire.'

It seemed to conclude our conversation. I wasn't sure that I felt any differently about Rita, but Delores seemed happier to have shared what she knew.

'Will I see you at Rita's funeral?' she asked.

'I didn't know it had been fixed.'

'Next Monday, ten a.m. at St Barnabas. Andrea doesn't want lots of fuss but I know you'd be welcome. She speaks highly of you.'

* * *

One thing my conversation with Delores had done was stir up memories of my own less-than-straightforward entry into the world, and I was lost in thought when I realised that Plum had returned from showing Delores out and was standing leaning on the door frame, arms folded, jaw working and watching me. The subject of my condition had only arisen between us on one occasion before.

'I looked you up,' she'd told me, one day, out of the blue. 'Cer-eebral palsy.'

'Yes.'

'Bummer,' she'd remarked.

'Yes.' It was the only time it had ever been discussed. Until now.

'What happened with you?' she asked, with her customary directness.

'The delivery was taking too long,' I told her. 'I was stuck in the birth canal and in distress, but the midwife ignored it. I was blue when I was born, and they spent five minutes trying to get me to breathe. If what Delores says is right, I doubt Mr Leonard would have bothered.'

Plum's brow furrowed. 'What shall I do with these?' she asked, holding up the notes she'd just taken. 'Rita Todd's case is closed, isn't it?'

'Yes, it is.'

'Except . . .'

I waited.

'From what Delores has just told us, Rita was getting to be a real pain in the butt, wasn't she? And she more or less said that Rita was getting ready to blow the whistle. Wouldn't that be . . . a reason for someone to want her out of the way?'

Plum looked as if she was expecting a telling off, but the reality was she'd only put into words what I was already thinking.

'Shame not to close it for good,' I said. 'Let's see if we can get hold of the hospital's mortality figures and see if what Delores says has any substance. We can't look up individual case notes, but the mortality rates might make for interesting reading — both before and after the reorganisation. If Rita was right, then we should be able to tell.'

'Are we allowed to see that kind of stuff?'

'Since the Freedom of Information Act, yes. You'll probably have to fill in endless forms but theoretically it should all be publicly available. See what you can do, will you?'

CHAPTER THIRTY-SIX

Liam Archer had appeared again, only this time it was in a skip underneath several sheets of plasterboard. Turned out he was smarter than anyone thought, and he'd somehow managed to locate the main arteries in his wrists and gouge them open using the neck of a broken bottle, after which it would have taken a matter of minutes until he bled out. Covered only by the same shabby parka I'd seen him wearing on that Friday evening, he had started to decompose, but had lain there for several days before being discovered by someone walking past who noticed the stench. Even Archer, with his limited intelligence and grasp of the real world, couldn't face up to or live with what he'd done. No doubt his 'voices' had guided his actions. In a sense, justice had been served, but it still left an unsatisfactory taste in the mouth.

It was unlikely that they'd tell us much this long after the event, but I offered to collect his clothing and personal effects from the mortuary in the hope that they might turn up something in the way of forensics. His pockets were a revelation, including a ridiculous number of spent lottery tickets, purchased at Davey's shop. How did he afford them, I wondered? What came as a shock was finding a flashy and very expensive-looking watch. The inscription on the back was To Stefan on your 21st birthday, *along with a date. How the hell had Liam Archer come by that?*

Before Matthew Westfield took over my life, there were a couple of things I wanted to do. The first was a call through to Natalie to follow up the DNA tests on Keeley's shoes. The lab must have been snowed under too — it took me several attempts to get through to Natalie and when I did at last speak to her, she sounded harassed.

'Did you manage to get anything off those shoes I sent you?' I asked.

She brightened. 'Yeah, we did a swab and there were a number of substances.'

'And DNA?'

'Traces, sure. One of my tasks today was to email through the results for you. Hold on a minute and I'll bring them up.' After a few seconds' silence, I heard her cursing under her breath. 'Oh, for God's sake . . .'

'What?'

'It's telling me "data not found". It's OK. We've been having problems with the software all morning, to be honest. Can I find it and get back to you?'

'Sure.'

A little later she called back, full of apologies.

'I can't understand it — the record has gone. I'm missing a couple of others, too, so I'm sure it just must be a glitch in the system. Soon as I can track it down, I'll get back to you.'

'Great, thanks.'

'And if I can't find the results, I'll just repeat the test. We've still got the shoes here.'

It was a long shot, but the only other way I could think of trying to break the deadlock on the case was the slim hope that Tracy Carrick could identify the thugs hanging around the flats where she and Jodie lived. I rang her and she agreed to see me, so armed with my trusty tablet, I called round again. But the explanation of my purpose didn't get the response I expected.

'I'm not sure that I'll be much help,' she said. 'I have severe nystagmus and photophobia. I'm registered blind.' She removed the sunglasses and now I could see the way her eyeballs danced in the sockets. 'It means faces are at most a blur, and I won't see much on your tablet either. I'm so sorry.'

'God, no,' I said, feeling a terrible mixture of shame, embarrassment and downright stupidity. 'I don't know why I hadn't worked that out for myself.'

She laughed. 'Why would you? I'm willing to give it a try, though, if you think it's worth it.'

This time when I went into her flat, I immediately saw the white stick propped by the front door, as if to confirm what I now knew. Hm, great detective I was going to make one day.

'So Jodie had a visual impairment, too?' I asked her.

'Oh yes, she was almost totally blind and she was epileptic too.'

'And Rory was an assistance dog.'

'That's right.'

* * *

On the drive back to the station, an idea that until then had been only ephemeral began to solidify and take shape. Back in the office, I went back to the PNC and those past crimes. There had been oddities that had struck me: Lloyd Jones, an eighteen-year-old still usually driven to computer club by his mum. Ian Whiteacre, no recorded employment. In isolation, those facts meant little, but put them together with Jodie Marshall and Stefan Greaves . . .

While Whiteacre's crime report was in front of me, I scoured it from top to bottom. There was no mention of him having been urinated on. Nor did it feature in any of the other cases known to me. Had it been deliberately omitted? It was a key component of Stefan Greaves' case and the kind of signature that might link with other cases. But perhaps it was part of the phenomenon Booth had described as low priority. If there was no real intention to investigate, there was no need for the crime records to be accurate.

Just out of interest, I did a keyword search on 'urinate'. It came up a couple of times, including on a couple of historic crimes from several years ago, but one of them brought me up short: a burglary attributed to a Bostwick. Not Sam Bostwick, but Gary Bostwick — his younger brother. I looked him up. Gary Bostwick's rap sheet was long and varied, from an early career in petty theft to more recent affray and a caution for possession with intent. The younger Bostwick had made a career out of crime, serving two prison sentences in the process. He was the spit of his older brother, hence Davey's mistake.

And there was the flag for a profile on the National DNA database. I couldn't believe it. Jesus, if we'd had a sample from Stefan Greaves' clothing, the case could have been sewn up. Had Denny realised that and deliberately let the clothing go? Sure, it could have been oversight or error, but then I recalled how he'd tried to discourage me from pursuing this one. Was it because it mirrored the others that he and Booth had given low priority? Booth had said there was a pattern to the crimes, but because we'd had to rush out and rescue the fence, I hadn't got back to asking him what. I wished I'd asked for his mobile number, supposing he had one. What I did have, though, was the address of the farm, and from that I was able to get a landline number. A woman answered, presumably the same one who'd directed me to Booth's caravan. I introduced myself and stated my inquiry. There followed a prolonged pause, during which I began to wonder if she had gone to fetch him, but eventually she spoke.

'I'm sorry, Kevin's dead.'

'Dead?' I echoed in disbelief. 'I don't understand.'

'It was sudden — an explosion, three nights ago.' Her voice cracked and there was a pause. 'Sorry, we're still, you know . . .'

'Of course. Take your time.'

'We think it was the gas canister. There must have been a fault, or he made a mistake in connecting it . . .' she tailed off again. 'He was killed outright.'

I replaced the receiver feeling numb. Booth had been getting his life together. How harsh was that? I sat for a while, head in hands, trying to make sense of it. Was this mere coincidence?

When I came to, I saw Bowers standing over me.

'Everything all right, Fraser?'

'Kevin Booth — Denny Sutton's former partner — he's dead.'

'Really? Poor chap,' said Bowers, all concern. 'But the man was an alcoholic. Probably the kind of accident that was waiting to happen. And it's doubtful that he would have known anything about it.'

'Known what, sir?'

Bowers blinked. 'About Denny Sutton's death. I don't think anyone managed to track him down.'

So he didn't know that I'd been to see Booth. And now Booth was dead. Booth knew about what had been going on. I thought about the man I'd met just a few days ago, who was very much not in a bad way, but I hadn't the energy to put him straight.

'You've handed on your cases, Fraser?' Bowers asked, moving on.

'Just about to,' I lied. But now I'd said it, there could be no more delay.

* * *

As it was, Sharon Petrowlski sought me out just a few hours later.

'The boss was asking me about a Stefan Greaves. I didn't know what he was talking about. Some case that you were meant to be sending over to me?'

'Sorry.'

'No worries. I didn't know what he was on about, so I felt a bit of a twat.' She smiled. 'But it's hardly the first time and I don't imagine it'll be the last either.'

True to form, she already knew the basic facts of the case. 'I read about it on the weekly bulletin. Anyone in the frame?' she asked.

I wondered whether to tell her about what I'd found in Denny's locker, but much as I liked Sharon, I couldn't trust anyone else not to jump to conclusions about Denny. I reiterated what I'd told Bowers.

'Bostwick, eh?' she said. 'He's a real little charmer.'

'But until we get any fresh evidence, there's not much more to be done, so it's probably a sleeper.' I handed her the file.

'OK, I'll keep my eyes and ears open, but can't promise to do much more than that. You know what it's like at the mo.'

'That's fine,' I said. 'I've got to know Stefan Greaves a bit. Is it OK with you if I check in once in a while?'

'Sure, but like I say — don't expect too much. What's the super got you doing instead, then?' she asked.

'Babysitting Matthew Westfield.'

Her eyes widened. 'Lucky you,' she mocked.

I paused. 'What do you think of the superintendent?' I asked, knowing I'd get an honest response.

'He's all right,' she said, looking surprised by her own assessment. 'Worked out better than a lot of us thought he would.'

'Oh?'

'Yeah, Chief Inspector Jim Hunnington was up for the job, and common consensus was that he'd get it. The next we heard, Hunnington had been hand-picked for some new special crime unit for the Home Office and Bowers appeared out of nowhere.'

'When did all this happen?'

'Let me think, must have been about four years ago.'

* * *

Since Keeley had asked, I'd realised it was a few days since I'd seen Greaves. I needed to fill him in about Petrowlski and it would be a good excuse to return his belongings to him. I knew that he'd cancelled his credit cards so I may as well remove them from his wallet, but what to do about the cash? If I left it in, he'd wonder what was going on. In the end, I decided that the wallet was too complicated and it would be better to hang on to it until I'd established what exactly it meant, but I could at least return his watch.

On the way, I called in at Davey's with a photo of Liam Archer. The shop owner recognised Archer at once.

'He hung around,' he said. 'Mainly foraging in the bins.'

'Did he buy his lottery tickets here?' I asked.

'No, the only times I remember him actually coming in, it was with used tickets — handfuls of them, sometimes — trying to convince me that he'd won big. He never bought anything.'

'How would Archer finish up with so many old lottery tickets?' I asked. I was wondering aloud, really.

'Beats me,' said Davey. 'Scratch cards would be different. But people don't throw away their lottery tickets until they've waited for the numbers to be announced.'

And then they can find their way anywhere, I thought, like to a person's front garden.

CHAPTER THIRTY-SEVEN

The buzzer sounded. It was Mick Fraser. When I opened my door to him, he was holding up something. 'Thought you might like this back.'

It was my watch.

'Wow! How did you . . ?'

'It was handed in,' he said. 'Someone must have found it.'

'Who? Where?'

'They didn't leave a name or anything. But I guess it must have been somewhere near where you were attacked.'

I was baffled. 'But why just dump it?' It didn't make sense. 'Couldn't it have been sold?'

'It's a good watch,' he said. 'And maybe, with the inscription, they thought it was too distinctive and could be traced back. Too much of a risk.' He sounded a little irritated.

I slipped the bracelet over my wrist. 'Funny,' I said. 'I hadn't appreciated how much I'd missed it, but didn't expect to see it again either. Thanks.'

'It looked as if it might be of sentimental value, too?'

I looked at the watch. 'Mm. You want to come in? I was just going to take a break for coffee.'

'OK. Cheers.' He followed me through to the kitchen. 'I went to see your friend Keeley,' he said. 'There's a chance we may get some DNA evidence from her shoes. She was asking after you.'

'Yeah?' I said, realising how long it had been. 'I should get in touch with her again. I might need to again soon, anyway.'

'That doesn't sound good,' he said. 'Sorry, it's just, I hadn't understood . . . er, your relationship. I do now.'

'Well, up until a couple of nights ago, I'd have said that things were on the up in that respect, and that Keeley might be consigned to the past. I'd met someone. Trouble is, now I don't know if I can really trust her or not.' I felt a pang of regret. 'Serves me right for counting my chickens, I suppose.' I told him what had happened with Cate. As I came to the end, a grin spread across his face.

'Did no one ever tell you? It's a woman's mission in life to change her man. Sonia's tried to change so many things about me, I've given up counting. Maybe Cate forgot herself and was speaking as a medic, or maybe she just miscalculated and went too far.'

'Thing is, I've come close before, and then something tends to come along and spoil it. You asked me about my watch? It represents the closest I've ever come to settling down with someone.'

A fellow student at university, Joanna had been a year ahead of me and was a high-flying mathematician. We'd met at the chess club of all things, though she was quite new to the game. We hit it off from the start — same interests, same sense of humour and she genuinely didn't seem to notice the rest of the crap. Until life started to get serious. In her final year, she was offered an internship with a multinational professional services company and part of the interview was a weekend at the country pile belonging to one of the directors, partners invited too. All part of the vetting process. It crossed my mind that she should take someone else, but she had been appalled at this suggestion.

'You're my boyfriend,' she'd said. 'Why wouldn't I take you?'

I'd wondered afterwards if it would have been better had I been black or gay, but I'm not so sure that it would have. Either way, they didn't quite know what to make of me. I couldn't ride and I couldn't shoot, though I would have loved to have been let loose with a twelve-bore with those particular boors. The conversation across the dinner table had been fast and furious, no time to let me have my say and after the first couple of contributions were greeted with an embarrassed and impatient silence, I'd given up. The final straw came when I'd overheard a conversation between Joanna and her prospective boss.

'You need a partner who can hold his own,' he had told her. I hadn't needed to think too hard about what he meant.

It had been a tough call. We'd lasted a little longer, long enough to go to the company's Christmas ball, when I'd followed the git into the gents and contrived to piss all over his trouser leg, but shortly after that I suggested we should call it a day, and Joanna didn't object.

After university there followed a few barren years before I realised that there would have to be times when regular sex was going to have to be a commercial undertaking, and I contacted a couple of escort agencies.

'And one of them sent me Keeley. She's great, it's simple and we both know where we stand. I don't have to second-guess what she's thinking. Now Cate has come along and complicated things again.'

'Well, for what it's worth, my experience is that any relationship with a woman is a guessing game. It's part of the fun. And it sounds like you and Cate might have something.'

'Honestly? I don't know. It was going pretty well, until she started talking about making me better.'

Fraser laughed. 'It's nothing unusual, believe me.'

'But maybe it depends on what it is they want to change. There you go.' I slid a coffee mug along the counter to him and we went back into the lounge.

Fraser took a long slug of coffee. 'The other thing I need to tell you is that I'm going off the radar for a few days. I've been asked to hand the case over temporarily to another officer for a week or so.'

I felt an irrational stab of disappointment. 'Why?'

'You know the ex-politician Matthew Westfield?'

'Oh, yes.'

'Wow. A lot of disapproval in those two words.'

'If I'm honest, I don't know that much about him. But let's say I don't share some of his more widely publicised views. And my boss, Jake, has never had anything good to say about him, and he must have a reason. I'd trust Jake's assessment of character any day.'

'Well, anyway, Westfield's visiting Charnford for a couple of days, from tomorrow,' said Fraser.

'Why?'

He snorted. 'It's funny, that's what everyone asks. I don't know. But Denny, my partner, was to act as liaison officer for the visit, and now that he's . . .' he tailed off. 'Well, the gaffer has asked me to do it. I've had to hand over any live cases to concentrate on that.'

'That sounds like a promotion.'

'I'm not sure about that, but it'll get me noticed so I need to do a decent job. Meantime, I've handed your case over to DS Sharon Petrowlski.'

'Gee, thanks,' I said. 'Couldn't you have found someone called Smith?'

'Ah, sorry,' he cringed. 'I didn't think about that.' He passed me a business card. 'Anyway, this is her number if you've got any questions. I'll pick things up again next week, but in case Sharon gets in touch, I wanted you to be up to speed with what's going on.'

'Cheers.'

Fraser leant forward. 'What did you think of the inquest — Rita Todd?' he asked.

'I suppose it was the right decision, based on the evidence,' I said, grudgingly.

'Take it from me,' he said. 'That's your conscience trying to say you could have done more. You couldn't.'

If he was looking to reassure me, it didn't really work.

CHAPTER THIRTY-EIGHT

I got to Fulford Road bright and early and polished to a shine the next morning. Westfield's train was due mid-morning and, unsure of how the superintendent was planning to play things, I went along to his office. The door was slightly ajar and, poised to knock, I hesitated, partly because of the expression on Bowers' face, which was flushed and excited, as if he was up to something illicit, like watching porn. It was nothing onscreen that had gripped his attention, though. Instead, he was gazing at a document of some kind. I knocked lightly on the door. After some hesitation, he reacted with an abrupt 'Come!'

As I entered the room, he closed the document and placed it face down on his desk. I wasn't quick enough to glimpse the title, only the logo, which looked like a drawing of an old-fashioned sailing ship. It was the same distinctive yet meaningless symbol I'd seen on the data report in the folder Denny had put together. I imagine that giving it a logo somehow elevated the importance of the enterprise and played to both Bowers' and Westfield's vanity.

'Mr Westfield's train is imminent, sir,' I said.

'Let's not keep him waiting then,' he said, taking his hat from where it hung on the back of the door.

* * *

After some initial hesitation on Westfield's part, he and Bowers greeted each other like the old pals they were. They spend a few minutes catching up before getting to me. The porcelain white smile turned on me seemed genuine, and reached Westfield's impossibly blue eyes, but then I reminded myself that he was an expert in all this.

'Constable Mick Fraser will be your body man for the trip,' Bowers told him. 'Anything you need, ask him.'

'Good to meet you, Mick.' We shook hands. Leaning in slightly, he lowered his voice. 'I'm sorry, this is going to be an incredibly tedious couple of days for you, but being able to travel independently means I get a bit of thinking space between gigs, and I really do appreciate that.' He turned back to Bowers. 'Right then, where first?'

The first appointment was a meet-and-greet lunch reception at the council house. I took him there and parked and then, since I wasn't exactly invited, did a lot of hanging around in the hallways. After that I brought him back to Fulford Road, where he was given the guided tour that lingered on the smart new bits and glossed over the scruffy. So, there I was, redundant in the middle of the afternoon on my first day of the job. After all the build-up it was something of an anticlimax.

With idle time on my hands, I called Natalie again to see if the DNA results had turned up.

'I'm baffled,' she admitted. 'They seem to have completely evaporated.'

'How does that work?'

'I don't know. I've never known it to happen before. We've got the techies in now trying to sort it out.'

'You think that's what it is, a technical fault?' I remembered the hate mail Keeley had received.

'Sure, what else would it be?' Natalie said.

I dug around on the desk until I found the envelope. It was stuck down, though it was hard to tell if it was self-adhesive or one that had to be moistened.

'Listen, it's a long shot, but I'm going to courier over something else for you. This time, if you get anything, can you make sure that I get any results before they go on the system?'

'It's unorthodox, but for you, Constable Fraser, I think I could manage that.'

214

'Thanks, Natalie, I'll be forever in your debt.'

'Hm, that's worth remembering,' she said, and there was that audible smile again.

* * *

After the police station visit, which went into the early evening, I was summoned to transport Westfield back to his hotel. For a few minutes we drove in silence, me allowing him his thinking time. But then it was Westfield who spoke first.

'Do you live locally, Mick?' he asked.

'Yes, sir.'

He laughed easily. 'I'm not your boss, you don't have to call me "sir". Matt will do fine. With that accent, I know you weren't born here. What made you come to live in this area?'

'My wife,' I said. 'I mean, we followed her job. She's a store manager.' I told him the name, though I doubted he'd ever shop there. 'My job was more flexible, so I put in for a transfer. In fairness, we had been told it would be a nice place to live.' It wasn't the whole story. Mostly, we'd moved to get away. I wondered again, as I often did, if it was possible to be the black sheep of a family if I was the one who operated on the right side of the law.

'That's what I'm hearing,' said Westfield. 'What is it that you like about it?'

It was hard to quantify, and I had to think for a moment.

'The atmosphere, I suppose,' I said. 'And the people. It's a pretty friendly place most of the time.'

'Hmm, that's what I'm being told. So you would agree?'

'Yes, sir . . . er, Matt.'

'From what I've seen of the crime data, you certainly seem to be getting a grip on it around here.'

I briefly wondered if I should enlighten him about the crimes that went uninvestigated, but decided not to spoil his day.

'We haven't lived here long, but I understand that Councillor Curzon has done a lot to improve the area in the last couple of years. Gentrification, they call it, don't they?' It's what had happened to me, in a sense, meeting Sonia and trying to make something of

215

myself. My brothers would piss themselves and my dad would turn in his grave — if he was dead and not inside. Mum would be proud, though.

'Ah yes, Councillor Curzon. He sounds like a useful man to have around.'

'Don't get me wrong,' I added, for the sake of balance. 'The place is not without its problems and in my line of work, I get to see the seedier side of it.'

He met my gaze in the rear-view mirror. 'Of course,' he said. 'Chief Superintendent Bowers told me what happened to your partner — a tragic waste of a good officer. But you guys must be doing a good job. I'm getting the message that Charnford has fewer of the social issues than many towns of this size.'

I thought about Liam Archer's friends and their convenient deaths but kept it to myself.

'Shame we can't just bottle that magic and sprinkle it elsewhere,' he went on. 'Don't know about you, but I love my country, Mick, and it grieves me to hear people running it down, politicians or others. I believe that we have the capacity to make Britain a major power again, we just have to look for the good.' He laughed again. 'Christ, listen to me. I'll be fighting them on the fucking beaches next.'

'So do you think you'll take us on, sir?' I asked, taking a punt.

'How do you mean?'

'Are you thinking of representing us in parliament?'

He seemed genuinely amused by that. 'Is that what you've been told?'

'Well, not exactly—'

'Had you heard of me before this week, Mick?'

'Of course, sir.'

'Then you must be familiar with my reputation. I'm not convinced that being an elected representative is entirely compatible with my nature. I'm too fond of saying what I think and somewhat averse to bowing and scraping to the public. I do have plans, though — you're right about that. It's just not yet clear if and where Charnford might fit into those. I only know that your local officials were keen for me to see for myself what goes on here.'

'Do they know that you're not going into parliament?'

He smiled. 'Probably not, but let's keep it between ourselves for now, eh, Mick?'

'Yes, sir.' I really couldn't get the hang of calling him Matt.

* * *

'So how's your day at high altitude been?' Sonia asked, that evening. 'Are you sure you're OK to mix with mere mortals again?'

'I'm just a glorified chauffeur, to be honest,' I said.

'But what's he like?'

'The way everyone kow-tows to him, you'd think he was royalty.'

'He's political royalty,' said Sonia.

'I suppose so, but in point of fact, he seems like a genuinely nice guy. I've yet to glimpse another side to him. He treats me as if we were colleagues.'

'Well, that can't be bad. Is he as handsome as he looks on TV?'

'That's kind of hard for me to judge, but yes, I guess he is,' I admitted. 'And he's got charisma all right, bucketloads of it.'

CHAPTER THIRTY-NINE

'Why is our office junior spending her time filling in Freedom of Information paperwork?' Jake wanted to know. I had just come back from lunch and, clearly, in my absence he'd been grilling Plum.

'Because Rita Todd was concerned about the children who were dying on the recovery ward, and that's the only way we can discover how many we're talking about.'

'I don't understand,' Jake said. 'Rita Todd was a woman, who *might have* — and I can't stress the uncertainty enough here — *might have* hired us to defend her on a disciplinary case. Sadly, Mrs Todd is no more, and therefore neither is her case. As far as we're concerned, it's closed.'

'Rita's daughter is convinced that her death was neither suicide nor an accident,' I countered.

'To be blunt, that's her problem and she needs to address that with the police,' said Jake. 'I know you feel bad about it, but it no longer concerns us. Harsh, I know, but true.'

'Thing is, I think Andrea might be right. I think there might be more to this than meets the eye.'

'Based on what?'

'Based on the fact that it appears Rita was planning to blow the whistle on some dubious practices within the hospital. I think there could be people who would have wanted to stop her from doing that.'

Jake looked at me as if I'd just announced that Martians were invading the town. I couldn't really blame him.

'Like who? Oh yes,' he continued, answering his own question. 'This would be one of the renowned NHS Hit Squads that go around "taking out" anyone who doesn't agree with their policies.' He was staring at me. 'Have you been overdoing the ju-jus? First off, where did you come up with that particular paranoid conspiracy theory? And second — if we indulge your fantasy for just a moment — how could you possibly hope to verify it?'

'To start with,' I said, more defensively than I'd intended, 'by looking more closely into what was happening to Rita Todd at work, as we would have done if she was still alive.'

'If she had wanted us to,' Jake reminded me.

Ignoring him, I told him what Delores had said. 'Trouble is, without direct access to any medical records, we've no way of knowing who was right or wrong.'

'Or,' Jake pointed out. 'It could simply be the case that Rita Todd was getting too attached to her patients. I'm sure that's not uncommon.'

'Administering overdoses could be construed as euthanasia, which as far as I'm aware is still illegal in this country.'

'But if it's to alleviate suffering? That's exactly where it gets tricky. There are guidelines for these things.'

'Which are subject to interpretation,' I reminded him.

'So this is why we're applying to FOI,' Jake concluded.

'You'd think the mortality figures would be readily available, but according to Delores, Rita came up against a brick wall. I thought I'd see if we encountered the same problem. Delores told us that one of the families at the centre of all this was the Dawson family. Couldn't we at least try talking to them?'

'What would that achieve?'

'It might help establish just how much trouble Rita was causing for the hospital, and how much someone might have wanted her silenced.'

'By driving her to suicide, you mean,' Jake said.

'Well, all right,' I conceded. It wasn't what I'd meant, but it was the only realistic possibility. 'Whatever it was, there's something going on here that smells off.' I considered Delores's words. 'And someone ought to be held to account.'

'Oh, for God's sake.' Jake sighed. 'All right, then.'

'After all,' I added. 'It's not as if we're overwhelmed with other work.'

Jake winced. 'That's below the belt.'

'About the Dawsons . . .' I continued. 'It'll be a delicate one. Can you do it?'

He shook his head with exasperation. 'Dog with a bone,' was all he said.

* * *

I hadn't been in there since the night I was attacked, but on my way home I called in at Davey's newsagents.

'I heard what happened to you,' Davey said, gazing at my fast-fading bruises. 'That's what they did? I can't believe it round here. Have they caught the men who did it?' He seemed a little nervous.

'Not yet,' I said. 'But I appreciate your help. The police said that you picked out a couple of faces.'

He was quick to respond. 'They were just people I've seen hanging round the shop. That's all,' he said.

'Well, thanks anyway.' I paid for my items and left.

CHAPTER FORTY

Superintendent Bowers' obsession with discretion seemed to have paid off and on the whole, no one seemed to have got wind of Westfield's presence in Charnford. The few passers-by we encountered paid scant attention to the chauffeur-driven car as it deposited its passenger outside the community centre on Thursday morning. Our secret was apparently safe.

For someone who wanted 'thinking time', Westfield was surprisingly chatty. We had barely pulled away from the kerb afterwards when he asked, 'Do you have children, Mick?'

'Not yet,' I said, intrigued.

'But you're planning them, you and your wife?'

I nodded to confirm.

'Well, good luck to you,' said Westfield. 'It was one of the things that Amelie and I didn't get around to. We'd talked about it, in an abstract sort of way, but once she'd had her diagnosis, she was worried about the risks. And by then it was too late. She had some of her eggs frozen, but what would be the sense of raising her children without her?'

I sensed he'd said more than he'd intended and there followed an awkward silence. 'I read about all that of course, sir, I mean, your wife's illness. I'm very sorry.' Our eyes met in the rear-view mirror. 'Nobody should have to go through all that.'

'Thanks, Mick. I appreciate it. You want my advice, if you want to start a family, don't hang about, just get on and do it.'

'I'll keep that in mind, sir,' I said, pulling into the hospital.

'Jesus . . .'

It took me a moment to realise that Westfield wasn't still talking to me, but then I saw what he had. We'd reached our destination a few minutes ahead of schedule, for which I was quite proud. But despite his request that the visits should be low key, a welcoming committee of hospital bigwigs was already assembled, lined up outside like in a costume drama, when the new master or mistress of the house arrives for the first time. I wasn't sure what to do once I'd let Westfield out of the car, so I stood by and watched for a moment. He behaved as if he was flattered, but I sensed that underneath he was fuming. As he began to make his way down the line, offering a handshake and a few words, a woman at the far end became increasingly agitated, hopping from foot to foot with anticipation — clearly a fan. When Westfield got to her, he seemed to recoil in surprise, but then took her outstretched hand as she leaned in and kissed him on the cheek, which surely went way beyond protocol. Simpering didn't begin to describe it. Westfield, ever the diplomat, handled it smoothly, with a hand on her forearm and a step back, his smile unwavering.

As was becoming the pattern, the visit ran over and I sat outside with the engine running, trying not to obstruct the emergency vehicles that were still trying to do their job. Eventually my fare appeared, still surrounded by hospital staff and deep in conversation with the woman from the line-up. As they parted company, Westfield managed to put enough distance between them for an arm's length handshake, before ducking in through the passenger door I held open for him.

Heeding the superintendent's instructions, I started the car and eased out back onto the main road without passing comment. But Westfield's blue eyes were staring steadily into the rear-view mirror, and met mine each time I used it. He let out a heavy sigh.

'Everything all right, sir?' I asked.

'Wonderful,' he frowned. 'This reception I'm going to tomorrow night, it's going to be a nightmare . . .'

'The lady at the hospital?'

'Was it that obvious?'

'She was all over you like a rash.'

'My past life catching up with me. I have no objection, you under-stand, but I'd prefer it not to be so inevitable. You wouldn't happen to have any friends who'd be prepared to act as a human shield, do you?'

I hadn't expected that. 'No, sir, I—'

'I'm kidding, Mick,' he said. 'Actually, no, I'm not. You don't know anyone that I could take along with me to enable me to keep a distance, do you? Someone whose company I might enjoy for the evening and perhaps into the night, but who would be discreet? No, sorry, you're a family man. Forget I even asked.'

We drove in silence for several minutes, then, unbidden, Keeley came into my head.

'As a matter of fact, sir, I might know someone.' He looked at me, curious. 'She's someone I know from a case I've been working on. A professional, if you get my meaning.'

'Is she respectable?'

'She's very classy, sir.'

'Discreet? I'm sure I don't need to point out what a risk it would be. You can imagine what the press would make of it. Are you and she . . . ?'

'Oh no, sir, but I've met her several times and had absolutely no idea what she did until she told me.'

'If your situation was different, would you go out with her?'

'Like a shot, sir.'

'Well then, she sounds perfect. Give her a call, will you? I think I should meet her beforehand too, perhaps tonight at my hotel if possible, at about ten?'

'I'll see what I can do, sir.'

CHAPTER FORTY-ONE

Jake hadn't needed any kind of direction in talking to the Dawsons. He knew what I wanted to find out, though we were both sceptical of uncovering anything of significance. He went armed with a Dictaphone and I played it back later, the digital recording as crystal clear as if I'd been there in the room with them.

'I realise this was only a matter of months ago. Do you mind talking about it?' Jake asked.

A male voice responded — Alex Dawson. 'As long as you don't mind talking to me. My wife isn't here at the moment, she's taken George to one of his numerous medical appointments. I'm sorry, could you just tell me again what your interest is?'

'My firm was due to be representing Rita Todd at a disciplinary hearing. Your case was one of those named in the allegations. Since then, of course, she has passed away, but there are one or two loose ends we need to tie up.'

'Did you say passed away? Rita? That must have been sudden. Was she ill?'

There was a slight pause while Jake chose the right words. 'It's not yet clear if it was an accident or suicide.'

'Oh my God, that's terrible. Rita was such a lovely woman, so kind.'

There followed a long pause, while Jake let him take in that information. Dawson spoke again. 'And a disciplinary hearing? Was that because of us? I don't understand — Rita was fantastic.'

Jake was tactful. 'There were some allegations of er . . . discrepancies. Rita had been suspended pending a hearing. I understand Rita nursed your child,' he continued, moving things along. 'Would you be able to tell me about what happened to you? I realise this it's a difficult time to look back on.'

'Actually, it helps to talk about it,' said Dawson. 'To acknowledge the difficulties George had when he was first born. Have you got children?'

'No, I haven't.'

'Well it was all a bit of shock, really. It was our first pregnancy and it was all going along nicely, then at twenty weeks, Jenny had a bleed. They took her into hospital to try and keep the baby in there for longer, but then at twenty-four weeks he was delivered, obviously much too small and very ill. He looked like a scarlet frog. Then on top of that, we found out that he had a rare metabolic condition. He was taken into NICU and that was when we met Rita for the first time. We were in shock, but she was wonderful. She always explained everything they were doing and why. The consultant, Mr Leonard, was good, but he didn't really have a lot of time to talk to us.'

Tell me about it, I thought.

'Anyway, those first few weeks are just a blur now. We lurched along from one day to the next, hardly eating or sleeping. Slowly George began to get stronger, I think he surprised everyone. He did so well that he was taken off the ventilator and transferred out of intensive care. We didn't see Rita much after that because it was a different staff team on the new ward. In fact, we didn't see much of anyone consistently after that, there always seemed to be temporary staff. Perhaps that's why we appreciated Rita so much. Anyway, George had only been there a few days, when some complications arose from his medical condition. Mr Leonard said that he felt George was in distress and that although we might be able to solve the problem in the short-term, it was likely to happen again and that it was probably going to be an ongoing problem that would require further interventions. He asked us to strongly consider whether we wanted to subject George to further invasive treatment that might not have positive outcomes.'

'How did you feel about that?'

He stopped to think for a minute. 'I've thought about it a lot,' he said. 'To be honest, it was rather out of the blue. Just prior to that, we had been given the impression that George was doing well. But suddenly Mr Leonard seemed to be saying that we were just prolonging George's suffering. It was the one time that we were quite at a loss. We didn't know what to do for the best.'

'Did you speak to Rita at that time?'

'Only because Jen bumped into her by chance. When she told Rita what was happening, she was very concerned.'

'Did you feel as if you were being put under any pressure to make a decision?'

'In truth, the way in which it was framed gave us little choice. No one wants their child to suffer. Mr Leonard said that even if George survived, which was by no means certain, the risk of severe disabilities and the need for ongoing treatment would be greater. He asked if we were prepared for that. And frankly? We weren't. I mean, it's hard enough these days for a child to cope with all the pressures of modern living without starting already at such a disadvantage.'

'Indeed,' I murmured to myself.

'Well between us we got as far as agreeing to turn off the life support machines,' Dawson said. 'It felt like the hardest decision of our lives. But then that evening, we had a call from Rita. She didn't say it outright but I knew that she was sticking her neck out for us. She gave me Mike and Sara's phone number.'

'Mike and Sara?' Jake queried.

'They have a little girl, Chantelle, who has the same metabolic condition. Like George, it was touch and go with her when she was first born and there were all kinds of dire predictions, but she's five now and doing very well. I think Rita wanted us to see another perspective before we made our decision. And she was right. We rang them and spoke to Sara and that was when we decided we wanted the hospital to do everything they could to keep George alive.'

'What kind of reaction did that get?' asked Jake.

'Mr Leonard made it very clear that he thought we were making a mistake. It was only when I made a vague threat about legal action that he backed down.'

'And what do you think now?'

'I'll be honest, it hasn't been plain sailing. George has had to go back into hospital for further treatment. Sometimes when he's poorly and I see how anxious my wife is, I genuinely wonder if we did the right thing, but I know that Jenny has never had any doubts. And when George is well, it's impossible to imagine life without him.'

Jake switched off the Dictaphone. 'Does that help?' he asked me.

'Lucky that the Dawsons are articulate and assertive people,' I remarked. 'Otherwise they might not have got what they wanted.'

* * *

Rita had uncovered some dubious practices, and now she was dead. Was she dead because she couldn't live with what was going on, or because someone wanted to abort her attempt to expose it? If the latter, then it meant that anyone in possession of such information could be under threat.

Plum had also had some limited success with FOI, and she and I were sitting in silence, each trying to make sense of the data, when there was a knock on the office door. We both looked up and were equally surprised when Cate's head appeared round it.

'Hello.'

'Hello,' I managed to reciprocate.

Cate glanced over at Plum, who was scowling. 'May I come in?'

'Of course.' Getting up, I indicated the chair opposite. 'Have a seat. Can you give us a minute?' I said to Plum. The atmosphere in the room had noticeably thickened. Folding her notebook with a slap, Plum got up and without a word, stomped out of the room, closing the door with more vigour than was necessary.

'Something I said?' Cate ventured, sitting and placing her handbag on the floor beside her.

I shook my head.

'Well, I wouldn't be surprised,' she said with a wry smile. 'It's becoming a habit. How are you?'

'I'm fine, thanks,' I said. 'Can I get you something — tea, coffee?' I'd sat down again, and here we were, like lawyer and client, facing each other across the desk. Formal. It suited me, for the moment.

'No, thanks.' She looked different today, but I couldn't quite identify why. She was as well-groomed as ever, in a tailored skirt and low-cut soft sweater, a tasteful chunky necklace at her throat. Then it came to me. It was her manner. There was a marked absence of her usual self-confidence, and in its place were disquiet and vulnerability. It made me want her even more.

'You haven't been returning my calls,' she observed.

'I'm not very good on the phone,' I said, though we both knew it wasn't the reason.

She hesitated. 'I've missed you.'

I nodded a silent assent, but said nothing. I wasn't going to make this easy for her. She needed to understand.

Smoothing her skirt, she looked up directly into my eyes.

'Stefan, I'm really sorry about what I said. I was trying to be helpful. I hadn't really thought through how tactless it might be.'

'It makes me think that I'm not good enough,' I said, running my fingertips along the edge of the desk.

'I can see that. It was a terrible and hurtful thing to say. But I hope you can appreciate that this is a new experience for me, and there are some things I'm learning the hard way. I think we have something, and I'd really like to give it another try, but I will understand if you don't want to.' She reached down to pick up her bag and began rifling through it. 'Anyway, I've got some tickets for the theatre, I mean, I don't even know if you like the theatre, but— Oh, now I'm waffling. Anyway, they're for tonight, which is probably too short notice, but . . .' Breaking off, she placed a ticket on the corner of the desk. 'I'll leave this one with you and if you feel you can give me another chance, I'll see you there.' Getting up, she leaned over to kiss my cheek, all subtle perfume and straining cleavage that sent a rush of heat to my groin. Then she turned and walked out of the office.

After Cate had gone, I just sat for a couple of minutes, before picking up the ticket from where she'd left it. It was a touring production of *Whose Life Is It Anyway?* Ten out of ten for irony. I'd think about it. It occurred to me that Cate might have access to the statistics we were after, and it might be helpful to pump her further about Guy Leonard. She might even know the identity of the mystery woman at the inquest. Would that make it a quid pro quo? The only other consideration was how far I was prepared to let my principles stand in the way of a decent shag.

'I'll be off now, then.' Plum stood in the doorway, coat and surly expression in place.

'OK,' I said. 'Thanks for your help today.'

'No probs,' she replied, making it sound second only to global warming in terms of inconvenience. 'Want a lift home?'

I did. It had been a long day and I was probably going to take Cate up on her offer. Getting home quickly would be a bonus.

'Thanks. You're a star.'

CHAPTER FORTY-TWO

I dropped Westfield off at his afternoon engagement at the old people's home.

'You don't need to hang around here,' he said. 'I'll get a cab back to the hotel. I'd be glad if you could deliver your friend there later.'

I called Keeley from the car. 'I've got another favour to ask.'

'You're a happily married man, PC Fraser,' she reminded me playfully.

'Yes, I am. It's not me. We have a, er . . . VIP visiting this week.'

'And who might that be?'

There was no sense in being coy. News of Westfield's visit would emerge soon enough.

'Do you know a man called Matthew Westfield?'

'The only man of that name I know is the politician.'

'Well he's here, in Charnford, right now.'

'Really? You're talking about business here?'

'In a manner of speaking,' I said. 'I'm not exactly sure what he has in mind.'

'Oh my God.' Keeley sounded almost star struck. 'I've made it to the big time. He's pretty fit for a politician, too. What's the deal?'

The deal is absolute discretion. He's inviting you to go with him to a reception he has to attend tomorrow evening. He's in need of protection.'

'From what?'

'Another woman has got her eye on him and he's not interested. He's asked to meet you first, tonight. Can you do that?'

'How important is it?' she asked.

'It's Matthew Westfield.'

'OK, I'll have to cancel another client, but I can plead sickness, I suppose.'

'I'm sure he'll make it worth your while. It'll be a visit to his hotel room tonight and nothing more, as far as I know. I'll come and pick you up just before ten. You'll be er . . . recompensed in line with, er, your usual . . . well, you know.'

She laughed. 'Yes, I do. I think I can manage that.'

'You're OK with it?'

'I'm fine. Don't sound so worried, PC Fraser. It's my job, remember?'

'I'll see you later, then.' Jesus, I thought, replacing the phone, I've just pimped for a former government adviser. Was that why I felt so grubby?

It didn't seem worth going home, so I went back into the station. Always plenty to do there.

* * *

Plum drove me home and pulled up just outside my apartment block. She seemed edgy, somehow, still not quite recovered from her strop in the office that afternoon.

'I'm gasping for a coffee,' she said, turning off the ignition, 'and I've never been in your flat.'

'All right.' I hadn't much time and I was tired, but she had helped me out, and the hint was hardly a subtle one. It seemed the least I could do. Once inside, she dropped her bag on the floor and surveyed the lounge.

'Very nice,' she said.

'Thanks. Coffee?'

'Or something stronger?'

'You're driving,' I reminded her.

'Oh yeah, coffee's great,' she beamed — somewhat unnaturally, I thought.

It took me a few minutes, and when I emerged from the kitchen Plum had vanished. What was going on? I hadn't heard the front door and her handbag was still on the floor.

'Everything OK?' I called, somehow apprehensive of the response.

'I'm in here.' Her voice didn't, as I might have expected, echo back at me from the bathroom, but seemed to come from further down the hall. That was taking curiosity a little too far. Putting down the mugs, I followed her down.

'What are you nosing at n—' I began, breaking off when I saw her lying in my bed. Although the duvet was pulled up to her chin, I could tell she was naked. Her clothes, underwear included, were in a none-too-neat pile on the floor. Momentarily, the power of speech deserted me.

'It's all right,' she said, with a mischievous smile, waving the pack at me. 'I've brought condoms.'

Shock, embarrassment, disbelief and fear surged through me in equal measure, culminating in an explosion of anger.

'What the fuck are you doing, Plum?' I strode across the room and picked up a handful of clothing, flinging it at her. 'Get dressed and get out!'

I went back into the kitchen to put as much space as I could between us. Moments later, I heard her hasty footsteps through the flat, followed by the slamming of the door. My reaction had been pure reflex, but I'd handled it badly. And now there was less than an hour before I was due to meet Cate.

* * *

I got to the theatre a little early, my nerves still jangling from the incident with Plum, and ordered a much-needed double Scotch at the bar. The barman took several attempts in the noisy environment to understand me, and I felt conspicuously single among a sea of couples. With the announcement that the performance would begin shortly, I began to get the first glimmer of unease that I might have been stood up. I had to decide whether to go in and see the play or cut my losses and go home. Then suddenly there she was, breathless and apologetic and planting a light kiss on my cheek, as her citrus-noted eau de cologne wafted over me.

'I'm so sorry,' she said. 'I just couldn't get away. But I'm so pleased to see you. Shall we go in?'

During the play, Cate took my hand and as we left the theatre, she slipped her arm into mine. We talked about the play a little but uppermost in my mind was the encounter with Plum.

'I can't understand it. Why the hell did she do that?'

'Because she fancies you,' said Cate. 'It's blindingly obvious. Why do you think she's so jealous of me? You saw the way she reacted this afternoon. Maybe she saw it as her last chance.'

'But she's just a kid. I'm almost old enough to be her dad.'

Cate stopped walking. 'Stefan, look at me.'

I stopped and turned. 'Sorry. I said . . .'

'I heard what you said.' She put a finger on my lips. 'I just wanted to do this.' And she leaned in and kissed me properly.

It was still early, so we ducked into a bar. It hadn't been my intention, but after a while I got to telling her about Rita and the Dawsons.

'It's a terrible decision to have to make,' she agreed. 'But they're not making that decision in a vacuum. They have support.'

'Who from, though? It didn't sound as if the Dawsons had much of that.'

'The medical professionals who are treating their child should help,' said Cate. 'And they, in turn, have guidelines to support any decisions they might make.'

'But who writes them?' I asked.

'The General Medical Council in the first instance, although there's always scope for individual interpretation. Additional guidance is set down by the local ethics committee that meets to review any cases that may be contentious. Sometimes decisions can have wider implications.'

'And decisions are based on what, the "viability" of the patient?'

'I would hope that it's first and foremost about the patient's quality of life. But yes, after that there may be a consideration of the long-term prognosis.'

'And effective use of resources?'

Cate sighed. 'This is the real world, Stefan. Yes, in some cases that has to be a factor.'

'But who has the final say?'

'It's a joint decision, hopefully, a consensus between the medics and the parents.'

'And is the ethics committee active in that?'

'To a degree. They have to ensure a fair and practical distribution of resources. And they determine local policy. Why the interest?' Cate wanted to know.

'It was something Guy Leonard said when I asked him about Rita Todd, about the pressure he was under from the committee.'

'That's true,' she said. 'The committee wields a lot of power, but it's for good. Ten years ago, the hospital was in the equivalent of special measures and now, since top-level staff have been replaced and new procedures introduced, it's thriving. Waiting lists are down and the health authority looks as if it could be operating within its budget before long. I can be confident about referring patients because I know they'll be seen quickly.'

'Are you governed by the ethics committee too?'

'It has more influence over what happens in the hospital than in general practice, but we still feel the ripples. The current chair seems to have some particular ideas about the way things should be done, and has tried to introduce some innovations.'

'Such as what?'

'I'm pretty sure the voluntary sterilisation programme I told you about was her idea.'

'Who else sits on this committee?'

'Medical professionals, of course, but also a legal representative and a cleric to provide moral guidance.'

'How often do they meet?'

'About once a month, at the hospital. Now, can we stop talking about work? Your place or mine?'

'Actually, would you mind if I gave it a miss tonight?' I had found myself wondering again about Rita and her priest. But it also seemed imperative that we find out whom it was she met when she left the church that night. Cate took it well, but the absolute truth was I still couldn't be sure of her.

CHAPTER FORTY-THREE

I took Keeley to Westfield's hotel and agreed to pick her up three hours later. This was beginning to get, as the man himself had predicted, tedious. I seemed to have become the force babysitter — first Denny and now Westfield. I hoped this gig wasn't going to turn out like the last one had. I didn't know what to do with all this waiting around, especially since the boss didn't want me engaged on anything else. But something that wouldn't be too taxing and that could usefully be done while the squad room was quiet would be to look at the CCTV for Rita Todd, as I'd promised Stefan Greaves.

Since the government's obsession with surveillance had waned, the number of cameras in Charnford had been substantially reduced. A lack of funding for repairs meant that many of them had fallen out of commission and only those dotted about the town centre were fully maintained. That left dozens that were still in place but not functional. It occurred to me then that this was a line of evidence I hadn't considered for Greaves' mugging. When I had my next bit of spare time, I'd see what, if any, public CCTV cameras there were between Davey's supermarket and his flat.

But first things first. There were no cameras in the immediate vicinity of the church, so I started to fan out to a wider radius. It had been a quiet night with not much activity at the time Rita was out. It took a while, but eventually I picked up two figures that could possibly be Rita

Todd and her companion. It was cold — I could see their breath misting as they walked. Trouble was, I'd only seen Rita horizontal on a gurney. It would help if Stefan could confirm that it was her. And he might also have more of a clue than I did about whom the companion might be.

The first time I called him it went straight to voicemail, so I left a message. I didn't expect to hear from him that evening, but he rang back about an hour later and once he knew what I'd found, despite the time, he was keen to come in.

While I waited, I did a quick scan to see if there were any cameras anywhere near Davey's supermarket. There weren't, of course, though there was one a bit further back down the street on the opposite side. I left a note to flag this up for Sharon Petrowlski. I'd just finished scribbling it when Greaves texted me to say he was outside.

'What are you doing here so late?' was his first question after I'd signed him in as a visitor.

'Running around after our friend Mr Westfield.'

'At this time of night?

'Can you keep a secret?'

'For you, anything,' he said with his lopsided grin.

'I've dropped off Keeley at his hotel and have agreed to go and pick her up later.'

'Keeley Moynihan?'

'Yeah, sorry, that was my idea. Westfield wants to take his own plus-one to this gala thing tomorrow night. It was quite funny, really. There was a woman massively coming on to him when he was up at the hospital and he wants some protection from her. Anyway, he asked if there was anyone I knew who would be a decoy, and the only name that came to mind was Keeley's. She seems OK with it. In fact, she's with him tonight, "getting to know him". I'm sorry, that must be weird.'

He shrugged. 'It's life, isn't it? Girl's got to earn a living. If you're collecting her, you can give me a lift home at the same time.'

We turned our attention to the CCTV I'd found.

'Could that be Rita Todd?' I asked.

'Looks like her,' said Greaves.

'So who is it with her?'

He studied the footage for several seconds and just when I thought he'd drawn a blank too, he spoke.

'It could be Guy Leonard, Rita's boss at the hospital. He's not too tall and has that kind of bearing. I wondered at one point if he and Rita might be more than just colleagues, but I'd discounted that idea — maybe too soon. Where are they going?'

We watched as the two figures walked towards the main market square. As they approached one of the roads that went down to the river, they stopped and Leonard turned towards Rita and put out his hand to touch hers.

'You sure there's nothing going on?' I asked. 'What's he doing there? Is he trying to hold her back, or comfort her?'

'I think he's giving her something,' said Greaves, peering at the screen. We watched Rita glance down at her hand before slipping whatever it was into her pocket. Then the pair spoke again briefly, before they went their separate ways. Once they'd disappeared down their respective side streets, there was no more footage to show where they went.

'What was it he gave her?' I wondered aloud. 'She was on strong antidepressants. Do you think he could have been supplying them?'

'Weren't they on prescription, though?' said Greaves. 'Why would he need to?'

'Unless he's supplying something else.' But there was no evidence to suggest it.

'What happened to Rita's clothes and backpack?' he asked.

'Those we do have,' I said, understanding at once. 'Wait here.'

It took me about ten minutes to locate the bag in the evidence store and to go through Rita's pockets. But the outcome was a disappointment.

'The contents of her pockets,' I said, depositing them on the desk, 'including one river-washed scrap of paper. If you can read it, you're a better man than me.'

'Guy Leonard knows what he gave her,' he said. 'We could always go and ask him. He might actually have been the last person to see Rita alive.'

'Have you got a number for him?'

'No, but I know where he lives.'

I glanced up at the clock. 'It's pretty late.'

'Which means we would take him by surprise. We'll be able to tell if there's anyone up and about in his house.'

And Keeley would need to be picked up soon, too.

239

'Has Sharon been in touch with you yet?' I asked Greaves, as we drove.

'Sharon?'

'Petrowlski.'

He shook his head.

'Hm, she probably hasn't had the chance to do anything yet. There's been a lot happening what with Denny and now Westfield.'

He waved away the apology. 'It's fine. To be honest, I didn't really expect anything.'

CHAPTER FORTY-FOUR

It was eleven thirty but there were lights still on in the Leonard household, so I had no qualms about ringing the doorbell. Leonard came to the door himself and was understandably startled to see us and reluctant to invite us in — at first.

'Why didn't you see fit to tell us that you met up with Rita Todd on the night of Friday, March fourth?' asked Fraser.

Turned out that was the password. Within minutes, we were sitting in the cosy lounge enjoying the warmth from the dying embers of the wood-burner. The rest of the house was quiet. Everyone else must have been in bed.

'You know that you were very likely the last person to see her alive?' said Fraser, his annoyance showing through.

Leonard was defensive. 'Not necessarily,' he replied.

'What did you give to Rita, just before you went your separate ways?'

Leonard hesitated.

'We can do this down at the station if you'd prefer,' said Fraser. 'Where we can all see the footage. I'll even get in the popcorn.'

A pause. 'It was an address,' Leonard said.

'Which was?'

'It was for one of the large properties that backed onto the river.'

'That would be upstream from where Rita was found, then,' said Fraser. 'What's at that address?'

'Not what, but who,' said Leonard, resigned. 'She was very persuasive. I have a family, a mortgage. I had no choice.'

'Who lives there?' I demanded.

'Margot Warren-Byrne.'

Fraser's eyes met mine and I gave him the merest nod. We'd got what we came for.

'I've seen that name somewhere recently,' said Fraser, once we were back in the car. 'You know who she is?'

'Only recently,' I said. 'She's the head of the medical ethics committee at the hospital. Broadly speaking, she heads up the group of people who moderate decisions about who gets to live or die.'

'What did Rita Todd want with her, do you think?' asked Fraser.

'Allegations had been made about Rita's professional conduct. Perhaps the committee, or even Warren-Byrne herself, have some kind of influence over disciplinary matters. If so, it would make sense for Rita to go and see her to plead her case.'

'And if Warren-Byrne refused, or was unable to help, that could have been what pushed Rita over the edge into taking her own life.'

I didn't like that version of events but I had to acknowledge that it added up.

The alarm on Fraser's phone sounded.

'Keeley. I've got to go and fetch her,' he said. 'I'll drop you off at your flat on the way.'

I spent a restless night going over everything I knew about Rita and still struggled to reconcile the woman I had met with someone about to take her own life. But then, how long had we met for? Five minutes? Ten? Not much more than that. No, the person who had known all about her frame of mind was the man she had spent evenings in the church with just talking — Father Adrian. He was the one person Rita might have confided in. I should have asked more questions when I could. Not for the first time, I cursed myself for having squandered the opportunity when I met him.

The following morning, I saw a message in my inbox from Mick Fraser: *Knew I'd seen that name somewhere before. Cast your eye over this unholy trinity.*

I clicked on the attached image. It was a poor definition, colour photo downloaded from the web that could only have been taken some years ago, a group shot from some kind of student society. It took me a few seconds to locate the youthful Matthew Westfield, but once I did, it took no time at all to identify the woman at his right shoulder. Fraser had circled another head and inserted a caption: *and this is my boss.*

CHAPTER FORTY-FIVE

As Plum and I walked through the town to St Barnabas for Rita's funeral, I realised that in the space of a week, I'd managed to piss off two of the women in my life. It was an uncomfortable walk, and not just because it was raining again. By the time we got to the church gates, I still hadn't worked out quite what, but I had to say something.

'Plum, about last night. I'm sorry. You're a lovely girl, but you're very young. You should be seeing someone your own age. Plus, I'm already seeing someone.'

'That doctor.' Two words imbued with contempt.

'Yes. We've got to work together, and I really value you as a colleague. I'd hate to spoil that. I count on you as a mate, too. I like your company. Tell you what — why don't we go out sometime, just the two of us?'

Her lip curled with suspicion. 'Really? You'd do that?'

'Place of your choosing,' I said in trepidation of what I might be letting myself in for. 'So we're OK? No hard feelings?'

She shrugged. 'I'll get over it.' I had to trust that she was telling the truth. She flashed me a sudden, cheeky grin. 'Maybe I'll try my luck with the priest.'

* * *

Andrea's wish to keep her mother's funeral low key was granted. In Father Adrian's continued absence, Deacon Robert was officiating, so there would be no communion and the service would lack the usual Catholic bells and whistles. The gloomy weather seemed only to underline the sadness of the occasion.

Even as the service got under way, there were no more than thirty of us present. Delores was the only representative from the hospital who I could see. Clearly those staff shortages were such that no one could be spared for even a couple of hours.

'I watched *The Wizard of Oz* again last night,' said Plum, as we got to our feet for the first hymn. 'It didn't help.'

On our way out, she paused by the noticeboard, where a new flyer had been pinned announcing a candlelight vigil for the rough sleepers who had perished in the town, including, controversially, Liam Archer. She took out a pen and wrote the details on the back of her hand.

'You're going to go?'

'I knew a couple of them.'

'Really?'

'From way back. Want to come?'

It was a challenge. She expected me to decline.

'Yeah, all right then. I said we could have a night out.'

* * *

We'd been invited back to Rita's house, where Andrea had laid on drinks and nibbles for the wake.

'It went well,' I said to her, noting the unlikely sight of Plum in earnest conversation with Dean Robert.

'Mm, looks like I was wrong,' Andrea said. 'Mum had planned it all — hymns, music and everything. I think she knew it was going to happen — and sooner rather than later. It's made me think again.'

Plum's voice rang out. 'Father Adrian said something really weird,' I heard her say. 'He told us he didn't have the

Lion's courage. We thought . . .' Plum hesitated as she caught sight of me watching. '*I* thought it must be to do with *The Wizard of Oz*,' she said, deliberately avoiding my gaze.

'Really?' The curate was taken aback by this statement. 'How extraordinary.'

'Was the vicar a fan?' Plum persisted.

'I really don't know,' said the curate. 'I can't remember it ever coming up in conversation.'

CHAPTER FORTY-SIX

Today was education day for Westfield, so I dropped him off at Millpool Primary School. There weren't many people about at the station when I got back, but Sharon Petrowlski was one of them.

'I've got to catch up on paperwork at some point,' she said, by way of explanation. 'I'm really behind and Bowers doesn't like that, does he? Thanks for the tip-off about the CCTV, by the way. Haven't had the chance to look yet, but I'll get onto it.'

'No worries,' I said. 'I'm effectively here twiddling my thumbs for the next couple of hours. Want me to have a look? I'll give you a shout if I find anything.'

'Thanks, I owe you one.'

I went back to the CCTV footage and sought out the camera from outside Davey's supermarket. I didn't hold out much hope. It was obviously intended to be a traffic camera designed to cover the speed bumps, so was angled too far to the right of the pavement. I could fast-forward without much risk of missing anything. But at least I might catch anyone going in the direction of Greaves' flat. Feet crossed the corner of the screen and thanks to his distinctive, jerky gait, I recognised them. Then nothing. Headlights approached from the end of the street — a lone driver, going slowly thanks to the traffic calming, and on his mobile. Why was I not surprised at that? The car moved off the bottom of the

247

screen. As the registration plate dipped in and out of focus, I hit pause and rewind. I'd seen that vehicle before.

Flicking through my pocketbook confirmed what I'd thought. It was the car that had been sitting on Evan Phelps' drive when I went to speak to him. It belonged to a Tyler Curzon. OK, this was a small town, but I didn't like it when names kept recurring. Sure, it could be a complete coincidence that the mate of the man Davey picked out was close to where Stefan Greaves had been mugged on the same night, at the same time, but really, what were the odds?

I called over to Sharon. 'Can I tear you away from your paperwork for a minute?'

'I thought you'd never ask.'

'Here's the thing.' I showed her Tyler Curzon's car. 'Is he any relation to the councillor?'

'Oh yes,' said Sharon. 'His son. He was the little scrote who got off that burglary charge with Evan Phelps, thanks to Daddy's influence. The Phelps parents were the ones with the common sense to make the misdemeanour a learning experience. Kid nearly got expelled from Cavendish as a result. It was touch and go, I seem to remember.'

'What's Cavendish?'

'It's the posh independent school over Hoyland way. The primary schools in Charnford are all right, but it's a different story at secondary level. Most parents who can afford it generally try and get their kids into Cavendish. My beat copper's salary doesn't quite stretch that far, so my kids lost touch with some of their friends when they moved up.'

'So Phelps and Curzon could be schoolmates?'

'They might have gone to primary school together, too,' said Sharon. 'I don't know about Phelps, but it's only really the last ten, fifteen years that Ashley Curzon has been raking it in. Curzon junior was involved in petty stuff from a young age — him and his little gang. Used to call himself something stupid . . . Oh yes, "Top Cat", that was it. The family moved off the Flatwood as soon as they could afford it, but you know what they say — you can take the man off the Flatwood . . .'

I thought about Bostwick and Phelps being only a couple of years apart.

'Would they have known the Bostwicks?'

'It's possible, again, especially at primary school.'

'You said that Phelps learned his lesson from the burglary bust. What about Curzon?'

'We've never had him back, as far as I'm aware, but he's a little thug who didn't strike me as being all that bright. And if his dad protected him once, he can do it again. He carries a lot of influence in this town.'

Returning to my desk, I found an email from Natalie. Regretfully, both Keeley's shoes and the test results had vanished into thin air. On a more positive note, she had managed to harvest enough DNA material from the envelope to build a profile, but it didn't match anything on the database. It was beginning to feel like one step forward and two steps back.

* * *

I'd gone back to the office when a call came through from Dean Robert.

'Father Adrian's returned?' I said, sounding more hopeful than I felt.

'No, it's something your partner said . . .'

'She's not . . .' I began.

'Sorry?'

'Nothing. Please, go on.'

'Well, what she told me was rather puzzling. But then it came to me. I'm sure the "Lion" Father Adrian was referring to must be an old bishop. He was nicknamed "the Lion" for taking a stand, speaking out against the authorities when no one else would.'

He and Rita had something in common, then, I thought. 'Do you have his contact details so that we can get in touch with him?'

'Hardly,' said the Dean. 'He died in 1946. I don't know much about him but old Father Aidan will be able to tell you more.'

'I thought he was in Rome.'

'Not Father *Adrian* — Father *Aidan*, his predecessor. He's long retired now and is rather infirm, but I understand his mind is still sharp and he was quite a scholar in his time. I'm sure it's of no consequence whatsoever, but it might clarify, for your partner at least, why Father Adrian might have made reference to him.'

'Does Father Aidan live locally?'

'Not too far away. He's in The Cedars nursing home.'

It occurred to me as I hung up that those flowers in Rita's house could have been from Father Aidan. There was a good chance we had been talking to the wrong priest.

* * *

Since she was the one who'd prompted the breakthrough, I took Plum with me to The Cedars Roman Catholic Care Home. Having signed in to the visitors' book, I flicked back through the pages and there was her name, time and time again. Rita, it seemed, had been a regular visitor here, going back a good few months before her death. Father Adrian was telling the truth when he said he hadn't seen Rita often. It was Father Aidan she'd been coming to see.

The staff member who signed us in went ahead to check if Father Aidan was up to seeing us. He was, but she was firm.

'Twenty minutes at most. He's very frail and tires easily.'

When we went in, I thought we must have been sent to the wrong room. The man who sat in the high-backed chair and looked up from the substantial volume he was reading looked little more than seventy years old, certainly not two decades older. He regarded us curiously as Plum introduced us, his eyes magnified by thick-lensed glasses. And as it appeared that he had both his wits and senses about him, I felt able to speak, too.

'We wanted to ask about a bishop known as the Lion,' I said. 'I understand you can tell us something about him.'

The old man regarded me carefully. 'He's suddenly in vogue again,' he observed, in a soft Irish accent. 'I wonder what he would make of that.'

'Someone else is interested in him?' I asked, feeling a murmur of anticipation in my gut.

'One of my old parishioners comes to visit me. She remembered my mention of him in one of my sermons from thirty years ago, would you believe?'

'Rita Todd?'

'Yes, Rita. She couldn't recall the man's name, of course, but the story was remarkably fresh in her mind. He'd made an impression on her and she wanted to know more about him.' He smiled. 'We churchmen always hope that what we spout from the pulpit will resonate and be relevant for our congregation, but we don't expect that to happen quite this far down the line.' Closing his book, he handed it to Plum, who put it on the nearby table. 'The man you are asking about is Bishop Clemens von Galen. He was the Bishop of Munster, in Germany, from 1933 to 1946. As you can imagine, it was not an easy time or place.'

'And what did he do that made him the Lion?' I asked.

'He spoke out against the injustices happening in his town and in his country, even though it meant putting himself in the gravest danger.' He glanced at each of us. 'It's quite a long story.'

'If you feel up to telling us, we have the time,' I said.

He settled back in his chair. 'Very well.'

CHAPTER FORTY-SEVEN

Münster, August 1941

By the time the young priest arrives, the thunder is a constant, rumbling around the city like a prowling beast, preparing to strike. But still the storm does not break. As my assistant shows him into my office, I see in him the same restlessness and indecision that I myself feel. Now it is he who paces the room while I wait calmly for him to collect himself. Finally, I persuade him to sit and explain.

'The first time I encountered Martha Keller,' *he begins, haltingly.* 'I had no idea why she made such an impression. She wasn't beautiful in the conventional sense, but there was a sharp intelligence and often a sense of mischief about her. She seemed somehow more alive than anyone around her. On the first Sunday she came to Mass, she sat with her children — but no husband — exuding confidence, and I felt an instant and unsettling reaction, which I can't adequately describe. There are enough of my parishioners who like to gossip, and I quickly learned that Frau Keller was from a wealthy family in the capital and was educated and well-travelled. Certainly, she seemed at odds with our tiny parochial town, too sophisticated. After the service that day she waited behind to introduce herself, at the same time quite unashamedly appraising me.

'"Since two-thirds of the congregation is female, I would say that's two-thirds of the congregation who have an improper affection for their priest," she said. It was a joke, but, subjected to her intense gaze, I found myself suddenly awkward, which only seemed to amuse her further. She added, "I'll look forward to confessing my sins to you, Father."

'I suppose the warning signs were there from the beginning — the new and unwelcome feelings in anticipation of Sunday mornings, her absence from Mass, which was rare, bringing with it a jolt of disappointment. When she was in the congregation, I had to make an effort not to address myself only to her. I told myself that what I looked forward to was the cut and thrust of our exchanges, the originality of her thoughts and ideas. Conversations with her were never dull. And she was fundamentally a good person, she regularly made donations of food and clothing for the needy, always with the utmost discretion. She once even denied to me that she did it, although I knew differently. She made her confession regularly and I came to recognise her footfall and perfume. Her confessions were unremarkable: she had been abrupt with the children, she had lacked tolerance or spoken unkindly to a neighbour. She was invariably bright and talkative, but sometimes she looked strained. Her husband, who seemed to have an important civil service job, was often away, and on the rare occasions he came to Mass there was a subtle change to her demeanour. Some of the brightness left her, and it seemed to me that her behaviour was more controlled.

'On occasion she would come to the church in the evening to sit in silence. It was on one such instance that she stole up behind me while I was working, watching and waiting while I finished what I was doing.

'"Would you like me to hear your confession, Mrs Keller?" When I turned to face her, I noticed immediately the bluish shadow, not quite concealed by make-up, that ran down her left cheek.

'She saw me observe it and turned away. "No, Father, but I would like to sit for a few moments, if you have time?"

'"Of course." I indicated the front row of the pews, before the altar, and when she sat down, I sat beside her. For a few moments we sat in quiet contemplation, just inches apart. I don't know if she was aware, as I was, of the thickness of the air between us.

'"Your husband is violent towards you," I said, after a while. There followed another lengthy pause. Perhaps she was deciding whether to deny it and fabricate an explanation for the bruise. That her eventual reply was an honest one came as no surprise.

'"Not often." She continued to stare straight ahead at the altar.

'"I don't understand," I ventured. "Why don't you—?"

'"What?" She rounded on me, her voice low and controlled. "Leave him? Where would I go? How would I live, and what would happen to my children?"

'I had no answer for her, recognising, not for the first time, my pitiful grasp on the realities of family life.

'"We all carry our burdens," she said after a long pause. Her tone had lightened, as if she was challenging or even teasing me.

'"All of us?" I responded in kind, knowing straight away that it was a mistake.

'She moved a little closer to me, so that her shoulder touched mine.

'"If I am not mistaken, you sometimes wish you were not a priest."

'I should have been appalled and heeded the warning, but I didn't. Some weeks later, I rode over to an outlying village, to visit a sick and elderly woman. A minor infection had turned into pneumonia, and as she was already frail, there was little hope. I blessed and anointed her and was heartened to find that she seemed better. My mood was lifted, but in my eagerness, cycling up the small incline out of the village, the chain on my bicycle snapped, which meant pushing it the five miles back. A low rumble in the darkening sky signalled an oncoming summer storm, so I took the quickest route, along the river path, across the fields. But I hadn't gone far when the rain began to fall in great sheets. I knew that there was a byre in one of the fields, so I pushed on to it and ran inside to shelter until the storm had passed. I think we were both equally startled when I came face to face with Martha Keller.

"'Father Franck! You were caught too," she said. "I came out for some air. The house is so stifling today."

By now the young priest is sitting forward in his seat, holding his head between his hands. I know what he is about to say next, and now I think I understand what it is that torments him. I feel a crushing disappointment, but wait patiently for him to continue, even though I now see how it will end.

'Common sense told me that this was stupid,' *he said eventually*. 'That I should walk on, regardless of the rain. But then the thunder crashed directly overhead, seeming to shake the foundations of the building, and she grabbed at my arm, drawing herself closer to me.

'I put a protective arm around her, and tried to reassure her.

"'It's only nature," I said. "It's nothing to be frightened of." I cannot make excuses for what happened next, except to say that it had been so long since I'd held another human being so close to me, and all control and reason left me. But just as quickly, the heat of desire was subsumed by the agony of guilt and shame.

'And do you know what she said?' *On his face is a sardonic smile.* "'It's only nature. It's nothing to be frightened of."

'Of course, I was worried about the . . . consequences of our actions. But she told me there could be none.

'She was so calm. "I am already expecting a child, by my husband. It's early and I haven't been to the doctor yet but I'm quite certain. I will tell Gregor when he returns home."

'And I naively thought that I was being spared for my recklessness, and that all I was left with, on the long trudge back to the church, was the revulsion I felt for my own weakness. Afterwards I was convinced that my guilt was visible, like stigmata, and spent hours in private prayer, asking for forgiveness.' *He pauses, lost in his own torment.*

'And after that?' I ask.

'We never alluded to that day,' *he says.* 'Though she stopped coming to the church in the evenings. She seemed more radiant than ever as the pregnancy began to show. It made me wonder if I had simply been a challenge for her to overcome. As time went on, my life returned to some semblance of normality.'

I make to say something to reassure him that one aberration need not damage his vocation, but he silences me with a hand. He hasn't finished.

'Some months later, I was awoken from deep sleep by the persistent ringing of the telephone. It was a little past three a.m. A call at this time of night means only one thing, doesn't it? Though I couldn't bring to mind any parishioners on the cusp of their final journey. Though thick with emotion, the voice I heard was instantly recognisable and I recoiled with shock.

'"Father Franck, you have to come. It's all going wrong. You have to come."

'The Keller residence was on the opposite side of the town and I pedalled for all I was worth through the deserted streets, the cobbles slick with rain and my heart clenched with anxiety. The house was the only one ablaze with lights. It was big and square, a testament to Gregor Keller's wealth and ambition. They had anticipated my arrival, and the door opened immediately. I climbed the steps. Maria, the help, greeted me with hope and expectation — now the Father was here, he would make things right. An agonised howl erupted from somewhere upstairs and as I handed my coat and hat to Maria, Gregor Keller descended the stairs towards me, for once lacking in composure.

'"Come in here, Father, the doctor and midwife are with her now." He took me into his study and offered me a drink. When I declined, he poured a large one for himself.

'We made rather desperate small talk while the cries from upstairs continued, then I asked if he would like to pray. Suddenly there was the loudest cry followed by a dreadful, ominous silence. When Doctor Vengt appeared, he was grim.

'"It's done," was all he said. "Your wife lost a good deal of blood, so she is weak, but with rest and a good diet she will recover. The baby seems robust," he added. "However . . . well, you will see for yourself." He placed a hand on Keller's shoulder. "Father Franck," he said. "Mrs Keller would like to see you now. She wants you to bless the child." He raised his eyebrows, as if this was an extraordinary request. Leaving the room, I lingered for a moment by the door and overheard the doctor.

'"I did suggest to your wife that we deal with things now, but she became rather distressed, and with the priest in the house. . ." I climbed the stairs, preparing for the worst.

'Pale and damp with exhaustion, Martha Keller sat up in bed cradling her baby, while the midwife fussed around her. She was in better spirits than expected.

'"I'm so glad you're here," she smiled. "Isn't she beautiful?" I realised that, until that moment, I had not known if the child was a girl or boy. I stepped closer to look, and wondered how the doctor could be so sure of his conclusions.

'"She is," I agreed.

'I blessed the child and afterwards I walked Fraulein Edelman — the midwife — back to her home.

'"One of my most difficult deliveries," she told me. "I was so afraid that one or both of them might die."

'"The doctor thinks the child should be sent away," I told her.

'She nodded. "Mrs Keller told him that she and her husband will decide when she is feeling stronger. She's a woman who knows her own mind."

'"She does indeed."

'As Isabel grew, the doctor's recommendations became all the more baffling. She perhaps did not progress in the same way as other children, but the only cloud over her young life was the seizures which seemed to occur with increasing regularity. She developed into a delightful toddler, fair-haired, blue-eyed and with chubby, pink cheeks. Her older siblings adored her and it seemed to me that she made the Keller family complete.

'A few months ago, Martha told me it had been suggested that Isabel be sent to a specialist clinic, where she could receive the most up to date therapies. Knowing that she must do the best thing for her little girl, she sought God's guidance and was persuaded. She would miss Isabel enormously, but would be able to visit in a few weeks, when Isabel had settled into her new life.

'On the Sunday after Isabel left for the hospital, Martha's distress was palpable. It was as if some of the light had gone out of her world. When the first visit was due, I called in at the bookseller's and bought a picture book of nursery stories, which I wrapped and took to the Keller house. Maria answered the door.

'"Who is it, Maria?"

'I heard her voice first, and then Martha herself appeared, her eyes raw from crying. I scrutinised her face for bruises, but could see none.

'"Is everything all right?" I asked, and followed her inside, where she handed me a letter.

'"This came yesterday." It was from the hospital and explained that regrettably Isabel had developed an infection, making it necessary to postpone the visit.

'"I'm sorry, you must be disappointed. I know how much you were looking forward to it." I gave her a reassuring smile. "Perhaps by next week—?"

'Her hand shaking, she passed me a second letter.

'"It came today," she said, her voice almost a whisper.

'In the starkest of terms, the letter stated that Isabel Keller was dead. The infection had worsened, and she had succumbed to it. Holy Mother of God. Martha wanted to collect her ashes right away, but her husband had forbidden her to go. With some reluctance, I agreed to help, which meant travelling to the hospital where Isabel had died, a twenty-mile bus ride away. To be honest, I was partly driven by curiosity — I wanted to see for myself. The director was businesslike. The nameplate on his door bore an impressive set of medical credentials. He seemed not the least bit perturbed by my visit, and explained to me the course that Isabel's illness had taken.

'"The speed of it took us all by surprise, Father," he said. "It was an especially virulent form of scarlet fever and Isabel Keller was one of several children we lost at the same time. It was distressing for everyone. I did tell Mr Keller all of this, and he seemed to accept it and understand." He gave me the urn containing a pitifully small quantity of remains. "Perhaps you would like to see more of the hospital?" he offered.

'It was saddening to see so many unfortunates together in the one place, though I would be able to tell Martha that Isabel's last days were spent in a pleasant environment. But when the director showed me out at the end of the visit, I felt . . . unsatisfied, as if it was somehow all too good to be true. I walked back down the long drive a little way behind three people, two men and a woman in hospital uniforms. They were talking and laughing, shaking off the cares of their working day.

'Guided by some inexplicable instinct, I followed them back to the town. As we reached a junction, the woman bid goodbye to her companions and peeled away from the men. In the town centre the men parted company, too — one making off along a side street, while the other went into a bar. I followed him inside, wrapping my scarf over my collar. He was at the bar paying for beer and a shot of something stronger, which he took to an empty corner of the room. The bar was a lively place, but the man avoided eye contact and ignored the banter. I ordered a beer and took it to an adjacent table. The young man emptied both glasses quickly and was soon ordering more. As he returned to his seat and passed my table, I raised my glass to him. His eyes fleetingly met mine, before he returned to his seat and went back to staring sightlessly in front of him.

'"You work at the hospital," I said, raising my voice a little.

'"How do you know that?" He was instantly on his guard.

'"I was visiting. I left at the same time you did." I loosened my scarf so that he would see my collar, knowing it would either reassure him or frighten him off. "It must be challenging work that you do."

'"If that's what you want to call it," he said. He was already halfway through his second beer.

'"Can I get you another?" After the smallest hesitation, he acquiesced and, returning with the drinks, I joined him. He didn't object.

'"Are you a Jesuit?" he asked.

'I shook my head. "Roman. And you?"

'He shook his head. "Were you at the hospital to pray for those poor souls?"

'"I knew a patient there, a child. She died."

'The combination of the drink and perhaps the implicit trust in a man of the cloth was loosening his tongue.

'"They'll all die," he said, contemptuously. "One by one."

'"Her name was Isabel Keller. Did you know her?"

'"We're not told their names," he said, staring into space. "They say that would make it harder."

'"Oh?" My heart began beating a little faster and I sipped my beer, my mouth suddenly dry.

'He looked at me sympathetically.

'"What were you told, Father?" he said. "That it's a wonderful hospital, with the latest up to date treatments, that the child benefited from the most modern interventions?" He sneered. "It's all lies. The child was brought here to die, along with all the others like her. I should know — we're the ones who carry out their sentences, my two colleagues and me. Everyone in the town here knows. They pretend not to, but they do." For the first time, he let his eyes sweep around the room. "That's why no one comes near me. But what frightens them most is that they're glad that it's done, and even more glad that it isn't them who has to do it, or has to live with it." He told me a little bit more about his job, about what he did every day at the hospital, and revulsion made my skin crawl and my stomach churn.

'"So," he said finally, swigging back what remained of his schnapps and wiping a hand across his mouth. "Ask your God to forgive me that."

'Placing his glass down on the table, he got up and lurched out of the bar before I could think of a rejoinder. Many pairs of eyes watched him go, I noticed, though no one spoke a word. After his departure, I drank a couple more beers to try and quell the turmoil inside me. I was the worse for wear when I returned late that night on the bus.'

* * *

A flicker of lightning illuminates the room.

'That was more than a week ago,' he tells me. 'I still have Isabel Keller's ashes — if that's what they really are. But how can I even face Martha Keller now that I know what goes on at that place? How can I stand in the pulpit and preach about a merciful God?' His eyes blaze at me. 'Do you know how it works, what they do to those children? In the early days, they were simply given an overdose of medication. The method was favoured over slow starvation as being more humane. But that was the old way. What they have now is much more efficient — a kind of a holding room into which noxious gas is introduced. It's over in minutes. The staff who administer this are paid handsomely for their work, and after every fifty deaths, they celebrate. They have a party with wine that Herr Director brings in specially, to toast their contribution to this great country of ours.'

I am stricken with shame and he sees it on my face.

'You know, don't you?' he says. 'You know all this and yet you say and do nothing.'

261

And I have no answer, none that would satisfy him. I could tell him that until now, I've had only hearsay and testimony within the seal of the confessional. I could fall back on the Fulda agreement, citing the fragility of our Church's relationship with the state. But he is right, it is not enough. The time for prevarication is over.

'Tell me,' I say, as I walk with him to the door, 'why are you so affected by this child? Martha Keller is one of your flock, but why do all this for her?' He says nothing. 'Is it because on that afternoon in the barn, she lied to you? Is it because you knew, from the night she was born, that Isabel Keller was your child?'

His silence is my answer.

* * *

When the young priest arrived, the storm had yet to break. Now, it seems like a portent. Shortly after his departure, at around six, when the heat and airlessness are suffocating, an enormous crack shakes the foundations of the Bishop's Palace. Clemens von Galen goes to the window and is dazzled by lightning that splits the sky in two, illuminating the cobbled streets that are soon slick with rain. Booming thunder rumbles all around while he grapples with what he has just been told. In his head now is the proof with which he'd hoped he would never be presented, in words so plain that he can, in good conscience, no longer ignore it. The young priest was right, for too long the Church had stood by and done nothing, or, even worse, looked the other way. Now, it is time to act. Rain batters the leaded windows as the storm rages. In this increasingly chaotic world, his would always be a difficult path to tread. He has recently been made aware of the nickname that is being attributed to him locally, and it seems now as if God Himself is challenging it through the elements: Do you deserve it, this title that has been bestowed? Are you a lion or merely a weak and feeble lamb? Closing the window and turning away from the wild night, the bishop sits down at his desk to compose the most significant sermon of his life.

* * *

'Few people realise that what ended in Holocaust began with the clandestine murder of sick and disabled children,' said Father Aidan, softly. 'It began in such an insignificant way, with the death of one child, the Knauer child. Unable to cope with her afflictions, her parents requested help and in doing so, played into the hands of those in authority who were already cognisant of the economic benefits of "mercy killing".'

'Now I get why Rita chose me,' I said. 'She must have thought I knew. But I'm ashamed to say that I didn't.'

'What terrifies Rita is that a resurgence of such ideas now is so much more dangerous because the force of science somehow legitimises them.'

'She thought history was about to repeat itself.'

'Rita hoped to persuade the present priest to intervene. She thought that citing von Galen to him would strengthen her argument and persuade him of his duty. But von Galen was an extraordinary man. It's a great deal to live up to.'

'Rita thought that Father Adrian could influence policy by preaching from the pulpit?' It seemed unlikely.

'Oh no.' Father Aidan shook his head regretfully. 'We cannot delude ourselves that the Church commands the same authority it did in von Galen's day. Father Adriano wields much more direct power, in this case, through his role on the ethics committee.'

Of course. 'He's the clerical representative,' I said.

'Rita saw him at the hospital one day and realised why he was there,' said Father Aidan.

'But his calling must surely mean he is pro-life, and therefore biased in his views.'

'That may be true,' admitted the old man. 'But he is there to present the theological arguments, which the committee use to inform their decisions. When she first asked for his help, Father Adrian told Rita that to speak out would compromise him. It is a rarefied existence in this place, but I am not entirely disengaged from the wider world. Personal sacrifice doesn't seem to count for much anymore.'

'It did for Rita,' I said. 'She paid with her life.'

His eyes, behind the thick lenses, grew huge. 'Rita is dead?'

'I'm afraid so.'

'Oh no, no . . .' For the first time, the old priest looked defeated.

'The official line is that she took her own life,' I said. 'But Rita's daughter has never believed that and now I no longer do either.'

Father Aidan hung his head. 'I knew what Rita was trying to do would carry risks,' he said, his voice barely audible. 'I should have tried to warn her.'

'Did you send her flowers?'

'I asked one of the care staff to do it for me. I was concerned for her. I could do nothing practical to help, but I wanted to remind her that she was not alone.'

CHAPTER FORTY-EIGHT

When the phone rang, it took me a couple of seconds to realise that the voice at the other end was Stefan Greaves.

'Rita Todd didn't take her own life,' he said. 'I think someone wanted to silence her.'

I found myself unable to speak.

'Hello?' he said. 'Are you still there?'

'You're saying what happened to her was deliberate?'

'When we asked Guy Leonard about giving Rita Warren-Byrne's address he said, "I had no choice". I thought he meant that Rita had strong-armed it from him because she wanted to plead her case regarding her disciplinary hearing, maybe even get Warren-Byrne to drop the allegations. But what if it was the other way around? Rita was becoming a thorn in the side of the hospital management. What if Warren-Byrne used Guy Leonard to lure Rita to her home? The bait might have been a promise to discuss Rita's concerns, but Warren-Byrne had other plans for Rita.'

'You think her death was premeditated? Jesus, that's a bit far-fetched, isn't it?' I said, taken aback by the notion. But as I turned things over in my mind, I couldn't dismiss it.

'It's a coincidence that Warren-Byrne's property backs onto the river in which Rita drowned, though, isn't it?' Greaves pressed.

'But what was the motive?' I asked.

'Rita was about to cause big trouble for the ethics committee,' he said. 'According to her friend Delores, she deliberately provoked the disciplinary action because she wanted to go to a tribunal. She wanted to be able to stand up in a public forum to shine a light on some dubious policy changes that were being introduced to her department — something that would have far-reaching consequences. She was planning to whistle-blow.'

'What's brought this on?' I was curious.

He replied by filling me in on what he and Plum had learned in the last couple of hours. I could hear the effort as he strove to articulate clearly and, in the absence of visual clues, I had to concentrate hard.

When he came to the end, I didn't know what to say. I wondered if he realised how crazy it sounded. And yet . . . Hairs stirred on the back of my neck. It felt like we were on the brink of something.

'There's something funny going on at our place too.' I said. 'And now I'm wondering if it isn't all part of the same thing.'

'What's that?' he asked.

'You'll have noticed, until now, a conspicuous lack of progress on your mugging?'

'There were no witnesses,' he pointed out.

'As far as we know,' I said. 'But it's more than that. It's been tactical, too.'

'How's that?'

'Your wallet and phone weren't stolen,' I said. 'I found them in Denny Sutton's locker. Your watch turned up on Liam Archer. I'm still trying to figure that one out.'

The other end of the line went quiet. And after a pause that seemed to go on for minutes, I told him about the rest of the haul I'd found. Once I'd started, the rest just poured out.

'I've been struggling to understand why these crimes are significant — what the common factor is. Then I found out that Jodie Marshall, another of the victims, was visually impaired, and Lloyd Jones was on the autistic spectrum. All these victims had a disability of some kind. According to Kevin Booth — Denny's ex-partner — there's been a kind of unofficial operation going on for years, Operation Beagle. There has been a whole spate of crimes, including homicides, against those he quoted as being called "undesirables". Your attack was the latest. None of these incidents has been properly investigated, under orders from above. And now the two people who knew about the scheme are dead. Denny was one and the other, Kevin Booth, was killed in a gas explosion a couple of days ago. Bowers blamed Booth's so-called accident on his alcoholism, but I met the man ten days ago. He might have been an alcoholic when he left Charnford, but he's been dry since then.'

We both took a moment, then, to think about what all this meant.

'If this is a coordinated effort, then it's huge,' said Greaves, putting my thoughts into words. 'What's Matthew Westfield been up to during this visit?' he asked.

'The usual,' I said, wondering where this was going. 'He's spent some time here at the nick discussing crime figures, then a school, an old people's home, the hospital and lunch with councillors.'

'But why, and why now?' he persisted.

'Believe me, I've been racking my brains to work that out too,' I said.

'You think he knows about what's been going on?'

'Maybe it's more than that,' I said, the thought coming into my head. 'What if he's behind all of this somehow? Everyone's been wondering when and how he'll make his re-entry into politics, and perhaps this is it.'

He seemed to buy it. 'Machiavelli on the job again, but in a whole new arena,' he said.

'Christ, I've been thick,' I said in sudden realisation. 'Westfield mentioned it. I was telling him what a good place Charnford is to live, and he said we needed to "sprinkle some of the magic" across the rest of the country. He actually told me that we could make Britain a world power again. He's using this town as some kind of template for what could be rolled out to the rest of the country.'

'It fits, doesn't it?' said Greaves. 'He's a great advocate of assisted dying, which is only a step away from mercy killing.' He snorted. 'And just look at him — how much more fucking Aryan can you get? That photo you sent me, it was some kind of student group, wasn't it?'

Tucking the phone under my chin, I grabbed the mouse and woke up the computer.

'Hang on, let me find it again.'

It took me minutes to locate it and to track down the original caption. But when I did, it suddenly made sense.

'OK,' I said, at last. 'It's the members of something called . . . Shit. Stronger Britain. Ever heard of it?'

'No,' said Greaves. 'But I've a feeling it's about to have a comeback.'

'Sharon Petrowlski told me that Bowers' appointment was sudden and unexpected.'

'Cate said the same about Warren-Byrne. They've wangled their way into positions of power in this town, and Westfield is pulling the strings. He's been getting his cronies to test out these approaches here ahead of getting into power nationally, where he can inflict them on the whole country.' He tailed off. 'Oh God, how many more are a part of this? If we're right about this, we need to get it out into the open. People have died for it, and might continue to die.'

'But we'll need evidence,' I said, stating what was obvious. 'Westfield is a powerful man, as are the people working for him. I know Bowers will have covered his back. Two key witnesses are dead and all I've got is a bag of victims' belongings. If I produce them, it will be Booth's and Denny's names that are dragged through the mud, and that'll only be if everyone can stop laughing for long enough.'

He sounded dejected. 'We're struggling to even get hold of any data from the hospital to support Rita's concerns, let alone prove them,' he said. 'A week or so before she died, Rita sent a text to her friend Delores, saying, "I'm right, it's pure strategy." It puzzled me. I mean, why "pure strategy"? Why not just say, "It's a strategy"?'

'She could have meant it's "only" a strategy or "simply" a strategy at this point,' I pointed out.

'That's what I thought,' he conceded. 'But what if she was let down by the punctuation? What if Rita wasn't just talking about any old strategy but had stumbled on some kind of plan — the Pure strategy.'

'That suggests something tangible, something in writing,' I said. 'Bowers may have some kind of documentation. I caught him reading some report that he obviously didn't want me to see. Had a picture of a sailing ship on the front.'

'What was that operational name you mentioned?' he asked.

'Beagle,' I told him. 'Bowers has got a dog. I mean, I don't know why they use these fucking stupid . . .'

'This is not named after his dog,' he scoffed, cutting me off. 'HMS Beagle *was the ship sailed by Charles Darwin. Survival of the fittest and all that.*' He let me absorb that morsel. 'Is there any way you can get hold of this report?' he asked.

'It'll be in Bowers' desk drawer, which will be locked, as will his office. I guess I could try getting in there.'

'And if you're caught?'

'I'd probably lose my job.'

'Then I think we should hold off on that for now. It can't be the only copy. If Westfield's driving the whole project, he'll have it, surely?'

'The man travels light,' I said. 'Apart from the suitcase in his hotel room, all he takes with him to meetings is a smartphone — and he keeps that pretty close. He's never asked me to carry anything for him. And we're running out of options,' I added. 'Westfield leaves tomorrow. The main thing left is some reception at a place called Mawton Manor, which Bowers called a "mopping up exercise".'

'Mawton Manor? That's Ashley Curzon's place. Shit, I'll bet he's in on it too. It'd be right up his street.'

'The event's swathed in more secrecy than a Lodge meeting.'

A beat of a pause. 'You're a . . . ?'

'Not a chance, mate. But whatever the purpose, it sounds like it's the big finale. Strictly invitation only and Westfield's opportunity to schmooze anyone he might have wanted to meet but hasn't already. Bowers was practically wetting himself with excitement over it. You know this Curzon guy?'

'It's a long story,' he said. 'He was the man we prosecuted for the possible manslaughter of a Syrian refugee baby. Also conveniently known for his right-of-centre beliefs. I wonder if Keeley would help.' He was thinking aloud, but all the same, I balked at the suggestion.

'It's a lot to ask,' I said. 'She's already doing me a massive favour.'

'She could always say no.'

He was right. It was worth a punt. 'How about I pick you up on the way over to her place — in about an hour?'

'Perfect,' he said. 'And if it confirms what we think?'

'We could always see if someone in the press is interested in doing some research,' I said. 'Don't know any friendly hacks, do you?'

269

'Actually, I do,' said Greaves. 'I know just the man.' He paused. 'You said "until now".'

'Sorry?'

'You said there was a lack of progress on my case "until now". Has something changed?'

'It just might have,' I said. 'I'll fill you in when I see you.'

CHAPTER FORTY-NINE

Keeley came to the door in a T-shirt and leggings, and as she leaned on the frame, my gaze couldn't help but linger on the fine red marks around her wrists.

'Did you have a nice time last night?'

'I'm sorry, does that concern you?' she said.

'Did he do that?' I asked, even though it was none of my business.

Keeley just looked at me. 'He has particular tastes, OK? What do you want, measurements, timing, positional diagrams? It's nothing I haven't done before. Grow up, Stefan. What did you want, anyway?'

'We are concerned about what Matthew Westfield might be doing here.' I said. 'Can we come in?'

Once inside, Fraser told her what we'd found out and where our thinking was taking us.

'Are you joking? You're trying to compare him with . . . ?'

'Of course not,' I said. 'But this is serious. Whatever this master plan is, people are being killed for it.'

'You don't know that.'

'Actually, I'm pretty sure that we do,' said Fraser.

She seemed to recognise the gravity of what we were saying. 'What do you want me to do?'

'We need proof. And that means getting access to his smartphone or his briefcase. You're his date for tonight. I imagine you'll be going back to his hotel with him, too?'

'Sure, I'll just ask him! Mind if I just have a skim through your emails before we get down to business?'

'Did he sleep last night?'

'Not while I was there. We did . . . what we did, and then I left.'

'You could drug him,' I suggested, with a thrill.

'How old are you two, ten?' she snapped. 'He might just notice that and I'd end up getting arrested. *You* should know better, Constable Fraser.'

Fraser raised his hands in defence. 'Not my idea.'

'Could you distract him?' I persisted.

'Well, I would hope so,' she said.

'No, I mean enough to let Fraser get in and take a look? If you could take him down to the hotel bar or something . . .'

'I don't see that working. He wants to keep it discreet. Anyway, it'll be late, and we'll have already spent the evening eating and drinking. He won't want to waste any more of my time on that. Even if we did leave the room, he'd take his phone with him, wouldn't he?'

Fraser was gloomy.

'Maybe,' I said, my frustration growing. 'But at least if we could catch a hint of something in his emails, we'd know for sure that we were onto something.'

'I thought you were sure.' Keeley ran her tongue over her teeth in thought. 'I suppose I could give him something that would disturb his digestion,' she said. 'Make it seem as if he'd eaten something that disagreed with him.'

'You can do that?'

'A girl I knew used it if she ever had a date with a guy she didn't really want to sleep with. She swore by it. She'd slip it into his drink at dinner and by the time they'd get back to the hotel, he'd be bent over double and have to spend all night in the bathroom. And there was no comeback — as it were.'

'Charming,' I said. And enterprising. 'It might do the trick, though, get him out of the room, leaving his things behind. I don't suppose he'd take his phone into the bathroom with him.'

'We don't know that,' said Keeley.

'Look,' I said. 'We wouldn't be asking you to do this unless we were desperate.' I didn't like to point out the biggest flaw in the plan. Even if we got hold of his smartphone, it would more than likely be password-protected — then what? We were hardly MI5 and a bit short on handy gadgets to help us download the contents. I kept this to myself, though, and we left Keeley to get ready.

CHAPTER FIFTY

I drove Greaves back to his flat, an atmosphere of despondency in the car. I wondered if he had the same doubts as I did about Keeley's plan.

Fulford Road was quiet when I got back. Most people had clocked off for the day and I had to squeeze past Gloria and her cleaning trolley in the corridor. I flopped down in my chair and switched on the PC, where I was absently staring at the screen as it went through the booting-up process when an idea surfaced. Gloria.

The next hour or so was agonising, as I pretended to work at the computer, monitoring the cleaner's progress as she gathered up empty sandwich packs and coffee beakers, wiped over surfaces and emptied bins. Finally, she wheeled her trolley towards the lift, which would take her up to the first floor.

In that time, I had located an empty manila folder, which I marked with a bold CONFIDENTIAL. *Tucking it under my arm, I followed her up. A glance out of the window at the car park had already told me that Bowers had left for the day, and when I got upstairs it appeared that Gloria was — as I'd hoped — the only human presence there. In full view, I knocked on Bowers' door. I waited a minute or so and knocked again, then did a bit of sighing and pacing, tapping the folder on my thigh to convey, I hoped, my frustration. Gloria was, by now, letting herself into one of the neighbouring offices and glanced up, catching my eye.*

'I can't believe I've missed him,' I said with a "just my luck" shake of the head. I held up the file. 'I was meant to have left this in his office. I'll get a bollocking tomorrow.' I eyed the chain loaded with keys around her waist. 'I don't suppose you could . . . Just for a couple of seconds . . . ?'

Even though there was clearly no one else around, Gloria checked behind her, and with a weary smile that suggested this wasn't the first time she'd had this kind of request, she shuffled along and unlocked the door.

'Two seconds,' she repeated, sternly, at which point the limitations of my venture became clear. However, having unlocked the door, Gloria returned to her work and as I moved across to Bowers' desk, I heard the door to the office next door being opened. Ideally, of course, the Beagle report would have been there on the desk or sitting at the top of the in-tray waiting for me. But the desk was immaculately tidy. I tried the first of the three desk drawers. It was locked. The second slid open easily, but contained only the usual office paraphernalia: pens, pencils, stapler, hole punch. The third drawer seemed empty, but as I closed it, something inside slid a couple of inches. Reaching to the back, I found a plastic bag containing a number of what looked like unused mobile phones and a corresponding number of unused SIM cards, their packaging intact. Burner phones. Why the hell did Bowers need these?

A door closed out in the corridor. I was running out of time. Heart pumping, I shoved the bag back in the drawer, and that's when I noticed what I first took to be a tiny scrap of paper on the floor by the leg of the desk. I bent and picked it up, slipping it into my pocket, and was practically running for the door when Gloria reappeared.

'Thanks, Gloria, you're one in a million,' I huffed, brushing past her and back out into the corridor. It wasn't until I was back at my desk that I realised I was still carrying the folder. I doubted she'd been fooled by the ruse in any case, but it was too late now. I'd have to trust her discretion.

The SIM card was burning a hole in my pocket. My phone was fiddly and my hands trembled as I rushed to take the back off, remove the SIM and replace it with the one from Bowers' office. All the risk had been worthwhile — it only took seconds for me to recognise the contents of Denny Sutton's phone. Many of the contact names were familiar to

275

me, but here and there were sets of initials, most of them meaningless to me. One sprang out at me, though: TC. I touched "Call". After several rings, voicemail cut in, short and to the point:

"You're through to Top Cat. Leave a message." Top Cat — Tyler Curzon.

Out of interest, I looked at the call history. There hadn't been many interactions between them, but I did note that the last call Denny had received from Curzon was on the evening of Friday 4 March, shortly before Stefan Greaves was mugged. It made me feel sick. I tried to work out if this was progress. This indisputably proved a link between Denny and Tyler Curzon, and further analysis could well confirm that it was Curzon who was tipping Denny off about the other Beagle crimes. That I'd found the SIM in Bowers' office was dodgy to start off with, but even more so given that Bowers had quizzed me about the whereabouts of Denny's phone. I felt sure that a forensic analysis would implicate more than just Denny and Curzon, so ripping out my phone battery again, I slid out the SIM and tucked it into my wallet for safekeeping.

Then, my heart still pumping hard, I called Stefan Greaves and told him what I'd found and — more pressingly — not found.

'I don't know what else we can do.'

'There's always my press contact,' he said. 'I could try and convince him that we're onto something?'

'Worth a shot,' I said, though my expectations were low. There wasn't much more I could do at this stage. Besides, it was coming up to the time I was due to collect Keeley.

276

CHAPTER FIFTY-ONE

I went round to Laura and Simon's house feeling less than certain that what I was about to say would be taken seriously. It was Simon who came to the door.

'Sorry, Laura's out with Grace . . .' he began.

'That's all right, it's you I want to see,' I said, and already his curiosity was piqued.

Bemused, he took me through to his office and we sat in the confined space while I tried my best to articulate my involvement with Rita Todd and what I thought had happened to her, followed by what Fraser had told me. Simon, with the true open-mindedness of a journalist, listened patiently and without judgement, but I had to admit that even to my ears it sounded fantastical. After all, this was Charnford we were talking about, a bog-standard town in Middle England. The frown between Simon's brows as I came to the end was no great surprise. His response, nevertheless, was measured.

'If what you're saying is true then it's a hell of a story,' he said. 'But even you know what's missing, don't you?'

'Evidence,' I said, with a sigh. It was what had let us down with Mr Asif and it had always been going to let me down now.

'Without it, all you've got is hearsay and speculation,' said Simon. 'I can't print that, I'm afraid.'

I was in no position to disagree.

'One of the things that interests me most here is that Westfield is flying under the radar,' he continued. 'Normally, a visit by someone of his profile, everyone would want it on the front page — for him and for Charnford. So why have we been cut out of it? Maybe I'll make some discreet enquiries.'

By which time, we both knew, Westfield would have departed, and it would be too late.

* * *

When she came to the door, Keeley took my breath away.

'You look terrific,' I said, truthfully. 'Did you manage to get . . . everything you need?'

She tapped her clutch bag.

'All in here,' she said. 'But I'm not promising anything. Do you understand?'

'Of course.'

We drove to Westfield's hotel. Watching him walk out of the hotel lobby, his white-blond hair slicked back and navy suit in perfect accord with his dazzlingly blue eyes, I wanted to leap out and throw him to the ground. As he got in the car, he looked from one to the other of us and turned on the smile that by now made me feel slightly queasy.

'I believe you two already know each other,' he said.

'Yes, sir.'

'I'm counting on your discretion, Mick,' Westfield said, putting a hand on my shoulder, though he didn't really sound as if he cared. 'Now to Mawton Manor. Do you know it?'

'Ashley Curzon's place,' I said, trying to sound as if I knew more than I did.

'So I understand. Finally, a chance to relax a bit and switch off the politician in me. Then I can get back to London and start to change the world.'

'Sounds ambitious,' I said.

He laughed. 'Hardly. But I've been offered what sounds like an interesting job. Sorry, I can't divulge any details,' he added, in anticipation. 'But I guess you'll hear about it in the fullness of time.'

My gaze met Keeley's in the rear-view mirror. What kind of job? As I dropped them off at the Palladian pile that was Ashley Curzon's home, I made a mental inventory of the other cars parked on the drive, including Superintendent Bowers'. The one thing they all told me was that there was a shedload of money here tonight. I made a note of the other licence plate numbers with the intention of running them through ANPR at the next opportunity. Then, parking up, I decided to take a stroll around the outside of the building to get a sense of the scale of the place.

CHAPTER FIFTY-TWO

Looking back on the meeting with Simon as I arrived home, I felt deflated. It would be about now that Fraser was delivering Westfield to Mawton Manor along with Keeley. What wouldn't I give to be a fly on that wall tonight? I tried to go over what Fraser and I had learned, tried to apply a rational analysis. Now I'd had time to really think it through, it seemed ludicrous. It was little wonder that Simon had reacted in the way that he had. So when the rap on my front door came a little later, it was a puzzle. Had Simon decided the story was worth chasing after all? I hoped so. Drawing up a plan of action — even if it went nowhere — might help to subdue the thoughts doing endless circuits of my brain. The astonishment must have been all over my face when I opened the door and found Guy Leonard standing in the hallway, a bottle of wine grasped in one hand.

'Peace offering,' he said. 'I've no wish to interrupt your Friday evening, but I feel we didn't get off to the best of starts. I was an arse. It's been happening a lot lately, as my wife's frequently pointed out. Cate is a lovely woman and a good friend, so I would like to make reparation.'

O-kay . . .

'And if you'll allow me the opportunity,' he went on, 'I'd also like to enlighten you about Rita Todd, also someone I am — was — fond of. I want to set the record straight regarding our relationship.'

This I had to hear. Now, no doubt, the failings of my overactive imagination would be revealed. I stepped back to let him in.

'Are you all right?' he asked, as he brushed past me and I followed him into the kitchen. 'You look a bit peaky.' Aware that he must have been staring, he held up the bottle. 'You do drink this stuff?'

I got out some glasses and he poured us each a generous measure, before we went to sit in the lounge.

'Cheers,' he said, sincerely. 'Here's to a fresh start.'

'Cheers.' I took a sizeable gulp. I'm no connoisseur, but I knew quality when I tasted it, enjoying the complex flavours which lingered on the palate. He'd overfilled my glass, though, and as I went to place it on the coffee table, an unexpected spasm threw a few drops onto the carpet.

'Whoops.' He looked long and hard at my twitching hand. 'I understand Cate mentioned surgery to you,' he said, lightly. 'Not my place to meddle, of course, but it might be worth serious thought.'

The flat was beginning to feel unbearably warm. It had been milder today and I'd meant to turn down the thermostat. I drank some more wine and held my tongue.

'I mean, I'm sure you know all this, but as you get older, your muscles will stiffen and you'll be in more pain. It's quite possible that surgery would help.' He took my stony silence as resistance. 'It might at least be worth having an assessment to see if it would be a suitable treatment. It would give you options.'

Leonard's face drifted out of focus. God, I hoped I wasn't about to have another seizure. Talk about bad timing. I took a deep breath to try and clear my head.

'Anyway, I digress,' he went on. 'We're here to talk about Rita. Rita . . .' He leaned forward in his seat. 'I'm happy to tell you all I know, but I'm afraid there's one con-dition. Rita was party to some very privileged information.'

'OK.' I was struggling to concentrate on what he was saying.

'In order to share this with you, I have to ask you to sign a simple non-disclosure agreement.'

A printed sheet of paper had appeared on the coffee table in front of me, and he brandished a pen.

'Like Delores,' I said, my tongue suddenly rubbery and slow.

He looked surprised. 'Yes. Like Delores. Would you mind?'

I wasn't at all sure, but the room had started moving away from me, curling into a long tunnel. Partly to anchor myself in the fast distorting space, I took the pen from him. Its grip was reassuringly tangible, something quite literally to hold on to. He pointed to a place on the paper, and I leaned forward to scrawl my name.

'Splendid,' he said. 'Now. Rita.'

But as I sat back to listen, Guy Leonard's face began to melt, finally vanishing behind an explosion of silent fireworks.

CHAPTER FIFTY-THREE

The circuit of Ashley Curzon's manor took me a leisurely fifteen min-
utes. Petrowlski had told me he'd picked up the property some years ago
at a knock-down price because of the state it was in. Less ostentatious
than I'd anticipated, it was built in a truncated U shape, with perhaps
six or eight rooms on each of the two levels, making it easy to navigate.
Apart from those at the front of the house where the reception was being
held, these were all in darkness and all I could make out inside were
the static shadows of the furniture. Tacked onto the end of one wing,
at right angles and almost completing the square, was a low timber-clad
construction. Sliding picture windows along each side opened onto the
landscaped gardens, and had views over the surrounding countryside.
An aquamarine, backlit rectangle in the floor cast an eerie glow over
the room. Ashley Curzon had an indoor swimming pool, lucky bugger.

At the far end, where the pool room linked to the house, was a
kind of indoor patio, with loungers and other garden furniture among
exotic pot plants and complete with what looked like a bar. At the
opposite end, an object the size of an armchair was covered with a sheet.
If that was the barbecue, it was modest for the otherwise upmarket
amenities.

Disappointed with my findings, I returned to the car and sat
weighing up the relative merits of sitting and freezing my arse off out
here for the next few hours or heading back to the nice warm station,

283

where I could at least be doing something useful. It crossed my mind that I could have another crack at Bowers' office — no danger of him turning up there. But then I realised that he'd have brought anything pertaining to Operation Beagle with him here tonight. The chance of anything useful happening here was pretty small and Keeley would be in it for the long haul, so I turned the key in the ignition and was just checking over my shoulder to reverse into a three-point turn when I spotted another vehicle making its way towards the parking area. It stood out from all the other cars in terms of both age and condition, and when the driver emerged, I recognised her. I saw her gaze sweep over the assorted cars, forcing a hesitation, so I rolled down my window and called out to her.

'Hey, what are you doing here?'

Her relief at seeing me was touching. She hurried over and got into the passenger seat beside me.

'They told me at the station that this is where you were. But I thought you must be inside,' she said.

'What is it?'

'I've just been round to Stefan's place, but he's not there. He'd promised to come out with me tonight. We were supposed to meet in the market square, but he didn't turn up and he didn't let me know he wasn't coming, which isn't like him at all, he would always let me know. And now I'm thinking, what if he's been beaten up again and left for dead in some alleyway somewhere . . .' She stopped to draw breath.

'Woah, steady on. Let's backtrack a bit. What makes you think he might have come to harm? How do you know he hasn't just made other plans and — I don't know — forgotten to tell you?'

'Because he wouldn't do that. He promised to come with me.'

'With you where?'

'The candlelight vigil for the homeless, in Charnford.'

'That's very noble.'

'It's what you do for friends.'

'You were friends with the rough sleepers?'

'Some of them, yes.' Her tone was defensive, belligerent. 'We were in the care system together: me, Tommo, Liam and that. I was lucky. I came out of it all right, but not everyone does and it's not always their fault.'

284

'You knew Liam Archer?' I said.

She nodded. 'I mean, I'm sorry Liam killed your mate and all that, but he was harmless. He wouldn't have done it unless someone put him up to it.'

'I was told it was the voices in his head.'

She pulled a face. 'Liam didn't hear voices. He wasn't the smartest and he was easily led, but that was all. He just always wanted to be part of the gang.'

'What gang?'

'I don't know now. When we were at school it was Bostwick and Sully and all that crowd — until he stopped coming to school.'

'Why?'

'Dunno. He just stopped. And no one seemed that bothered.'

What Plum had just said was significant, but my thought process was interrupted by my mobile buzzing into life. It was Keeley.

'Sorry, I need to get this.' Plum made to get out of the car, but I signalled to her to stay.

'Where are you?' asked Keeley.

'I'm outside, why?'

'Westfield's gone off somewhere. A guy who looked like staff came and got him. Your boss and Ashley Curzon have also disappeared and there was a woman who was all over Westfield when we got here, and I can't see her anywhere now.'

Apart from Plum's old banger, nothing had moved out of the car park so they couldn't have gone far.

Before doing anything else, I put a call through to Sharon Petrowlski and asked her to call round to Stefan Greaves' flat, though I felt sure there'd be nothing to find.

'And you stay right here,' I told Plum. Then I got out of the car and headed for the hall.

I showed my ID at the door. 'I'm Matthew Westfield's driver,' I said. 'I'm burstin' for a piss, do you mind?'

As I'd hoped, he let me in. Now I just had to find them. Inside, it was clear where the official action was taking place. Crossing the chandeliered vestibule, I came to double doors that opened onto a room big enough to be called a ballroom. I saw men in black tie and women in dresses of all colours and levels of sophistication, but no one whose face

285

I immediately recognised. In one corner a petite, pretty woman with a strident voice seemed to be holding court with half a dozen or so couples. Flunkeys circulated, balancing trays of champagne flutes and canapés. Nodding at one confidently, as if I was meant to be there, I scanned the room until I saw Keeley. She was involved in what looked like a less than riveting conversation with a short, red-faced man. I willed her to glance in my direction, which eventually she did. Her eyes met mine and, making her apologies, she hurried over. Her kiss on the cheek took me aback, until I realised this was role-play. Over her shoulder, the red-faced man stared regretfully into his drink.

'Any idea where Westfield's gone?' I asked, my voice low.

'Sorry, your guess is as good as mine,' said Keeley. 'I tried telling one of the waiters I needed to speak to him, but was told he would be back in due course. I haven't had the chance to spike his drink yet.'

'Don't worry about it,' I said. 'It was a stupid idea anyway. Who's the woman in the corner?'

'Our hostess, you mean? That's Ashley Curzon's wife — Tamara, I think someone said. Seems that her husband has abandoned her too.'

'And I don't see my gaffer anywhere. Ah well, I came in on the pretext of using the loo, so looks as if I'll just have to get lost along the way, doesn't it? You OK?'

She rolled her eyes. 'Apart from the slow death by boredom? I'll survive.'

Before leaving the room, I approached the waiter who was standing in the doorway and seemed to be directing the others.

'I wanted to speak to Matthew Westfield this evening,' I said. 'When's he due to arrive?'

'He's already here, sir,' the waiter said. 'He's been temporarily called away, but he'll be back shortly.'

'Ah,' I nodded acceptance. 'And sorry, where's the gents'?' He gestured right behind me to where a computer-printed notice with a giant arrow pointing along a hallway was stuck to the wall. 'Great. Thanks.' Under his scrutiny I was forced to head in that direction, but as I set off, there came a crash from inside the room and I saw Keeley's hand fly to her mouth as she stooped to attend to the glass she'd just dropped. The doorman went to help, so, seizing my chance, I headed off in the opposite direction to the toilets, along a wood-panelled corridor.

I don't know what I'd hoped for, really — perhaps a door left conveniently ajar so that I could listen in unnoticed. It wasn't to be. The three doors along here were all firmly closed. I had to resort to pressing my ear against each to see if I could catch even the faintest murmur of conversation. At the third I got my break, sort of, when I saw the unmistakable sliver of light along the base of the door. I heard a bark of laughter from within, but any hope that I would be able to overhear the conversation was stymied. The solid oak door was shut. I'd have to try a different strategy. Retracing my steps to the lobby, I went out again into the cold. This time it was easy enough to find the room where the action was — I simply looked for the lights. Edging up to the uncurtained windows, I peered into what looked like a library or study, with book-lined walls and leather Chesterfields. Ashley Curzon was at a drinks table, pouring and passing round glasses, while the others were standing around as if waiting for something. It was now or never.

I was about to make myself visible when I was grabbed from behind and a hand covered my mouth, stifling my instinctive cry. Off balance, I felt myself dragged back from the windows by someone strong, and I fought and twisted, trying to get a glimpse of my assailant. Turning, I lunged at him and we fell on the dewy grass, wrestling in eerie silence, until I managed to gain the advantage and get him pinned on his back. I expected to see one of the minions from inside, but I'd never seen this man before.

'Go easy,' he whispered furiously, his hands raised in defence. 'We're on the same side!' I glanced back at the house, but our commotion didn't seem to have attracted any attention from inside the room.

Instead, what we did hear were tyres on gravel, driving fast. Headlight beams swept across us as the vehicle skidded to an abrupt halt. I flattened myself to the ground, keeping stock still, and my captive did the same. I hoped Plum had been sensible and ducked out of sight. The headlights blacked out and we heard voices alongside some unidentifiable grunting and car doors slamming. Gradually the sounds faded as the car's occupants entered the hall.

'Who the fuck are you?' I whispered at the man beside me.

'Simon Montgomery. Stefan Greaves is a mate. I'm a journalist, so he tipped me off that Matthew Westfield was here. You must be Mick Fraser? Pleased to meet you.'

The threat over, I released my grip, but ignored the hand he offered me. We both got to our feet, taking care to stay back from the light cast by the windows.

'I was trying to get your attention,' Montgomery said. 'You didn't hear me, so I had to do something.'

'What the hell are you doing here?' I demanded.

'Like I said, Stefan told me about Westfield and what you think this visit's about. I thought I'd come and see for myself what was going on. I saw Plum in the car park and she told me you were around, but I didn't think you'd be outside. Sorry, I've probably fucked things up for you.'

I thought for a moment. 'Actually, I think you might have given us a ticket inside,' I said, though there was no guarantee it would play out as I intended. 'How do you fancy reprising our fight, but with an added soundtrack?'

'Sure, but just give me a minute, will you?'

But while Montgomery was setting up his phone to record any conversations we might overhear, I wandered back over to the windows. The room was empty.

'Shit, they've moved on.'

'What?'

'They've gone.' I kept on walking around the house and as I rounded the corner to where the swimming pool was, lights flickered on and I saw people filing into the patio area.

'Crap, we need to get to the swimming pool.' With Montgomery trailing behind, I hurried back to the main doors of the house. The hallway was empty except for a man crossing it on his return from the gents', and once inside, we walked casually across and along the corridor that would take us round to the back of the house. Making two right turns, we came to a door that opened to our left onto a darkened anteroom, which had the unmistakable aroma of chlorine. Inside were the benches and hooks you might have for a changing area, along with a couple of large freestanding storage cupboards. Through the next door, I could see the glow of the pool and hear voices echoing around the dimly lit chamber. Keeping to the shadows, Montgomery and I moved forward and positioned ourselves at either side of the door, from where we could hear and see what was unfolding.

CHAPTER FIFTY-FOUR

When I first came round, it was with a stonking hangover, a mouth like sandpaper, and the smell of laundered linen in my nostrils. I opened my eyes slowly to allow them to adjust to the light, and was subjected to a nasty attack of déjà vu.

'Hello, Stefan.' Margot Warren-Byrne's face appeared, horribly close to mine, before morphing into someone also familiar but more benign. 'What are you doing back here?' she wanted to know.

I closed my eyes again, struggling to comprehend. Was I still here? Had I never left? Had I dreamed . . . ? No. She'd said *back*. I felt exhausted, my limbs like stone, and it would have been so easy to turn over and drift back to sleep, but I had to know why I was in here. I opened my eyes and she was still there, smiling at me but in a forced kind of way. Things must be really bad.

'Not in Oz, then,' I said, stupidly.

The 'no' that came back was strangely measured, as if I'd missed something.

'I mean it,' said Freckle-face — Claire. 'Do you know why you're here?'

Through the fog that shrouded my cognitive functioning, I tried to grasp the last thing I could remember. The visit from Guy Leonard, feeling unwell. And now I was back in hospital. I must have either passed out or had another seizure. Or was it something to do with the aftertaste of that wine? He'd come to talk about Rita, but I could remember nothing he'd said about her. Mostly he'd talked about me:

…as you get older, you'll be in more pain… surgery would help… it might at least be worth having an assessment…

Was that what Guy Leonard's visit had really been about?

'Don't know,' I said, shaking my head, which triggered a sickening wave of nausea. 'Doctor? Notes?'

'That's what bothers me,' she said. 'There aren't any, and you've been put down here in a room that isn't used any more. I had to track down a master key to unlock it. And you seem to still be fully clothed. Your shoes are under the bed.'

'So how did you . . . ?'

'Fluke,' she said. 'I was getting a coke from the machine in the foyer when I saw you come in. But when I checked on the system to see why you'd been admitted, there's no record at all. And the two guys who were with you — something didn't look right. You really don't know why you're here?'

Slowly and falteringly, I explained the whole sorry story to her, including what Fraser and I thought we had uncovered, knowing that there was absolutely no reason why she should believe me. It took for ever, my slurring at its worst, but she seemed to understand and take me seriously.

'Shit,' she said. 'You know there have been rumblings in the geriatric wards here about the unusual amounts of opioid painkillers being used. Talk was, there was going to be some kind of enquiry. But it never happened. And Warren-Byrne's a ball-breaker. Fires her PAs on a regular basis for all kinds of spurious reasons.' She was thoughtful. 'I caught her hanging around your room once before, when you were in the last time.'

So that was where I'd seen her.

While we'd been talking, I'd drunk about a litre of water, and my head was beginning to clear. 'She must have an office here in the hospital?'

'Yes, of course.'

'Have you still got that master key?'

'Yes. I could . . .'

'No! You've got a good job. And I know what I'm looking for. At least, I'm sure I will when I see it.'

'I'm coming with you,' she insisted and, when I pulled a face, added, 'You're in no fit state to do it alone and you're less likely to be challenged if I'm with you.'

I couldn't fault her logic.

'I just need to make a quick call,' she said.

'Oh yes?'

'Calling in a couple of favours. Might be good if you see if you can stand up.'

There was a paranoid gremlin in my head that wondered if she was about to call for reinforcements to subdue me again, but that was a chance I'd have to take. There was little I could do about it.

Meanwhile, she was right. Whatever the eventuality, I needed to get out of this bed. I started small, lifting my head off the pillow, which set the lights flashing behind my eyes again and forced an involuntary retch. But after a moment the flashes subsided and little by little, I was able to get myself to a sitting position. Then, since I hadn't thrown up, even though my gut was advising me differently, I swung my legs over the edge of the bed. By the time Claire came back, I was on my feet, although my head felt somehow detached from the rest of me.

It was like an out-of-body experience tramping past silent, abandoned rooms, our footsteps ringing back at us. When we emerged into the hospital proper, the sudden glare and noise made for a particularly intense experience of sensory overload. Warren-Byrne's office was part of the executive wing, separated from the rest of the hospital by a door with a key code. Through the glass, it was clear that the automatic lighting had gone out, meaning that everyone had clocked off for the night. Consulting her phone, Claire punched numbers into the pad.

'The favour?' I said.

'First of several,' she grinned.

Warren-Byrne's brass nameplate, with the many letters after the double-barrel, took up almost the width of the door. We unlocked it with the master key. As we stepped over the threshold, Claire stooped to pick up a sheet of A4 that had been slid under the door.

'God, that smell!' I said, the source of the strong floral smell a huge vase of wilting lilies on the edge of the desk. But Claire didn't seem to be listening. She thrust the paper in front of me.

'Is this your signature?'

I looked at the indistinct squiggle. 'More or less. Guy Leonard got me to sign some non-disclosure thing.'

'This is nothing to do with confidentiality,' said Claire. 'You were giving your permission to go ahead with corrective surgery.'

Fuck. 'Shortly before I was drugged and brought here.'

'It explains why you were in the abandoned wing. Lucky I saw you.'

I shuddered. Lucky didn't come close to describing the reprieve I'd had.

'Right,' she said. 'Let's crack on. Favour number two.' The computer was naturally enough password-protected, but phone out again, Claire tapped in a sequence of letters, numbers and symbols. An error message bounced onto the screen. 'Bugger.' She repeated the exercise and on the third attempt, we were locked out completely. 'I can't believe it.' She flopped back in the chair. Eva was so certain.' But while she'd been trying the computer, I'd been conducting my own more conventional search. Outwardly, the box beside the printer looked like the usual supply of new paper. But when I lifted the lid, inside was a pile of booklets labelled Operation Beagle, with the clipper logo on the cover. Hidden in plain sight.

'Eureka,' I said, but we both turned to the corridor as we heard the outer door open and close.

'Bernie,' said Claire.

'Is that supposed to mean something?

'He's Warren-Byrne's tame security man. Ensures that she's not disturbed, keeps out unwanted intruders — that kind of thing. Leave him to me.'

Of all Claire's many talents, her ability to charm us back past the security guard was probably one of the least surprising. We made it back to one of the public waiting areas before the adrenalin that had sustained me dissipated and I folded to the ground.

CHAPTER FIFTY-FIVE

As Montgomery and I edged our way towards the light, the voices got louder. Though they remained standing, they had congregated among the pot plants and garden chairs. They must have felt safe here — the last one in had left the inner glass door open by a couple of inches.

'Well, this is different,' I heard Superintendent Bowers say.

'We've got privacy down here,' said the man I recognised to be Ashley Curzon. 'We had the pool put in years ago but now the kids have grown up it hardly gets used.'

I was so busy straining to catch what they were saying that it was only when Montgomery grabbed my shoulder that I heard what he did — footsteps and voices approaching from behind us in the main house. Moving quietly away from the door, we blended into the shadows cast by the storage cupboards and held our breath as Margot Warren-Byrne breezed through in a lingering cloud of perfume, closely followed by a stocky youth. They were careless enough to leave the door even further ajar and I breathed out again as we edged back to our listening post. By hanging back a bit, I found that I could see most of their faces, too.

'Good evening, gentlemen,' I heard Warren-Byrne say. 'I'm sorry to be late. There was another urgent matter requiring my attention. But now that we're all here, perhaps we can begin?' She held something unidentifiable in the crook of her arm.

'Tyler, thanks for showing Miss Warren-Byrne in, but you can go now,' said Curzon. So that's who he was. If it wasn't for the bigger fish on offer, I'd be tempted to grab the kid now, on his way out.

'On the contrary,' said Warren-Byrne, 'I think Tyler should stay. After all, he's very much a part of the initiative, isn't he, Inspector?'

Uncomprehending, Ashley Curzon turned to Bowers, who had at once become preoccupied with the contents of the cut glass tumbler in his hand. Tyler remained where he was.

There followed a moment's hiatus, in which the tension in the room was palpable. Warren-Byrne cleared her throat and addressed Westfield.

'So, Matthew, now that you've spent some time here, what do you think of our humble town?'

'It's an agreeable place,' Westfield said smoothly, though his expression was wary. 'Clearly people are working hard to create a pleasant environment. I'd like to congratulate you all. I'm just not sure why . . .'

Warren-Byrne spoke over him. 'Yes, hard work but also strategy, Matthew. We invited you here because we think we have something unique to offer that will benefit the whole country. And you could just be the person to deliver it.' She smiled knowingly, but Westfield just looked baffled.

I had a moment's clarity, then. Westfield didn't know. He wasn't in on it.

'Haven't you guessed?' Warren-Byrne went on, with the barely contained excitement of a child playing a game. 'All of us in this room have something in common.'

'I'm sorry . . . ?'

'A vision of the future,' said Warren-Byrne. 'We all share a passion for doing what's best for our communities and our nation. It's for that reason that we have the same concerns about the turn things have taken over the last decades. Successive governments have tried to shape our society by a number of different means, attempting to change behaviour through monitoring, guidance and occasionally legislation. But this nudge effect isn't working. We think — we know — that a more . . . direct approach is more successful, and is what is required.'

'Approach to what?'

'To neutralise the impact of what we might call the more . . . challenging elements of our communities.' Warren-Byrne produced some booklets and, as she distributed them, I caught a glimpse of the sailing ship logo. It was the report I'd caught Bowers reading.

'I'd appreciate it if we could keep these confidential for the moment, gents.' While Westfield flicked through the pages, Warren-Byrne continued her speech. 'We need to think about where our dwindling resources can be most effectively distributed to develop a healthy and resilient population. As you can see, it's what some of the country's most respectable institutions are striving to achieve, and this plan sets out exactly how to take this forward into the future. In turn, strengthening our many communities will inevitably strengthen our nation, making us more forward thinking and better equipped for the contemporary world. All we need is to have the right, charismatic leader in place.' Warren-Byrne was staring with intent at Westfield, though he seemed not to notice. 'When we do, others will follow his lead. It has happened before.'

'I think that might be enough for now, Margot,' said Bowers, taking a step towards her. 'We should let Matthew read the report and mull things over.'

But Warren-Byrne was warming to her theme, so she ignored him and pushed on, reminding me of what Stefan Greaves had said about the arrogance of medics.

'This is our time,' she said, in an increasingly impassioned voice. 'We have science and common sense on our side. Of course, people have their rights, but at a time when resources are running short, we must balance the rights of the individual against the rights and welfare of the majority. It's for the greater good. Medicine now enables us to eliminate physical weakness through termination, genetic counselling and embryo selection. We know for example that, thanks to more effective neonatal testing, conditions such as Down's syndrome can be a thing of the past, as is already the case in Scandinavia. Our increased understanding of brain development and genetic propensity allows us to address social and moral weakness. Institutions such as law enforcement can support this and sometimes even lead—'

'Perhaps we should show Matthew what we propose,' said Bowers, stepping in.

Warren-Byrne glared at him for a second, before yielding. 'Of course, of course.'

And this was where our luck ran out. In preparation for the big reveal, Curzon began shepherding his guests further into the room, across to where the shrouded entity stood (probably not a barbecue, after all). It effectively took them beyond the range of our hearing and of Montgomery's phone recording. He made a "what do we do now?" gesture at me. The door still wasn't open sufficiently wide for us to slip through, so, praying that it wouldn't creak, I gave it a gentle nudge. It moved a couple of inches, then stopped. It was enough. I waved Montgomery in ahead of me and crept forward into the room, taking cover behind the potted palms. I was just getting into position, when I kicked the leg of a chair. It bounced and scraped on the tiled floor and everyone spun round in our direction.

'What's that? Who's there?' called Curzon senior.

The only option was to brazen it out. I lunged at Montgomery, grabbing him by the arm.

'You've got an intruder, sir.' I stepped out into full view of everyone.

'What the hell . . . ?'

'This is PC Mick Fraser,' Westfield said, making eye contact with me. 'He's been my body man while I've been here.'

I addressed Bowers. 'I was waiting in the car when I thought I saw someone approaching the house, sir. I was right. I followed him in here.'

'Who is he?' demanded Warren-Byrne.

'Simon Montgomery, a reporter from the local rag.' Bowers sneered. 'Hoping to make his name, I suppose.'

Warren-Byrne arched an eyebrow. 'Well perhaps we should let him,' she said. 'Once our plans are signed and sealed, this news is going to be public anyway. It seems fitting that a local journalist should take the credit for breaking the story.' Her expression hardened. 'And we can make sure that he reports the facts of it accurately. Shape the message.'

She turned to Ashley Curzon, who, with a flourish, threw off the sheet to reveal a table, on top of which was an architectural model of what appeared to be the two floors of this very building, side by side.

'What is it?' It was Westfield who had voiced the question in my head.

Curzon stepped forward, his chest puffed with pride. 'It's a reimagining of Mawton Manor,' he said. 'This place is far too big for my family now, and I'm willing to let the health trust have it at a reasonable price. Plus, my teams will be on hand to do the conversion work.'

'We're going to develop our own centre for differential treatment, right here in Charnford.' Warren-Byrne beamed at Westfield.

It took him a moment to process the information.

'You mean assisted suicide,' he said.

Bowers spoke up. 'For years now, there have been calls on the government to make it legal, and surely it's only a matter of time before the will of the people triumphs. We want to offer our citizens choice, you see,' he said. 'The centre will offer a range of services that will enable people to make informed decisions about their lives that would benefit society as a whole.'

Warren-Byrne cut in, with the fervour of a sales rep closing a deal. 'We will continue to promote our voluntary sterilisation programme,' she said. 'Persistent offenders could be offered it as a way of commuting their prison sentences. And there will be relief for the families of disabled people and children who feel that they can no longer manage.'

'Hang on a minute . . .' Ashley Curzon cut in, confused. Some of this was news to him, too.

'It will dovetail neatly with our prioritised law enforcement policy,' said Bowers.

This was my chance. I took a deep breath.

'That would be Operation Beagle you're referring to, sir?'

'In part, yes, Constable Fraser.' Bowers shot me a warning look. 'You haven't been with us long, so you can't be expected to understand its subtleties, or appreciate the difference it's made in making Charnford a safer, more welcoming place.'

My heart was thudding. 'But at what cost?' I asked. 'And I don't mean the economic cost, I'm talking about the human cost. When I saw the name on the folder, I thought it was named for your dog, but it's not, is it, sir?'

'What are you talking about, Mick?' said Westfield.

'Operation Beagle,' I told him, 'is a police initiative to ensure that certain crimes — depending on the victim's perceived worth — go uninvestigated.'

298

'Is this true?' asked Westfield.

Bowers stood his ground. 'You said it yourself, Matthew. Our crime data is impressive, and we operate within budget. How many forces can say that?' He attempted a dismissive laugh. 'Fraser here's just got hold of the wrong end of the stick.'

'Actually, sir, what I've got hold of is Denny Sutton's SIM card,' I said. 'The one that you were so keen to hang on to. It's very informative. And I'm sure will be even more so, when cross-referenced with the data from phones belonging to other people in this room.'

Bowers seemed to momentarily lose the power of speech.

'Be very careful, PC Fraser,' he said eventually, a strain in his voice.

'Why? What will you do?' I challenged him. 'Silence me in the same way that Rita Todd was silenced?'

Nobody spoke up to deny it, but when I saw the look Warren-Byrne and Tyler Curzon exchanged, my stomach lurched. They were thinking about it, and not 'if' but 'how'.

'Rita Todd should have focused on doing her job,' said Warren-Byrne. 'And left wider policy to those of us who understand the bigger picture.' It was practically an admission of guilt.

'You mean . . . ?' Now it was Bowers' turn to look discomfited.

Warren-Byrne was quick to respond. 'Something had to be done,' she said, as if that was justification enough.

'What do you want?' Westfield demanded of her.

'When you return to government, we want you to endorse and match our funding for these initiatives,' said Warren-Byrne, a little less sure of herself now. 'In return, you'd get the blueprint of what we have done here, to roll out across the rest of the country. You've seen the proof, Matthew. It works. And when other towns and cities see our accomplishments, they will be desperate to adopt the same strategy. This is what will get you to the top of our political system once again.'

Westfield looked appalled. 'I want nothing to do with this,' he said. 'In fact, I think you're out of your minds. There's a precedent for such a plan and you seem to have overlooked its catastrophic outcome. And thank God, humankind has learned from it and moved on.'

There was a foreboding silence. Ashley Curzon shifted his position.

'Of course.' Warren-Byrne smiled. 'But there is much to be learned from our history, no matter how the positive aspects of such *interventions might have been misremembered. There are and always have been people in this country who understand that the intentions behind such historical strategies were sound. It's just that, in recent years, we haven't had the opportunity to make our voices heard.'*

'And things are different now,' Bowers chipped in. He cast around at the others for support. 'Evidence supports this as the only sustainable long-term option.'

'And you promised!' Her cry was one of such desperation that we all, as one, turned to look at Margot Warren-Byrne.

'When?' demanded Westfield.

She opened a book she held in her hands. I saw the gold number on the cover. It was an old diary. '"October sixteenth,"' she read. '"Matthew Westfield spoke at the Union today. He said we can change the world. Talked into the night about how we would make it happen."' Triumphant, she was oblivious to the embarrassment of her colleagues.

'I was twenty-two years old!' Westfield exclaimed.

'But I did this all for you!' Warren-Byrne was aghast. 'What about Amelie? Don't you think this is exactly what she would have wanted?'

Westfield stepped forward, and for a second I thought he might hit her. Instead he jabbed a finger at her, pure anger showing on his face. 'What happened to my wife is nothing to do with you. You should all know that I plan to resign as a government advisor before the next general election. But rest assured, I will certainly take your ideas back to the prime minister. I think someone needs to know exactly what is going on here.' He turned to Montgomery. 'I think you've got more than a story here this evening. If you stick to the truth, I'll endorse every word, although I think the people of Charnford and beyond will find it utterly incredible.'

Warren-Byrne looked devastated, but the pragmatist in her didn't take long to kick in.

'You won't be needing these, then, will you?' she said, and snatched back the incriminating evidence.

Ashley Curzon was staring at her with disbelief.

'Jesus. How naïve am I?' he said. 'I thought you wanted a hospice. I thought you genuinely wanted the best for this town, not some . . . glorified social engineering experiment. I wash my hands of it. All of it.' He threw the report back at her. 'You'll have to find yourselves

some other premises. And now I'd like you all to leave my house, please. Tyler, come with me.'

'Oh, I think Tyler's old enough to make his own decisions,' said Warren-Byrne. 'And he can't so easily turn his back on all this. He's been doing a sterling job on our behalf for some time. I don't think you appreciate him at all. He's extremely versatile.'

Curzon's eyes narrowed as he turned his attention to Tyler. 'What have you been up to, son?'

'Oh, I know he'll be far too modest to say,' said Warren-Byrne. 'But your offspring is a born leader, especially among those in the under-class. It's really quite invigorating to have — what's the colloquial term? — "muscle" at one's disposal. And those young men from the Flatwood estate respond to his every request.'

'What kind of request?'

'Tyler provides an invaluable service,' Warren-Byrne continued. 'How would they cope without those little "extras" he provides that make their miserable lives a little more bearable? And in return, they would do almost anything for him. I imagine they enjoy it, the violence, I mean.'

'You stupid little . . .' Curzon was white with rage. 'You're still dealing? What are you doing hanging around with those people? We don't even live there anymore.'

'I've been helping to rid the town of benefit-scrounging scum, Dad,' Tyler protested. 'I thought that's what you wanted.'

'He's his father's son,' went on Warren-Byrne. 'It was Tyler him-self who realised what a carefully placed rag in a boiler vent could do.'

It took several seconds for Curzon to understand the implications of what she'd said.

'You sabotaged the Asif family's boiler?' he said, realisation dawning. 'Christ.' He turned on Warren-Byrne. 'What have you done to him?'

Tyler Curzon looked at Bowers, then at me, then made a dash for the door. In another moment, he was through it and running down the corridor. As I turned to give chase, I heard scuffling behind me, a splash, and Montgomery shouting, before a door slammed shut.

* * *

301

We were a motley crew that left Mawton Manor that night. I called for reinforcements and two uniforms came and removed Tyler Curzon. It took a while to find his phone, which he'd shoved into a plant pot on his way past. That left Matthew Westfield in the front seat with me, and Keeley and Plum in the back — two ends of the sartorial spectrum. Plum was the last person I delivered home.

'So, what's with the name?' I asked, to break the awkward silence. She told me.

'That fella has a lot to answer for, doesn't he?'

CHAPTER FIFTY-SIX

I awoke from what had been a deep but troubled sleep to find Laura and Grace fussing over me and a lot of questions I needed answering — the first being how I finished up at their place.

'Jake brought you,' said Laura, as if that explained it. It made more sense when she added that Jake and Freckle-face Claire were an item.

* * *

When I was back in my flat, Mick Fraser came to visit. He arrived just as I was returning my chess pieces to their starting positions.

'Did you win?' he asked.

'We agreed a draw,' I said. 'And Crusader got suddenly chatty. He's been having treatment for a serious illness, but has just been given the all clear.'

'So that's why he kept to himself,' he said. 'D'you know, for a short time I even wondered if . . .'

'Yeah, me too,' I admitted.

Fraser had come to fill me in on what I'd missed.

'Best part of the caper and you slept right through it,' he said.

What he told me made for chilling listening, and I shuddered to think how differently it might have ended. 'But Margot Warren-Byrne and Bowers had made a massive miscalculation with Matthew Westfield. They seem to have overlooked the fact that most people grow up and mature.'

'And we thought he was behind it all.'

He looked rueful. 'Yeah, we didn't get it quite right.'

'And it was Tyler Curzon, not his dad, who was responsible for the death of the Asifs' baby?'

'Tyler or Warren-Byrne, depending on how you look at it. Curzon senior was genuinely horrified.' Fraser shook his head in disbelief. 'And there's a catalogue of other offences. Tyler Curzon has been more or less running the Flatwood, using his power as a drug dealer to exert a hold over the lads he'd grown up with, most of whom had few other options open to them, including Gary Bostwick and Liam Archer.'

'The man who killed your partner?'

'We may never know if it was him or Curzon who wielded the knife, but my money is on Archer simply being the lure. All it took was a bit of weed and a handful of spent lottery tickets,' said Fraser, grimly. 'They convinced him they were winning numbers and that all he had to do was cash them in. That little lot have committed so many offences between them over the last few years, it's going to take a hell of a lot of sorting out. Something on that scale, even though we discussed it, I don't think I really believed — it seemed . . . unimaginable.'

I knew exactly what he meant. 'But what about evidence?'

'We've got layers of it.' He told me about the SIM card he'd found and young Curzon's phone. 'The mobile links between him, Bowers, Denny and Warren-Byrne have got more strands to them than a cat's-cradle. And backed up by the testimony of an influential politician, there's enough to indict all four of them even without your friend Simon's recording, which unfortunately went into the pool when he did.'

'Really?'

'Yes, Bowers apparently gave him a shove. It was quick thinking, really. Simon's phone was irretrievably damaged.' He looked askance at me. 'And don't be modest — you were pretty busy too.'

'I just made the most of an opportunity,' I pointed out. 'Made possible by the ingenuity of a friend.'

'I've no doubt that Bowers and Warren-Byrne will deny that the Pure strategy was a serious proposition, but it's hard to refute when it's there in black and white. Bowers tendered his resignation on the spot. Claimed he was leaving the force anyway.'

'To spend more time with his conscience?'

'Or his ego. He'll still face the anti-corruption squad, who may yet bring criminal charges. It's all taking a bit of untangling.'

'And Rita?' I asked.

'Her case will be reopened,' said Fraser. 'Along with the circumstantial evidence, we now have a big, fat, publicly declared motive — and it'll be down to the CPS, but I think Warren-Byrne pretty much incriminated herself in front of everyone.'

'So, Rita did exactly what she set out to do when Andrea first brought her to our offices,' I said. 'She exposed what was going on. But I only had half the picture until I talked to you.'

'I never asked,' said Fraser. 'How did you . . . ?'

'Put simply, we talked to a priest about another priest, who, it turned out, had no interest in *The Wizard of Oz* whatsoever.'

EPILOGUE

When I met Mick Fraser some weeks later for a drink, he was in a buoyant mood. The CPS had sanctioned the charges being brought against Margot Warren-Byrne and Tyler Curzon.

'I ended up feeling sorry for Ashley Curzon,' he admitted. 'Tyler's likely to go down for a charge of culpable homicide at the very least. Idiot wiped his prints off the knife he used to stab Denny, but left clothing fibres. Thanks to his confession in front of witnesses, he'll also face charges relating to the Asifs' baby, though he'll doubtless claim ignorance and get it reduced to manslaughter. Interviews are ongoing with the various "persons of interest" who were bribed into doing Warren-Byrne's other dirty work, including your assailants. The custody suite's never seen so much business.'

'Any of your guests called Cate?' I asked.

'No, and for what it's worth I don't think she had any part in it at all. You're really letting her go?'

'It's a trust thing. What she said to me, it couldn't just be unsaid, and however much we could try to move on, it would always be there, in the background.'

Simon's write-up, along with a copy of the Operation Beagle document, was making a good story at both local and national levels, too. Mick told me he was thinking about taking his sergeant's exams, with a view to getting into CID. But most exciting of all, he'd just found out that he was going to be a dad.

My news was more mixed. The end for PGW had come sooner than we expected. Jake had invited Barbara, Plum and me into his office to tell us that the firm as it was would be unlikely to survive much beyond the end of the financial year. And Jake had decided to move away. To Australia. With Freckle-face. A fresh start, he'd called it.

'So where does that leave you and Plum?' Mick asked.

'Jake will give us glowing references and he's convinced that we'll get snapped up by one of the other local law firms.'

'Is that what you want?'

'I'm not sure,' I said.

'Well, I've worked with worse private investigators,' said Fraser. He grinned. 'You two make quite a team.'

Now there was a thought.

THE END

AUTHOR'S NOTE

The Truth About Murder is a work of fiction, but, although I have been selective, it includes some real people and events.

In 1939, a father, Herr Knauer, lobbied Hitler to put an end to the life of his severely disabled child. The family's doctor was subsequently directed to proceed with euthanasia, an act that presaged the start of the T4 programme — the systematic eradication of over 70,000 elderly, disabled and mentally ill children and adults.

In 1941, Clemens von Galen, Bishop of Munster 1933–1946, was lobbied by a nun, Sister Baudelerta and Father Lackmann, the chaplain at the Marienthal asylum, who raised concerns about the programme of euthanasia being implemented at the institution.

Von Galen's response — after some deliberation — was to preach about this turn of events in a series of sermons. In the third of these in July 1941, he described the removal of patients from the Marienthal institution, reminding his congregation that killing is wrong and that euthanasia is a violation of God's law. It was a forthright challenge to state-sanctioned murder. In August 1941, the adult euthanasia programme was suspended, although the 'mercy killing' of incurably ill children continued until 1945, authorized at local level by individual institutions.

The idea for *The Truth About Murder* was sparked during the time I spent teaching and discussing disability history with undergraduate students. In further researching the book, the sources I found both fascinating and invaluable were Michael Burleigh's *Death and Deliverance* (2002), Hugh Gregory Gallagher's *By Trust Betrayed* (1989), and *Bishop von Galen: German Catholicism and National Socialism* by Beth Griech-Polelle (2008).

Chris Collett, Dec 2019

KEY CHARACTERS

Stefan Greaves: a forty-year-old paralegal at Perry, Goodman and Wright (PGW), who has mild cerebral palsy.

PC Mick Fraser: married to Sonia, he recently moved to Charnford to work at Fulford Road police station with partner PC Denny Sutton.

Jake Goodman: managing, and sole remaining partner of PGW.

Plum: the office junior at PGW, she spent time in the care system and sleeping rough before Jake's ex-wife secured her the job.

Rita Todd: a paediatric nurse, widow and mother to grown up daughter Andrea.

PC Denny Sutton: constable of thirty years' service who is due to retire imminently and move to Portugal with his wife, Sheila.

Kevin Booth: Denny Sutton's former partner, who left the police in disgrace some time ago.

Guy Leonard: consultant paediatrician at the local hospital, and Rita Todd's boss. Married to Joss, a GP.

Laura Montgomery: long-term friend of Stefan Greaves; married to Simon, a local journalist, and mother to Grace (aged 3) and Zoe (18)

ALSO BY CHRIS COLLETT

DI MARINER SERIES
Book 1: Deadly Lies
Book 2: Innocent Lies
Book 3: Killer Lies
Book 4: Baby Lies
Book 5: Married Lies
Book 6: Buried Lies
Book 7: Missing Lies

FREE KINDLE BOOKS

Printed in Great Britain
by Amazon